ANTONIO IN LOVE

Alfred A. Knopf   New York   1968

ANTONIO IN LOVE

(LA COSA BUFFA)

———◆———

by Giuseppe Berto

translated from the Italian by William Weaver

THIS IS A *BORZOI BOOK*
PUBLISHED BY *ALFRED A. KNOPF, INC.*

First American Edition
Copyright © 1968 by Alfred A. Knopf, Inc.

Library of Congress Catalog Card Number: 68–12680

Manufactured in the United States of America
Originally published in Italian as *La Cosa buffa*.
© Rizzoli Editore, Milano, 1966.

Droll thing life is—that mysterious arrangement of merciless logic for a futile purpose. The most you can hope from it is some knowledge of yourself—that comes too late.

—Joseph Conrad   (*Heart of Darkness*)

There is only one great adventure, and it is to the inside, toward the I, and for it neither time nor space nor even the facts count.

—Henry Miller

We are, instead, at the mercy of the thing.

—Robert Musil

Let's have it clear that

I'm in favor of order,

and that being so is useless.

CONTENTS

ANTONIO IN LOVE

CHAPTER
I

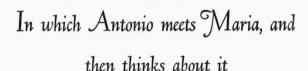

In which Antonio meets Maria, and
then thinks about it

In that long midwinter, though he went every sunny afternoon to the terrace of the café on the Zattere, a far from disagreeable place cheered in fact by the few happy things to be found in a damp city like Venice in the bad season, Antonio most of all wanted to die. Expressed in these terms, his behavior might easily seem somewhat erratic indicating a confused psychological state to say the least, but apart from the consideration that when a man wants to leave this world he usually seeks out places where remaining in it seems least painful, in the case of Antonio there is the enlightening circumstance that it was precisely on the terrace of the café on the Zattere that he had seen Maria for the first time and this Maria though through little fault of her own was connected with his present and consequential desire to die.

Now these two adjectives, applied to his desire to die, are also, when you think about it, fairly risky, because somebody might be led to argue, assuming an absurd hypothesis, that Antonio, if he had been able to forget about the girl and the painful events connected with her, would at that time have been happy to live, an absolutely erroneous supposition because, while it's true that the story with Maria had excited and we could also say enforced his desire to leave this world, it is also true that even in his least wretched moments he had been fairly full of the generic and youthful conviction that it would have been better from every point of view if his parents had at the time spared themselves the effort of bringing him into the world, a sad conviction really but then not after all entirely harmful since Antonio's romantic fascination though not superabundant perhaps seemed to derive chiefly from this not wholly eccentric idea.

The story with Maria is one of the most unusual and tearful stories that could nowadays befall a young man in the flower of his youth, and since not even Antonio could deny his being the greatest and almost sole artificer of his own misfortunes it is quite natural that in the end he should be filled with a firm desire not for what we might call self-destruction or voluntary annihilation but for a natural death, and he gave the matter much thought at that time and he wouldn't at all have minded for example an abrupt and unconscious decease, preferably while asleep, in fact he attached great importance to this last detail and in the period of his most acute and intense suffering, that is when the idea of a definitive escape from his earthly woes seemed dearest to him, he was careful at night to put on clean pajamas, so that he wouldn't make a poor showing if such good luck came his way.

The strange thing is that when he was most longing for death and without exaggeration almost enjoying the idea as the only way to treat a suffering too great to bear and also unjust all things considered, when it came to Maria who was the object and to say the very least a partial cause of his grief his image of her had become vague and hazy by then at times even without consistency so one of the greatest components of his excessive suffering was the fact that he suffered greatly without even knowing exactly why, but these are the very griefs that as a rule lead to the desire for death since they attack our existence at its roots, assuming proportions of existential frustration, the kind that cuts the ground from under any desire to keep going. To tell the truth immediately after the rupture, perhaps through the functioning of an unconscious defense mechanism against the excessive pressure of suffering due more than anything to the catastrophic and to some extent unexpected way in which the rupture had taken place, his beloved Maria had become somewhat cloudy and confused in his mind so that he couldn't even reconstruct her with the aid of the passport-size photograph, the only one he had been left with at the moment of the disaster, where she appeared with a slightly fixed stare, a not very intelligent expression, her lips clenched, something that hardly ever happened with her although she always tried to keep them closed because she had a crooked front tooth which upset her greatly, just as she was upset by the freckles that especially in summer came out on her nose and the upper part of her cheeks.

According to Antonio, Maria was downright silly to be upset by those little defects which for that matter weren't at all unbecoming since the tooth for example was only slightly crooked and lightened the otherwise too severe and melancholy aspect of her face with a gay and slightly childish touch without which Antonio would probably never have fallen so boundlessly in love, and as for the freckles, he must have had some innate tendency toward them because on a later occasion, namely when he met Marika and plunged into a new and even more eccentric story but at least in some ways a revealing one, it was in fact her freckles which at the start lured him into the trap.

The meeting with Maria had been to the extent that human affairs can be determined by good intentions a voluntary and conscious act in the sense that Antonio in those days was in fact looking for a girl, and he was looking with proper resolution for various reasons among which we could if we chose also count the circumstance that following the death of his maternal grandfather he had suddenly found himself with the sum of eight hundred and ninety thousand lire at his disposal, an extraordinarily unusual sum for him, and since he had never had a girl all his own and he attributed this deficiency chiefly to lack of money he was now of the opinion that with eight hundred and ninety thousand lire in his pocket it was absolutely urgent to have a girl. Naturally he had no notion of buying one, but being poor by condition and parsimonious by nature he was inclined to attribute to money an importance that went beyond its strictly economic value, that is he endowed it with a kind of spiritual power not primal perhaps but achieved through the goodness of the things that can be bought with money, and so in the present instance he knew all too well that unless a young man possesses the supernatural gift of making an impression at first sight he has few chances of arousing the interest of even the most unmercenary girl if he doesn't have in his pocket at least the money for a movie ticket or for some drinks when they go dancing.

So Antonio was aware of his own right to look for a girl and he was also prepared to expend in this search a reasonable part of the spiritual buying power connected with that little heap of money that had unexpectedly come to him, however he didn't have a very precise idea of the girl he was looking for, that is he didn't have any preconceived notions about whether she was to be blonde or brunette or with a turned-up nose or not, still he knew that apart from some minor defect such as in fact freckles or a very slightly crooked tooth she had to be perfect. Obviously he knew that with girls there are numerous and exceedingly various ways of being perfect inwardly if not on the exterior, and therefore there are many probabilities of making a blunder in judging their perfection so he didn't underestimate the difficulties and the risks even economic ones in his search, nevertheless quite irrationally he was sure that as soon as he came upon the creature made to measure for him a special inner impulse or twinge would alert him. Strange as it may seem this is exactly what happened, and in fact as soon as Maria turned up before his eyes he was immediately seized by the turbulent certainty that she was the girl he was looking for, and just as immediately he felt that this girl excluded any possibility of his having another girl different from her at least at the same time, and in short he found himself in the condition most propitious to an amorous explosion even greater than he could have desired and foreseen.

Now on that late October afternoon when the significant encounter took place, on the terrace of the café on the Zattere which was a kind of wharf attached to the shore of the broad Giudecca Canal, in addition to Maria there were two other girls alone also attractive to look at and also with their pack of textbooks on the table beside their glasses, and the only immediately evident difference between Maria and these two was that while the latter held their faces ostentatiously up to the sun to preserve their summer tan Maria not only turned her back to the sun but also wore a broad-brimmed white piqué hat such as children usually wear at the beach, and perhaps it was this unseasonal and obviously also unfashionable hat which along with the freckles and the crooked tooth and the hair loose over her neck that gave Antonio the decisive shock, because all this endowed Maria with an irrationally young appearance like a high-school girl, and since she couldn't be all that young since she was studying at the University as was obvious from her books then a young man who felt the ambivalent urge to protect and to be protected at the same time and who was moreover driven by a somewhat rash eagerness to fall in love in a hurry found himself so to speak at her mercy.

Still though the internal symptoms had rapidly become seething and indubitable Antonio didn't abandon himself without some caution to the certainty of having found exactly what he was looking for and indeed he was by nature prudent at times to the point of irresolution and besides a tendency to foresee always the worst, never disproved for that matter by previous experiences, made him consider it quite improbable that just when he needed a girl who had properly to be considered extraordinary he should happen upon such a girl without any effort exactly as he had dreamed she would be, because despite the stormy emotional upheaval caused by the sight of her and indeed because of it, though a moment before he had had no idea of how the girl should be he now was suddenly sure she could be only like this.

Naturally it wasn't that he thought he could have foreseen she would have precisely that long chestnut hair tending to red or rather with bright coppery glints or that face which seemed sweet every time she decided to glance up from her textbook, or still less the freckles or the even more remarkable tooth just a shade crooked, however Antonio hadn't staked his hopes and satisfaction only on a physical image but rather on a more metaphysical concept in which interior beauty insofar as it could be perceived influenced the outer appearance, but interior beauty has virtually endless ways of revealing itself so the seriousness and the grace that Maria possessed in what he could see of her could very well correspond to the ideal portrait Antonio had created of his girl.

Obviously at the point where things then stood there was still the possibility of some irritating surprise, since for example this girl was seated and almost huddled over in her effort to memorize the material in the textbook therefore nobody at that moment could have dismissed the possibility of her being awkward in her person or having crooked or stumpy legs, however as Antonio was amorously and hence mysteriously sure that the face was in harmony with the spirit, so he hoped that the body was in harmony with the face, sufficiently lovely in other words and without coarse defects, but meanwhile as he waited for her to stand up so he could check any drawbacks he felt it was useful if he was to achieve a rapid development of the matter already so happily begun for the girl to notice him and feel at least to a slight degree the same emotional turmoil he had felt on glimpsing her, and since an inevitable condition was that she should somehow see him he settled himself at a table opposite her keeping his eyes fixed on her waiting in fact for her gaze to meet his.

Sitting near the girl like this, opposite her even, had been for Antonio an exceptionally bold action at which he felt an almost anguished fear to a large degree unfounded, however he couldn't bring himself to repent the position assumed because he was sustained by the conviction that he had all sorts of good reasons for behaving in this otherwise somewhat arbitrary way, and he honestly felt he was on the point of making a definitive choice and even more on the brink of one of those opportunities that normally don't happen twice in a lifetime which justified any boldness on his part and even obligated him to run some risks, among them the greatest was no doubt the risk that the girl in looking at him as he was looking at her might not notice him, and unfortunately this is exactly what seemed to happen.

To tell the truth Antonio was a nice-looking boy only in the ordinary sense of that expression meaning somebody young and in good health, but he surely wasn't one of those lucky men who stand out thanks to that almost divine power that has always been the privilege of true beauty, in other words he was completely unsuited to arousing emotions at first sight with his pensive face rather lacking in special distinction which had to be examined and appreciated by anyone seeing it with willing not to say benevolent attention, and as for his body it was tall all right and slim and therefore not exactly unattractive, but on that afternoon he had covered it with a suit that though it was his best had still been made without any elegance by the village tailor, and therefore was surely not designed to enhance his figure. As a rule Antonio didn't suffer much about his own appearance also because he rightly believed that the fact of being the way he was and in addition being badly dressed was only a marginal misfortune and quite negligible compared to the other more complete and decisive misfortune of having come into the world, but feeling now that his existence might even take on sudden meaning from the encounter with the girl, when her gaze resting on his person went right through him as if he offered no obstacle to her looking at what was beyond him, he perceived a precise unhappiness at his condition and appearance of a country boy rather lacking in the gift of communicating externally and of course automatically the great spiritual riches that not without pride he felt he possessed, so in the present situation he would gladly have changed places with anyone even less rich in spiritual qualities provided he was more interesting to look at or at least dressed a bit better.

In effect Antonio's impression that the girl when she happened to look up from her textbook didn't see him at all was quite correct, however the truth is that she didn't see the other people near him either and still less those behind him or those passing by in the distance on the street picking their way among the baby carriages and the children playing in the sun, because she was entirely absorbed in her determination to memorize certain youthful doubts and conflicts of the poet Percy Bysshe Shelley on the problem of evil and she had so to speak burned her bridges to the outside world and therefore wouldn't have noticed Antonio even if Antonio had been the way he regretted not being, and this completely absolved her of any specific guilt for the suffering that her obvious lack of attention was causing in her hapless admirer.

Unfortunately the fact that at least for the moment she was completely innocent of the suffering she caused didn't in any way reduce the strength and importance of the suffering itself on the part of the person undergoing it, and Antonio who for that matter didn't know that she was ignoring the rest of the world just as she ignored him was suffering rather a lot, and thank goodness the poor young man was so accustomed to the pangs of dejection that in a way he was better off when he suffered than when he didn't, at least when he did suffer he also felt at times that his perceptive capacities became considerably greater and also his reflective ones to a secondary degree, and this was in fact happening to him now since there was nothing legitimate and opportune he could do at present to arouse the girl's attention and so he felt almost naturally drawn to utilize the pause her unawareness granted him to put some order in the thoroughly confused feelings that had gripped him at his first sight of her.

To begin with he had honestly to admit that emotional ferment of the sort he was now feeling he had felt though not as immediate and profound various times recently, that is since the fortunate inheritance of eight hundred and ninety thousand lire had stimulated his search for a girl all his own, and in fact often on seeing a girl at random in the street perhaps from behind or in any case

only vaguely he had been seized with palpitations and shortness of
breath and at times by a diminution of his visual and motory
powers, however on closer examination he had promptly realized
he had become upset over nothing whereas with this girl the
business was growing increasingly substantial and giving more
and more propitious signs as in Antonio's spirit the first tangle of
upheavals was being followed by a certain order still temporary
of course, and for example as he gazed at her he found no end of
comfort and reassurance whether she had her head bent over her
book or whether she occasionally raised her serious concentrated
face with her eyes wide open and her upper lip carelessly raised
so that the slightly crooked tooth could be easily glimpsed, and in
conclusion there was no doubt that she was the right one, in addition to being beautiful naturally, and it was surely not an accident
that Antonio obeying an instinct of a probably religious nature soon
was comparing her to a musician-angel in the nearby Accademia
Gallery, especially because of her manner, enchanted and contented by some inner fullness.

In addition to her personal perfection Antonio didn't fail to
underline and put in the pile of favorable auguries also the perfection of the things that had somehow collected around her on
that October afternoon, namely the fairly warm sun, the canal that
spread out luminous behind her between the Stucky mills and the
harbor station, the big barges that now and then passed near the
shore or others farther off which tried to catch the slight wind with
their sails, the bustle of the vaporetto between the Zattere and the
Giudecca and even the noises, the loud shouting of the children
on the street, the throbbing of the motorboats, and the slaps as
they hit the waves, the frequent and various sound of bells from
one or the other of the many churches in the neighborhood, and
all that penetrating into the spirit of a young man who after all
asked nothing better than to fall in love seemed extraordinarily
appropriate to her, to her quiet studious composure, so that Antonio
finally abandoning all hesitation and prudence allowed himself
to be seized by a downright cosmic exaltation, that is directly related

to the boundless concepts of time and space, whereby the meeting with the girl was no longer casual or dependent on him or her or both together, but rather the result of an uninterrupted and rigorous series of events which had begun with the creation of the universe and had fatally ended there on the terrace of that café on the Zattere, where two beings who had been eternally seeking each other in the infinity of the worlds had at last met once and for all.

This was an idea that such a well-meaning young man could formulate to his satisfaction both sentimental and intellectual and actually it offered various advantages because while on the one hand he succeeded in establishing himself in the very center of creation a quite acceptable thing since creation being infinite must also have infinite centers, on the other hand he was able to evade any responsibility for action since he had set himself in the flux of ineluctable things which would happen in any case, so finally Antonio had only to let himself go a bit, but he soon realized that the comfort he derived from such thoughts couldn't be long-lived because as the minutes went by and nothing happened it became clearer and clearer that for the moment the only one seeking was himself, whereas she continued blissfully unconscious of what must also be her destiny. In short the sun was sinking and a big ship coming from Marghera seemed motionless against the gray background of the lagoon and except for the fact that she had taken off her piqué hat, no important change could be noted in the girl only the red sun struck redder glints in her brown hair, and in this sense she was perhaps even more beautiful, without her showing any awareness of it however.

Unfortunately she showed no awareness of Antonio either and so the young man felt a gradual waning of his faith in the destiny that was to lead him into her arms quite independently of his great ineptitude in such undertakings, and as for his own position in the center of creation he finally abandoned that too choosing another at the outer edge and even too wretched so that now he felt absolutely nobody, to such a degree that he felt he deserved even the supreme misfortune which would have been some other boy's arriving and sitting beside her and Antonio would then see her chat with him happily and easily like other girls who have a steady young man, and in fact it was surprising that this hadn't already happened and that the girl with all her marvelous array of good qualities was still so to speak at his disposal, and considering that an event of such importance as getting to meet her was open to any number of pitfalls that could stupidly have ruined the whole thing Antonio was again filled with turmoil and he swung frightfully between fatalism and activism, at times taking refuge in a tormented apathy and at times arousing himself to an even more tormented urgency to force events and wrest the girl from her persistent neglect of him, and in the aroused phase he felt ready for anything, that is he would rush to pick up her pencil or book if by chance they fell from her hand, as he would rush to light her cigarette if she put one in her mouth, since however ordinary and short of the ideal these actions were they would have been enough to submit himself for better or worse to her attention, but the girl seemed not to be in the habit of smoking or of dropping objects or of offering any other excuse for outsiders to penetrate her virtuous solitude, showing also in this composed behavior that she complied with the notion of the perfect girl Antonio had constructed and so he trembled all the more at the idea that she might elude him or worse still that somebody else might come and take her away from him.

Meanwhile the ship that seemed motionless in the background had come forward into the Giudecca Canal and it was a large rusty tanker with its waterline well above the surface heading toward the San Marco Basin and the sea beyond it, and then the sun just before it touched the horizon vanished in the slight haze that had risen from the lagoon and the air quickly turned cold and damp, and nearly all the people had now left the terrace of the café, and the children had also gone indoors, and finally collecting her books and her purse and her piqué hat the girl stood up revealing that she was not very tall but harmonious of body and certainly without crooked legs, and therefore it was even more heart-rending that she should go off not showing by any of her actions and movements and gestures that she was aware of the boy who only a few feet away from her had been dying on her account for at least a couple of hours.

In which Antonio accosts Maria and

comes off fairly well

Some time afterwards but not a long time afterwards unfortunately inasmuch as the story with Maria lasted in all just one season, when Antonio in drawing up a kind of final balance attempted meditating with special attention on the real start of the matter that is on the fact that the girl hadn't even finished crossing the Zattere presumably on her way to the Fondamenta Nani when he had already rushed after her, although by nature he tended rather firmly toward a sense of responsibility that is toward a concrete and recognizable intervention of the will in human behavior and actions, in this special case which moreover already in the phase preceding the actual start had entered the list of events hard to explain because of the idea of the two spirits seeking each other from all eternity in the worlds' infinity, he felt rather inclined to depart slightly from his general principles that is substantially to lean if not toward total determinism at least toward a strong conditioning, and though he certainly didn't come to profound conclusions since in the final analysis the problem was really the question of free will, nevertheless to free his conscience of remorse at least partially he came to admit that very little free will could be found in his act of pursuit, and in other words he opted for an insufficient mental control of his motory centers, basing this opinion chiefly on the detail that he had over-taken poor Maria before he knew what he was doing.

Once he caught up with her he still had to do something else and in fact without thinking twice though stammering audibly he managed to ask if she would allow him to walk with her, and im-mediately afterwards gradually realizing that he was there in person with her he was plunged into a progressive confusion with blushes and general trembling, and he hastened to add that what he had said was the stupidest thing a person could say whereas in fact it was stupid only up to a point since when a young man wants to walk with a girl it's natural to ask her and there is no more simple or suitable way to ask than with the words he had in-stinctively used, however getting everything wrong from the very beginning, he wanted to use words with this girl that nobody had ever said before, and this ambition was certainly excessive and above all unnecessary.

The girl in fact had stopped immediately where he had over-taken her under the portico in front of the branch office of the Cassa di Risparmio and at first she seemed filled only with amaze-ment but then once she was sure she was really the object of all this concern she blushed as much as he though far more prettily of course, and this indicated shyness and a gentle spirit and basically also pleasure, and in fact the poor thing showed no intention of eluding the encounter but instead when she had overcome her initial surprise she started smiling in a somewhat forced way admittedly since she was making an effort to conceal that tooth but it was encouraging on the whole though at the same time entreating, as if having decided abruptly to entrust herself to him she was begging him above all not to hurt her, so Antonio was then like those soldiers who are frightened to death but pluck up courage when they realize the enemy is more afraid than they are, and there-fore cutting things short he again asked her if she would really allow him to walk with her.

The question basically wasn't even a question but more a manifestation of justified and cautious wonder, so the girl could have answered yes without diminishing herself in the least, and certainly she was tempted to answer yes that was obvious, but still there was a persistent restraint in her and almost a kind of shyness that prevented her, and in this impasse which for that matter made her more attractive than ever also because it confirmed both her seriousness and her charm she solved the problem by saying that she really lived at quite a distance namely toward the Campo San Polo and perhaps it would therefore take him too far out of his way to see her home.

This obviously was not quite a yes though on further thought it could also be something more than a mere yes and besides the timid and docile way in which the girl had after all entrusted the decision to him and especially the fact that she was waiting for him was enough to give an affirmative meaning to her words, so it was easy for Antonio to answer politely that it was no trouble for him especially since he had to go to the Piazzale Roma which was practically in the same direction she was going and seeing that she didn't seem to reject the idea he would be very pleased if they could go a bit of the way together.

So they were soon walking side by side along the narrow Fondamenta Nani which is the street that follows the Rio di San Trovaso and poor Antonio was already less content and sure than he had been a moment before as if the very fact of moving had abruptly robbed him of the lucidity and self-assurance which he had enjoyed as long as he had remained still, all the same though the business of walking obviously drew attention to his shoes which were shapeless from excessive and protracted wear, and though he also was somewhat clumsy in keeping his pace in harmony with hers which was measured and perhaps even reserved, it wasn't only the incidental fact of being in motion rather than still which caused the uneasiness that had seized him again, but also and especially it was his own particular cockeyed way of reasoning, according to which since things had so far gone even too pleasantly and smoothly it was only justice that obscure and perhaps insurmountable difficulties would follow.

Truth to tell however from what he could see of the girl at his side with the oblique glances he cast at her now and then, there was nothing in her to make him fear complications because she walked along confident and composed with her head bowed as if she were profoundly interested in the slabs of the pavement and with her half-red hair swaying at every step and all in all not hostile but on the contrary apparently ready to receive with great benevolence anything he might decide to proffer, except that he couldn't decide to proffer anything because he could only brood over ideas which he immediately rejected either because they were too complicated and hence hard to communicate or because they were too elementary for this encounter which was in no way to be allowed to decline into a commonplace meeting, and it really wasn't so easy to find something to say which would even approximately rise to the level of the event as he conceived it in his heart, namely the level more or less of the theory of the two souls eternally seeking each other in the infinity of the worlds, and so fishing stubbornly for some phrase that wouldn't sound too bad he forced his brain to excessive and exhausting not to say sterile labor, and in fact although she had looked at him several times along the street in a way that could without exaggeration be called encouraging, he reached the point when they had to turn, namely the Ponte delle Maravegie, without managing to utter a word and with his original fine nonchalance all shot to pieces.

It's entirely natural then that afterwards, in the Calle della Toleta walking in the midst of the confused crowd going to the Accademia or coming from there and hence physically prevented from launching a sufficiently elevated conversation, Antonio renounced at least for the moment his search for things to say and turned to an examination however summary of the situation as it had developed thus far, and from a certain standpoint there was no lack of positive factors since the girl was undeniably walking at his side and if he for example had abruptly stopped with a curt good evening and had gone off in the other direction he would have sworn that this move would have caused her a certain displeasure or at least amazement, but from another standpoint considering how she moved deftly among the people and quickly chose her way along streets and through squares you might also think she had a kind of haste to arrive where she was going, and if considered seriously this might also mean that in spite of having first accepted the idea with pleasure she no longer had much desire to enjoy the company of a young man who in the long run had proved over-reticent if not simple-minded.

Unfortunately as they proceeded beyond the Campo San Barnaba along the Calle delle Botteghe and then along the Calle del Fabro with mounting self-commiseration Antonio couldn't help tending toward the second and more pessimistic view also because the only people who passed along those streets were all in a hurry and moreover the public illumination had not yet been turned on so there were large zones of darkness very favorable to enterprises of a sentimental nature and more than one example was visible thereabouts namely couples who were talking intently or hugging and kissing especially if there was some recess to shelter them but basically not giving a damn even about shelter, and in short the environmental conditions certainly didn't help justify the behavior of a young man who having asked to see a girl home and after having received permission in a tone that was inviting to say the least now walked there beside her like a dope without even the nerve to open his mouth, and if after such a favorable and promising start the affair had ended in nothing Antonio in all probability could only have blamed himself, and this would hardly have been a good thing in view of his already insecure faith in his own capacities and his already overdeveloped sense of guilt about life in general.

Luckily when they had gone a bit farther the girl had the sense to start the conversation herself and of course she did it simply by asking him if he came from Venice or from somewhere else, and stimulated in this way he could answer without too much difficulty that he wasn't from Venice and that he was in fact going to the Piazzale Roma to catch the Number Eight which would take him to Marocco where he lived with his family, that is with his father and a sister slightly older than himself, however thinking that the girl might have received a bad impression from the fact that he came from the country whereas she was no doubt a Venetian he hastened to explain that his grandfather was a hundred per cent Venetian who had moved to the country after the First World War because the air in Venice wasn't good for him, in short although he had been born and still lived in the country he could be considered a Venetian in view of his family background, but the girl didn't seem to care about his background country or city in fact she had started chatting with happy simplicity about Marocco where she had gone a couple of times on her bicycle and she had enjoyed it a lot because she loved bicycle excursions and naturally like all good Venetians she loved the country, and then he felt encouraged to describe the countryside around Marocco with the old Venetian villas and the slow, limpid river and the lazy canals and the rows of poplars lining the fields, and since she had been to Marocco twice he asked her if she recalled the road after the Dese bridge the one on the right that went to Favaro and Tessera because on that very road about three hundred yards or so from the old Terraglio highway was where he lived, in short after all his silence he poured out far more information than was opportune but the girl showed no sign of being surprised by this and answered that she couldn't seem to remember the road but anyway the next time she went to Marocco on her bicycle she would look out for it because from the way he described it that is from the poetry he put into his description it must surely be a lovely road and one worth knowing, so their dialogue went along very well and though the subject matter of the conversation was quite different and remote from what Antonio had dreamed of saying until a moment before he chatted gladly because she showed she enjoyed listening to him and this was a sure sign of a sensitive nature or in any case a generous one.

In reality as soon as the subject of the country seemed about to reach its inevitable depletion she promptly suggested another, and since at that moment they were going along the the Calle Foscari stopping in front of the closed gate of the Ca' Foscari she was prompted to tell him that she studied there at the University and then he was prompted to ask her what she studied and she answered that she was in her second year of foreign languages which amazed him very much in fact he said it was impossible because she looked like a little girl and she replied that she was almost nineteen and he protested that she didn't look it and then he made a rapid calculation and said in any case it was fantastic for a girl of eighteen to be in her second year at the University and she admitted that in fact she was doing fairly well but she didn't give herself any airs as she said so.

Then it was up to him to furnish information about himself and he revealed that he was studying Italian Literature at the ancient and glorious University of Padua but unfortunately he wasn't bright like her in fact he wasn't doing well at all because he was almost twenty-five and was behind but he could take his degree within a year if he buckled down and he might very well decide to one of these days especially if he were encouraged by certain special events, and though she didn't display the proper interest or curiosity about these special events he hinted at the girl continued the conversation saying she was sure he would take his degree within the year and in any case she said he wasn't to be discouraged about being behind at the age of almost twenty-five because in her department there were students who were thirty and one was even thirty-two and this one surely wouldn't take his degree that year no matter how hard he worked because he still had to pass twelve exams and everybody knows you can't prepare for twelve exams in a year.

Antonio would really never have imagined that you could talk with such pleasure about ordinary things and since this obviously derived from the fact that the girl could speak sweetly and listen benevolently it was logical for him to want to press his acquaintance forward a bit so he felt authorized to ask her if she called those older classmates of hers *tu* or not and she said *tu* naturally because this was the custom among fellow students and it would have been funny not to address them that way really funny she insisted with a half-smile and then he seized the opportunity to remark that the two of them even though from different universities were still both students, and perhaps after all it wouldn't have been exactly wrong or indiscreet for them to call each other *tu* and finally he asked her outright if she thought it improper for them to use the *tu* form, and she answered that she didn't think it the least bit improper in fact she thought it would be the right thing however they had to make up their minds somehow after all the Russians or the Americans would soon be putting a man on the moon and in times like these it was so to speak practically obligatory to be open-minded and modern at least while you were young, however if he went on addressing her formally even when he was asking permission to call her *tu* they could continue like this to infinity without ever getting started.

Now perhaps her remark was a bit too severe or sharp but admittedly she made sense so Antonio couldn't be annoyed at it however he was now clearly being forced to say something quickly to her involving the word *tu,* and of course he didn't lack ideas to express in a language that could even be intimate because in reality he had all sorts of things ready and in an instant he could blurt out some of the sentences that were violently racing through his mind like I'm very fond of you or you mustn't be surprised if I say I'm in love with you and please don't doubt what I say because I know one thing you don't know namely that the two of us have been seeking each other eternally in the infinity of the worlds and now that we've finally found each other I don't want to lose you or let you go and you wouldn't be happy with anyone else anyhow and it's enough for me just to look at you or even look at the courtyard of your university with you near me and I feel complete in a way I've never felt before in my unhappy life complete thanks to you who are near me and give me meaning otherwise I would be maimed and useless, and as can easily be seen these concepts Antonio wanted to blurt out were anything but simple still he could have expressed them with great fluency and even with adequate language since they were merely the synthesis of all the intellectual and emotional activity of his last two hours and a quarter not counting obviously the previous preparatory period and other dreams as old in him as his inner being itself perhaps, but first of all he had the impression somehow that it would be easier for the Russian or the American to arrive on the moon than for him to let such expressions escape his lips, and in fact he had only to imagine that the girl might be offended or perhaps simply annoyed and he lost his nerve about uttering them, and in short the little courage required for him rightfully to unburden his feelings continued to fail him to the great embarrassment also of the girl whose expectation was becoming more obvious every moment, so Antonio clearly understanding that it wasn't possible to remain silent any longer without disgracing himself said to her that maybe it was downright stupid of him but then and there he couldn't think of anything to say involving *tu* and maybe it was better for her to start.

After all that waiting the girl wasn't happy at hearing such a ridiculous proposition of course, still she had her own way of being displeased rather subdued and almost imploring like a person accustomed to assuming responsibility for the disappointments that came to her through the fault of others and whose first impulse in every situation is to apologize, and added to this was a slight awkwardness because Antonio had shifted to her the task of starting to say something and this something after the importance that it had accumulated during the long evasion couldn't of course be one of those remarks made just to be saying something, still judging by what could be seen of the half of her face left visible by her flowing hair she must have been more perplexed than pensive as if she too had a fine assortment of sentiments ready and not too different from those stirring within him but she also seemed to lack the courage to bring them forth and that disturbed her but also irked her since basically it wasn't up to her to speak first, and in short the girl was caught in a turmoil of feelings to which however annoyance finally seemed to get the upper hand, and in fact at a given moment she moved resolutely from the gate and started up the Ponte Foscari saying that as he could clearly see she was stupider than he was after all.

Antonio naturally started after her without hesitation and was quite happy because in saying as you can see she had called him *tu* perhaps without even being aware of it so she had carried the whole business a step forward a short step if you like but in a sense a basic one; however when he pointed this out to her with no doubt excessive euphoria since after all he hadn't been the one to take this step, she answered that it wasn't hard, a reply all too simple in appearance which however on further examination seemed evasive and even mysterious because it wasn't clear what wasn't hard and substantially this might even be a reference or an allusion to his awkwardness which even the most kindly people apparently found ridiculous in the long run, anyhow it wasn't surely a sentence that could encourage him to go on with the conversation and in reality he didn't even try to answer, and as for her it seemed that after having expressed her idea of the lack of difficulty in using the *tu* or whatever it was she had nothing to add so they were silent perhaps both convinced that in this story of theirs which in a way could be said not to have yet begun, recriminations and even regrets were already beginning to crop up.

Now they were walking along the street which had widened somewhat after the bridge and in fact this stretch was called Calle Larga Foscari instead of simply Calle Foscari, and they were both proceeding with bowed heads as if in the grip of a kind of inertia caused probably by the poor outcome of the efforts made so far, and Antonio now did nothing to prevent the comparison of his shoes with hers which needless to say were new and beautifully shaped, on the contrary he wished his had been even more shapeless and old so that the evident lack of harmony might suggest to her also a wider meaning namely the complete impossibility of achieving what was lofty and good and possible for the two of them in common on earth, and naturally such reflections seemed made on purpose to aggravate the sense of frustration he felt rapidly coming over him and in fact he had the impression he had reached a sufficiently advanced stage in this process when she stopped before the end of the street and worsened things greatly by saying now he had to turn left for the Crosera in order to go directly to the Piazzale Roma whereas she would go ahead to the Campo San Polo, and before Antonio could translate into words the imploration legible in his eyes she added explicitly that she couldn't let him accompany her any farther because in the rest of the street she might easily be seen by her father who usually came home about that time and her father didn't like her going around with boys even if they were her classmates, a category which for that matter couldn't strictly be applied in the present case.

A rejection like this which on top of everything else sounded very much like an excuse to get rid of him quickly was exactly what Antonio was expecting if not consciously at least in his unconscious mind, he needed it as a final confirmation that what he had after all foreseen from the first moment was actually coming true, namely that he was losing her irreparably and would never see her again in his whole life and nothing remained to him but desperate loneliness and it was only right that this should happen because he was foolish and weak-willed and deserved the worst misfortunes in fact he was a mistake of conception and should never have seen the light of day, and in short he forced himself deeper and deeper into these lugubrious thoughts with the same intoxication others feel in plunging into dreams of joy because he knew that after all he would enter a phase of lacerating and fertile satisfaction during which there was virtually no action so bold he wouldn't feel capable of performing it especially if there was a prospect of coming to a dire end, and in fact now that he had lost all restraint he seized the hands of the astonished girl and suddenly said that he couldn't let her go away because first he had to speak to her.

Naturally in doing this he expected to be laughed at or even slapped and he wouldn't have cared much since any catastrophe was preferable to a colorless and irremediable separation, but she certainly wasn't thinking of slapping him or laughing at him and she seemed rather to be torn between fear and expectation like a frozen sparrow that he had picked up one frosty morning or else she was full of poetry and therefore oblivious or at least careless of the fact that in the meanwhile she was leaving her hands in his in any case she didn't hesitate to ask him to speak to her quickly if he had to because any moment her father might pass by, and this new reference to her father was enough slightly to deflate Antonio who found himself in a state of miraculous but extremely precarious audacity, that is whereas a moment before he had been on the brink of spilling everything not excluding the business of the two souls in search of each other and in addition had been convinced that revealing this to her would have been marvelous as well as definitive he was now assailed again by doubts and palpitation so he had the impression that it would after all have been much better if she had slapped him, but since she hadn't and presumably didn't intend to he confessed to her that despite the probable imminent conquest of the moon by the Russians or the Americans he didn't feel the least bit modern when feelings were involved and to his way of thinking these words were fairly provocative in the sense that she might easily have asked him then what feelings were involved and in this case he felt he could have told her the whole business and that would be that; instead the girl remarked sweetly and simply that if being modern meant toying with people's feelings irresponsibly then she preferred old-fashioned people and as far as the difficulty of opening one's heart was concerned she understood that and forgave it also because there are some things that can be said clearly without speaking at all, and of course Antonio approved her line of reasoning however it was a question of whether or not she was capable of understanding those things he was saying to her without speaking and since the matter meant a lot to him he asked her outright and she answered with the same sweetness as before that sometimes she understood such things hinting probably that this could certainly be one of those times, but Antonio at this moment wasn't satisfied with hints, he wanted the naked truth and he asked her and then she seemed finally to realize the fact that she had left her hands in his and she tried to withdraw them but without any strength or conviction and then lowering her eyes she answered that she had realized he didn't dislike her.

Now this was no slight admission in fact if he thought about it, knowing the girl, he found it a big confession less than half an hour after she had found him facing her, however Antonio didn't yet know the girl well and besides he was in such a passionate state that he couldn't reflect on her words, so when he heard her say that after all the efforts of communication he had been making so far she had understood only that he didn't dislike her he was almost offended however instead of pulling himself together and speaking clearly he asked her in a slightly irritated tone if that was all she had understood, and with her eyes still lowered she tried shyly to answer or at least to find a way of expressing what she wanted to answer and when she obviously couldn't find it she finally shook her head meaning no several times not rebelliously or resolutely but rather as if she were denying herself first of all a joy that was in any case hazardous, and then gasping a bit for breath she begged him to let her go because she couldn't be late, but he had to exploit her submission and assume a bit of aggressiveness so he didn't let her go at all and asked her curtly if she disliked him by any chance.

At this point the girl had to look up not to decide whether or not she disliked him but because she felt the conversation had reached such a degree of intensity that they had to look into each other's eyes, and so with her eyes raised to his without any bewilderment but with a kind of voluntary forbearance she answered no as if she were conceding some part of herself and as if she meant with that little word to assume a large share of responsibility in the pleasures and the sorrows that would inevitably derive from it, and Antonio suspected that her no was important however he couldn't dwell on it because all this happened as they were taking leave of each other and naturally the main thing was to establish some practical bridge toward the future, that is to decide where they could meet the next time, tomorrow for example at four o'clock at the Zattere again, and at every question she answered yes with her eyes and her head and all of herself but not with words since a fair amount of alarm persisted even in her decision to entrust herself to him and so was easier for her to say it without words though it was no less binding, still she couldn't go too far in this silence either and so as soon as she had granted what he wanted she begged him once more to let her go, and reluctantly he was about to let go of her when he realized he didn't even know her name so he asked her and she answered hastily that her name was Maria and she slipped from his hands.

In which Antonio, transformed into
a bloodhound, makes a consoling discovery

For Antonio this was clearly a day of pursuits made without thinking twice or rather without thinking even once, and in fact as he watched Maria go off rather in a hurry he supposed that for the moment he had done enough partly because of the weariness which set in after all his tension and partly because he was going to see her tomorrow anyway, but as soon as she had disappeared into the crowd in the narrow Calle di Dona Onesta which opens right at the end of the Calle Larga Foscari he suddenly and automatically felt impelled to follow her realizing only later that he had gone off after her again not so much out of a desire to discover exactly where she was headed and if possible who she was as out of a necessity to combat his own profound and frightening sense of insecurity which customarily appeared at the least opportune moments and which could attack both himself as subject and external reality as object, and in this case Maria still hadn't so to speak withdrawn from his sight when he was already beginning to suspect she was nothing but an abstract fiction of his spirit which thirsted too much for love and naturally if he had let himself go he would soon have come also to doubt himself, risking perhaps some form of depersonalization or of existential irrelevance, hence the need to gaze upon her again even from a distance and in absolute humility, that is without attracting attention or causing any disturbance but strengthening his certainty that she existed in flesh and blood and that in consequence he also existed at least as an entity capable of love if not as anything else.

Driven by these impulses he managed to glimpse her as she turned from the Fondamenta del Forner into the Calle del Cristo, and before she reached the Campo San Tomà he was almost behind her so he didn't lose sight of her after that because there were many people coming and going along that route which meant he could follow her closely reassuring himself of her existence but with a kind of mental paralysis as far as the rest was concerned, that is he succeeded in thinking only of the fact that her name was Maria managing however to accumulate in that name despite its being common his anxiety and tenderness and gratitude and other still stronger sentiments which taken all together might not improperly be called love or anyhow something that sufficiently satisfied his long need for love, and from that he derived an excessive joy which in fact he was able only with some effort to contain without shouting it all around at anyone passing by, and naturally along with the joy there was also a sense of fullness and of vigor born from the hope or rather from the certainty of being loved and in fact she not only hadn't rejected him but had accepted him and you might say even encouraged him, and all this had happened with an unbelievable rapidity which for that matter filled him or at least should have filled him with justifiable pride.

And instead it was precisely this unbelievable rapidity that struck the first blow at Antonio's joy and though he hastened to defend his nascent love telling himself that the many doubts about to attack him were only the fruit of his long lack of aptitude for happiness and full enjoyment in general of both material and spiritual benefits, the doubts attacked him all the same and he had to analyze them mercilessly one by one, and what's more without slowing his pace so as not to lose touch with the girl who was walking faster all the time. The basic fact then namely the one which it was impossible to doubt was that the girl had allowed herself to be won with extraordinary ease since it was undeniable that from the moment he had approached her brusquely under the portico of the Cassa di Risparmio she had shown nothing really but docility and submission, in fact every time he had been on the verge of giving way to despair or inexperience or shyness she had been the one to save the situation promptly smiling or giving him a heartening look or even suggesting new subjects for conversation so it wasn't farfetched to suppose that she wanted to be won by him even more than he himself wanted to win her, and this was a supposition that led directly to other imputations fairly ruinous not only because of the lessening of his own importance since it emerged that instead of having taken the initiative he had followed hers, but also and especially because of the suspicion that Maria might be one of those modern girls who are a bit too inclined to involve themselves in love affairs.

From such a suspicion which to tell the truth he didn't go so far as to formulate completely Antonio recoiled immediately repentant and grieved and he had only to look at her present way of walking which was even too absorbed and to think also of the purity of her face and the hesitation in her smile and the limpid depths of her gaze to realize how thoughtless and unfair it was to be suspicious of her behavior, however the incredible ease of his conquest still had to be explained and since with the admitted scarcity of his physical attractions he was the first to be unable to deceive himself that he had fascinated her simply by appearing before her and since it was also best for the moment to leave out metaphysical explanations since with all those Russians and Americans who were now strolling around in the cosmos the theory of the two souls seeking each other in infinity really looked like a piece of nonsense he was forced to think up something else and so as he went on thinking he began to have the idea that Maria wasn't exactly beautiful the way she had seemed to him until then and she was actually a bit plain and she had seemed beautiful to him only because he had met her under special circumstances namely when an impelling necessity to fall in love was capable of playing some nasty tricks on his ability to judge female beauty, and to tell the truth looking at her now from behind as she walked in front of him she didn't seem so terribly beautiful, instead she was just a girl like dozens of others with a gray coat and a bucket-like bag full of textbooks and legs which weren't crooked but weren't particularly slender no more than normal, and her hair was Venetian blond that is to say brown with a tendency toward red that is in the final analysis an ambiguous and rather ordinary color.

Now Antonio was capable of recalling very clearly that her first expression when he had stopped her under the portico of the Cassa di Risparmio had been more of amazement than anything else that is in effect she had displayed chiefly wonder that a boy had had the idea of stopping her and this could only stem from the fact that they didn't pay much attention to her and obviously they didn't pay much attention to her because they didn't consider her at all beautiful since nowadays a girl was hardly shown respect for any other reason, in short following this line of reasoning he came to re-establish the propriety of her behavior however it also emerged dammit that the girl wasn't beautiful any longer and this obviously made him very sorry so he also tried to back away from this new set of notions by recapturing his first impression of her when he had seen her at once as beautiful not to say very very beautiful but this beauty might also be of a sort that was valid only for him in which case it would be absolutely mistaken to call her beautiful because what is considered beautiful becomes so thanks to a consensus and not thanks to the passing whim of people who might be in a mental fog so to speak, and in short Antonio no longer felt sure of having made a fairly prudent and shrewd choice especially when he considered that all the good qualities the girl seemed to possess were on the verge of becoming defects a bit like the freckles and the crooked tooth for example so it would be wise for him to think it over a moment before going any farther.

He had achieved this splendid result which rightly depressed and embittered him considerably when still following the girl's footsteps closely he came out after her in the Campo San Polo and here since the vast square was almost deserted he promptly slowed his pace to keep her at a distance and in fact he was fairly unsure whether to go on with his shadowing, whose objective of recovering his sense of existing seemed at present all too fully achieved, however now that the first aim was gone it could immediately be replaced by another namely since he was there he might as well see where the girl was going, especially since she was walking toward the end of the square namely more or less in the direction he would have to follow to go on to the Piazzale Roma, however at a certain point she turned toward the entrance of one of the buildings that formed the square's northern boundary that is toward a handsome upper-class palazzo with Gothic windows and inlaid marble decorations on the façade, and after having rung the doorbell and waited pensively for them to open as soon as the lock clicked she pushed the door and disappeared inside. At this point Antonio was a bit dumfounded because by going into such a fine building where people loaded with money must live the girl had done something he really hadn't expected, however to tell the truth he hadn't been expecting anything different on this score namely that she would go into a less elegant building or even a poor one, and in fact the problem of her belonging to one social level rather than another was one he hadn't yet considered partly because to his way of thinking these were hardly relevant questions and also a bit because until now other problems far more lofty and pressing had kept his spirit busy, however seeing that she had after all gone into a building which so to speak inspired awe he felt it wasn't a bad idea to investigate and to learn the last name of this Maria with whom he had one way or another already begun a love story, and his curiosity soon led him to a heavy shiny painted door where there was a single bell with a brass plate in the form of a fluttering ribbon with the name Cavalier Ilario Borghetto written on it.

At first that name Borghetto rang no bells at all with Antonio

who was however sure he had heard or at least seen it hundreds if
not thousands of times so he began to ponder it as he walked back
and forth on the wide damp cobbles of the Campo San Polo though
in the end he solved nothing that is he couldn't connect the name
with anything known to him until he finally decided to do the
only logical thing in such a situation namely to go into the café at
the corner of the Sottoportico della Madonneta and order a coffee
while he looked up the name Borghetto in the telephone directory,
and having done this he found that Cavalier Ilario in addition to
the address San Polo 3142 had another written in larger and bolder
letters which declared that he was the proprietor of Borghetto
Maritime Supplies which had its headquarters at Dorsoduro 1217.

Now Antonio could remember clearly that he had in fact seen
that name Cavalier Ilario Borghetto Maritime Supplies many times
even painted in aggressive lettering on the sides of the motor barges
that sped through the various canals of the city laden with mer-
chandise especially in the neighborhood of the station either at the
Piazzale Roma or the harbor station, and if Maria was really the
daughter of such a cavaliere it meant that she was rich, that she had
a whole mountain of money at least from our hero's point of view
and therefore it's possible to understand how as a result he was
seized with great excitement and having drunk his coffee he went
back again to pace up and down the Campo San Polo in the dusk
heedless of the cold and damp and feeling beyond the shadow of a
doubt that this love of his which he had wretchedly succeeded in
smashing to bits by rationalizing over it was now regaining strength
and fabulous dimensions, and not surely for reasons of self-interest
and practical utility as some might think but for different and
almost opposed motives and in fact Maria's wealth restored her to
a fairly remote sphere where he could desire her with the alarm
and frustration necessary to the nourishment of a great love, and
also his doubts about her beauty and propriety no longer had any
foundation inasmuch as she was the presumably favorite daughter
of Cavalier Ilario Borghetto so now Antonio could see with absolute
clarity that the error he had made and the cause of his temporary

confusion was his having brought her down too close to himself, however everything now returned to its proper place because he was poor and she rich and therefore inaccessible and all the same she hadn't rejected him and perhaps who knows she might even allow him to love her, with torment and despair as was necessary, and also with his vanity completely satisfied.

CHAPTER
IV

In which Antonio and Maria
become certain they requite each other's love

The following day at exactly a quarter to four when Antonio turned up on the Zattere wearing a magnificent pair of English-style shoes he had just bought in an elegant shop in the Mercerie in other words the street in Venice which has the greatest abundance of shops that are elegant, unfortunately it was already raining for all it was worth and this was because that morning as not infrequently in autumn the weather had undergone an abrupt change and the sirocco was blowing up from the sea a great number of clouds that had become heavier and heavier and thicker and thicker until the whole sky over the city and the lagoon was filled with rain, and now all this rain was finally coming down.

This was an event that our young man had quite culpably not foreseen so while he stood under the portico of the branch of the Cassa di Risparmio and watched the rain fall with increasing abundance on the pavement and on the café's empty terrace and beyond on the wan surface of the Giudecca Canal he felt a double melancholy come over him both because of his new shoes which were beginning their life in such adverse conditions and for another far graver and quite different factor which however very mysteriously became linked with his sadness for his shoes, namely his thoughtlessness to say the least in not arranging with Maria a different meeting place in case of bad weather since it certainly wasn't easy or even justified to hope that from the Campo San Polo she would venture as far as the Zattere with all that water the heavens were pouring down. In different circumstances, to be specific if he hadn't had the bright idea of following her to the door of the handsome palazzo with the Gothic windows and marble tracery he wouldn't have known a thing about Maria now neither her last name nor where she lived and so with this bad weather he would have been in grave danger of losing her perhaps for a long time or even forever, and as he considered it now after almost twenty-four hours of incessant lucubration during which she had become something that for him corresponded absolutely to the very idea of love, that danger was more unbearable than any grief or misfortune he had undergone before then in his life.

The knowledge of Maria's last name and address was in any case more valuable as a guarantee for the future or a privilege from which he could somehow extract consolation than as an element of immediate usefulness and in fact it didn't seem possible that Antonio could make use of his discovery by casually telephoning her to stay at home and not catch cold because in telephoning her he would have had to reveal how he came to know her telephone number and that would not have been good or suitable at the very beginning of their story, so he decided to wait without setting any time limit there beneath the portico and so much the better if he should be the one to catch cold as was more than likely because he was of the opinion that the joys of this world are always achieved through a good portion of sufferings and though he didn't dare establish any connection and still less any direct relationship between a head cold and the hope of loving Maria properly, still he was sure that even a simple cold would help make him at least a little less unworthy of her, something which in view of the abyss that separated them seemed to represent a real need. Moreover though the idea was absurd if Maria were to brave the rain which was falling harder all the time and appear at a certain point then he would know the extent of her interest in him, an extent that in this circumstance would be enough to kill even the slightest suspicion that she might not be prepared to let him love her despite everything, and his desire to love her was so great that the fairly absurd hypothesis of her coming soon became almost a hope and he even began to imagine how she would suddenly turn up, coming from the direction of the Rio di San Trovaso and in order not to spoil his own joy in her sudden appearance at the corner and also not to give his waiting a trepidation which all things considered was best avoided he forbade himself to go and cast an inquisitive glance along the Fondamenta Nani, and in short he was in a state of inner turmoil because on one hand to offset disappointment he wanted to remain sure she wasn't coming but on the other hand he didn't want to give up the pleasure of waiting for her and even of imagining how she would look in case she did come, and all this confusion still had a positive aspect in that it meant remissive acceptance of whatever was going to happen, a suitable sentiment which in the end increased his merits thus diminishing of course the distance that separated him from his beloved.

Then when it was exactly a quarter to six and practically night it so happened that Maria turned up from the direction opposite the one Antonio had imagined in other words from the Gesuati and so he was faced by an apparition even more sudden than he had foreseen and in a different frame from what he had pictured and what's more her hair was clotted with the dampness and she seemed even less tall than yesterday because of her little rubber boots with their low heels, and in conclusion now that all his meticulous mental preparation for this second meeting had gone up in smoke there was more than one reason for him to be quite confused and to allow her to apologize for her lateness at greater length than was proper because after all though the lateness was considerable it wasn't her fault because in such weather she couldn't tell her mother she was going to study on the terrace of the café on the Zattere and so she had to invent the pretext of getting a needed book from the library and then think up endless excuses to wait till her mother had gone out because since she did have to go out she had decided to accompany Maria and this was why she was so shamefully late and she hadn't hoped she would find him there but she had come all the same and now she was happy to find him that is happy he hadn't waited and waited for nothing.

During her speech which was fairly long even if uttered in great agitation Antonio had all the time necessary to recover from his initial perturbation and to examine her calmly and almost in a critical spirit discovering that she was much more beautiful than he had remembered her also because he had prudently forced himself not to remember her as too beautiful and instead here she was very beautiful in the truest and most profound sense and not of course common and showy, and not even her hair all matted from the dampness could detract from her face's luminous animation which for that matter she probably hadn't had or rather surely hadn't had yesterday so this was an exceptional aspect, that is it was to be connected with her present action almost as if her coming here signified a number of things that her reserve kept her from saying but which in any case she allowed to transpire through her expression which was to be precise animated and luminous, and also probably not entirely unconnected with a display however indirect of her feelings was the fact that she was dressed in a way that might lead one to believe she had prepared carefully for the meeting, in short she was wearing an elegant raincoat of a rather dark brown with all the accessories harmonizing including a little girl's rainhat with a strap under the chin so that in addition to his gratitude that she had come in this cloudburst he also felt a mounting almost paternal tenderness because she was so tiny and visibly helpless and maybe even in spite of her boots her feet were wet or at least damp, so he said to her it would be best if they moved from under the portico and went inside the café to have a rum punch or a good cup of hot tea, and she didn't say no but she could only stay five minutes because at six-thirty the library closed and anyhow she would have to go home quickly in fact almost immediately.

So when they had entered the warm and smoky air of the café they waited for their punch sitting opposite each other at a little marble table oblivious of the other people around them and naturally looking at each other with shy trust or to be more precise piercing each other with glances and each giving the other as much as possible of himself, but while in Maria this giving ripened in the knowledge of something that would probably be sad but was in any case inevitable and already accepted, in him it didn't ripen at all or rather it was restrained by an irksome uneasiness which in turn stemmed from a need for sincerity not so much in his feelings which were pressing all too vitally and unmistakably as in certain marginal matters which were contaminating these sentiments making them difficult and we might as well say painful and in fact the day before he had told her a slightly distorted truth when he had claimed to be a university student because for a couple of years now he hadn't taken any exams or paid tuition fees and if he had to come out with the naked truth he would have to confess that he had long since given up his university studies and was merely a teacher in the fourth grade of the Marocco coeducational elementary school or to put it baldly he was an elementary school teacher, however he couldn't reveal this to her, not to the daughter of Cavalier Borghetto of the Maritime Supplies or in any case not now during this still uncertain beginning, and since she had become quite aware of his tormented hesitation she was saying that if he had anything to say, even something unpleasant he was to say it without any hesitation in short she was inviting him to speak frankly on whatever subject so he took her hand across the table and though knowing he was thus blocking the way to the revelation of other less attractive truths put perhaps no less important foreseeing a real love story he said that he felt afraid because he was already falling in love with her.

This statement at first sight perhaps downright brilliant on closer examination wasn't after all so judicious since apart from the men-

tion of fear which was out of place there was the fact that the girl
might also become suspicious at the ease and haste with which he
revealed sentiments of a certain gravity, that is she might have been
led to think he was accustomed to scattering such declarations at
random more or less everywhere, but the poor thing at present had
her head in the clouds that is she was quite impervious to nasty suspicions and more than anything else she seemed eager that this
thing which was apparently going to happen to her although in
all probability it might easily lead to disaster should happen to her
as soon as possible and in fact she asked him with wonderful heedlessness why he spoke of fear, thus confirming the no doubt mistaken but still fairly widespread principle that love should never
be frightening.

Now with the small amount of time they had it surely wouldn't
have been wise for Antonio to pursue this subject and explain
how though in general what she seemed to think about love was
quite correct still there could be special cases where a young man
of very humble circumstances and what's more already in trouble
as far as fibs were concerned might really be afraid of falling in
love with a girl who was probably a millionairess in addition to
being a mirror of frankness and simplicity, and in fact trapping
himself in such questions would have spoiled the enjoyment of
the good things within their reach such as devouring each other
with their eyes inextricably mingling their ineffable inner trepida-
tions, and besides he had hinted at fear more to make an impression than for any other reason and actually he had made a certain
impression so it would no doubt be all to his gain if he stuck to
such slightly theatrical remarks therefore he said he was afraid
because maybe he would be the only one of the two of them to fall
in love and who could say how much it would make him suffer, a
less clever remark than he would have imagined since it allowed
her to attribute a degree of egoism to him which he really didn't
possess at least not in the present situation that is to say a moment
when he would gladly have had himself flayed alive in order to
become more worthy of loving her, but she couldn't see into his

mind and examine what was really inside it so she had perforce to judge by the words he spoke and thinking he was worried only about himself she then seemed a bit upset not to say demoralized so she replied with a touch of resentment that she too might happen to fall in love alone but it wouldn't frighten her at all.

This was an expression that could be interpreted in several ways but the most logical since she continued sweetly to leave her hand in his was as concrete encouragement to proceed with his sentiments not lingering to quibble over them so much or thinking so much about the complications which would in any case arise as soon as they both were a little more deeply in love, but Antonio was troubled by a bad conscience and also firmly convinced that this dialogue had necessarily to be complicated and difficult so he took her to mean she was reproaching him for lack of courage and he even attributed to her the intention of placing herself on a spiritual and intellectual plane superior to his own, something he couldn't accept since he already realized his inferiority in too many other ways thanks to unfortunate and generally unjust circumstances and he wanted to retain his superiority at least in the field of experience of life and then to clarify the situation at once he asked her if she had ever been in love before, wanting to imply that a girl like herself completely ignorant of love matters was in no position to judge the enormous suffering of unrequited love, however when he had tossed out this question with no doubt excessive self-confidence she unexpectedly began to reflect and after perceptible hesitation she answered that she had never been in love though her expression was quite odd almost as if she were at pains to exclude a memory or worse as if she were perhaps feeling an inner satisfaction because of it, so Antonio was cut to the quick and had good reason to ask her if this was really the truth and she blushed slightly at first and then smiled as if apologizing and also wanting to be free of her confusion until she finally admitted she could never tell lies because anyone could see the minute she told one.

If he hadn't also been obliged to square his conscience after his reticence about his elementary school teacher position, Antonio would have accepted her statement with the proper common sense since there was really nothing extraordinary in the fact that a girl of eighteen should have been in love with somebody at some time and it was even less extraordinary that she should try not to spill the information to the first boy who came along, but instead he was not only irritated at not being the first man she had loved or was falling in love with but he also had this necessity to square things and so he aimed at enlarging her guilt in order to put her so to speak with her back to the wall therefore he insisted on knowing every detail about the person she had loved before, and then half-bewildered and half-amused and perhaps also a little flattered if there was room for that as well, she answered that she had been in love with a boatman a man who ran a public motorboat who was more or less Antonio's age but already with a wife and children she thought it was at least two children when she was just nine and a half and she had cried for ages in secret without telling anybody about it of course and least of all the boatman, and perhaps she was hoping Antonio would smile at this childish misadventure of hers but seeing he didn't smile at all she added in a somewhat apologetic tone that she had told him this only so he would realize why she wasn't afraid of unrequited love.

It was evident that in this fashion the conversation wasn't going smoothly for Antonio who had first set the fencing-match tone and was now getting the worse and becoming irritated, and perhaps this was why instead of finding the boatman story fairly consoling at least as far as he personally was concerned since it might suggest a tendency on her part to fall unhappily in love with people of an inferior rank he became unreasonably annoyed and allowed himself to be seized by a sudden and ill-advised desire to hurt her as well as himself so he asked her point-blank if she wasn't rich by any chance, and he saw immediately from her expression that the unexpected question didn't please her a bit and that of all the subjects Antonio might have touched upon this was probably the least welcome so instead of answering she asked him in turn in a rather reserved tone why he had asked that, and immediately outdoing her as far as reserved tones went he answered that he wasn't really asking her at all it was more of a verification since her belonging to a privileged class to say the least was quite clear from her manner of dressing and speaking and her general attitude, and having heard this she seemed to have nothing to reply and in fact it wasn't so easy to find an answer also because he had spoken aggressively as if he wanted to reproach her for something, so at this point she wasn't in the least well-disposed toward him and when the waiter came to bring the punch she wanted to pay immediately to be free to leave as soon as she had finished drinking it and moreover she insisted punctiliously on paying half saying that this was the custom among students thus depriving their meeting of its emotional basis, unless her intention was even worse and she wanted to underline the notion that he probably had much less money than she and therefore he would be wise not to squander it, and this is precisely how Antonio interpreted it and since they couldn't go on he thought he might as well ruin what little there was left to ruin and without any preamble he revealed that the night before he had followed her and having seen where she lived and who she was he had thought all night that he shouldn't come to their appointment and should never see her again and so it had been a mistake for him to come.

To tell the truth this wasn't the serious, firm speech he would have liked to make to her nor was his tone the most suited to express a perhaps pained but still courageous dignity, and actually in those few sentences uttered not without effort he had showed not only that he was weak but also capable of more than one compromise if she had given him the slightest excuse, however she seemed to feel no reply was necessary, in fact she took back her hand which she had in all events left in his until then and moving it toward their glasses she said they had better drink their punch before it became cold, and though she said this with every intention of easing the atmosphere, the suggestion could also be understood in a context of dismissal and Antonio as you can well imagine was hardly the type to miss the opportunity of understand-

ing it exactly this way and in fact convinced that the moment had
come to risk all he grasped her hand again preventing her from
drinking her punch and saying that first she had to answer, but
she insisted that as far as she was concerned there was nothing to
say or to argue about and then he put the question directly if by
chance she thought he had done wrong to come back today and
meet her and she answered that she thought only one thing
namely that all these problems he seemed so worried about had
nothing to do with the two of them the way they were.

An assertion of this nature corresponded exactly to the nucleus
of Antonio's thoughts or at least his desires for though all during
the night he had done nothing but writhe in desperation at the
various abysses that separated him from her he was basically in
favor of a superior classification of human beings, that is an arrangement that overlooked all social and economic and geographical differences and made him equal to her or still better left him that
slight margin of advantage due him thanks to his greater experience
of life and suffering, and he should therefore have felt happy at her
clearly expressed opinion and he should wisely have directed the
conversation toward less involved themes, but by now he was so
bent on a lacerating need of sincerity that he couldn't stop himself
and after having stated that the problems she so generously tended
to dismiss were instead all too pertinent he said that his own father
wasn't a millionaire like certain *cavalieri* who trafficked in maritime
supplies but was instead a second-category stationmaster retired
to whom the government granted a pension of seventy-seven thousand lire a month and this was all the money they had to live on
and at present they were full of worries because they didn't know
how to buy wood for the winter, and having said this he checked
himself right on the brink of disastrous emotion since another word
would have made him burst into tears and naturally he couldn't
start crying in front of her good God anything but not that not
crying since he would have all too much time to cry in the future
as far as he could foresee whereas for the moment it was better
to shield oneself with decorum thinking that anyway he had

spoken for once with courage and stout-heartedness and that the most important thing after all was to love like a man, and so after having asserted that she should know these things before it was too late he picked up his glass of punch and began to drink it in little sips because it was still boiling hot.

Naturally he was fairly convinced he was fighting a hard battle precisely to lose this Maria without any delay and to cut short their story which in an ill-starred moment like this one they were living in could surely not go forward, still because of the great suffering that losing her caused him as he tried hard to burn his bridges on the one hand he also took care on the other to leave her some chance to reconstruct them, and for example the expression you should know this before it was too late which he had used to conclude his speech about family poverty and the difficulty of buying wood for the winter was not so final that it didn't leave some room for puzzlement and curiosity, and in fact instead of taking her punch and drinking it as he was ostentatiously doing she asked what he meant by the words too late so he could answer her with suitable vigor that it didn't mean anything at least not as far as he was concerned since he was already irremediably in love with her but in any case that wasn't of the slightest importance because he had already made up his mind independently that they were never to see each other again.

To tell the truth this idea may have been too bold and though he didn't regret expressing it bluntly as it had to be expressed while Antonio waited now his heart skipped a few beats and his guts twisted expecting her to react, but she sat there with her head bowed and motionless as if under the weight of a resignation that made any reply useless so Antonio could believe he had finally achieved a precise result, namely that this story was also finished thank God it was finished because it was better to break it off at once though he would afterwards regret even the moments of suffering not consummated together, in short he was now seized by an excited desire for her to answer that what he had decided independently was all right with her too and instead after a little while in an open and helpless manner more than resigned to the inevitability of the troubles that were about to befall her she asked him if he would want them never to see each other again even if she were already in love with him.

Certainly Antonio in some profound part of his being was prepared for this in the sense that he had never completely doubted his own capacity to make her fall in love, but to hear her utter such a confession in such a knowing and yet remissive way was enough to fill even a fairly well fortified narcissistic spirit with dangerous exultation, still though half-overcome he understood it would have been absolutely irrational as well as disrespectful to let himself go now in demonstrations of excessive happiness especially since he had obtained his best results so far chiefly through melancholy so in a fairly subdued tone as if he still couldn't entirely believe it he asked her if it would really make her happy for the two of them to go on seeing each other more frequently and seriously, and raising her face in which there seemed to be more suffering than anything else she answered that she would be more than happy but he had to stop saying she was rich and he was poor because this was very mortifying for her and maybe it wasn't even true that she was as rich as he thought since her father was a self-made man and at times he was terribly worried because business wasn't going as well as it ought to go.

Undoubtedly Antonio was able to imagine the difference between the worries of her father who by all appearances made business deals involving millions at a time and the worries of his own poor father who always grumbled at the least expenditure and therefore also at the wood that had to be bought, however it was still a consolation to learn that not even Cavalier Borghetto of Maritime Supplies hit the bull's-eye every time and he was even tempted to say as much so she would at least understand his general way of thinking but this would obviously have led him off the track therefore he kept quiet and meanwhile she misunderstood his silence but was also contagiously affected by the great desire for self-laceration he had displayed until a moment before with forced and bitter stubbornness so she went on to say that her father had come up the hard way since he had only finished elementary school and before the war he had been an errand boy running around for the man he worked for, and she said this not only because the way things stood it was right for Antonio to know it but also because it wouldn't be surprising if one day his good luck vanished as it had come, and in conclusion what she wanted to know at once was whether he would be just as fond of her if she were to suddenly become poor.

In Antonio's view this remark was made just for the sake of making it that is he didn't believe Cavalier Borghetto could stop earning millions so easily and it was still less easy for him to conceive even hypothetically of her being poor since poverty wasn't the least bit suited to her, yet overcoming these numerous contradictions he thought it would be marvelous if suddenly she were to turn out to be poor, still retaining her rich girl's fascination which obviously she couldn't lose, and imagining her as poor as himself finally encouraged him considerably so after having first stated that yesterday he had fallen in love with her without knowing she was rich and she apparently had fallen in love with him not knowing he was poor or not caring at all he ventured the opinion that it was a kind of destiny that had led them to meet or in other words it was more than probable that the two of them had been seeking each other for God knows how long though without knowing it perhaps and at last they had fatally found each other.

This final proposition contained a cautious reference to his long-cherished theory of twin souls seeking each other in the infinity of space and time and he felt rather content at having managed to produce it even in this approximate form after he had been working it out for twenty-four hours, but Maria perhaps didn't grasp its full value or in any case she seemed unwilling to follow him along this metaphysical path and in fact she said with disarming simplicity that according to her the two of them had fallen in love if it could be called that because they were young and it was right and beautiful for young people to fall in love if they appealed to each other without ulterior motives and that between them there were as Goethe put it elective affinities, and then with some effort because the subject was becoming delicate she added that Antonio attracted her a great deal both because of the delicacy of spirit he had already revealed even in their brief relationship and because of his general appearance, but she wasn't equally sure that she appealed to him and if he were really to examine her calmly he would notice that she wasn't at all beautiful because her face was full of freckles especially now after all the summer sun and what's more she had a crooked tooth and a front tooth at that which unhappily was the first thing anyone noticed about her and in short she couldn't understand how Antonio could have fallen in love with her if he really was in love and it wasn't just a passing infatuation and Antonio answered that if she had been able to see inside his heart she would see clearly how deeply he was in love and she wouldn't have mentioned infatuations and as far as the rest was concerned he could certainly tell her he had fallen so completely in love and at first sight precisely because of what she considered her defects because in his eyes she was beyond comparison the most beautiful girl in the world because of the light in her eyes and the color of her hair and her expression and lots of other things but above all because of her freckles and that tooth that was just a tiny bit crooked, and as he spoke he looked at her with such overpowering adoration that at a certain point she had to lower her eyes out of modesty and so she noticed her wrist watch and saw it was already six-fifteen and she was frightened because at half-past six they closed the library.

Naturally, seeing all that water pouring down from the heavens which were dark by now she didn't want Antonio to accompany her because by taking the circolare to San Marco and then the motoscafo he could reach the Piazzale Roma without exposing himself to the rain which moreover was coming down at a slant because of the sirocco's blowing, but Antonio as could easily have been foreseen answered that for no reason in the world would he sacrifice a single minute he could spend in her company unless she was trying to get rid of him of course but she wasn't in the least thinking of getting rid of him and had spoken only out of concern for his getting wet, and so since both of them were basically of the opinion that it was best to stay together as long as possible, they huddled under her umbrella and set off hastily along the streets they had walked the evening before, first down the Rio di San Trovaso and then toward the Campo San Barnaba.

They didn't speak much as they walked because she really seemed concerned with reaching the Ca' Foscari before they closed the library while he was fairly engaged in fixing in his memory all those instants which he rightly felt were decisive in his life and obviously in such an intense atmosphere every detail even the most insignificant took on an extraordinary importance until it became unquestionably worthy of being remembered forever so he concentrated on putting together, perhaps heaping them up a bit, events and feelings and perceptions both lofty and trivial, her nearness for example connected with the color of the raincoat and the slightly funny shape of her hat, or else her way of avoiding a puddle at the very last minute and the heavy sound of the rain on the umbrella's nylon and the water which was copiously soaking through to his thigh all mixed with commiseration for his new and not very lucky shoes and with the sacrosanct observation that there had to be something unlucky in a day so full of good luck, in short though somewhat confusedly he paid attention to everything because he was convinced that all these things and others like them which would be added from day to day as long as the story lasted would then nourish his loneliness when he was left without her because naturally it was unthinkable that their love would last for all eternity also because imagining its limits now caused a sweet torment which helped him enjoy it more fully in its precariousness, or rather it was precisely by thinking that one day she would be taken from him that Antonio succeeded in savoring fully the present joy of having her near and in love, so considering the resistance he usually put up against the conquest of happiness it was correct to say he was fairly happy, and he could have been even more so if he had managed to dismiss a slight remorse that still gnawed at his heart. In fact although in that afternoon of truths he had pulled out all too many even exaggerating as in the case of his father who didn't know how to buy the wood, it had still been impossible for him to tell her the truth about his being an elementary school teacher, and he couldn't tell her now point-blank because he had the impression she would have rebelled against such meanness, or rather he felt that after she had passed over so many far more serious indications of social inequality this was the very one she didn't seem the type to overlook, and naturally he couldn't have explained the exact reasons why he thought a thing that after all wasn't too kindly toward her but he could see she took a perhaps excessive pride in being a university student and that obviously could be attributed to the fact that she was so smart in school but perhaps it wasn't mistaken to imagine a different motive for example a kind of revenge or rivalry toward her father who had barely finished elementary school if he really had finished it, and obviously Antonio certainly didn't dream of putting himself on the level of her father however it seemed to him that her excessive pride in her university student's status was a little shortcoming in the great heap of her perfections and it inspired in him an annoyance all the greater since it created a necessity for him to go back to being a student a step of not inconsiderable moment if you thought about it, in any case there was no enterprise of which he felt incapable in the present situation and in fact ipso facto he decided that as soon as possible he would pay up his back tuition fees so that he could be properly enrolled again and he even thought that in a single year he could take the dozen exams still required for his degree which he would also take, just to show her it wasn't impossible to pass twelve exams in a single year.

Meanwhile they had reached the Ca' Foscari and luckily the library of the English seminar was still open so Maria could go and hunt for the book to show her mother while he stayed in the hall on the ground floor facing the great glass window over the curving Grand Canal looking at the palazzi on the opposite bank which appeared of a fantastic beauty since they could barely be discerned, and over the dark water boats and motoscafi and vaporetti with red lights passed almost continually, and although you couldn't say it was downright beautiful still the amorous sentiments which were overflowing from his heart were somehow poured out also on the bold-faced magnificent city toward which he had always felt a country boy's aversion and resentment, but naturally like all the other things of the world this feeling too was subject to modification and on careful examination it was already being modified since there was nothing strange in the fact that since he now was loved by the daughter of a character whose boats and motor launches sped freely through canals and basins he should overcome his old uneasiness and somehow take part in the sumptuousness of a city with which he had never felt any intimacy before.

Maria came back in a few minutes carrying a thick volume on the remote poetical experiences of Percy Bysshe Shelley and with this evidence to demonstrate at home to justify her brief absence she seemed much happier than before so Antonio had no trouble in perceiving her timorous submission to her mother as well of course to her father, and though if he had chosen he could have found in this too a good side in the sense that she became enriched by the virtue of being an obedient and respectful daughter which did no harm in a girl to be loved without any hesitation still he wouldn't have been displeased by even a circumspect display of independence at least on the question of what time she had to be home, but instead she said promptly that now she had to go and though it had been clear from the beginning that she couldn't stay with him eternally and therefore the moment when she had to go would have come perforce now the imminence of this event was something that suddenly seemed to drain all the content from the happiness he had painfully accumulated and naturally he feared that as soon as she had escaped his gaze his unconscious sense of insecurity would stir up all his existential doubts again.

Anxious as she was to arrive home quickly she still didn't have

the heart to leave him in too much haste and so once she came
out of the building though the rain was still pouring down she
stopped against the wall of the courtyard and perhaps she hadn't
really done it on purpose however it so happened that the place
where they stopped was not very well lighted and he was very
close to her in order to take what shelter he could under the
umbrella but also to be as close to her as possible of course, and
moreover there wasn't much need of talking since their sadness
at having to separate soon was sufficiently expressed by their sighs
and there was nothing else to talk about at that moment so then
Antonio began to tremble because he realized the moment had come
for him to kiss her and naturally kissing a girl wasn't an entirely
new undertaking for him since he had had occasion to kiss perhaps a dozen before then however with this girl whom he loved
as he had never believed it possible to love a girl the affair took on
a completely extraordinary aspect full of uncertainties also because
like it or not the socioeconomic differences had their importance
even in this sort of event where they shouldn't have counted, still
he had the impression that there was simply no way for him to avoid
the issue because she had already been looking at him for some
while with total devotion expecting something that in all common
sense could only be a kiss even if perhaps she wasn't fully aware of
that, and in fact outside of waiting she did nothing else though her
expectation was constant so he had to make up his mind to satisfy
for better or worse this anticipation and he began by resting his
mouth on hers with his lips closed which in a sense could already
be considered a kiss though it was all a question of guessing
whether this was enough for her, but how could he guess when
she gave him no hint that is she kept her mouth closed however not
closed tight and therefore perhaps hoping he would go farther,
the fact was in any case that she was as docile as a little girl full
of curiosity although on second thought curiosity wasn't the
appropriate term for this and full of love might perhaps be a
more suitable expression though the word love in the end wasn't
without ambiguities since at this very moment it was spreading into
a new sphere rich in danger, but in any case since doing something

more than what he was already doing seemed now unavoidable he overcame his paralyzing fear of a misstep and pressed her mouth harder until gradually her lips parted.

It was a complete and very long kiss from which Antonio derived much less satisfaction than one might think because all that time he was filled with torment wondering whether what he was doing was good or bad toward her and there were external complications too like the question of the umbrella which it wasn't clear who was to hold erect and in fact it didn't remain erect at all but that had no importance since the only thing that counted then was Maria's reaction to that no doubt ruinous kiss assailing her after an acquaintanceship of twenty-four hours, but her only surely perceptible reaction was so to speak a lack of reactions or to put it bluntly she was so abandoned that she allowed him to do as he pleased as if she no longer had any will of her own or as if she were even half-fainting, and really only her rapid breathing and her hands' weak clutching indicated she was still conscious.

When the kiss finally ended she remained huddled against the wall for a full minute or two recovering herself with difficulty from her deep languor, then making an effort she looked at him her eyes soft with gratitude and still a bit lost in an unbearable sweetness and she said she was slightly ashamed but she would never have imagined a kiss could be the marvelous thing she had just experienced, and realizing that this must have been the first time anybody had kissed her seriously Antonio was gripped by an emotion so intense it was impossible to find words for it so he limited himself to asking her rather banally if she had liked it, and almost weeping she answered she didn't know and she asked him to forgive her for answering like an idiot but she was so overwhelmed that she couldn't think and she was certain only of one thing that she loved him with all her heart, and then he was filled with an immense happiness that left no empty space inside or outside him and so after infinite uncertainty and anguish he felt he had finally discovered a plausible reason for his having been brought into the world.

———◆◇◆———

In which Antonio and Maria make colossal progress and get into trouble

The time that followed was a time
of beautiful love and according to the opinion Antonio formed
when things were all over and therefore with a sufficiently lucid
mind it was without doubt the most beautiful period of love in
the whole story with Maria because in the times after that although
their affection continued developing according to a natural and
in a sense irrepressible crescendo and therefore reached very high
peaks not commonly achieved by others such complications set
in that in the end the affair was filled with annoyances and tribulation. This doesn't mean that the first period or phase of Antonio's
and Maria's love was completely free of troubles and obstacles, but
at least these troubles and obstacles sprang exclusively from the
couple themselves or to be more precise from him because of the
peculiarly complicated character which by chance or by misfortune
was his, though on second thought the very fact that they loved
each other to such an extraordinary degree lent a hand when it
came to complications since excesses are by nature contrary to the
peaceful enjoyment of whatever affection and in fact according to
popular opinion they must always be paid for. In any case compared to what happened later the first period of the story can

without exaggeration be called the period of complete happiness and it lasted about a month namely from about the end of October to the end of November, not a long period certainly but all things considered not such a short one either and when you measure a period you must never overlook the number or the variety or the intensity of the events that take place within it, and in this case if the number of events wasn't basically considerable nor even their variety to tell the truth the intensity on the other hand was so great that both Maria and Antonio were often on the brink of foundering body and soul in that love whose special qualities were from the very beginning torment and destruction, and if they didn't founder it was only because of lack of method and inability to find the right way because as far as willingness was concerned they had no lack of that, and in fact if for example it had been granted them to devour each other with their eyes and with repeating to the point of boredom I love you and I love you too then without thinking twice about it they would soon have wasted each other away.

Naturally to destroy oneself or each other in such a brisk and basically rather unsatisfying fashion is not in the list of eventualities granted humankind and therefore Antonio and Maria also had to pass through the practical questions that loom over every love affair and make love troubled to say the least, and though the two of them possessed an unusual harmony of purpose and were moreover armed with a prodigious desire to content each other reciprocally in whatever situation things still couldn't all be smooth sailing, but at least they always tried to avoid superfluous annoyances and Maria especially not only shunned even casual references to her family but also did everything she could to keep from reminding him she was a rich girl and even pretended not to see the motorboats that sped along the canals bearing her father's glorious name painted on their sides and she turned up at their appointments dressed in great simplicity wearing as a rule a skirt and a pullover and a woolen overcoat like all the other girls, and only a closer inspection revealed that skirt and pullover and coat were wondrously soft and warm and in other words very expensive but perhaps she didn't have any cheaper ones and in any case they were very becoming.

During this first phase and especially after Maria had fairly successfully taken her exam on the painful beginnings of the poet Shelley's career the two of them spent several hours of the afternoon together generally from four to seven, and at first they continued meeting at the café on the Zattere where each came with his books and notebooks and they started studying indoors or outdoors according to the weather and it was nice to study and look up every so often to exchange an intense glance perhaps clasping hands at the same time under the table but they soon realized that in this way it was impossible to study with that minimum of application indispensable if any results were to be achieved, and besides in a short while they began to arouse the curiosity more or less discreet of other people since such an unusually fervid love could hardly pass unnoticed so at a certain point they would get up and go off for a stroll and as they enjoyed that much more they took to meeting directly at the corner of a street or behind a church or near a bridge and from there they would set out for walks lasting hours and hours never tiring, and really that first and favorable phase of their love was primarily deambulatory.

It was the time of year when autumn is hurrying toward winter which in Venice is a particularly wretched season and the one least suited to life in the open air, and in fact there was little to rejoice in whether it rained or whether there was thick penetrating fog, and the situation wasn't much better even when the sun was out because by then the sun was low and weak and always accompanied by a strong wind from the west or by an east wind which seemed to slash your face at every street corner, however they were so in love they found good whatever came and indeed the worse the weather was the more pleased they were because with the fog or the rain it grew dark earlier and then they could start kissing each other that much sooner.

For their walks they generally preferred that far section of the city toward the gasworks and the warehouses and although this choice had first been dictated more by cultural motives than anything else namely because of the presence of the church of San Sebastiano rich in fairly distinguished works of the painter Paolo Veronese on whom Antonio was thinking of resuming special studies toward his degree Maria and he became fond of the area after the cultural attraction proved baseless since any interest in Paolo Veronese was soon overpowered by the urgent necessity they felt to communicate to each other in every licit way their great love and so they visited San Sebastiano only occasionally when it was raining too hard outside and even in these circumstances it wasn't possible to study the paintings because the church then was so dark that the works were barely visible, but still it was very sweet to sit side by side in a pew at the back and hold hands without kissing because they couldn't forget that this was a holy place and besides there was always the sacristan who kept his eye on them precisely so they wouldn't forget.

The city they had been led to prefer was a minor and humble Venice with little canals full of gondolas and sandalos retired for the winter and little squares with laundry hanging in the weak sun when there was sun and songs from the radio or the television which pursued one another from street to street endlessly and with fewer and fewer people about as Antonio and Maria neared the point where the city ended at the pale lagoon or against the fence of the port, and it must have been the quarter's special tranquillity that made it remain a favorite even after Paolo Veronese's decline because there it was easy to find a passageway or a deserted street or a dimly lighted spot along some little canal or any place where as soon as it was decently dark they began to kiss each other madly with the sudden awareness that everything that had happened before that moment, namely the ever-renewed joy of their daily meeting and then their long walk arm in arm and the tireless succession of sighs and glances and words in which they indulged to let each other know how much they loved and in short that whole complex of wonderful actions which lovers generally use to express love of whatever quantity and quality, for them these things were fine only during daylight whereas with darkness they revealed a mysterious insufficiency and inadequacy so to compensate the couple had to hug and kiss each other, and precisely at this moment along with the greatest of pleasures Antonio also began to feel great uneasiness.

Our young friend had in fact been accustomed for some time to the idea of the intercommunion or mutual compensation of sorrows and pleasures and experience had taught him that sorrows are not always even accompanied by pleasures so he was now surprised that he should experience some pleasures which temporarily at least came without their corresponding sorrows, and it was also for this reason that he was eager for night to fall and he blessed the season which led to a progressive shortening of the days however at this point the question became still further complicated in the sense that despite the impression that their kisses were absolute and full as the evenings passed there seemed to be an obscure lack, that is just as the day's glances and words became insufficient as soon as night fell so the kisses of the previous day seemed defective the following day and from this failure to live up to their promises apparently came a necessity to proceed toward other deeper experiences which insofar as one could foretell once experienced would in turn become inadequate and therefore would demand with mounting urgency other satisfactions progressively approaching the final one, which Antonio tended to consider a kind of definitive profanation. Now he wasn't so backward that he didn't know that these progressive stimuli however disturbing were quite legitimate since they coincided exactly with certain plans of nature's connected with the continuation of the species, however it was one thing to argue abstractly and quite another to face the problems concretely and in the present case he felt a strong resistance to lumping Maria together with the problems of the continuation of the species in fact if he could have had his way he would have exempted her from all general principles of this sort and not for

hedonistic reasons obviously but precisely to obey his lofty impulses toward idealization, and this was just where the whole
thing broke down because it certainly wasn't possible to idealize
and paw over a girl at the same time and since it was impossible
to shelter Maria from the weakness of the flesh he wanted her to
be at least aware of it or in other words he wished she too would
suspect that at the end of this in all likelihood the definitive profanation would come.

Instead Maria seemed to be completely ignorant of the dangers
toward which after all she was also heading and to tell the truth
his chief impression was that for her everything was fine that is
she demonstrated an absolute and tangible adaptability to his
whims and this could indeed be a proof of submissiveness and
perhaps also of satisfaction however it was much more probably
a sign of perfect innocence and since according to a good principle
a maiden's innocence is to be respected this is how he came to face
the exquisitely moral problem of respecting it and he faced it with
the best will in the world every evening beginning to kiss her
hands and her hair and her forehead and her closed eyes and then
on the mouth with his lips shut meaning to linger over those actions as long as possible perhaps for the whole evening, but instead
it so happened that each evening with greater and greater speed
and impatience he parted her lips driving his kisses more and more
deeply as she denied him nothing and summoned to her mouth
all her sweetness and desire and passion ready to give him whatever
he wanted of her no doubt because she loved him desperately but
in the final analysis also unloading on him the total responsibility
for what happened and even more for what was bound to happen
in the very near future.

This wasn't a responsibility Antonio could take lightly especially
since he knew all too well that Maria's most appealing quality
that is the one thanks to which he had fallen so excessively in love
was her purity and it was this very purity that evening after
evening he was damaging and his sorrow at this inspired him to
find further motives for suffering perhaps not of equal intensity

but unquestionably more vast and complete such as for example the impression that they were leaving behind them the most beautiful and happiest part of love and of life itself, and the awareness of the vanity of trying to arrest the progressive yieldings in the hope of reaching total contentment in actions that still retained some residue of modesty, and the fruitless aspiration to suppress his overpowering desire to keep spoiling new things which he would never have again, and in short the wish not only to combat time but also to combat something much more mysterious and inflexible that even faster than time led existence to decline.

And a thornier problem than the kisses were the caresses, those direct and rather complicated contacts of his hands with her body where he ventured though torn by all sorts of fears and bewilderments since on the one hand there was the risk that his desire to clasp and touch would drive him even inadvertently beyond the boundaries of the licit and on the other hand there was the no less embarrassing probability that his inexperience or worse still some obscure fear of the female body might keep him from doing what a girl virtuous as you please but still sufficiently in love might expect, and his doubts and fears concentrated in greatest number precisely on this expectation of hers since it was quite clear that also in this troublesome field of the flesh she allowed him to do what he pleased without setting up obstacles and therefore probably furnishing an encouraging consent, however her real intentions in so doing remained to be seen since just as he never performed an action without first asking himself if she would like it or not presumably in her own behavior she placed first the idea of complying as far as possible with his desires and so she was there offering herself and waiting more to content him than to please herself.

The caresses began one evening when a strong wind was blowing and Maria in touching his hands noticed how cold they were and said poor darling how icy your hands are and had tried to warm them with her breath and also with various kisses but then seeing that no great results were achieved in this way she had opened her coat and invited him to warm himself better against her since at that moment she didn't feel the cold at all, and he had entered the sweet warmth of her cashmere pullover leaving his hands there gently pressing her thin hips and feeling her ribs and the little spaces between one rib and the next and the slightly rapid movement of her breathing and he experienced directly the enormous tenderness of that contact which as he saw it was of an exemplary purity because his dominant impression was that her ribs were childishly fragile, however in the long run anyone would have understood that keeping his hands still against her body without clasping or roving was a fairly ridiculous thing and not natural in any case and indeed Antonio himself began to think he would have behaved quite differently if instead of Maria he had had his hands on a somewhat less unblemished girl but naturally with her he couldn't behave as he had with the dozen at most girls of a less unblemished nature whom he had known before although to be completely honest he had to admit that his kisses with Maria had by now far surpassed both in depth and completeness any kiss he had known in the past, but this argument was correct only up to a point or rather it wasn't correct at all because a comparison between Maria and the other girls was completely off the track and in conclusion that first evening he had withdrawn his hands which still weren't very warm saying that was enough.

But the following evening when the wind was even more icy and piercing he warmed his hands against her once more and touched or rather involuntarily grazed her breast, an action that was imprudent to say the least and in fact she shuddered in a way that could have been dismay or even disapproval though in any event she should have logically taken into consideration that the very location of the breasts was such that one could bump into them without having any specific intention of doing so, in any case the intersubjective relationship in that quite intersubjective incident was very difficult for Antonio to work out also because he was not supported by sufficient knowledge of the argument and really had no idea of what was going on inside her as a result of his accidental contact with the touched or grazed breast, but luckily as soon as that unfathomable shudder had passed she hastened to say darling to him darling darling four or five times in a row in such a languid tone of voice that even an imbecile would have realized that if he had enjoyed caressing her breast she had also been fairly content to have it caressed, and so he felt called upon to repeat deliberately the action he had previously performed by accident and he did so with great fear and yet with amazement both at the thing in itself which was soft and sensitive and at the pleasure which however gradually he began to derive from it.

And obviously it wasn't possible to retreat from this step either also because when the moment came neither of them really wanted him to and so now immediately after the first two or three kisses without further ado he fell to caressing her and in fact his hands went straight under the pullover and sought warmth and a timid sweetness against her bare skin with the problem of finding a sufficiently unobstructed path between slip and bra and straps until his fingers arrived at the yielding curve of the breasts and then she stretched back against the wall and trembled and uttered with gasping breath a quantity of tender words like my love and darling and my sweetheart so there could now be no doubt she enjoyed it very much and Antonio also enjoyed it very much of course however at the end of these exhausting exercises he felt weighing upon him a considerable and complex burden of remorse which instead of dismissing or repressing he almost cultivated until he reached the impression that she had no responsibility in this matter or only a marginal one, an impression he was the first to admit was quite fallacious but which he needed since it was only by drawing the guilt for those actions upon himself that he could exculpate her that is despite everything preserve her innocence which on sober consideration was an obligatory process if they were to continue with the caresses or better still if they were to proceed further as now seemed more and more inevitable.

To tell the truth though caressing her breast was an extraordinarily beautiful and sweet action it couldn't be called a complete one in every sense and in fact at the end of all that caressing a state of tension remained that was the more disturbing and frustrated the more the contact had been long and intense and so it wasn't hard to understand that there was another and more secret part of her body which demanded to be caressed with an abandon and indeed with a demand that might be called autonomous in the sense that she couldn't have been wholly aware of it but which was still so effective that Antonio's hand finally summoned courage and seeking a narrow path between her skirt and her abdomen which for that matter drew back to ease his passage the hand moved down farther until it found that low point of the body which seemed to attract it and there it lingered in caresses or something similar while something not entirely clear took place within her a kind of yielding rigidity or rigid yielding and she even stopped saying tender words because she bit her lips perhaps afraid of shouting and she breathed with her nose more and more frequently and at the end after an alarming outburst full of shudders she said stop and sank into an exhausted lassitude her face flushed and her eyes dazed but much more luminous than before, and in short she became all tenderness after her solitary gratification.

The first time the thing happened Antonio had been mostly frightened not so much however by the frank way she had revealed her pleasure as because he had the idea he had gone too far along the road to definitive profanation and naturally the fault was more his than hers because even though she was in a sense the principal beneficiary of that long maneuvering Maria had made it possible also to please him that is to satisfy his frenzy to lead her somehow to the end of all that aroused excitement that affected them both, and he felt that no one could judge this matter better than he since he was the one who felt that frenzy, and as if this weren't enough once the peak of pleasure had been past she had put her head on his shoulder and started crying and if she wept it could only be from shame at what had happened to her that is in the final analysis from what he had been in a frenzy to do to her so he had asked her forgiveness assuring her moreover that he would never do it again, but she told him not to torment himself about anything because she wasn't crying in shame or regret but with tenderness at that mysterious thing that had happened to her and now she at last felt completely his and utterly happy and in short now there should be no further doubts that they would be married at once or rather as soon as it was possible.

At this point Antonio's real uneasiness began although he wasn't entirely averse to considering matrimony the inevitable consequence of a love as great and complete as his for Maria and therefore he had never had any illusions that this problem wouldn't crop up one fine day still he wasn't very prepared to hear it set before him so soon that is after less than three weeks of their acquaintance and moreover he had thought that though they would inescapably have to talk about the subject it would be discussed as something extremely complicated to be placed in any case in the not too concrete category of conjecture and instead she referred to it with such simple immediacy that the question became not just affective but effective, and this meant that the careful reflection normally granted such events could no longer be postponed.

Naturally also in this matrimonial matter the first complication that stood out was the socioeconomic one namely the familiar fact that she was rich and he poor and she from the city and he from the country and she from the upper middle class and he from a petit bourgeois background, and although he knew quite well that such disparities have always been irrelevant in the birth of a great love and could even be considered at times favorable circumstances he was not unaware of how the petty calculation of who is more or has more takes on tiresome importance again the moment love descends from the lofty spheres which are its own and lowers itself to the level of marriage or a contract properly speaking.

Now isolating a single part of the problem from the rest when it came to Maria's considerable wealth and his own burdensome poverty Antonio could make some reflections which were debatable to say the least and which from one day to the next were influenced by extraneous factors such as poor digestion or lack of family affection or difficult relations with the assistant principal of the Marocco elementary school and so on, still striking a balance of his arguments considered calmly and without stomach upsets and in a neutral state as far as other mishaps were concerned, in the economic fortune of Maria who moreover was an only child and therefore most likely sole heiress of the Maritime Supplies, Antonio tended to see both a present annoyance and a kind of remote guarantee in case he fell ill or God forbid died and also in no less unpleasant situations such as the hypothetical event pictured only in an excess of prudence that Maria should prove less perfect than she now appeared and that the marriage should then turn out less happy and lasting than one might think at present. All of this naturally didn't stem from uncertainties Antonio might have had about Maria because at that same period she did nothing but amaze him with the revelation of ever new perfections and even her willing submission to the evening caresses of her breast and elsewhere took place with increasing spontaneity and freshness and was to be judged a proof if not of innocence at least of good health both physical and mental, but it was the nature of matrimony in itself that rightly caused our young man to stop and think also because there wasn't a person in the world especially a married one who didn't believe that in this particular matter you could never be sure of anything and therefore it's best to go slowly, and of course Antonio was just the type to accept such constant and general invitations to prudence however this was the very place where the otherwise repugnant wealth of Maria had to be reconsidered since it supported the notion that in this hybrid thing namely matrimony she being rich would get along all right even in the event of a mortal defection on his part or some similar misfortune, and in short he could even accept her being so rich in the present situation whereas in different circumstances the thing would have frightened him with good reason or would have depressed him immeasurably.

Now it isn't that this rather twisted and generally disconnected reasoning completely satisfied Antonio who was quite aware he didn't emerge from it exactly in the guise of a hero, but luckily

there were other much less contrived considerations which he set
into motion when he reflected that his and Maria's love was the
most sublime love that had ever appeared on the earth and therefore
naturally suited to elude all general and mean rules so it was possible to presume that no contractual pettiness could have distorted
or diminished it, and in the face of that love obviously Maria's
wealth was less than nothing or rather it took on moral if not
economic irrelevance and at this point it was clear he might as
well accept it rather than reject it provided things were regarded
from a sufficiently lofty point of view, but if for example he tried
to foresee his reception when he presented himself to Cavalier
Ilario to ask for his daughter's hand then it seemed better to reject
the idea of wealth altogether, and this was in fact the course
Antonio followed more or less working out a plan that finally
saved both his personal dignity and the uncommon quality of his
and Maria's love, namely they wouldn't be married at once but
after she had reached the age of twenty-one when she could dispose
of herself independently of her father's or mother's attitude, and
in the meanwhile he would obviously not remain idle but having
taken his degree in literature he would start teaching on a higher
level and with his professor's salary they could both live perhaps
not as comfortably as Maria was accustomed to because naturally
at the moment of their marriage she would have renounced any
dowry and all goods and chattels but two people who loved each
other as they loved each other could live happily even if they had
to do without a few luxuries.

Maria pounced on this plan with an enthusiasm and a fervor so
extraordinary that in the end they could only seem suspect that is
to say they aroused the impression that she too believed Antonio's
going to the cavaliere and asking for her hand wasn't a simple
matter so the way out he had devised was finally also from her
point of view the best to evade the difficulty and perhaps even
escape family nightmares so she did nothing but repeat that what
Antonio had thought up was marvelous and there was just one
little correction she felt she might make which was that he wasn't

going to be the only one who would work because at the age of twenty-one or a little more she would also take her degree and she would teach in some high school, and with two teachers' salaries they would earn enough for the two of them and their numerous children, because naturally she wanted numerous children and she wouldn't be satisfied only with two as Antonio suggested and insisted.

Perhaps this was the highest moment of their love as they were confidently constructing a sensible future in front of shops selling furniture and sanitary articles, and they thought nothing in the world could harm them since they loved each other immensely and theirs was the most perfect love on earth, and even his caresses in the darkness had lost their annoying flavor of something improper since now they were sure they were going to be married and it was really as if they already were because only a few unfortunate side issues prevented them from marrying at once, and in their conviction that they were in the right or that they would set everything to rights as soon as possible he found it more beautiful to caress her and she found it more beautiful to be caressed so that exploiting these pleasures he gradually succeeded in curing the unpleasant agitation that overcame her when she saw it was late and she wouldn't be home on time, and in fact each evening he wrested a few extra minutes from her and moreover persuaded her to let him accompany her a bit closer to the Campo San Polo along that stretch of street where she was afraid of being seen by her father, and there too at the Sottoportico Gaspare Gozzi or at the corner behind the church of San Tomà they found some hole where they could exchange a last kiss though in great haste and fear, until one evening when they were walking along the Rio Terrà dei Nomboli quite near San Polo and they were in the midst of a crowd of people coming and going he saw her suddenly turn pale and then equally suddenly blush and struggle vainly to conceal the fact that something unpleasant had happened, and even after he had begun to question her she kept on saying no nothing had happened but in the end she burst out crying desperately as she had never cried before and said that her father had gone by a little earlier and he had surely noticed her because he had looked at her for a long time and had even turned his head to get a better look at her.

The next day Maria came to their appointment very late and with great melancholy because her parents had discovered she was changed and she was too often dreamy and was always tired and listless with red, hollow eyes, and they had never seen her so pale and run down, and in conclusion they had realized she must be excessively in love and she hadn't had the strength to deny it because it would have been useless anyway because her father had seen her all right the previous evening so now he had inevitably to go to her house and talk with her mother but he had nothing to fear on that score because she had already explained everything namely that she was going to marry at twenty-one of her own free will and without taking a penny from anybody.

In which Antonio pays a call on
Signora Borghetto and everybody is upset

The inkling Antonio had felt al-
most daily during the first and happy phase of his story with
Maria that is the notion that they were experiencing but also
leaving behind them the most beautiful part of love and perhaps
of life itself received a vigorous confirmation at the point which
marked the end of that first phase and touched off the second
namely at the not entirely spontaneous or willing visit that he in
some indefinite capacity paid to Maria's mother Signora Amalia
Borghetto. Though he had the distinct impression he was acting
somewhat recklessly Antonio prepared himself with all due scruple
to make the acquaintance of this person who until the day before
had remained in a quite marginal area of his interests whereas she
had now suddenly become terribly important, in other words he
paid the greatest attention to his clothing and to his personal
hygiene having his hair cut not by the usual barber at Marocco
but by one near the Rialto who everybody said was very good, and
also to the end he had hesitated whether or not to present himself
with a bunch of flowers rejecting the idea finally not so much because a bunch of flowers suited to the situation and to Signora
Borghetto's economic power would have cost the earth but more

because of his presentiment that no floral tribute in the world would have succeeded in dispelling the enormous quantity of repugance that the lady in question must already have accumulated toward him even though she had never seen him and until the previous day had never heard his name mentioned.

From this way of foreseeing the situation one might deduce that Antonio was going to meet the lady who after all might even be his future mother-in-law without the support of an adequate amount of self-confidence and this in fact was the pure and simple truth, however since all or almost all the events of this life found him equally unprepared for optimism and he had always regarded the happy beginnings of his story with Maria basically as a kind of temporary not to say fictitious miracle which sooner or later he would have to pay for heavily, he cannot then be held particularly to blame for his all too renunciatory spiritual attitude and in any case to speak of blame would be entirely out of place because if one looks at the facts as a whole it can safely be said that nothing better than what did happen could have happened to him not even if he had presented himself to the dear lady with his spirit laden with flattery and his arms filled with the most costly flowers.

Moreover in order to form the most accurate possible idea of the event one must also realize that he went to pay that deplorable visit in a highly overwrought condition after about twenty hours of conflicting elucubrations whereby at one moment he suffered because of his poverty and more because of his excessively modest position as an elementary school teacher feeling quite unworthy of becoming the virtually official fiancé of Signorina Maria Borghetto, but then the following moment naturally without anything new taking place he felt downright trapped in a kind of plot which sooner or later would drag him to the altar, and this was a horrible suspicion because if intrigue were present then not even the above-mentioned Signorina Maria could be extraneous to it and then all her pristine chastity in which he had believed blindly and the innocence so to speak with which she had fairly promptly for that matter abandoned herself to pleasures leaning against the wall were not chastity or innocence but the keystone in a far from clean machination.

To arrive at such a conclusion though it was fairly disastrous and indeed enough to destroy forever all hope for anything beautiful in the world would have had at least one good aspect namely it would have resolved matters for better or worse if Antonio had had the good sense to stick to it but instead the poor young man when he reached that point began to wonder if Cavalier Ilario Borghetto's money wouldn't have been sufficient no matter how shopworn Maria's virtue and how feigned her innocence to procure her a husband a bit more suitable than himself, and the answer to this question was so simple that he was horrified at his own sacrilegious conjectures and realized he was still more unworthy not only of becoming engaged to Maria but even of raising his eyes to her unless of course she had already descended to an unspeakable stage of corruption that is with a past full of depravity at the very least and a minimum of three or four abortions because to cover up a situation like that even he would be a prize, but these were mostly mad ravings and in reality when he had thought them he felt truly mad and he kept whirling deeper into a state of progressive depression, surely the least propitious for nourishing any illusions about a complicated and even recondite encounter like the one he was girding himself to face.

Though now convinced the visit to Signora Borghetto had become ineluctable if for no other reason than the fact that he was more likely to lose Maria by not making the visit than by making it, Antonio was tormented to the end by a kind of constant sentiment of superiority toward the event which in practice was manifested in the awareness of the ultimate spontaneity of what he was doing and therefore also of his power not to do it if he had felt like not doing it, and in fact the temptation to retrace his steps was still present even when he had pressed the bell under Cavalier Ilario's name plate in the form of a fluttering ribbon and had entered a vestibule quite bare of bric-à-brac and without doors or windows but with a flight of steps at one side obviously leading to the *piano nobile* or the master apartments and since not a sound was heard nor was a living soul to be seen Antonio realized he was to go up those steps and so in effect it was a crumb of mystery that caused him to lose the marginal power of backing out of the whole business, and in fact once he had gone up the stairs it was too late to retreat because at the top waiting for him there was a maid with a starched cap and a white apron who first of all made Antonio give her the overcoat he had only recently bought in an elegant shop in the Piazza San Marco and this was the garment on which he had chiefly counted to make a good impression on Signora Borghetto as if he had expected to find her at the head of the steps instead of the servant.

Once in possession of his overcoat the maid opened a door for him saying he was to be so kind as to wait in there and she would immediately tell them he had come and Antonio found himself alone in a living room vast but dimly lighted at that moment by a single bulb at the top of the raised arm of a little Venetian blackamoor giving a more than adequate idea of what the Borghettos could allow themselves in the way of elegance at least in the receiving rooms and in fact there were three doors on one side and three narrow arched windows in the background the marble tracery windows that overlooked the Campo San Polo, and between one door and the other there were eighteenth-century chairs and sofas covered with brocade and great gilded consoles with mirrors and Chinese vases, and on the walls there were huge baroque pictures probably of religious subjects as far as you could tell in outsize frames with curlicues also gilded, and even if you admitted all this might not be original and authentic it must still have cost a pile of money not to mention the monumental Murano glass chandelier which hung from the top of the ceiling over a large marble table with twisted gold legs, a chandelier with infinite arms each furnished with numerous light bulbs turned off at the moment and the fact that they hadn't lighted them didn't suggest domestic economy to him since in a house on that scale they would hardly try to save money on electricity but rather he felt this was a somewhat indirect indication of the lack of consideration that surrounded his visit and adding this to all his other already accumulated reasons for dejection he became more lost than ever and though nothing in that sumptuous atmosphere could prompt the idea he began to have the impression he was in a dentist's waiting room or even a surgeon's for an operation that wasn't really necessary but which would become inescapable as soon as he had walked through one of the six doors and among other things he couldn't even imagine which one it would be.

Naturally this fantasy about being in a surgeon's waiting room was also a half-unconscious defense mechanism on Antonio's part in the sense that to pass into the true realm of inevitability he still had to cross a threshold and he might still possess the power of not crossing it, however he only had to think about it for a moment to see that this way of considering the thing was ridiculous that is even admitting that he really hadn't much desire to have his guts cut open it was now too late to think about it, in other words if Antonio really wanted to set up an efficient defense mechanism it would be better to try to form a less ugly notion of what was waiting for him beyond one of the six doors, and really it would have been enough to think a bit more about Maria and a bit less about her mother however the fact was that in the present situation it was very difficult for him to think about Maria in such a way as to derive comfort from that thought and indeed when he reflected that he was in the mess he was in only because he had assented a bit too passively to her inopportune eagerness to rush things the thought of Maria finally disheartened him altogether also because after having drawn him into the golden trap of the six doors the girl was taking an inexplicably long time to appear and he might even believe she wanted to allow him plenty of time to admire at leisure the splendor of the house where she lived in order to under-line certain distances.

Now even overlooking the little fact that in his present disheart-ened state it would be quite hard for him to be impressed by his sur-roundings even if the room had been for example more luxurious and imposing than it was, if Maria was by chance counting on impressing him with that gilt she was making a big mistake and in fact as he contemplated the excess of all that stuff he felt a deeper sense of confusion which was poured out against her since there was no conceivable connection between the room they were making him admire for too long and Maria who to him possessed humble and happy grace and above all reserve and a sense of proportion, unless he had been wrong in his judgment of her a thing after all possible and indeed as the minutes went by it seemed more and more likely to him and if an entirely unexpected Maria had popped up all of a sudden he wouldn't have had much reason to be surprised in view of the house where she lived.

This line of reasoning was quite unfair and Antonio himself could have realized as much if for example he had considered how little he corresponded to the house in Marocco where for better or worse he lived but this certainly was not a moment in which our young man could reason sensibly and to tell the truth he had never felt so far from Maria as he did now in her house or so ill-disposed toward her so when the poor girl finally slipped through the first door to the right of the entrance and came toward him saying hello and asking if he had been waiting long because they had just told her and she had run to him at once, the doubts and the resentment which filled him despite himself enabled him to notice that this time her simplicity was artificial like the forced smile she had no doubt thought to cheer him with as if she wanted to make him believe this painful ceremony wasn't merely the only way out of the mess into which chiefly through her fault they had got themselves but was a step that all things considered it should be pleasant to make. Faced with such an effort at pretense which still had nothing sinister or malicious about it but if judged properly revealed even a kind of remorse mixed with a desperate display of confidence Antonio realized she was in a much worse mess than he was and she was kept going only by her extraordinary moral strength and so he suddenly dropped the rancor and the suspicions he had brooded over during his wait in the grand living room and forcing

himself in turn to simulate serenity and self-confidence he allowed
her to take his hand and lead him into a room that seemed really
another world it was in such contrast with the first in substance
and form and in fact it was filled with furniture and pictures and
rubbish that certainly dated back to the time when Cavalier Ilario
hadn't made the excessive fortune he had been able to make afterwards, to a time that is when he or his wife for him or both together had cultivated a taste for cumbersome Mussolini-modern
furniture and for oleographic scenes from *Othello* in the line of
pictures, and in short this must have been the room where the
family still bound to its origins felt most at home and therefore
passed the hours when business obligations didn't require them to
appear in quite different surroundings, in any case though Antonio
had no particular fondness for cumbersome furniture or for oleo-
graphs of Othello all this would have been fine if at the end of this
humble room Signora Amalia Borghetto hadn't been in a chair
knitting.

Although in his natural attempts to imagine this lady Antonio
had made no special effort to picture her as less terrible than would
be natural, he had fallen far short of reality in the sense that the
person was one of the most repulsive creatures he could have met
and not so much because of her physical aspect which was neither
beautiful nor ugly but typical of a wife and mother of humble
origins though full of airs but rather because of the extraordinarily
intense hostility which she was able to display with a single look
when Maria went to tell her that the young man she had brought
in was Antonio and forced her to raise her eyes from her knitting
which at that moment seemed to absorb her more than anything
else, and if it had been merely a simple glance it wouldn't have
been so bad but disregarding the rules of proper behavior which
can't have been very familiar to her the signora went on staring
at him with calculated aversion for quite a while without even
dreaming in the meantime of uttering one of the conventional
remarks people make on such occasions so Antonio hadn't the
slightest trouble in realizing that among all mortals he was the

very one Maria's mother least preferred as the husband of her daughter a thing which would have rendered ineffectual any eagerness or aspiration to win the lady's favor if he had harbored any, and yet with a bit of attention and good will it was possible to perceive in the lady's disgust a hint of control or of restraint, in short she managed to make it clear to him that she could have expressed quite rightfully a far greater amount of disgust if she hadn't been checked by something that could be awareness of her duties as a person of station or more probably a previous agreement with Maria which had established that whatever happened his presence in that house would be tolerated with at least minimal good manners.

Now if this interpretation of the lady's attitude in one respect allowed Antonio to believe himself protected against the worst in another it certainly didn't help him patch up his dignity which had been sorely offended by the reception, however he couldn't promptly tell Signora Borghetto to go to hell as he had basically every right to do because the unexpressed part of the mother's hostility indicated what heroic if futile courage the daughter had shown in having him penetrate her house at present in the form of an intruder but with hopes of a better future, and out of respect for this courage which poor Maria continued stubbornly to display as if the matter had begun and was proceeding in a way that after all wasn't so bad Antonio checked his own aggressive impulses which weren't ter- ribly strong and with the best manner he could at present muster he told the lady he felt highly honored at making her acquaintance, and for a moment it seemed the remark which she no doubt con- sidered entirely her due made a slight breach in her heavy malevo- lence but immediately afterwards no doubt following a prearranged plan she ordered her daughter to go to the kitchen and make tea, however perhaps there had already been something defective in the execution of the plan so far that is very probably the mother despite her reserve and the margin of inexpressed hostility had behaved more nastily than agreed because Maria tried to disobey the command saying perhaps Antonio didn't like tea and anyhow the maid could prepare it perfectly well, but then the signora repeated the command energetically and explained with great clarity that she wanted to remain alone with the young man because she had something to say to him.

So Maria had to go out of the room sadly leaving him alone with her mother who after heaving a deep sigh to be interpreted no doubt as a suitable preface to the exposition of her sorrows took up the burden of her speech saying that when her daughter had confessed perhaps with some effort that she was in love, even before learning who the girl was in love with both she and her husband had almost had apoplectic fits because Maria had grown up before their eyes and they hadn't realized it, that is they thought she was still a little girl and had no idea of such things since she was a long way from finishing her studies and instead she had fallen in love and falling in love is always a disaster even if young people never want to understand that, in short on finding out the girl was in love both of them were upset however they hoped that since this misfortune had befallen her she had at least fallen in love with somebody who had a position, and by this she didn't mean he had to own property or have money because her husband was a democratic man and understood these things that is he didn't pay attention to class distinctions though naturally it's always better for a person to have some money and not be a tramp, in any case even if Maria fell in love with a tramp that would be that because you couldn't give orders to a girl's heart as the saying goes but her husband thought he should have at least a degree in economics or business administration because then he could be given a job in the business but a young man who was still studying and would have to wait perhaps years before taking a degree and what a degree too because it was in literature and nobody had ever heard of a degree in literature helping you to a position a man like that in short would be of no use to her husband in his business or rather he wouldn't have any place to put him and without a position there was no point in even thinking of marriage he could put the thought right out of his head if he was thinking about it, and on the other hand she didn't care for long engagements because she well knew how modern young people keep changing their minds overnight because they lack moral sense and then gossip gets about and perhaps a girl's reputation is ruined and you can't imagine what people will say in these cases especially about them since with the Lord's help they had made a certain name for themselves and so had attracted a lot of envy and Venice was full of people who were dying to speak ill and gossip about them but instead there was nothing they could say because when it came to proper behavior the Borghettos could set an example at least until yesterday that is until Maria had had this disaster and fallen in love and unfortunately nothing could be done because she was more stubborn than a mule, but Antonio had to examine his conscience and remember that she was a mother and she asked him frankly was she or wasn't she right to be worried.

This speech based as it was on the universal common sense of mothers faced by an aspiring son-in-law with no position didn't surprise Antonio who in fact apart from the frequent slips made by the lady's supreme dignity into somewhat vulgar gestures and expressions had been expecting even worse that is he wouldn't have been at all amazed if for example they had offered him a sum even a considerable sum of money on the understanding he would clear out at once, and so he wouldn't have found anything substantially to criticize in Signora Borghetto who basically was only looking after her affairs if in doing so she hadn't also insisted on preaching for that matter from the quite wrong and brazen pulpit because in all her argumentation full of virtuous reasonableness she hadn't allowed the slightest place for the admittedly supremely irrational motives for which Maria had made him come to that house and he poor thing had come, namely the lady refused to concede or was incapable of conceiving that he and Maria might love each other with let's not say the most marvelous love that had ever existed on earth but even with a normal love of the sort that might rightfully belong to any boy and girl on this earth, and since this was the way things were it was quite useless for him to examine his conscience and defend his right to love which could be sustained by nothing but the irrational motives that made love exist in and for itself despite all good mothers, however on the other hand it wasn't possible either for him to go off without saying anything or perhaps cursing and swearing also because although at the moment it seemed unlikely or improbable he and Maria really did love each other with the most marvelous love that could exist on earth and for such a love a man had to fight even though chances of success were fairly slim.

So as Signora Borghetto had begun already to assume an all too satisfied manner as if she thought she had already made short work of him Antonio spoke up with dignified firmness though perhaps with inadequate warmth of conviction and not because he didn't believe fully in the ideas he was expounding but because he was quite aware of their present incommunicability, saying he didn't want to contradict her when she was concerned with her daughter's reputation and future and this was a part of her strict responsibility as a mother but the fact was that he and Maria loved each other and were confident that their love would last all their lives and in their opinion this was enough for the present since the other problems like marriage and possible children would be faced when the time came, still as of now he was able to assure her that they would solve these problems on their own and he was particularly anxious to make it clear that he couldn't allow questions of money to enter into this matter because as he came from a modest background he would make Maria his wife only if Maria had previously given up the privileges of her family's wealth or to put it more bluntly he wanted Signora Borghetto to understand that he would take Maria only with the clothes on her back or even without them, and this was something he and she had already discussed and they were in perfect agreement.

As Antonio had clearly foreseen his speech produced no beneficial effect on the lady however after having heard if not really understood it she was filled with a disturbing mixture of distrust and contempt as if uncertain whether to become angry because the young man's appeal to love rang false to her or because it rang true, in either case the way she looked at things at least she should become angry and so she did however as she grew angry she managed to realize that the real cause of her annoyance or grief since the poor woman really was suffering considerably was that Antonio's convictions surely coinciding with those Maria must have explained to her previously were as firm and as indestructible as her own, so she dropped the persuasive tone that for better or worse had dominated the first part of her action and went on to certain injunctions, if that word can be used to describe conditions expressed chiefly in a threatening tone.

She said then that her husband left all responsibility for their daughter in her hands and God alone knew what a responsibility it was nowadays when young people had lost all self-control and common sense and religious feeling excepting her own daughter of course but as for the others you couldn't trust anybody, and first she didn't like at all absolutely not at all the idea that Maria met him outside their home, if the girl really couldn't do without seeing him which would have been the wisest course for a while anyway then she would have to see him properly at least under her mother's supervision, and for this purpose they were making a great exception and Antonio was to be allowed to visit the Borghetto home on Wednesday and Friday afternoons at tea time or at five o'clock to be precise staying until seven but on the other days of the week no because on the other days except Sunday which she devoted entirely to her husband Signora Borghetto was engaged in playing cards and in various other charitable activities of the San Simeone Grande Ladies Aid whose president she was, however she wanted to make one thing quite clear from the very beginning namely that the fact he was really being received in the Borghetto home didn't authorize him to believe or still less to announce to others that he was engaged to Maria and in fact the signora was of the opinion that engagements were serious matters to be given long thought before being undertaken whereas he and Maria unless she was mistaken had known each other a month or perhaps a little longer and she really couldn't think what had come over her daughter to insist the way she had why you'd think she'd found the son of the Agha Khan. In conclusion Antonio was to have the honesty and the good taste not to divulge the information that he and Maria were seeing each other and in this respect he was to be very careful because if her husband heard any talk about an engagement he would be capable of throwing Antonio out of the house quite unceremoniously because on this point he wasn't the sort of man who joked since he liked things to be open and aboveboard and he called a spade a spade and didn't let anybody get the better of him unlike herself who always allowed herself to be overcome with compassion at the wrong moment. Moreover since Maria until this time had given them nothing but satisfactions Antonio was to be careful not to harm her health either and now even a blind man could see the way she was run down till she looked like a TB case nor was he to distract her from her studies in which she had always shone and her husband wanted her to go on shining until she had her degree which is always a great honor but especially a kind of security because you never know what might happen in the future and she might have to earn her living, especially a girl like Maria who wouldn't hear of thinking ahead and good advice was lost on her, and in short without wasting any more breath on these conditions with Antonio who was already old enough to know by himself how to behave with a young girl of a more than respectable family who had been brought up not by modern methods but the good old-fashioned way in the fear of God and with healthy regard for moral principles so it wasn't even to be suggested in jest that she wasn't chaste and pure as the day she came into the world because the care she had taken in bringing up this only child was more than other mothers took surely, and now she felt like crying when she thought that Maria wasn't a little girl any longer and was being exposed to so many snares and dangers.

At this point namely at the end thank God of her speech Signora Borghetto really did have tears in her eyes which wasn't so amazing since in her own way she loved her daughter, and as far as the snares and dangers to which Maria was exposed was concerned they did exist and to a much greater extent than her good mother could imagine, however Antonio felt that her final emotional weakness was at most a rhetorical expedient moreover not even directed toward him because he obviously had no importance whatever but rather to the Almighty so that He would realize from her tears that she had now done everything humanly possible to safeguard her daughter's virtue and the family's honor and now it was up to Him to take action as was only His duty after all since proper behavior and the maintenance of chastity should mean as much to Him as they did to her, and after having expressed all this with a tearful glance at the ceiling Signora Borghetto lowered her eyes at once and immediately resumed her knitting with a kind of angry alacrity to underline precisely the fact that her emotion didn't concern Antonio who was therefore excused from making any comment or argument.

Now the most discouraging thing for Antonio was that he had no desire to comment or argue in other words though the lady's avalanche of unctuous abuse to which he had to add the unspoken but fairly transparent accusation that he was plotting to marry money should have aroused him to stronger and more consequential counterattacks such as wrath or open revolt, though he tried to bestir his spirit to something worthy he was still entangled in vaguely melancholy and hardly virile sentiments even cowardly ones because in effect while the signora was making her speech he had taken a kind of cheap revenge by thinking of all the impure acts or rather the downright filth he had performed with Maria in back streets and dark passageways, and he went on thinking of them even now that Signora Borghetto had stopped talking and he felt comforted even reassured by them since these meditations were directed chiefly against the mother and he could easily imagine how furious they would have made her and how her vainglory would have been destroyed if she had known even a part of the truth, but unfortunately Antonio was unable to forget that from another point of view all this was highly unfair toward Maria to whom he certainly could attach no blame for having a mother like the one she had, just as by reverse logical process the mother could be given no credit for the especially spiritual beauty of her daughter, anyhow dejected and sad as he was he felt he had a right even regarding Maria to assert in the only possible way his possession of her remembering precisely the impure acts perhaps even exalting and exaggerating them or rather heightening the obscenity of his own caresses and the unseemliness of the pleasure Maria derived from them, and contemplating these pleasures he had been absently gazing at the signora who was still knitting so at a certain point he almost lost his sense of reality as if he were seeing the mother in Maria's place as she abandoned herself to licentious pleasures and naturally as soon as he was aware of this confusion he retreated from it at full speed all too frightened because in that absurd substitution far from recognizing an unconscious and highly praiseworthy effort which tended to rescue Maria from the insults of his imagination he saw simply a danger of confusion between mother and daughter with the very dangerous consequence of being tempted perhaps to see how much of Signora Borghetto there might be in Maria whereas for the very safety of his love he should if anything have racked his brain to do the opposite that is to establish the most distinct separation between mother and daughter a hardly impossible enterprise since it is well known how aleatory and improbable the so-called blood ties can be.

Antonio was thus immersed in a thoroughly reproachful and risky confusion of thoughts when luckily for him Maria arrived pushing the tea cart on which she had arranged the good silver service and the best porcelain and she revealed such domestic grace in handling pot and cups and in asking lemon or milk that Antonio was brought immediately back to more worthy reflections and he might even have forgotten however temporarily about Signora Borghetto if that lady hadn't started urging her daughter with grim but quite audible grumblings to handle the cups with care and she even asked if it had been absolutely necessary to bring out the best service because things are always broken and then when an important guest came they couldn't receive him properly, and with this she meant to signify explicitly that Antonio wasn't somebody who had to be treated especially well even on his first visit, and the remark wouldn't have been so offensive if it could have been interpreted to mean that on his first visit he was already considered one of the family however this interpretation was in contrast to the preceding insults as well as the general tone of his welcome.

In any case Antonio for the sake of peace swallowed even this last vulgarity of the signora's and began to drink his tea as far as possible from her that is to say on an uncomfortable bony sofa where Maria joined him with great and sympathetic desire to conduct some sort of conversation but he couldn't manage to answer more than yes and no and meanwhile he was trying to understand what was happening to him because he felt sure that finally something was happening to him and though it wasn't nice especially in the present difficult moment to think that such a great and wonderful love could not of course decrease but certainly undergo some damage or check because of adversities that all things considered were merely exterior since Maria was only marginally connected with them, still this is what he did think and he had to admit that on the practical level at least his love story as a result of that unfortunate meeting had come so to speak to a point of suspension or inertia from which it would be hard to shift it in the direction of progress or to draw back in the sense that even if apparently all roads to retreat were more open to him than ever in reality if he didn't want to call the whole thing off and lose Maria he was involved in a condition which on one hand offered him no privileges while on the other it created a number of duties for him and from now on he would have to behave like a fiancé with all the nuisances that derive from that state without however being exactly engaged or still less being able to say he was according to the signora's precise instructions, and naturally when he thought of the engagement's nuisances he had a specially nasty and painful one in mind namely the obligation to see Maria only in her home and under the surveillance of such a mother who was at present still knitting and was in fact so skilled at this occupation that she could do it while keeping her angry, inquisitive eye on them at length.

Now if Signora Borghetto had dictated these crippling terms with such self-confidence it must have been because she had previously come to an overall agreement with her daughter namely Maria and it didn't matter if Maria had been to a great extent coerced into it because he was in any case forced to the conclusion that the way desired by the mother was the only way that their relationship could continue, but this still didn't mean that of all imaginable ways it wasn't absolutely the worst from Antonio's point of view and indeed though with infinite pain and suffering he was beginning to wonder if it was really worth the trouble to go ahead since apart from the constant outrages to his personal dignity it was also difficult to hope that with Maria there would be any more kisses and secret meetings much less caresses or anything further, and even in the event that miraculously there were, nothing could now eliminate the thought that over everything there existed a creature like Signora Borghetto repulsive and harmful to loving sentiments.

When it was a quarter past six that is to say three quarters of an hour before the expiration of the period allowed for his visits in that household Antonio rose to take his leave and in doing so took a bit more time than necessary hoping Maria would make some effort to keep him there and not of course in order then to give in but to go off letting her understand how offended he was and how determined to leave, instead with great resignation she allowed him to say good-bye to her mother and start for the door and only at the last minute despite the disapproval which Signora Borghetto tried to communicate to her in various ways she decided to accompany him down the steps to the entrance on the ground floor, however she was so downcast it was pathetic and she too seemed to have given up any idea of speaking since there was nothing to be said and so now he had only to open the door of the building and

that story would in one way or another be over but when he
reached for the latch Maria stood in front of him to prevent him
and began to cling to him and kiss him with a kind of frenzy
pressing herself to him as if she wanted to offer herself body and
soul then and there, and perhaps she was aroused by an angry
fury to avenge herself like this for the way her mother was hurting
her or else to make him feel that in spite of everything she was
unconditionally his and ready perhaps to ruin herself meaning to
help him overcome the confusion into which he had fallen but it
would take far more than that and in fact he remained inert and
reserved and she gradually stopped kissing him and clutching him,
and as the apparent strength that until then had sustained her suddenly failed she burst into tears and asked him if it was all over
and he answered sadly yes it was all over.

Perhaps this was the very answer she was expecting and indeed
for a few moments she seemed to accept it weeping motionless
and hanging her head in total desolation but then she recovered
herself and said angrily I hate her oh how I hate her referring of
course to her mother who for that matter deserved every word and
she added that nobody understood her at home and they had
wrecked her life and she was all alone and desperate, and for a few
days she had deceived herself that Antonio might be her salvation
but if he left her now she would kill herself she already knew how
to do it because she had foreseen what would happen and she didn't
want to live any more, in short she revealed such great grief at the
bad course things had taken that Antonio was about to let himself
go and clasp her in his arms forgetting everything when the harsh
voice of Signora Borghetto was heard from the top of the stairs
calling Maria Maria and immediately Maria was filled with incomprehensible fear and dismay and she answered I'm coming Mamma
however she didn't have the courage to break away from her beloved and she wept on his shoulder begging him in a whisper to
tell her it wasn't over that it couldn't be over, and Antonio simply
didn't know what to answer but he thought that if she were to
kill herself he would follow her immediately as Romeo did Juliet

or rather as Juliet did Romeo and perhaps this wouldn't be the worst solution with all the misfortunes that could be foreseen if they went on living, and he felt such compassion at the idea of their joint deaths that he started patting her hair with boundless tenderness and probably if he had continued he would have reached the conclusion that it wasn't all over but from the top of the steps Signora Borghetto again was heard threatening that if Maria didn't come up at once she would come down after her and for Antonio this was such a horrid idea that he stiffened again immediately saying to Maria in a detached voice that she should go on up to her mother, but naturally Maria couldn't go away like that and in fact she wouldn't go up if he didn't first say he still loved her and he told her he still loved her but with a tone as if he were saying some commonplace thing just to be saying it and this couldn't satisfy her so she demanded a more precise pledge namely that he meet her the next morning at the Ca' Foscari where she had her Italian class at ten past eleven.

Now unfortunately Antonio wasn't in a position to make this engagement so hastily not of course because of scruples about obeying Signora Borghetto's intimidations since he couldn't wait to affront her but because at eleven-thirty he would be teaching at Marocco and as he didn't possess the gift of ubiquity like Saint Anthony he couldn't be simultaneously at the Ca' Foscari unless he decided to cut his class a matter which required opportune reflection for a moment in view of the dislike the assistant principal already felt for him and naturally this wasn't the only matter it would have been opportune to consider awhile but now there was anything but time to reflect because in the meanwhile Signora Borghetto hadn't stopped calling from above with increasing harshness and repeated threats and still Maria wouldn't move if he didn't promise he would come to the Ca' Foscari the next morning and at one point it even occurred to her to run off with him at once and forever, and for Antonio this would have been the most beautiful solution in the world if he had known where to take her but obviously on the spur of the moment he didn't know, so under the imminent threat of a new and more disastrous encounter with Signora Borghetto he told her and swore in great haste that he would come to the Ca' Foscari, and then she ran up the steps while he also without wasting time opened the door and found himself in the Campo San Polo walking into it as if into a dark universe, thinking a little that love was now a withered flower to press as a souvenir between the months of his again futile life, and on the other hand with the slight feeling that he was on the brink of truly extraordinary resolutions.

Where, for want of anything better,

certain serious observations are made

concerning Antonio

After a night of almost complete insomnia when after turning and tossing in his bed and debating about the past and the future he even reached the conclusion that for him it would have been much better not only not to come into the world which he already knew but as he was unfortunately in it he would have been better off if he had never known Maria or at least hadn't fallen so excessively in love with her, Antonio succumbed to the extraordinary power of this love which now finally was becoming the true center not only of the emotions but also of the events of his life and he decided to make some extraordinary resolutions that is he decided as the first and most concrete thing to continue with his love story even in the atmosphere of dramatic tension following the visit to the Borghetto home.

This primary decision as it might be called which in the current state of things could also have been on sober reflection a providential change of course capable of straightening out his drifting life had to be made by Antonio somewhat to the disadvantage of his own family because he had one too composed of an older and very sad sister whom a Southerner had married many years before only to abandon her inexplicably immediately thereafter and his father who had retired from the railroad and who had always predicted the worst disasters for his only son often hitting the nail on the head though still unlucky in what had been his favorite and most frequent prophecy namely that one fine day Antonio would end up in jail. To be honest if one excepted a generic indolence and listlessness in his studies both secondary and university Antonio hadn't provided real motives for predicting such a disastrous future, but his father was a man of stern principles and he had based his son's training on the concept that since he was taking the bread from his mouth to maintain Antonio the latter was obliged to repay him with equivalent sacrifices and in reality up to the present moment this had not come about. Antonio's mother had been chiefly a meek and quiet woman whom he would probably have loved very much if she had lived but instead she had died about a dozen years earlier and he had felt so little grief at her loss that there remained in him a sense of ethical debt or an impression that in the future he would have to suffer for this death much more than he would have suffered if he had suffered at the right moment, and all things considered this too was one way of feeling orphaned and ill-starred. In short since his mother had died before the opportune moment and since the rest of his family was what it was our hero's domestic ties couldn't be called strong or in any way intense and to tell the truth the morning after that night of tossing and turning he was able without excessive inner turmoil to put a few books and some things in a leatherette suitcase and walk out saying he was giving up schoolteaching and moving to Padua in order to finish his university studies, and the announcement afforded his father the opportunity of making more or less the same prophecies made two or three years before when Antonio had performed the operation in reverse interrupting his studies at Padua to undertake a schoolmaster's career in Marocco.

So having thus taken the first step Antonio also took the second that is he went to the coeducational elementary school and there instead of sitting at his usual desk he announced to the assistant principal his decision to retire from teaching since he was wasted in body and in spirit, and he did this without batting an eye or rather with great relief and inner delight since he had already abundantly suffered the grave spiritual torments connected with it in the sense that the decision to leave the school unlike that of leaving his home which was moreover the necessary premise had already cost him the longer and harder part of his nocturnal torture and in fact that teaching job even though fairly wretched in its socioeconomic aspects still represented a position though not of the sort or to the extent desired by Signora Borghetto nor even by her daughter Maria if he thought about it.

Though not hiding from himself the fact that this last thought at least in the part concerning Maria was at the center of the whole business because if Maria hadn't belonged to that particular family and station there wouldn't have been all this need to give up teaching, Antonio felt a fundamental need for clarity and we might well say honesty and he wanted to make his decision even independently of Maria partly because it was only right for him to assume the final responsibility and partly because he wanted very much to examine the situation in itself and to act according to rational prudence, and the reasons he was able to work out on this subject during the troubled night were substantially interdependent but of two different kinds and qualities, namely of a generally materialistic nature on the one hand and of a spiritual nature on the other, and while the former led him to the conviction that with strict economy and by studying dutifully with the seven hundred and seventy-two thousand lire left him at the moment he would manage to take his degree without his schoolmaster's salary, and the latter reasons obviously far more fertile finally roused him to a state of subtle intellectual fervor which truthfully he had not achieved for too long a time.

To understand properly the nature of this fervor and also to arrive at the most exact possible evaluation of Antonio's behavior in fleeing his family and his job it must be explained how like many others of whatever period he had often had the impression during his early youth that he had been born for great things and it had been this impression in other cases beneficent which had on the contrary led him perhaps because of a rare perception of the imbalance between the scarcity of real prospects and the grandeur of his imagined aspirations to settle into the wretched condition into which he had fallen namely taking a teacher's certificate and accepting a job in the elementary school, and really to say he had ended up there through sloth as for example his father said was a gross oversimplification because in a young man fairly rich in intelligence and above all in spiritual ferment neither the sloth nor the laziness which accompanied them could be without a reason, and this reason was precisely the unusual perception of the above-mentioned imbalance since anyone can see that if examined in a logical perspective the difference between an elementary schoolmaster and a high school professor as he would become if he had continued his studies to his degree was nothing compared to the truly enormous difference between a high-school professor and what Antonio thought he might have become if the things of this world had functioned properly, and so he felt he might as well stop at the less laborious rung and live in peace if nothing else.

On the subject of what he might have become through proper functioning of the things of this world Antonio had no specific idea in fact he had no ideas at all if you except the rather vague notion that if he had been born at a different time and place and above all in different family circumstances he would surely have become somebody, and since the expression to become somebody had the merit of absolute indefiniteness and moreover any projects took place on a completely theoretical plane he not only saw no reason to set limits to his potential abilities to progress but was almost indifferent as to whether he should dream of being a great poet or dramatist or the first man to set foot on the moon or the discoverer of a vaccine against cancer, to tell the truth he felt more inclined for practical considerations toward poetry than toward anything else however he would have accepted success also in other fields because what really counted for him was success or at least an exceptional position deservedly won of course, but meanwhile this tendency of his always toward the best without passing through the good and the better in the long run had led him to sloth, since he knew very well that even if he had made every possible effort some exterior obstacle would have kept him from arriving at the place where it would have been right for him to arrive, and this confirmed his conviction that he had been born ill-starred which was beyond any doubt one of his firmest convictions. To sustain this way of thinking which he had gradually raised to a system of idle life Antonio could adduce the far from uncommon concept that all the great men listed in the history of the arts or sciences or wars at a certain point had always had a sizable pinch of good luck without which they surely would not have become great men, and from this observation it was quite evident that it was useless to struggle or even to make an effort if one didn't have the hope that sooner or later the pinch of luck would lend a hand, and this was precisely the hope that Antonio perhaps not without reason lacked or to be precise had lacked until now because now almost forced into it by recent events he was beginning rightfully to wonder whether in a systematic and overall view of his life the meeting with Maria which had taken place in a generally chance or random fashion in its imaginable developments couldn't be that lucky accident which at a certain moment takes an existence otherwise condemned to mediocrity and abruptly addresses it toward marvelous destinations.

Of course when the matter was considered abruptly like this, apart from being enrolled at the University again which was still a matter of mere bureaucratic efficiency it could be objected that the meeting with Maria hadn't brought about useful structural modifications and indeed considering the state in which his personal dignity had emerged from the visit to Signora Borghetto he had every good reason to fear as in fact he did fear for a great part of the night that a severe blow had been dealt even to his most

elementary prerogatives such as for example the right to survival
not to mention that of procreation, but on further pondering one
could also see how those pinches of luck which Antonio surely overestimated in judging them determinative in the greatness of great
men were in most cases downright disasters like Leopardi's
humpback or Dante's exile, and in short there was nothing to
prevent the dire encounter with Maria's mother from becoming if
it wasn't already the event that taken in the right way would drive
him to achieve a form of greatness which vague as it was he felt
he now had within reach to the confounding above all of Signora
Borghetto, and it was precisely thanks to this important conclusion
that Antonio about five in the morning had come to the extraordinary resolution of changing his life after which he had finally fallen
asleep.

Naturally two hours later when his sad sister had come to bring
him his coffee with a piece of toast and he had waked up to a cold
and foggy morning with the bare branches of the trees appearing
outside the panes of the window like uncertain survivals his
thoughts of the night had already lost a great deal of their vivid
fluency and indeed in his sleep-heavy brain they stirred like the
remains of a badly digested binge and in particular the indetermi-
nate form of greatness no longer seemed quite within reach and in
any case it was absolutely base to have imagined it only to con-
found Signora Borghetto who surely didn't deserve his throwing
away for her sake an elementary schoolmaster's salary modest as
you please but still respectable and above all secure, and in short in
that already difficult hour of waking when to postpone the moment
of getting out of bed he usually fell to meditating on his own
affairs though it would have been much better not to meditate on
them at all Antonio had found himself on the brink of a frightening
smash and had realized that if he didn't hasten to cling to some
particularly energetic coefficient of the fervor he had laboriously
developed during the night he would barely have enough strength
left to get up and go to school, and he would have lost perhaps the
last opportunity to escape both a family and professional situation

which were hard to reconcile with ideas of success and happiness.

Now at that moment anyone would have realized that there could be no energetic coefficient except certain amorous sentiments assuming they still existed of course, but though he was so to speak spasmodically sure of those sentiments which in this difficult pass comprised his sole vital center he was reluctant to bring them up so as not to have to face again the problems which precisely during the night had been overcome on the subject of the expediency of assuming Maria as the driving force in a series of operations that involved as he couldn't forget not only the loss of his teacher's salary but also a considerable amount of expenditures, and to tell the truth having reached independently of her or at least keeping her very much at the margin of the basic line of reasoning the decision to fling himself recklessly into the fray had been for Antonio a kind of victory of logic over sentimentalism except that now in his cold morning depression it seemed all too obvious that his nighttime fervor which had supported the decision had in its turn grown from bases even more irrational than an amorous sentiment that is from certain dreams of glory which now in the light of day had become more withered than the branches of the trees outside his window, and in conclusion as far as Antonio could understand at that moment it wasn't possible to use only the intellect to find sufficient reasons for abandoning a home where he paid very little to live and a job that one way or another brought him more than a hundred thousand lire a month and in consequence he had to admit that if the situation still had a strong point that point was Maria even with all the drawbacks stemming from the circumstance that she had a mother like Signora Borghetto and a father who was God knows what perhaps worse, but on the other hand the Borghetto parents entered into this only relatively since the true kernel of the question was something else namely whether he and Maria loved each other with such an exceptional love that he could believe great things would be born from it. Now after the previous evening when Maria had declared herself ready to abandon father and mother and all the rest to follow him anywhere it was no longer possible to doubt that her love for him was sufficiently exceptional, and as to his own love for her he felt he had only to recall her smile and her gestures and her crooked tooth and a thousand other tiny things which all together constituted her ineffable fascination, and in a different field more mysterious and confused but surely no less seductive to recall her warm abandon at his caresses and the exhausted joy that followed and the well-founded hope that from there in a short time something similar for him might be achieved, this then was sufficient and it certainly was no small thing to feel more than sure of loving her to a degree that authorized any audacity especially since apart from the ridiculous teacher's salary and the certainty of cheap board and lodging in the family home the things he had to sacrifice were a depressed sister and a boring father and the unruly students of the coeducational fourth grade. At this point it was evident that the problem was not so much one of choice as of courage and indeed because the word courage frightened Antonio slightly it was really a matter of common sense or even of self-interest since basically he had only to decide between a gloomy condition with no way out and a future which in any case couldn't be worse than the past and finally the whole affair was reaching a phase of absolute logicality which permitted him to carry out with conscious firmness the steps necessary to leave the house and his job, and in so doing he had the impression that he was gradually acquiring a new dignity and a boldness which almost brought him to the same level of heroism Maria had reached in declaring herself ready to give up for him the comforts of her all too sumptuous house. Now amid a landscape of foggy countryside and ugly houses and then of ugly factories and foggy lagoon as he was going on the Number Eight toward Venice after so many tribulations and false moves he felt himself finally worthy of housing in his spirit a marvelous but far from easy love such as his for Maria and he didn't experience the least regret at what he had done in fact he was exultant when he thought of the hard times that lay ahead of him the days of furious study and of scanty meals eaten mostly in cafeterias or snack bars and of hard-won meetings with Maria from which however he would derive much of the strength necessary to go on with, but above all he was excited by the idea of having burned his bridges behind him in a state of perfect availability for the future with no fixed plans except to study and to love Maria with all his being and to hunt for a room in Venice because naturally the idea of going to Padua had never crossed his mind and he had produced it only to stave off to some extent his father's catastrophic predictions.

CHAPTER
VIII

In which Antonio, perhaps not too wisely, settles
in the Fondamenta della Parona

If life were made up only of
dreams and of fervors anyone provided with a bit of imagination
could live happily but instead it so happens that there are also practical difficulties and banal obligations and so our happiness even if
it moves in quite superior spheres is dependent in the final analysis
on the greater or lesser annoyance experienced in checking somewhere a heavy imitation-leather suitcase and then hunting for a
furnished room, and Antonio obviously was just the sort to feel
wretched when faced by problems of this sort and in addition at
times and almost by surprise he was gripped by a remainder of
alarm because he was there instead of at a desk looking down at
thirty or so kids male and female to perform an activity that among
other things would have caused him to receive on the twenty-seventh
of the month a salary that nobody was going to give him now,
but to be strictly truthful these moments of alarm were fleeting and
he soon recovered from them by observing that he had had in any
case the courage to turn his back on a closed routine and to put
himself on the right path toward achieving the distinguished things
for which he too was born or so it seemed and therefore the event
on the whole was positive and stimulating but this didn't mean he

could overlook certain fundamental rules of prudence which now more than ever consisted in economizing to the bone maybe even denying himself a cup of coffee or a cigarette when he wanted them and obviously also in the choice of a furnished room he had to take into account the criterion that there was little money to be squandered or rather none. Still there were other criteria which had perforce to be considered and in fact of the dozen want ads offering furnished rooms published in that morning's *Gazzettino* Antonio immediately rejected more than half because he surely couldn't go and bury himself at Cannaregio or at Castello nor even in the neighborhood of San Giovanni e Paolo since it was all too clear that he had to settle within a quadrilateral whose vertices on one side were the Piazza San Marco and the Accademia and on the other the Frari and the Ca' Foscari and from this topographical specification he derived above all a sense of teleological security since it evidenced so to speak the aims of his change of residence namely Maria in the first place and the desire to be as close to her as possible to breathe the same air and hear the same sounds she did and then in the second place the study of art history in which he would be assisted by the view of the monuments around the Piazza and the famous works of art in the galleries of the Accademia. When it came to rooms for rent in the chosen quadrilateral the *Gazzettino* advertised three one of which could be rejected out of hand because it was only a step away from that same Rio Terrà dei Nomboli where Maria's father had made the fine discovery that his daughter allowed herself to be walked home by a young man and so two rooms were left both of them in an apparently safe situation on the other side of the Grand Canal one in the Salizada San Samuele 3722 and the other in the Fondamenta della Parona 4247, and both were available for a respectable gentleman and were centrally located and had all modern conveniences and they differed only in that the first boasted central heating while the second called particular attention to the fact that it was independent.

In view of how things went subsequently with Maria one might

suspect that Antonio in choosing as he did after a careful inspection
of both rooms the one in the Fondamenta della Parona that is the
independent one which as far as heating was concerned displayed
only an ancient and rather smelly little terra-cotta stove for which
on top of everything else he would have to pay for wood, showing
thus incontrovertibly that above all things he valued the independence of the room which after all wasn't so independent as they
said because the door opened not on the stairs but into a vestibule
in common with other rooms and in fact on this score Antonio
had explicitly questioned the landlady who in herself was neither
old nor ugly and had an obvious understanding of what might
happen when you rent a room to a young man in the prime of
life and in fact she explained to him that he could bring in anyone
he liked and she would see nothing or no one but she begged him
not to bring up any streetwalkers because of the good name of the
house, in short considering all this one might suspect that Antonio
in choosing precisely the independent room in the Fondamenta
della Parona intended to bring somebody up to it, but though in
this world one can never be certain still in this particular circumstance it can legitimately be stated that such a suspicion would be
unjust and Antonio himself later meditated at length and probingly
on the matter more out of need for clarification than anything else
and he reached the conclusion that on the morning when he was
choosing the room the idea that he might one day bring Maria up
to it never remotely occurred to him, but this obviously is valid
only as far as his conscious mind is concerned whereas we know
full well that the unconscious has a dynamics all its own which is
far from negligible and therefore it might well be that inside
Antonio in a subtle but decisive way the impulse to have a room
with a bed whereon to lie with Maria was pressing him or if not
exactly with her with some other girl capable of absorbing those
desires which the intimate contacts with Maria aroused for better
or worse and these as anyone can realize were quite natural and
legitimate desires and it would have been a worrying thought if
they hadn't existed, however Antonio though accepting the dy-

namics of his unconscious was prepared to accept it with a different interpretation according to which since he had left home chiefly because of the need for independence he was satisfying this need even in the choice of a room which was therefore independent without any necessity to foresee the use he might make of it even with Maria.

So he paid the full month's rent which the landlady following the custom asked for in advance and in addition he disbursed three thousand lire for the purchase of a first supply of firewood and then he hastened toward the Ca' Foscari taking the San Samuele ferry to save time but still arriving when the Italian Literature class for the students in the second year of the English course had already been in progress for ten minutes however Maria instead of going into the classroom had remained in the corridor to wait for him her spirit filled with sufferings and a lump in her throat and one glance was enough for him to see that while the night however tormented had been for him a source of decisions which in the end had raised his spirits her morale on the other hand was even lower than it had been the previous evening when at the door of the house he had promised her he would come to the Ca' Foscari but making the promise under certain pressure from above that would also have excused him if he had promised idly just to get out of that house in some way, and in fact the first thing the poor girl said when she finally managed to speak was that in those ten minutes he had been late she had been assailed a thousand times by anguish at the thought that he would never come today or ever again and so those were to be considered the most tormented ten minutes of her life till then, and Antonio who had been so absorbed in practical obligations and the problem of the independent room had culpably not calculated that he would cause her such great suffering with a slight delay and he apologized saying that two buses had passed Marocco without stopping because they were full and he would never have imagined so many people were traveling at that hour or else he would have got up earlier maybe even at six in order to arrive on time at ten, and as he was telling her this he was saying to himself almost amazed here I am telling her a pack of lies and he even asked himself why he was telling her so many lies and oddly enough he found that he wasn't terribly sorry about telling them because he realized that he had finally put an end to the indecision that had racked him up till then namely whether or not to tell her that he had moved to Venice and now finally it seemed to him that on the whole it was best not to tell her so as not to drag her into a new series of worries and concerns which she surely didn't need poor thing, however not telling her meant putting himself in the position of having to dish out God knows how many lies to her afterwards and this behavior of his was if you thought about it sufficiently incoherent since one of the chief reasons he had left home was the opportunity of giving up his teaching job in order to make a full return to the status of university student in order after so much painful lying in the past to establish a relationship of absolute honesty with her and instead he hadn't even finished with the old lies when he was shelling out a new one surely subject to proliferation, still apart from the fact that this seemed inevitable it should also be observed that these lies were purely functional and in no way marred the great truth that he loved her more than ever and indeed to compensate some-how for the accessory fibs he had been forced to tell her he now told her he loved her more than ever and she answered that she could die of all the love she felt for him really die provided she could do so loving him, and naturally with these ideas on her mind there was certainly no point in her going to the Italian lesson so they went out and found a little café opposite the school which perhaps not by accident was called the Caffè della Speranza, the Café of Hope.

The café's name however didn't seem to reassure Maria very much and in fact while she was waiting for the coffee she had ordered she kept her head down and made swirling marks on the little table's marble top and the swirls were so visibly disconsolate that Antonio finally felt called upon to cheer her up repeating once again how much he loved her and naturally the remark can't

always have such a big effect if repeated after such a short time and
Maria kept on making marks with her finger for a while before she
said that she loved him too but loving each other didn't mean much
if they didn't know what to do, and Antonio at this expression felt
his heart fail since naturally he could only interpret it in the worst
sense namely as a perhaps too sudden manifestation of a total dejection on her part due no doubt to prohibitions and threats made by
her mother after his departure to which she had in her sorrow
agreed, but if this was true then it was her duty to say so clearly
and so to urge her on he asked her if by any chance she meant that
all was over between them, and the poor thing was so downcast
that the basically tragic question didn't surprise her in the least and
indeed in all probability she couldn't find anything really inter-
rogative about it as if properly speaking it hadn't been so much a
question as an indirect statement to the effect that according to
him despite their great love there was little to be done after the
disastrous visit of the previous evening, and consequently as far
as she was concerned it would have been downright indelicate and
inopportune to insist on patching up something that could not and
should not be patched up, and in fact she didn't insist at all but
looking up at him in search chiefly of sympathy she asked him if
he wanted it all to come to an end.

This was a question which could have been sufficiently and
opportunely answered with a simple no but Antonio didn't find
that suitable because to his way of thinking it required something
stronger and more binding which would contain among other
things at least a veiled hint at the enormous disaster into which he
would have plunged for more than one reason if he were to lose
her abruptly like this just now when he had even left home in order
to be more worthy of her and to be closer to her day and night,
however an answer so rich and intense wasn't easy to find point-
blank and in his deeply bewildered state, and moreover the two of
them seemed fated to proceed like two heedless creatures on the
edge of colossal desperations almost enjoying the prediction of irreparable catastrophes, so he rejected the easy answer and lowering

his gaze with perhaps a greater resignation than the situation demanded he answered if that's what you want meaning that he
wanted it all to come to an end only if she did implicitly declaring
himself ready to accept her decision however cruel, but she just
wasn't up to making decisions of that kind poor thing and in fact
she was only able to check her tears for a little while because then
she pulled out her handkerchief and tried to hide them by blowing
her nose but there was precious little to blow about and fairly
soon she was crying into her handkerchief with some childlike sobs
that tore at his heart and if they hadn't been in a public place and
if one of them at least hadn't had to be strong in the current
delicate pass he too would have started crying with all his heart.
But he resisted the temptation and pressing her to him he informed
her that as far as he was concerned he would never leave her and
she had to struggle a little to find the necessary breath but in the
end she managed to ask him to swear that and he swore over and
over again by what he held most dear namely in the final analysis
herself and he begged her not to cry because those were the most
unjust tears he had ever seen and to think she was crying through
his fault was an unbearable sorrow and she said I'm not crying
any more really I'm not crying now and instead she went on crying
perhaps more than before though differently from before thank
heaven that is now almost sweetly, but then thinking that probably
even in this way she was upsetting him she forced herself not to
cry any more and in the end she also started sipping her coffee and
even tried to joke saying thank goodness I'm not wearing any
makeup otherwise it would have been a real disaster and she even
managed to smile slightly almost forgetting the crooked tooth which
for that matter seemed more than ever in the right place in her
little-girl's face with her nose red and her eyes swollen from weeping and as he looked at her he felt overwhelmed with love and as
usual he sought the words to tell her about it in a way that was
not only adequate and lofty but also a tiny bit new, however he
had the impression that the phrases most suited to expressing lofty
and intense feelings of love had already been all used up by

Petrarch in his remote century precluding or at least making difficult any later innovation, and so he really loved her more than he
had ever before and at the same time he was saying to himself look
what a fool I am to think about these things now of all times and to
compensate in some way he clasped her with increasing tenderness
and she allowed herself to be clasped and to be loved as he loved
her without however completely forgetting all the woes through
which they were passing and in fact at a certain moment she said
to him you still haven't told me what we're going to do and their
not knowing what to do which was a subject that a moment before
had unleashed in him a turmoil of fears and consternation now
instead proved the most opportune and natural thing in the world,
in other words she simply wanted to know how are we going to
manage to see each other and speak to each other now that my
Mamma knows we're in love and won't take her eyes off me, and
naturally in speaking of this she had a special tone of apprehension
and perhaps also of remorse since she had been the one after all to
bring on the disaster which instead with a bit of cleverness she
could have avoided or at least kept from being so huge, however if
nothing else she was thinking of it in a concrete way whereas he
had had worries and concerns of every sort and had even revolu-
tionized his life and come to extreme resolutions which he would
never have dreamed of making but when it came to practical questions like how to continue now with Maria he hadn't even given
them a moment's thought perhaps because he was also basically ill-
suited to solving them, and really even as she urged him and he was
thinking intensely no solution came into his head and he finally
ended by wretchedly asking her if by any chance she had some idea
as to what they were going to do.

Luckily the practical sense in which Antonio was completely
lacking was only partially lacking in Maria who despite the sufferings and the torments that Antonio's introduction into her home
had caused her had not neglected to think up a kind of workable
plan in the event that this difficult love so opposed by her family
was destined to last as she hoped and desired with every fiber of

her body and soul, and in particular she had diligently copied out
the schedule of her weekly lessons and she gave the copy to Antonio
to guide him because in the future their meetings outside could
take place only during class hours excluding as if that weren't
bad enough the afternoon lessons from four o'clock on since her
mother had ordered her to be home before dark inasmuch as she
preferred having an ignorant daughter to leaving Maria exposed
to horrible snares and dangers, and in short the two of them would
no longer be able to take their evening walks behind San Raffaelle
Arcangelo and Santa Maria Maggiore and it was bitter to think they
would no longer take those walks nor would they give each other
all those kisses she liked so terribly however they had to be patient
because in a little over two years they would be married and then
they would kiss each other from morning to night as well as from
night to morning naturally, but in the meanwhile they were com-
pelled to do without and nobody was sorrier about it than she was
although they could console themselves a bit with the thought
that every cloud has a silver lining and for example in the future
he could telephone her at home whenever he felt like it now that
her mother knew, and also for better or worse there were those
two visiting hours on Wednesdays and Fridays and though there
was good reason to fear they wouldn't exactly be marvelous hours
they were nevertheless time the two of them could spend together
and this was the only thing that really mattered.

So the new situation altogether wasn't in the least desperate
especially if they remembered it could easily have been worse and
in fact the most surprising thing was this namely that it was no
worse than it was, but though Antonio tried in good faith to see all
the good aspects which in truth weren't lacking he was filled with
sadness and unhappily oppressed by the schedule of her classes and
the visits at home, and strange to say the only detail in the new
order that made him breathe a bit easier was that it would now be
very difficult in the future to start caressing Maria in the manner
and to the degree that had already become inevitable whenever
there was an opportunity, and though these things were not un-

pleasant and were instead very pleasant indeed they were however things that pleased him at the moment and made him even yearn to do them and to lead Maria to that confused exhaustion but afterward he was left with a bitter taste because of the profanation of her purity as well as a restlessness and dissatisfaction in himself of course, and in short they were things which on sober consideration were best avoided and to avoid them the best way was in fact to have no opportunity of doing them however this was a very meager satisfaction to add to the use of the telephone and the visits to the house under the surveillance of the knitting Signora Borghetto, my God there was his unhappiness coming back and growing until it gave him a dangerous power of penetration into the whole affair that is he began to wonder why this great love of theirs was always so poor in happiness whereas other lovers at least to look at them all seemed happier than they, even in this café for example there was a boy who was doing God knows what with his hands under the table because every now and then his girl told him to behave himself and pushed him aside but laughing and without any real wish for him to stop and Antonio couldn't recall that he and Maria had ever been so carefree as those two not even in their best moments because always even when there was no reason they carried their burden of worry and torment, he far more than Maria to tell the truth since she sometimes showed she knew how to live if not in outright joy at least with a natural heedlessness but he always seemed to be weighed down by a congenital inability to enjoy simply what it was right to enjoy in this world namely youth if nothing else and love, and this surely derived from the unhappy character he had been endowed with on coming into the world however if he thought about it there was also the fact that he loved Maria more than any man had ever loved a woman on this earth, except perhaps very famous lovers like Orpheus had loved his Eurydice and Abelard his Héloïse and Eduard his Ottilie, namely with a superabundance of feeling which willy-nilly tended to complicate things a bit, yes this must have been the chief if not the only reason and Antonio was fairly content at having been able to find it and indeed he thought it would be a good idea to involve Maria too in that fairly risky super-production of love and so with a great sigh he asked her why they had to love each other so much and naturally this wasn't a question but a rather smug statement of fact, and it was precisely in this sense that Maria took it and she in turn heaved a deep sigh and confirmed that for her part at least nobody in the world loved the way the two of them did however it was already past noon and she had to hurry home so as not to arouse her mother's suspicions and to keep her as calm as possible, in any case according to the class schedule they would meet the next morning at ten unless of course Antonio had to study or go to Padua for some important lecture but obviously Antonio had to do none of this or indeed of anything else to tell the truth the only thing he had to do was await the moment when he could see her again, and so once she had gone that moment was very far off too far really with a whole afternoon of loneliness to which he was no longer accustomed since they had fallen into the habit of seeing each other every weekday afternoon, my God he really felt a sense of heart-rending and unbearable emptiness that she had left behind as she went off so swiftly and simply from that café where instead other lovers had stayed loving each other good-humoredly as far as he could see and so he quickly paid for the two coffees and without wasting time went to claim his suitcase at the station in the Piazzale Roma and with the vaporetto he took it to Sant'Angelo and then covered on foot despite its considerable weight the long stretch of the Sant'Angelo imbarcadero to the Fondamenta della Parona where he stopped to buy bread and salami and cheese and also a fresh egg and with these things he ate in his room chewing and looking out the window at what little there was to look at namely the cold green canal where no boats passed and the buildings opposite which were fairly handsome but gave the impression they were about to collapse and to the right the Ponte della Parona which some bundled-up people were crossing, and as he ate and looked at these things which were new to him the sense of emptiness increased rather than diminished and as it did it frightened him a little because who could say what would happen next if he started analyzing it, anyhow when he had eaten he stretched out on the bed under the blankets because it was very cold in the room however it wasn't worth lighting the stove which anyway he had sworn he would light only to study but today after his agitated night and his morning of decisions and action there was surely no use studying and therefore wasting wood, so he stayed under the blankets shivering a bit from the cold or from something else and listened to the footsteps of people on the Ponte della Parona and the occasional cries and the hours being struck perhaps by the Moors at the clock tower which as the crow flies couldn't have been so far away, and he looked at the lines and the cracks and the stains of this room where he had come to live and the sense of emptiness increased still more until it became a kind of oppression and in fact it was very improbable that Maria in the Campo San Polo even if she listened carefully could hear the Moors striking the bell in the square and anyway that wasn't so important or rather it would have been much the same if she had heard them because the idea of being closer to her by listening to the same sounds she could hear was maybe a lovely thought but all things considered not very practical since he felt farther from her in this room which oppressed him than he had ever felt when he was in Marocco and in short it was the very goal of his escape that seemed unclear since at the moment the link with the hypothetical great things of the future had weakened and it emerged that the independence he had won with no small sacrifice and tribulation had been won just when he needed it least since Maria wasn't there to enjoy it with him.

In which Antonio and Maria

go ahead as best they can

In the days that followed Antonio several times and in various forms felt that same annoying sensation of uselessness and waste which though it stemmed from such a basically futile cause as the abandonment of a paternal roof so scarce in tenderness toward him still managed to disturb certain rather deeper spheres in him connected with productivity or even with love, but in fact he saw that abandonment above all as cause of increase in expenditures or rather the too rapid loss of the economic potential indispensable in arriving somewhere, and the thing made such an impression on him that he spent a great part of his time in programming strict economies which then behaving like some government authority he couldn't put into practice not that he allowed himself extravagances poor thing and he even solved the problem of one of the main meals of the day by eating bread and cheese and salami in his room adding a coffee which he prepared himself with a little Neapolitan machine over a spirit lamp and he ate the second meal in a milk bar nearby in the Calle dei Fuseri and only when his will was sapped by excessive appetite he went into a little restaurant in the Calle della Mandorla and though the place looked anything but expensive he ended by

paying even for the cheapest dishes certain bills that made him
remember his sad sister without excessive repulsion and the soups
and cutlets and stews she was capable of making, however one
must make sacrifices for love not to mention future glory which
ordinarily demands a high price from the man who wants to
achieve it, but this is exactly where the irritating confusion began
and in fact he was led almost constantly to ask himself what real
link existed between the life of hardship he was leading and a not
too distant future of glory since three or four times now he had
lighted the stove and always with dubious results not only as far
as the heat itself was concerned but also in what he had managed
to achieve in the field of studies and of artistic production. Our
young man as we have already had occasion to point out intended
to take as soon as possible a great number of examinations beginning with one in art history based on the works of the painter
Giorgione da Castelfranco, however rather than study the works
of others he was interested in producing works of his own and he
could hardly wait to test his strength in some poetical creation
which was a somewhat brusque way of entering that world of art
which had always attracted him and which attracted him more
than ever now since he had the impression that if by any chance
he managed to publish a few lyrics in a sufficiently important
magazine or if he succeeded in winning a poetry prize even a minor
one he would have something after all to set against the economic
power of the Borghettos, but with all the things he had on his mind
it wasn't so easy to think up verses suited to this goal and in fact it
took a whole afternoon's work to achieve the beginning of a com-
position which opened beautifully in this way The world and I
Have met here Each to say What we have in common, and apart
from the fact that neither the world nor he seemed in a mood to
spit out promptly what they promised to say he still had to find a
relationship of necessity between those four lines of verse and his
having moved to Venice that is he could imagine that had he
worked with a will he could have written the very same lines if
not better ones staying on in Marocco, and so at this point the

reasonable thing to do was to save on wood at least and in fact he decided not to light the stove any more and to prepare meanwhile for the general part of the examination by going to admire on the spot the works of art of which in Venice there was surely no shortage and then perhaps to go and study in the famous Querini Spampalia library or the even more famous Marciana where the central heating was excellent and free of charge however in this respect also the relationship of necessity broke down somewhat since he had the impression that the mosaics of the Basilica or the structure of the Doges' Palace with its mad inversion of masses could be studied better from illustrations in books than from reality, to say nothing of the works of the illustrious Giorgione only a handful of which were to be found in Venice since the others had ended up in Vienna for the most part but also in Oxford and even in San Diego California so he had to conclude that even for the study of art history in situ his coming to Venice had been a step of dubious utility and that in sum the only plausible reason for the move should have been Maria and this was something Antonio tried to think about as little as possible because living only a few steps away from Maria not only had no immediate practical advantages but also made him furious because it was cruel to live just those few steps apart and not to be able to see each other when they felt like it.

Still in the moments of most serious doubt when his economic programs seemed especially uncertain and he faced the frightening prospect of spending all his nest egg without achieving anything worthwhile Antonio could only swallow his anger and think intensely of Maria and of the unquestioned love that united them though he was prudent to handle Maria much as he did his dreams of glory namely shifting everything or almost everything to a vague future since when it came to the present not even thoughts of love could exist without bitterness as we have clearly seen chiefly through the fault of Signora Borghetto, and for example the telephone which in itself could have been a perfect system for uniting two lovers unable to be united otherwise proved instead a horrid device whose use led to outrageous surprises and to subsequent bestial rages since it frequently happened that a female voice and perhaps even that of Signora Borghetto in answering Antonio's specific question would say Maria was not at home when according to their previous understanding she was to be there, and this was a source of grave turmoil whether he thought she was really there or whether he thought she wasn't so after two or three of these little tricks they decided he should telephone at a set time when she could take her position next to the telephone as if by chance and answer personally, and obviously they set the moment on the basis chiefly of the hours when Signora Borghetto went out except that she had fallen into the habit of neglecting even her card games and the charitable activities of San Simeone Grande in order to guard her daughter's virtue with a more assiduous eye, and from Maria's uncertain and evasive manner of speaking Antonio realized at once when the old slut was in the vicinity listening and if in fact he asked Maria though of course not calling her mother an old slut and Maria answered yes then the conversation proceeded painfully with long questions from his end and with a yes or no from hers until they couldn't stand it any longer and said good-bye and hung up, so the telephone wasn't after all the great resource it had seemed a priori since even when things went well that is when Maria happened to be alone in the room and could say freely how much she loved him and how she longed for kisses and things of that sort, even in this extremely lucky circumstance they were doomed to suffer because the more fervent their love was the more they wanted to have the beloved person there in flesh and blood to caress, and in short the telephone after all as a means of exchanging amorous transports was highly unsuitable so in the end they developed a kind of contempt for it though they didn't break off such communications even if they felt worse than before when they had ended.

Hardly more satisfactory than the phone calls were the visits Antonio paid to Maria at fixed hours as in prisons and boarding schools on Wednesdays and Fridays with Signora Borghetto settled there knitting and heaving sighs that filled the whole room with noise and as far as one could tell those sighs were the only form of communication involving breath that she was prepared now to make with Antonio because she no longer replied in any way to his good afternoon or good-bye when he arrived and left limiting herself to a glance expressing enormous amounts of scorn or some equivalent sentiment, and she repeated glances of the same sort countless times in the course of the visit raising her eyes without interrupting her knitting or sighing so even though the distance to the little sofa where Antonio and Maria usually sat was sufficient to allow a fairly private conversation they had no desire to talk of lovely things with those two ugly eyes constantly trained on them and they remained silent for fifteen minutes at a time also sighing like a pair of bellows while their only consolation was to hold hands or rather press their hands together but this was a consolation only if they considered the irritation the vigilant signora felt since in itself it offered only meager satisfaction especially when compared as it inevitably was to the more substantial contacts of the past, so from those visits more sorrow was derived than anything else so after a while they decided not to give them up which would have made the knitting lady suspect that they met elsewhere but rather to employ those two hours in a more profitable fashion and thereafter during the visits they took to studying each his own subjects but in this way making up a bit for the time lost elsewhere, and the fact that they studied seriously only exchanging a very chaste smile every so often should at least have filled with comfort the old slut of a mother and instead she must really have been impossible to please out of principle because her long gazes lost none of their malevolence and even gained more if that were possible.

So also the visits to Maria at home finally became a trial to be undergone and it was more evident than ever that Signora Borghetto aimed at tiring the two of them as soon as possible or at least at tiring Maria since if Maria weakened her mother couldn't care less whether Antonio did, however well aware of these openly hostile aims they became still more determined to hold fast and they suc-

ceeded fairly well and moreover everyone knows that loves which
encounter the most opposition are often the most tenacious and
flourishing, and in any case apart from the utility they derived by
studying even in the wretched visits in the Borghetto home when
they were patient the right moment came which was the moment
of farewell which didn't now take place in the entrance hall on
the ground floor to which Maria after the first escapade had been
strictly forbidden to descend but in the great reception room where
the little blackamoor held the solitary lamp as high as possible, and
in any case even there that is to say in the immediate vicinity of
the hostile signora they could calculate on having at their disposal
perhaps fifteen or twenty seconds before the maid appeared with
Antonio's coat without going away again, and it was a period
they exploited intensely in hugs and kisses and burning words but
with all that it wasn't a very long time certainly and so it was fully
legitimate for them to go back to deceit and meet secretly during
class periods however Maria didn't have classes every day and on
Tuesday and Saturday for example she hadn't any in the morning or
in the afternoon and these were days of unspeakable sadness for
Antonio exceeded only by the ghastly dreariness of Sunday when
he got up at eleven and crossed the Grand Canal to the church of
Santa Maria Gloriosa dei Frari where hiding behind a column
like Jean Sorel he espied Maria in the distance hearing Mass with
Cavalier Ilario on one side of her and the Signora Amalia on the
other all dressed in their best and conscious of their fairly high
social position, and then at the end of Mass outside the church
they exchanged greetings and remarks joining the group that was
theirs by right thanks to the well worked out distinctions that
divide respectable society and if there was some young and perhaps
good-looking man around Maria our hero suffered the torments
of hell imagining that this was a son-in-law acceptable to Signora
Borghetto and perhaps who knows in the long run Maria might
allow herself to be convinced, then afterwards she went off to
the nearby Campo San Polo still escorted by her parents and Antonio could only return to his icy room filled with the smell of the

spent stove where he went back to bed perhaps without eating and listened through the long afternoon to the sound of bells which came to him from all sides since there were plenty of churches around and he could distinguish only the deeper sound of the bells of San Marco while the others became confused as they were fairly similar, and looking at the stains and cracks on the ceiling and the walls which had gradually become familiar to him and were now props for his imagination he began to dream that soon he would fill the world with his glory and then when he came out of the noon Mass at Santa Maria Gloriosa dei Frari everyone would bow as he went by and more than the others Signora Borghetto of course and forgetting the past he would perhaps give her a tolerant smile, but naturally the afternoon was long and so there was time also for different thoughts namely that he wouldn't fill the world with his glory so soon and that if he had left home to spend holiday afternoons in bed in a rented room on the Fondamenta della Parona it had been a great stupidity from every point of view and not only economically and in fact he couldn't dismiss the possibility that once the month paid for in advance was over he might go back to Marocco to the house in short that for better or worse was his, and for God's sake couldn't he have fallen in love with a girl just like Maria of course only less rich or if nothing else with a less unpleasant family because though it was no fault of Maria's and indeed she did everything possible to remedy and compensate for the disasters of family origin his love for her was a bit too mixed with humiliations and annoyances and torments, and as can clearly be seen these were dangerous thoughts which Antonio tried to avoid but without succeeding completely, indeed he found himself totally immersed in them during the week between the sixth and the twelfth of December when Maria had influenza and didn't come to class at the Ca' Foscari and when he tried to telephone without however insisting too much so as not to arouse suspicions they answered that the signorina had a fever and couldn't come to the phone, and even when he turned up for his Wednesday visit the maid rather haughtily told him that the signorina had the flu and couldn't get out of bed and asked him to excuse her, and Antonio suddenly imagined the most frightening things namely that Maria might have galloping pneumonia which didn't react to antibiotics, or else that she was perfectly well but since she had rightly tired of him she could find no better way to make him understand, or else that her father and mother joining forces had shipped her off abruptly to some religious college in London where among other things she would learn English much better than in Venice, and being so to speak left to his own resources without even the possibility of discussing his sorrows with others Antonio made incredible progress in the development of these and other grim imaginings until luckily on Thursday in the late afternoon Maria answered the phone herself and told him that she had had a fairly high fever namely a hundred and four but now she was better and had only ninety-nine and she had got out of bed especially to await his call since she was sure it would come and so it had, and in a moment when she could speak freely she told him her mother had raised the maid's wages to buy her loyalty and maybe the maid had answered nastily when he had called and in short her falling ill was really a disaster because all it took was a bit of flu and the two of them were suddenly as far apart as if one were at the North Pole and the other at the South so it was urgent for them to figure out an emergency plan to guarantee communications somehow if such misfortunes were to be repeated, but thank heaven she thought she was cured by now so he could come to the house the next day for his customary Friday visit.

He went in fact and was shown into the family living room already occupied as usual by Signora Borghetto more than ever full of tacit disapproval and Maria appeared shortly wearing a couple of pullovers her eyes red and her face drawn and with still a bit of cold which made her sniff continually but in a low voice she told him that since she loved him so terribly she would really have died of grief if she hadn't seen him only she hoped he wouldn't catch her flu, and in fact he did catch it with such alacrity that the next morning his temperature was already well over a hundred as his amiable

landlady soon ascertained when the poor youth had to call her
because he really couldn't stand up to go buy aspirin and vitamin
C, and toward evening his temperature rose still higher until it
was a hundred and four its increase also indicating its provenance
and he was a bit happy about that since all in all this too was a
form of communion and he was a bit annoyed because his landlady
had no telephone and so to call he would have had to go out but
there could be no question of that as he felt dizzy if he even tried
to get out of the bed however having to let Maria know somehow of
this obstacle which in itself was nothing of course but it forced
him to break off the visits and the rest he wrote her a nice letter
begging her to be patient until he got in touch with her over the
phone in a few days, but once the letter was written there was the
matter of stamps also for special delivery and taking it to the
main post office at the Rialto so it would go out faster and this too
was a mess because he wanted no one least of all the landlady who
basically was a curious person to know that he had such pressing
need to send information to the daughter of Cavalier Borghetto
of Maritime Supplies, but it had inevitably to pass through that
landlady's hands since at the moment she was the only person who
could buy stamps and mail a letter for him and moreover contrary
to what one might have supposed at first sight she proved to be a
kindly and discreet woman who made no fuss about going to the
central post office and back and even pretended not to have read
the address on the envelope though from then on she showed a
new solicitude toward Antonio and to begin with she squeezed a
couple of oranges for him because she believed that natural vitamins
were more efficacious than pills and she told him that through the
fault of the government which was opposed to divorce she was in
a somewhat awkward position since she was engaged so to speak to
a household appliance dealer who couldn't marry her as he was
already married and the beast was cruel to her and even beat her
when he had been drinking and she had to bear it all because in
the end he loved her and besides the house was his and he even gave
her a little money each month not much but still if she had chosen

she could have done without renting the room but she liked renting it because at times she had nice polite guests like Antonio though the one who had been there before she had had to send away because in addition to being late with the rent he had tried to take advantage of her, and in short in spilling out all these confidences she hoped to stimulate if not the same number at least a few from Antonio who however was running a high fever and in any case wasn't the least disposed to make any revelations about the urgent relationship that bound him to the daughter of Cavalier Borghetto, and though the landlady was quite downcast at his lack of expansiveness good woman that she was she continued to nurse him as best she could and even wanted to call a doctor but he considered this a superfluous expense since he knew quite well he had influenza and he also knew what medicines to take, and in conclusion since he really did have influenza and not another different and complicated disease thanks to aspirin in three days the fever went down and then risking a relapse the moment he was able to stand on his feet he went to the Campo San Fantin where there was a café with a public telephone and luckily she was sitting right beside her phone waiting for his call and she told him she felt guilty because she had surely given him the flu and for three days she had been in a state of unspeakable grief because among other things he had forgotten to put his home address on the special delivery and she didn't know where to write him though perhaps Marocco alone would have been enough, anyhow thank goodness now he was well and they had both had the flu and so they wouldn't worry about that any more, and meanwhile she had more or less recovered however she wasn't going to the Ca' Foscari in any case because the Christmas vacation had begun and besides her mother said she was run-down and wanted to take her to Cortina where there was snow and she would get her color back if nothing else but since she had fallen somewhat behind with her studies lately she was worried about catching up and so even if the vacation had begun she went on studying anyhow going to the Marciana to consult some volumes on English literature which she was sure she couldn't find in Cortina, and so he realized her mother was there listening and he asked her and she answered yes and then through a series of yesses and nos he had her confirm his impression that the mention of the Marciana was an appointment for the next day in the early afternoon, and so the next day as soon as they opened the library in the afternoon he settled there anxiously waiting at the first table on the left from which he could see her as soon as she arrived but he had to wait over an hour before she appeared and when at the end she did appear he saw immediately there was something wrong so he wanted to leave the library where naturally they couldn't talk and avoiding the square they passed the royal gardens and the Bucintoro to walk along certain back streets full of melancholy cats between the Frezzeria and the Campo San Fantin and it was more and more apparent that there was something wrong with her it was written all over her face which avoided his gaze and evident in her bitter and depressed manner but she kept stubbornly saying no there wasn't anything wrong every time he asked her and then since he insisted she admitted yes there was something but it wasn't worth talking about however as she said this she indicated that on the contrary the matter was very serious and that it would be necessary to clear it up, and then Antonio said that if she was so obstinate in keeping things to herself it meant she didn't love him enough and therefore it was best for them to give up the idea of going on, and at this point she made up her mind to spill the works which she had in any case a great desire to spill and she said that very morning her mother had told her she had collected some information about him as was only right for that matter since he was the person to whom her daughter was to be given in marriage and from this information it had emerged that he was an elementary school teacher in Marocco and naturally her mother had been very angry and she too had been well not angry but a bit downcast especially because she didn't know how to answer her mother who was overjoyed at being able to call him a liar, and naturally she herself didn't believe he was a liar such an idea would never cross her mind still she wished her blind faith in him had been in some way confirmed, and he allowed her to speak purposely remaining silent so she would go farther and farther with this talk which could also be the end of their love and he almost took pleasure in believing this because he thought at the moment he felt more rancor than love for her or at least considerable rancor mixed with love because among other things he felt insulted also from the social standpoint in his position as son of a poor man with a pension of a few thousand lire a month namely the amount that in all probability Cavalier Borghetto earned in half a day trafficking in Maritime Supplies, and this poor but honest man's son was being defamed for being an elementary school teacher instead of a wholesale dealer in salami and mineral water, and if Maria really felt that way she was surely falling in with certain family attitudes which dangerously lowered her so he didn't even choose to answer her and would let her think what she liked however in the meanwhile he was leading her with a kind of obscure premeditation to the Campo San Fantin and then turning into the Calle della Parona toward the Ponte della Parona at the top of which he finally stopped while evidently grieved but also rather confused she begged him to answer something because after all she too had the right to know the truth, and then with great calm he told her that the truth was so simple and banal that strictly speaking it wouldn't have been worth talking about but since it seemed to mean so much to her well yes for a certain period he had in fact taught in the elementary schools at Marocco just to do a favor to the assistant principal who was a close friend of his father's and had been short of teachers, but between this occasional assistance and being a real elementary schoolmaster there was quite a difference and he certainly wasn't surprised at her mother who after all was ignorant of many things but at her Maria yes he had reason to be amazed and in fact he would like her to explain how it would be possible to be an elementary school teacher and at the same time run after her morning and afternoon during the hours she herself settled on, and anyhow if she still had any doubts he could show her his university card or even get a legalized certificate which would show not only that he was enrolled but that he had paid all tuition fees in advance to the end of the scholastic year, and at this point the poor girl was already repentant and upset at what she had said and the horrid thoughts she had had and so he could and should easily have felt satisfied with such a victory but instead with the clear awareness that he was doing something outrageous but feeling fully justified in doing it because if nothing else he had to defend his humble origins he invited her to look at a certain window on the second floor of a certain house in the Fondamenta della Parona right before her eyes and he told her that this was the window of the room where he lived and she couldn't want more obvious proof that he wasn't teaching school in Marocco and she naturally had no desire to ask him for further proof of any kind and she only felt the need to do something extraordinary and extreme to expiate the guilt of having suspected him of deceit, and this action of such a lofty nature could only be to go up to his room, and surely she didn't have an idea of what she might go there to do but she wanted to go there with all her strength and to go at once, and he tried a bit to dissuade her and with diminishing warmth he explained how she had to behave so as not to attract attention or risk meeting somebody on the stairs, in short he would go a minute ahead of her and then from behind the window he would signal to her and she could move from the bridge and come confidently to the door which she would find open and climb the steps and at the top of the steps she would find him.

CHAPTER

X

In which Antonio and Maria

make several big missteps

When at a later date Antonio felt obliged to place his story with Maria in a predominately moral framework to overcome its statistical irrelevance and make it as was only right the critical and painful core of his young manhood, the step she took that day quick as a wink making her decision to come up into his room was one of the most ticklish and controversial passages in the whole matter since on the one hand it couldn't be ignored that Maria was acting in a state of great emotion not to say distress, on the other hand reasonable prominence could surely be given to the detail that slipping into a boy's bedroom for a girl however moved she may be is a procedure of some gravity especially since the emotion couldn't be all that great if the procedure in itself in its every phase involved the use of prudence and diligence namely in waiting for the signal from the window and in reaching the street door pushing it open and climbing the flight of stairs, in short there was more than enough time for her to realize sufficiently what she was doing, and also to draw back if she began to suspect she was doing something a bit too daring.

Now this posthumous and somewhat too great insistence on the share of responsibility which for better or worse fell to Maria was for Antonio a not very loyal means of freeing himself from his own burden of responsibility which was so heavy that he wouldn't have been able to bear it with the feeble strength with which he emerged from the affair, and in fact as he reflected on his conduct as a whole from the instant when he had had the bright idea of leaving Marocco to the moment when he had subtly and even theatrically driven Maria to the state of exasperation essential to her decision to come up to his room as straight as a rocket this conduct seemed that of a spider weaving his web with the firm determination to eat the fly, and in short his share of responsibility would truly have been intolerable if he hadn't unloaded a part of it on Maria and above all if he hadn't been able to recall that while things were happening so precipitately there had remained in him a kind of innocence or at least of obnubilation both because he was amply occupied in organizing the necessary moves so she would reach the room without anyone's seeing her and more especially because the idea of what would soon happen was taking shape in his mind in excessive fantasies such as Maria's shutting the door and throwing herself in his arms half-fainting and telling him to possess her because she was his or else of her in a much more modern way simply undressing very quickly and slipping into the bed asking him to join her promptly because it was freezing cold.

Imagining such unusual scenes was for Antonio a defense mechanism since at the very moment he imagined them he sensibly told himself they wouldn't happen like that though it remained clear that some event connected in one way or another with sex was going to take place and this filled him with such fright that he longed for it not to be true but this longing came too late that is when after his signal she had already moved from the bridge toward the building and there was now nothing for him to do but press the button opening the downstairs door then go wait for her at the top of the steps praying heaven the landlady wouldn't pop out at that very moment or worse still the landlady's lover, and there

Maria was tiptoeing toward him with her face uplifted and perhaps because this angle foreshortened her or because of her dazed expression she looked more childlike than ever and what's more she was gasping so that instead of a flight of stairs you would have thought she had climbed to the top of the campanile of San Marco running all the way, and this was certainly not a thing that could give him the courage he needed badly so the first thing he did when she got to the top was to whisper a sincere suggestion that she go back down again but she said no and then since she really wasn't able to talk she looked interrogatively at the three doors in the vestibule as if to ask which was the right one to open with no further tergiversation, and so he realized she possessed an extraordinary firmness of inner purpose in what she was doing and it didn't matter that this firmness wasn't exactly awareness as ever since he had begun to love her she had developed a total acceptance of everything and therefore also of anything.

But once she was in the room and he had reassuringly locked the door behind her like him she didn't seem to have practical ideas about what was to be done and obviously she made no motion toward half-fainting or throwing herself in his arms and still less toward stripping rapidly however on the other hand she didn't seem to stiffen in an attitude of even temporary defense of the flower of her virginity so she stood there more than anything else awaiting a suggestion from him but on that score she would have had a long wait poor girl and finally though her precise intentions weren't clear she stared at the bed which wasn't much of a piece of furniture in itself but it was still an instrument suited to making love comfortably or at least more comfortably than they had had grounds to hope for so soon however after she had taken a good look at the bed she turned her gaze with equal intensity to the wardrobe and to the dresser and the washstand and finally she decided to attach greater importance to the little table where along with his books and papers there was a dish with cheese rinds and date pits testifying to the frugality of his most recent meal and furthermore a dirty coffee cup and the Neapolitan coffeepot and looking at them she was visibly moved perhaps because she felt pity for his straitened circumstances or rather because since these were the things among which he lived she managed to fill them with love even if in themselves they were wholly unworthy.

In effect after having admired at ample length what there was to be seen she said you live here in a very low voice but with very high fervor and then taking off her fur coat and pulling up the sleeves of her pullover and asking rather resolutely where shall I throw this and where do I wash this she began to straighten up and to wash the coffeepot in the washbasin with icy water because despite the assurance of modern conveniences there was no hot water and he followed her partly trying to be helpful and partly trying to dissuade her from those tasks which he considered too lowly and saying he would do it later himself however at the same time he watched her cleaning up he was thinking with satisfaction that also when it came to domestic qualities he certainly wouldn't make a mistake in marrying her though he also had the impression that at this moment all her alacrity was bit out of proportion in the sense that if she had come to his room with the sole intention of straightening it up it would have been as if an amateur climber had scaled Mont Blanc only for the pleasure of eating a salami sandwich at the top, but then since that fervid demonstration of homely virtues was taking a bit too much time it was finally clear even to Antonio that her eager bustle was chiefly to postpone the moment when something else would have to be done or at least to disguise a basic embarrassment since for her too especially with that family background it couldn't have been a trifle to sacrifice the flower of her virginity and on this score his conscience was quite clear since the last thing he was thinking of was to press matters to the point of premarital defloration and yet to press them a bit farther than they had gone in the back streets and passageways seemed only right and proper bearing in mind the conveniences they happened to have at hand but how much farther my God this wasn't an easy question to decide also because in their present situation to act or not to act seemed equally wrong, and then when she had finished washing and drying and putting in order finding no other pretext she suggested lighting the stove and he then made himself go over to her and answer that in view of the brief time at their disposal it wasn't worth lighting this stove which took at least an hour before making the place even moderately warm but she didn't give a damn about the stove any more as could easily be guessed from the way she looked at him giving him all of herself and at the same time retaining in the depths of her eyes a residue of that expression which he had first noticed that day under the portico of the Cassa di Risparmio when it had seemed to him that more than anything else she was begging him not to hurt her, in short the matter wasn't simple even from that aspect in fact it was less simple than ever on second thought and he couldn't do anything and stood there looking at her with growing embarrassment until she asked him aren't you going to give me a kiss and she asked it so naïvely that it seemed she wanted the kiss chiefly for having washed the coffeepot, however the minute he started kissing her he felt her soft mouth express a surrender and a desire never reached before so fully but instead of being encouraged to progress with their experiences as she surely was expecting he remained almost blocked by a superabundant sense of responsibility and perhaps even more by the fear of not being able to translate his natural stimuli into action she would accept, anyhow he derived more dismay than pleasure from a kiss that according to common procedure should have been an exceptional spur whereas it didn't spur him on in the least and in conclusion he didn't know exactly what to do however it seemed important to him that she shouldn't become aware of his embarrassing behavioral confusion which she might mistake for coldness so he made an effort to simulate a transport which even in the best of cases would have been out of proportion but after a while she must have noticed something wasn't working properly insofar as sincerity of feelings was concerned naturally and in fact breaking away and looking at him anxiously she asked if he really loved her and really with all his soul, and he could answer yes to such a question without the least hesitation because he was especially convinced that the transitory difficulty of the relationship derived precisely from the fact that he loved her too much because if instead he had had before him a girl he loved a bit less he would already have thrown her on the bed to say the least, but Maria who couldn't read his mind demanded yet another confirmation asking him in a whisper to swear he loved her as much as she loved him and he answered passionately I swear.

This was probably a thing she was anxious to establish beyond all doubt in order to proceed herself seeing that he wasn't proceeding and in fact as soon as she had his oath she seemed to breathe more easily and she told him rather forcefully to face the wall an operation he performed without dreaming of asking her for an explanation because he would have done anything even something stranger than facing the wall provided he didn't have to make the decision, and when after a little while she said he could turn around again he turned immediately and was almost ready to collapse because he saw her in his bed with the blankets pulled up to her chin so she could even have been completely naked but luckily on the floor only her shoes and skirt were to be seen so it was likely that she had tucked herself in wearing all the rest which in the final analysis was more than enough, and so having recovered from his shock he approached the bed but looking chiefly at the floor and first he picked up the skirt to put it on the chair over her fur coat and then finding nothing better to do he asked her if she really knew what she was doing which was in many ways an inopportune question and she poor devil who was there trembling all alone with her teeth chattering too because of the cold answered with a shrug as if to say at the point she had reached awareness of what she was doing would have been cumbersome to say the least, and in any case since the most decorous as well as appropriate thing to be done at the moment was to hurry she said in what voice she could muster you come in too.

Having dramatically dismissed the hope that this invitation meant something different from what it reasonably meant Antonio rapidly examined the hypothesis of refusing however in Maria's gaze along with emotions like confusion and eagerness for perdition and desire for pity which for one reason or another might well have encouraged his tendency to virtuous renunciation he could also see a mass of other sentiments ranging from acceptance to enjoyment and exhortation and God knows maybe even to provocation until by looking closely it was even possible to notice a slight hint of hilarity which must perforce have been connected with his protracted indecision, and at this point Antonio could rightfully conclude that in the end he had done all too much to safeguard her chastity and he was now free to attack it as he pleased exempt from delays and scruples joining her obviously under the blankets without further hesitation, but good heavens now he was struck by the thought that he couldn't join her with his shoes and everything on that is to say it was clear he would have to take off his shoes but not equally clear about his pants and first of all he might ask himself whether a young man's pants corresponded exactly to a girl's skirt because if the answer was affirmative since she had taken off her skirt all right he couldn't avoid taking off his pants and since the reasonable answer was that skirt and pants were equal in their function then he couldn't let her see he lacked the nerve to take his off any more than he could expect her to believe he habitually went to bed without removing them, in short it seemed there was no way of evading the pants issue and so he asked her now to turn toward the wall and he made this request with such anxiety that she almost laughed in fact she did laugh but simply and without maliciousness and naturally she didn't turn toward the wall in the least but on the contrary kept her eyes fixed on him and perhaps she wanted to let him know that since she loved him in the complete way she did he shouldn't feel any shame not even in taking off his pants in front of her because it was precisely by overcoming the uneasiness of such troublesome operations that two people could find the degree of intimacy suited to going ahead, but at this point Antonio was quite ready to turn back toward the renunciations which in his heart he had never for a moment ceased to entertain

and he wasn't entirely wrong since she who now seemed so bold
only a few moments earlier had insisted he turn his back while she
took off her skirt so he said firmly that if she didn't look away he
wouldn't get into the bed and then without dropping entirely her
amused manner she shut her eyes and swore she would keep them
shut until she felt him at her side and with hasty and clumsy movements he freed himself first of his pants and then of his jacket after
which without any further hesitation he slipped in next to her.

For a while they lay there embracing a bit awkwardly and trembling with shyness their hearts pounding so that each could hear
the other's beating as well as his own but then despite the resistance
Antonio continued to set up against the natural course of events a
considerable warmness was created both under the blankets and
between their two bodies and it was surely beneficial in that it also
put our hero again in a condition to act but naturally before taking
any step it was wisest to consider it from more than one point of
view if possible and though the dominant thought was that it was
insane for a boy like him to let a beautiful young girl like her get
away since they were together in one bed and he surely hadn't
forced her into it there also remained to establish what value to
assign the phrase get away since she was so young and inexperienced
and besides in love to a degree generally and not incorrectly defined
with the adverb madly the responsibility lay chiefly with him to see
that irreparable things didn't take place and on that score he was
quite convinced that once the present moment of weakness and
abandon was passed she would be extremely grateful to him if she
emerged with the flower of her virginity saved, however the flower
in itself wasn't actually more important than anything else because
their love was surely one of those destined to last and besides they
were going to marry as soon as possible but here to be honest one
had to admit that this damn flower if it had no importance in one
sense it logically should have had none in the other that is it still
seemed somehow preferable for him to save her virginity as a symbol
if nothing else of the spirituality of their love although it wasn't
really right to place such an important abstraction in a female

location of weak resistance and of rather dubious respectability according to current language so it was much better to think of it as being distributed everywhere namely in the heart and the brain and the bloodstream and the skin as well as in the way of feeling and behaving of course, and so it must have been however after reaching this stage of reasoning it was inevitable to admit that Maria's diffuse spirituality had already undergone numerous jolts in the past through his groping in back streets and passageways and if it had come through intact as was indubitable since he still loved her spiritually it would then survive intact more serious situations and who knows perhaps the most serious of all, however in the final analysis it wasn't wise to think of this with so much premeditation and it was better to press on to the point where they had pressed other times and then leave to improvisation or mood or the enterprise of one of the two of them the task of pressing perhaps a little farther still though not too far.

Once he had established this it was very easy to begin because Maria had been waiting quite a while for him to make up his mind to do something and now obviously he took great pleasure in kissing her and in feeling her respond by clasping herself to him with increasing warmth and lessening restraint, but well aware of the greater risk the arousal of the senses might involve with these superior conveniences he kept watch with a far greater solicitude than when they were kissing and hugging against walls and in certain moments he even had the impression he had split in two that is in addition to a self lying and kissing Maria there was another self looking on from above with censorious intentions and not infrequently with ironic ones, and for example in the present pass this other self did not find it at all proper for him to allow Maria to perceive the consistency of his sex which she could now finally perceive all too distinctly and obeying the censor at first he tried to keep as separate as possible from her with that perceptible member but then the reclining self began to wonder if it was really right to deprive her of a contact that couldn't really be called coarse since she didn't seem in the least to disdain it and when they finally were both opposed to the censor however the matter threatened to take a very sharp and heedless turn compared to previous experiences since it was clear that being in bed she let herself go much more than she had when she was leaning against walls if for no other reason because here she was in no danger of falling having in a sense already fallen and moreover they were alone and quite sure nobody could take them by surprise and finally though abundantly provided with other garments she was without her skirt and he his pants, in short considering the circumstances it was more than likely that if he hadn't kept a firm grip on the rudder it would have been very difficult for the ship to reach shore without trouble therefore just as the prudent navigator never leaves the old course for a new one so he hastened to fall back on an already familiar itinerary that is he decided that despite the favorable opportunity to do much more he would meticulously and measuredly limit himself to repeating the practices already performed numerous times outdoors and since those external maneuvers generally began with some caressing of the breast he decided to seek her left breast which was more convenient to him and he found it with unexpected facility not only because it was easy to introduce his hand from below without the obstacle of the skirt but also because she had foresightedly undone the snap of her brassière.

This undoing which must perforce have occurred at the moment when she slipped into bed while his back was turned that is during a phase of relatively moderate sexual arousal could only be interpreted as a conscious invitation to him to act with more alacrity and perhaps adding some novelty with respect to the past and according to his knowledge of the amatory art a considerable progress might be kissing her breast instead of simply caressing it and doing so first with delicacy and then more suitably and truth to tell not even this operation was very difficult since she helped the liberation of the breast without making much show of doing it and in fact of both breasts raising her slip to her shoulders but naturally keeping well under the covers so that nothing could be seen and since because of the temperature and various other factors there was

surely no question of exposing her he had to move below and as
he was under there doing what he had to do it was easy for him
to imagine his censorious self snickering from above if for no other
reason because it wasn't at all easy to breathe under there and
moreover also because of the lack of proper circulation of the air
he perceived more acutely than ever before the odor of her skin
which was absolutely virginal in the sense that it suggested the
odor of milk slightly soured if you thought about it a minute, and
finally as he was doing his best he began to worry about his own
inexperience especially technical in the event that it proved necessary to progress in amatory actions as seemed inevitable since
Maria's breasts were very sensitive and already as a rule when he
caressed them she quickly moved on to ecstasies so imagine now
when she felt him kissing them however awkwardly we may fear
and in fact she soon began to yearn and writhe and moan and tell
him she loved him oh how she loved him but also these professions
though entirely spontaneous were enough to upset Antonio who
always wanted distinctions and subdivisions with erotic practices
on one side and amorous sentiments on the other thus making
another great mistake which for that matter was providential at
the moment because all those disturbing sensations granted him
an extraordinary clarity of ideas and therefore an excellent control
of the situation, and so as she raved more and more and had abundant transports he thought it was a good idea to go ahead but without departing from the usual pattern that is he moved a hand down
easily finding the path to her sex which was soft and damp also
with a rather sharp odor of which he was all too aware since he still
had his head under the blankets kissing her breast and yet in the
pressure of events he happened to think that according to nature's
plans that pungency should have provided a stimulus to sensual
pleasures whereas he would have preferred to forego it, and for
this reason one might even think there was something wrong with
him but he couldn't remedy that suddenly in the current juncture
so the only sensible thing to do was to caress her as quickly and
expertly as possible and finish rapidly if nothing else however be-

fore reaching the conclusion she seemed gripped by a new and powerful wave of desires or to be more precise by a single desire because while she moved and moaned and said take me take me you could realize that more than anything else she ardently wished to be penetrated so he once again thought it was a good thing he had a head on his shoulders as he did so soundly and he was content when for better or worse she reached her usual denouement full of shudders and passionate half-articulate words and finally her tears and childish sobs which she had often assured him were tears of love and he held her tight with gentleness now that thank heaven he didn't have so many thoughts not that it wouldn't have been wise to have them but because he tried to keep them in a state of preformal flux that is to prevent them from assuming consistency since this surely wasn't the moment to face problems and for that matter perhaps there weren't any problems because she loved him with her whole self and therefore they should be happy and content, and by and large he was happy and content and so he remained until as if heavily following a tortuous route among narrow streets and canals the sound of the great bell of San Marco arrived and he said oh my God it's four-thirty and she would have to hurry if she didn't want to arouse suspicions in her mother.

In which the situation is examined still further, in an effort to understand it somehow

On the following occasions things luckily went much smoother at least from the organizational point of view and for example on the days when it was agreed she would come to him Antonio took care to light the stove in the morning and keep it going so she found a bit of warmth and moreover since the visits took place in the afternoon though unfortunately not until five o'clock he bought a teapot and a couple of teacups and she generally turned up with a big box of cookies or pastries and insisted on serving tea though not with the luxury or ceremony customary in the Borghetto home of course, in short they did everything possible to give those meetings in a furnished room a respectable tone somewhere between family ménage and courtesy call but this remained mostly in the realm of intentions because in practice the first thing they did was go straight to bed and he had only to slip his hands under her fur coat to clasp her tenderly to himself and kiss her lips which were very cool because of the weather outside and immediately the desire which anyway they both had all ready and waiting inside flashed up with such urgency that fur coat and skirt fell to the floor without delay and then she allowed herself more than willingly to be led to the bed where the undressing continued though only up to a certain point as we shall see.

Our young man in fact though he derived a certain sensation of power from the undeniable fact that he was going to bed with the only daughter of Cavalier Borghetto of Maritime Supplies was still so to speak in turmoil that is he was far from the state of inner satisfaction and hence of confidence that persons lucky in love achieve however transiently and to remedy this confusion he set himself more passionately than ever to search for those definitive and absolute values never found in nature however he didn't suspect that this grave and sublime elaboration of spirituality stemmed in part from the chaotic fear of being in the wrong and hence exposed to all the demands for expiation this would later produce and in part from a still less noble consideration namely that whereas in their encumbered erotic maneuverings Maria somehow reached orgasm he in the final analysis remained so to speak high and dry. This was a kind of distress that affected Antonio all the more seriously since without knowing the reason he could clearly see that things appeared to him one moment in one way and another moment in another in a lack of stability which in the end Maria also had to pay for since the unused energy blocked within him and not entirely spent in the outbursts which led him to take altruistic pleasure in her satisfaction as if it were his own caused him harmful and almost dire upheavals and a trifle for example a little misunderstanding about telephone calls or an extra insult during a visit to the Borghetto home was enough to make him think with excessive bitterness and violence that the only daughter of the cavaliere and his wife was fairly easy if he recalled her in her less decent postures those she assumed only fleetingly when as a consequence of his caresses her desire gripped her most powerfully or when she was already close to orgasm.

Now it isn't that Antonio wanted to deny Maria the right to manifest the great desire to make love which assailed her at times or to display in her own fashion the immense pleasure which she suddenly reached thanks to his maneuvering on the contrary he liked these sincere demonstrations a lot however he liked them at the time but then afterwards on thinking about them they caused him a kind of sick feeling derived as far as he could tell from the fact that he was led mentally to connect Maria's behavior with certain quite crude and at times downright coarse expressions which being common usage are commonly used but which seemed entirely unsuitable to Maria though she was doing precisely what those expressions denoted, in short he generally deplored more than anything else the lack of an entirely new language which would be suited to his love in its every aspect both material and spiritual but at the moment this language apparently didn't exist and given his inclinations Antonio passed easily from this linguistic fault to moralistic scorn that is he moved from the inevitable coarseness of the language used to illustrate acts and attitudes and arrived at attributing to them a baseness that otherwise at least in Maria's case they wouldn't have had, and in substance it was precisely the baseness thus arrived at or rather contrived at which made them despite everything a bit repellent, but then gradually on thinking it over and naturally without any precise intention on his part his inner attitude was mysteriously reversed so that suddenly he was moved no longer by moralizing inhibitions but by erotic satisfactions that is he was now the one whose imagination drove the cavaliere's only daughter farther on the road to perdition surely much farther than her real capacities would allow imagining her in the center of the room freeing herself of upper and nether garments with a sophisticated grace more captivating than that of the most famous strippers, or else he saw her arrive already boldly naked under the fur coat which she dropped as soon as she came in as if it were nothing on the floor and lay down immediately thereafter happy and smiling on the bed inviting him with much charm and coyness to kiss her here and there and everywhere and after overcoming a very slight but dutiful resistance he started kissing her where and how she liked with a slow and knowing technique that practically speaking he was also dreaming of, and then thanks to the pleasure she received and the desire to receive much more she began to stir and writhe and twist and arch her back and spread her legs and finally offer herself in the most frank way until he decided to cause her orgasm kissing her right there and remaining excluded from it because naturally even when he made love in his imagination he adopted a certain abnegation not disassociated from prudence.

Unfortunately all this fantasticating in which he now indulged a bit too often both during the day and at night emerging from it obviously rather exhausted was not designed to ease his actual relations with Maria both because of his remorse at having imagined her so dissolute and because the poor girl dealing with garter belts and bras and other intimate frivolities displayed more clumsiness than sophisticated grace also because of many not yet overcome mental obstacles so he preferred not to look at her although she now no longer asked him to turn his back, but his preferring not to look at her originated not so much from the spectacle of inexperience she gave in undressing before another as from his own stubborn lack of preparation since according to him Maria was still divided into two parts of which he accepted one with joyous immediacy while the other required some effort for him to accept, and the immediately accepted part was what he always saw of her namely face hair crooked tooth and the clothed form and also the legs, instead the part hard to accept also because he couldn't remember it very well was the portion of the body from the shoulders to the knees which was usually covered up and on seeing it uncovered he considered it with great sorrow of course less perfect than the rest also because thanks to God knows what perverse tendency of his he dwelt more on the details he didn't like much than on those he liked a little more. Now if this really rather uncharitable method of examination had derived only from slight experience of female bodies and therefore from the critical confusion they generally arouse in the inexperienced there wouldn't have been so much to worry about because with time and familiarity he would have in the end found beautiful what at present didn't seem beautiful or wasn't beautiful as happens with great lovers who often come to love a body's defects and anomalies more than its perfections, however the trouble was that his strictness of judgment was nourished by deeply rooted distorted ideas since on the subject of female beauty he adopted a somewhat abstruse criterion of moral rectitude and was convinced that virtue had perforce to be linked with perfection of form and from this idiocy he deduced ipso facto another still more idiotic notion namely that imperfection was linked with vice or at least with questionable habits so that in forming an irreprehensible idea of the female breast he relied not on the splendid women painted by Titian and by Renaissance artists in general or still less on the equally famous female nude of Goya depicted with bold nipples but rather on the semispherical and firm and static and in short absolutely improbable breasts that the painter Jean Fouquet stuck onto a famous Madonna of his.

Maria instead possessed a pair of breasts neither too large nor too small neither too firm nor too soft neither too short nor too long and in other words she had a bosom like most normal respectable girls who aren't photographed for *Playboy* and moreover this fairly ordinary bosom had a number of those freckles which looked so fine on her face but there on the milky skin of her bosom were a bit out of place to tell the truth and also the nipples weren't exactly the way Antonio would have liked them since they gave form and relief to a certain material quality of the breast which from a certain viewpoint was also opportune considering the purpose for which the female body was endowed with breasts that is he realized quite well they hadn't been put there to delight the eye and the spirit so much as to offer the first nutrition to offspring and yet he felt that at least as far as Maria was concerned there was something unjust about it and if he had been the Almighty he would somehow have arranged things differently, and of course these were harmful and eccentric thoughts for which however he was guilty only to a small degree inasmuch as he had been driven to them by a carefully organized educational method tending to make him despise carnal love as something unclean and to make him appreciate spiritual love as sublime and though father Dante didn't then know it spiritual love was only a sublimated extension of the carnal of which it retained certain alarming traces, and on the other hand following the Bible the story of the human race really began with that mixup which we are still expiating if it's true that we're born already branded or probably predisposed to sins of the flesh, and who knows why the human race instead of accepting this condition and taking it in the best spirit which would amount to saying go ahead and make love as much and as joyfully as possible instead fell to thinking about it and producing in some exceptional cases ideas like the immaculate conception, and though our hero at this stage of his life no longer believed in God or in the saints he certainly wasn't the sort to rid himself of all those fine prejudices which he would no doubt have invented himself if someone else hadn't already invented them since he was so prone to engulfing himself in them partly with pleasure and partly with torment almost enjoying his own confusion and his own imperfection in the light of original sin so that at heart his ambition would have been to go beyond such a sin that is in some way fuse the acts of sex with the religious spirit making one whole and it was precisely for this reason that in his moments of great fervor he started imagining women's bodies that were completely odorless and without pores and possibly hairless and with barely indicated sexual attributes, and it seemed to him that if Maria had been made more or less in this way or at least had had highly spiritual and perfect forms she would have been safe from the profanation that is he would have loved her boundlessly without even touching her or better still he would have been able to touch her and enjoy her but without contaminating her or himself.

All this toilsome argumentation was basically not very magnanimous toward Maria since no matter how clearly Antonio himself recognized his motives were indirect and fantastic he tended to give her much of the blame for those sexual contacts which they practiced with abundant eagerness and even some expertise, however to tell the truth the argumentation was quite abstract and when confronted by real facts it lost all meaning and force, that is when the chips were down our hero was always ready to assume full responsibility and in the final analysis to accept as a natural circumstance the hair and pores and the other imperfections which allowed him when he thought about it to desire her and to treat her like a creature of flesh and blood destined you might say eschatologically to profanations and in fact he profaned her gladly experiencing at times an obscure and almost angry delight and then of course remaining quite dismayed at it but he hastily overcame doubts and remorse thanks mostly to the naturalness with which Maria the minute she had enjoyed him began to cry deriving according to him a sweet purification which if it settled things for her should have settled things even more for him who from the point of view of the remission of sins had the advantage of having been left high and dry, except that even this advantage was as we have clearly seen a two-edged weapon and tended rapidly to disappear since Maria was hastily developing a very lively curiosity about the physiological and mechanical aspects of love and asked him to explain to her in detail how the sexual organs both male and female were made and their function in pleasure and in reproduction, things that at least insofar as reproduction was concerned she should have known fairly well because among other things they taught them in school and she admitted they had taught them to her in school true enough but in a completely unreal way so it was as if they had taught them but without making her learn them or rather they had made her learn them but hadn't taught them to her or made her understand them however it must have been largely her fault because she had been so stupid when she studied science in high school that unlike many of the other girls she had no yen to know those things in a manner less theoretical than the school offered, but now that she had had the good luck to meet Antonio and to fall in love with him so deeply and completely she was all filled with desire to know a lot more also because knowing more meant with their present conveniences experimenting more and experimenting more meant entering a more blissful world of extraordinary joys whose existence she had never suspected until a few weeks before, and in conclusion although Antonio explained over and over that this would involve the definitive and irreparable rupture of the hymen or membrane of virginity she insisted he should penetrate her with that implement of his which for that matter she hadn't yet seen or known since all this talk and all these exercises went on when they were under the blankets and also provided with highly impeding garments such as underwear, however at a certain point of the story she suddenly took off her underwear with surprising resolve and insisted he do the same and after he had finally obeyed her she pressed herself completely against him with such abandon that she seemed to have lost her reason or rather to have acquired a superior way of reasoning because in all clarity she said she wanted him to deflower her then and there since she realized this was the most complete way of loving that two creatures desirous of loving each other could attain and this was exactly what she wanted namely for them to succeed in loving each other as much and as well as was granted to human beings, and poor Antonio though from a philosophical point of view he was forced to agree with her was torn between yes and no also because he was vague as to the real difficulties he might encounter in doing his duty nor did he neglect the apprehensions and uneasiness about the far from trifling risks of procreation and finally he couldn't completely dispel from some corner of his spirit the shadow of the suspicion that he was on the verge of trapping himself irreparably, but taking it all together the fact that he loved her and desired her with his whole being prevailed and therefore he felt himself impelled by natural forces to give her that boon she so yearned for and in short although the torments of indecision continued to seize him from various directions he climbed upon her and there he maneuvered so much that as best she could she reached a delirious orgasm and he also arrived at one a little later on his own managing at the last moment to cast elsewhere the fruit of his ejaculation so that she wasn't stained with it and remaining as never before in his life pierced by the profound mystery of sin and the disconsolate conviction that all things considered it would have been better to die.

But Maria was not in the least of his opinion and in fact limiting her usual emotional manifestation to barely a few tears she continued embracing him pronouncing very tender words of joy and exultation because having sensed in some way that he too had experienced that marvelous eruption which had happened to her she felt ineffably content and even grateful however all in all she mustn't have understood much of what had happened because she never tired of saying now she was forever and indissolubly his and now nothing in the world could separate them after they had been joined and mingled in such a way, and then Antonio to avoid confusion and misunderstanding felt called upon to explain that according to him the irreparable hadn't really happened and not because he didn't love her enough or because he was afraid of assuming the responsibility but because at the very moment when he had been on the verge of letting himself go it had occurred to him that at least three years would have to go by before they could marry and in that period of time many things might happen such as he might die leaving unpaid the great ethical debt a boy assumes when he deflowers a girl of good family, and she was rather tormented at hearing these fine words and answered that if there was really any danger of his dying so soon that was all the more reason for her wanting to be entirely his because in any case she would never be anyone else's, and she was so firm in this idea that she wanted and long to be deflowered at once so they wouldn't have to think about it again, but Antonio with all the things he had on his mind certainly didn't feel equipped for such an undertaking and he said it was too late now but if she were to continue in this determination until their next meeting then the next time he would certainly give it to her good and proper.

CHAPTER
XII

In which an extraordinary catastrophe
takes place

Antonio prepared himself for the fateful meeting in the best possible way dividing his time between appropriate erotic fantasies and elaborate scruples of conscience applied not so much to the defloration in itself which was by now so certain it was best to think it had already happened as to naturally his own portion of responsibility in the matter since while it was true that Maria in the absolute fullness of her feelings would turn up quite determined to have it given to her good and proper and therefore in the final analysis he could consider himself a mere instrument of her will it was also true that she had arrived at this extreme resolution and had maintained it after a process of progressive corruption on his part beginning with still half-innocent kisses and arriving through more and more elaborate manipulations in alleys and passages at orgasm or quasi-orgasm according to your point of view in his rented room, so one could easily understand and forgive her if she now wanted to come to the legitimate conclusion of the premises whereas he after all would have been satisfied with a chiefly spiritual result and with the little messes that with some adjustment they could indulge in without her having to sacrifice the membrane or the flower of virtue, however also to take a girl and artfully lead her to such a degree of infatuation that she wants to have it more than anything in the world and then tell her it would be better to think it over and wait was not such a wholesome action apart from the consideration that as a result of the inevitable frustration the poor thing might well fall into some dangerous mental depression from which there was no telling when she would recover if she ever did recover, in short in the present state of things an upright youth even though there was some doubt as to his being still upright had only one way out or rather one way in, and so our youth though still concerned with problems of sexual mechanics which also were not to be taken lightly had the general impression that he was ready for everything except that when he saw her climbing up the steps laden with packages large and small and with a festive air that was all falsity since it accentuated rather than hid her inner turmoil he thought perhaps not even this time would be the right one and strangely enough he was more annoyed than happy at this since in the end it didn't seem right for all his diligent preparation to be wasted.

In addition to the big package of tea cakes with which she usually arrived in the probably unconscious desire to contribute to his sustenance, this time as Christmas was imminent Maria had also brought a fruitcake and a plastic tree stylized like an abstract sculpture and a dressing gown for him and a pair of slippers for herself and a pair for him all very much in honeymoon style, and as a special present for him she had brought a book of Charlie Brown comics which wasn't really a comic book but actually a volume of poetry as was diffusely explained in the long introduction written by a university professor no less and she thought how lucky those students were who had a professor who probably even taught Charlie Brown in class while her professor was interested only in phenomenology and in a rather unpleasant way at that, anyhow she had brought the Charlie Brown book which for that matter was already out of fashion not to impress him with university professors' introductions but because she felt Antonio himself was a kind of grown-up Charlie Brown in the sense that he was always thinking about this and that and wanted to understand everything and perhaps was upset in the end, however she loved him for this too namely for his being just like Charlie Brown who anyhow lived in a beautiful poetic world and in fact in analyzing carefully her feelings she had discovered that in her love for Antonio precisely because of his being helpless against the wickedness and complexities of life there was a considerable protective and maternal element which however shouldn't offend him since it was abundantly clear that she loved him also and above all as a man that is with every sense and sentiment but anyway Freud had clearly proved how many forces of different nature came together in sexuality or perhaps it was the opposite namely that sexuality became manifest under various forms which could perhaps deceive, in short she wouldn't stop saying whatever came into her head and it was as if she were afraid of stopping and Antonio who meanwhile had slipped his hands under her fur coat to clasp her, as usual to himself felt her rigid and absent that is occupied by a painful thought which wasn't dispelled even by his attempts to caress her hips and elsewhere, and then interrupting her he said that if by any chance she was distressed at the thought of having him give it to her that day he was ready and willing to postpone the job to a later and better occasion and this wouldn't represent a sacrifice for him because he loved her with all his being body and soul however he didn't see anything odd in the prospect of keeping their relations within the limits in which they had been contained so far and maybe even within more severe ones if necessary but she answered that this wasn't her idea in the least and that the program previously established had to be carried out even though to tell the truth she did feel a bit concerned as he with his sensitiveness had guessed, but more than concerned she was you might say irritated by an episode that was for that matter very stupid and in fact so stupid she was even ashamed to mention it however since he had noticed her uneasiness she simply had to explain the reason also because at other times they had sworn to each other they would confide whatever thought came to them even the silliest, and so to make a long story short it had happened that as she was coming with the fruitcake from the Colussi bakery at the corner of the Frezzeria she had noticed an elderly woman looking at her hard with an ugly face and with those hollow eyes that suggest the evil eye and then she had come upon the same woman in the Campo San Fantin just a few yards from here and again that sort of witch had stared at her nastily and she had become nervous and was about to speak to her but then she had let it go because it wasn't worth the trouble however she had remained considerably irked as Antonio had correctly observed, and at this point Antonio naturally suggested renunciation again since it seemed to him rather imprudent to give it to her with the evil eye about and when he too felt a bit ill-at-ease, so it was much better to go out and maybe take in a movie if there was enough time but she answered that it would have been primitive on their part to succumb to the fear of the evil eye and superstitions of a medieval order in this scientific and technological age to which for better or worse they belonged, so they certainly weren't going to ruin their meeting just because she had let herself be slightly upset by some nonsense and she was sorry only for one thing namely that she hadn't thought to bring a bottle of champagne along with the cake so they could have toasted their love and they also would have felt more gay and prepared to do the thing they had decided to do.

Anyhow since the champagne hadn't occurred to her there was no point now in going out for it so they might as well try to work up gaiety and preparation with the traditional methods and so to begin she pressed her whole body against him in fact in his opinion she was particularly pressing the lower abdomen that is insisting in the offer of that special part of herself which was the center of so many doubts and sufferings, and drawing strength not so much from his own natural impulses as from the thought that this thing which was about to befall Maria had befallen several billion girls before her the majority of whom hadn't had too much to complain about he managed to feel both spiritually and physically fit for the task, however he wasn't unaware that behind her devoted ardor there persisted something alien and in truth the ardor itself displayed in an unquestionably excessive degree was proof of a stubborn worry of which the encounter with the evil-eye woman might be a pretext but not a cause, and of course if she wasn't entirely spontaneous and sincere then neither could he be with that outsize responsibility of his, and obviously in this way events proceeded painfully and artificially and in Antonio's opinion this surely wasn't the ideal atmosphere for giving it to a girl though heaven only knew if an ideal atmosphere exists for a process difficult and complex in itself according to what he had been told therefore a proper combination of this operation with real sentiment was practically speaking unattainable, and in addition it was well known that a girl doesn't even feel much pleasure the first time and indeed it seemed there were many who even felt disgust however he didn't have the impression Maria would be one of these though poor thing after having warmed herself in embraces and kisses she was now undressing with great diligence but with at least a part of her thoughts elsewhere, so Antonio in that series of maneuvers which was a kind of highly complicated mechanism of communicating chambers for the shifting of responsibility felt his own guilt increase progressively as it became more evident she had forced herself into this mess with the spirit of a victim though a voluntary one and not with the spirit of a bacchante or even of a pleasure-seeker, and actually since they had established in advance that this time they would completely and shamelessly undress each before the eyes of the other she was keeping her word removing one by one the outer and inner garments but she was doing this without any bliss whatsoever but rather austerely suggesting the idea of one who out of devotion or on a bet rips away bits of flesh, but she still came to the end that is to removing the last veil consisting of bra and pants and she remained standing there before him like Eve Progenetrix in the garden of Eden but shuddering all over and perhaps also full of melancholy but nevertheless in an attitude of obstinate surrender with her arms at her sides and not bent to cover her pudenda, and he who in the meanwhile had succeeded in removing only his jacket and shoes was looking at her and though his attention was particularly drawn to the horizontal red marks which bra and garters had left on her skin he was thinking that altogether even in the nude she was a beautiful girl but unfortunately not sufficiently beautiful to support his cockeyed theory of the correlation between virtue and perfection of form, still what disturbed him most at that moment was not so much Maria's failure to achieve formal excellence as the thought that by the terms of the agreement he too would have to undress and she who one way or another had overcome the shock of her own undressing at present seemed only to be waiting for his, and he then told her he was ready to do it but considering how the male body is by almost unanimous consensus less beautiful than the female perhaps it was only right and opportune for her to turn away a bit or better still for her to slip under the covers since the stove wasn't making the place too warm, but she resolutely objected saying he hadn't the right to evade his obligation and not because she had undressed in front of him and demanded the same out of pique but because it was a question of his showing himself as he was without hypocrisy or false adornments, and so before her eyes which betrayed a seriousness out of proportion to the occasion he stripped very rapidly since he had reached the conclusion that at this point the faster he did it the better and then as if gripped by an abstract amazement at what was happening he stood before her naked entrusting himself now for the practical part to the benevolence of heaven, and she too as far as he could tell must have been engaged in a rapid and not too easy adaptation of the visible to her ideal of male physique derived almost entirely from her admiration of classical and Renaissance nudes and this was not so much because Antonio's undressed body revealed notable imperfections of structure as because of that disconcerting-looking member which the Greek or Roman statues she had seen didn't display in similar form or to the same degree and though her previous contacts with his body had honestly warned her that it was a considerable object having it now before her eyes in full evidence made her suspect that it was deformed or at least slightly exaggerated except that a particular agitation of the blood and an anxiety of spirit suggested to her that against all reason that implement so long and heavy in appearance was the very device arranged by nature to penetrate her properly and if that was the case then she was to welcome it with all its force and violence bringing her pain and love infinite love and infinite pain and whatever else, and naturally this enflamed thought now shone in her face and transpired from her dewy eyes and was displayed in a remissive not to say inviting attitude of her whole body so in Antonio there was produced an almost miraculous fusion between the erotic fantasies on which he had formerly nourished himself and the barely credible reality which was before him and in fact now he could indeed entrust himself completely to his impulses and take her in his arms and clasp her and kiss her as he had intensely longed to do and since Maria wanted nothing else they began to clasp and kiss each other madly deriving a marvelous pleasure which seemed limitless and instead kept suggesting incessantly new horizons of pleasure still more remote and in consequence destinations that perhaps were beyond human capacity of enjoyment moving toward definitive release which could also be suffering or even sense of death but which anyhow wanted to be achieved as soon as possible until now nothing seemed to be important but to act in haste, however since with such a great charge of passion it had now become troublesome to stand up they headed embracing and swaying for the bed where Maria arrived so languid and open that to violate her was now no more than a technical detail whereas vice versa in him the obligation to guide their steps and regulate their movement so that both would finally fall on the bed and not elsewhere had produced a kind of distraction and a partial repentance, that is he didn't exactly think of drawing back but in a certain sense he would have liked for the thing to take place so to speak on its own or to put it bluntly he imagined that in maneuvering on top of her with a remainder of respect as he had done the last time the respect would disappear in the course of the action of its own accord and the defloration would ensue without his really wanting it, and so lying on top of her as she held her breath for long moments waiting for the desired laceration he began dealing with his turgid instrument at moments admonishing it to restrain itself safely and perhaps immediately thereafter urging it to boldness to end once and for all this nonsense about which far too much literature had been created, and in short to achieve the rupture of that veil which nature had questionably placed to guard female virtue and the inherent pleasures now only a trifle would have sufficed since to tell the truth our hero was on the verge of doing it when all of a sudden an unexpected knocking at the door abruptly blocked all his good intentions and capacity of action and basically of reasoning since his first thought was that this was a sort of supernatural intervention meant to save what was still salvageable of Maria's virtue, and to be sure one couldn't dismiss a priori the providential character of the incident however the knocking in itself was a real fact inasmuch as it was immediately repeated a bit louder accompanied by the mellifluous voice of the landlady who after begging his pardon announced that there with her namely just outside the door there was a lady who seemed to need urgently to speak to him and even before Antonio could make some plausible conjecture about the identity of such an importunate person Maria who had remained half-dead at the first knock collected what breath she could still collect and murmured that the lady outside was surely her mother and at the idea Antonio rightly felt faint and said to her in a whisper that this was no time for joking and insisted on knowing what had inspired such a dire supposition but the poor girl once she had made the announcement probably had nothing else to say and even if she had she couldn't have said it because of lack of breath, and meanwhile of course from outside the landlady went on asking if he heard her and what he had to answer and then Antonio began by telling her to ask the unknown lady to forgive him but that day he couldn't see anyone however at this point his words were interrupted by new knocks of unspeakable violence and by the very voice of the never sufficiently execrated Signora

Borghetto who excitedly and aggressively demanded that the door
be opened without delay because she knew very well her daughter
was in there, and at these words Maria let out a scream and covered
her face with her hands saying desperately no no no and nothing
but that so in view of her defection the task of facing the uncomfortable situation fell completely on the shoulders of Antonio who
to tell the truth went into action at once, jumping out of bed and
hunting feverishly on the floor for his undershirt and shorts and
the socks which he had dropped a short time before in complete
disorder to tell the truth and meanwhile as if that weren't enough
he was also trying to establish with the invisible but quite present
Signora Borghetto a conversation to let her know that in his room
he did indeed have a woman as she had happily guessed but not
of course her daughter but another who out of elementary chivalry
he couldn't let her see since in addition to everything else his guest
was a respectable person, but the signora surely wasn't going to
be taken in by such inventions since she had been well informed
and knew for a certainty that her daughter was in there and she
wanted to enter at once and take her away and she hammered
more and more furiously on the door and threatened to call the
carabinieri so Antonio would end up in jail because among other
things her daughter was a minor and that criminal had seduced
her hoping to get his hands on the dowry but she would give him
the dowry he deserved, and at that moment Antonio didn't give
a damn about her vulgar insinuations or about prison either since
Signora Borghetto's threats were destitute of legal basis as her
daughter was over eighteen, but even though the situation wasn't
as dangerous as the madwoman envisaged it was nevertheless delicate and above all he had to try to get out of it in some way but
it so happened that the person most involved in getting out of it
was unquestionably Maria and she seemed to take no part in the
events except with total retreat that is kneeling naked on the bed
moving her hands from her face to her hair and then from her
hair to her face, and when Antonio went over to her to ask her
about what to do namely and bluntly whether or not he should

open the door she said no no with renewed terror and asked him
mercifully to kill her then and there to save her from suffering and
shame, and on hearing this proposal he was amazed he hadn't
thought of it first himself it was so fine and also practical since
with another pair of corpses like Romeo and Juliet maybe people
would finally decide not to persecute young love, however the
matter was too pressing to be resolved so worthily because actually
he didn't know what to do nor was there any way of thinking it
over with Signora Borghetto outside yelling more and more heat-
edly though no longer so much against him as against the landlady
who at a certain point had invited her to lower the tone of her
voice since they could surely hear her in the Campo San Fantin
in one direction and in the Campo Sant'Angelo in the other and
she was properly concerned that her house shouldn't be taken for
a bordello, and Signora Borghetto replied that if people took it for
a bordello then they would be taking it exactly for what it was and
in fact she would report it to the carabinieri too and then they
would see and the other woman told her to wise up and stop yelling
in that way because if the story came out in the *Gazzettino* there
was no telling who had the most to lose, but Signora Borghetto
was in such an overwrought state she couldn't take this good advice
and she yelled with renewed insistence that Antonio was to open
the door or she would knock it down and he really had the impression she was trying to do that since she was now knocking so hard
and in short the thing was taking a nasty and clamorous turn because the landlady had also abandoned all caution and had started
yelling against people who didn't know how to behave civilly even
in fur coats and jewels and so Antonio decided that the best solution also for Maria's own good was to open the door and face as
best he could the signora so gravely outraged and wounded in her
carnal affections and propriety, still it seemed necessary first of all
for Maria to dress a bit in order to present herself decently covered
to her mother's eyes, but it wasn't easy to achieve this with the hapless girl who seemed suddenly to have become idiotic because he
handed her the various garments and she dropped them shaking

her head no and saying incoherent words about the pain of living and the woman with the evil eye, however with difficulty he made her put on the slip and then barefoot and disheveled in his shirt-sleeves and with his pants sensationally unbuttoned in front he went to the door and turned the key offering himself to Signora Borghetto's wrath.

Later in the sad and solitary period that followed the event Antonio had occasion to meditate at will on this decision of his to open the door to the signora and as he kept asking himself whether opening had been good or bad he ended by endowing the act of opening with an importance objectively undue but subjectively very advantageous in that with his profound psychological schemes he was obeying the need to take his sense of guilt which was based on substantial facts such as for example his uncertain behavior toward Maria or a sensation of being at the moment more outside than within the event and then to shift this guilt to a marginal incident which among other things since they surely couldn't remain locked in that room indefinitely or escape from it together with Maria in that crazed state by dropping from the window into the Fondamenta della Parona enjoyed the property of being inevitable and in view of the knocking also of being imperative, and it is precisely in situations where nothing else can be done that remorse is best appeased. To be sure in bowing to the necessity of opening the door Antonio could have done so with the fly of his pants buttoned however this buttoning though praiseworthy in itself would have done little or nothing to modify what happened then or later and in fact Signora Borghetto on finding Antonio before her looked him up and down but surely didn't notice this unfortunate detail because the act of looking at him for her wasn't aimed at seeing but solely at expressing an otherwise inexpressible mixture of dislike and contempt after which as was right she directed her gaze forward in search of her only daughter who knows perhaps still hoping it wasn't her daughter but indeed it was the flesh of her flesh kneeling on a rumpled bed prostrate like a confirmed sinner and dressed only in her slip and at this sight Signora

Borghetto received such a strong blow that she staggered and her face went white and her features contracted in an expression of very great suffering so Antonio thinking that a mamma is always a mamma felt almost ready to forgive her for a number of things and finally to display toward her a certain solidarity in her misfortune but he didn't have time to do anything because the signora stifled within herself all human feeling and suddenly shouted with anger and vehemence the word sow, an insult which though aimed at the daughter first struck Antonio who was in front of her and it hit him so hard he would in all probability have succumbed if he hadn't been sustained by the guilty pleasure of seeing Maria's mother finally behave like the old slut he had always thought she was.

In all honesty Signora Borghetto on that occasion was unable to rise to the height of the really painful situation and in fact she didn't limit herself to shouting sow once but repeated the insult a number of times with a kind of indecent insistence and then she hurled herself angrily toward the hapless girl on the bed with the intention of seizing her and doing God knows what to her however as she moved she found her way blocked by Antonio whom she intended not to see and still less to touch but who in any case was there if nothing else as an obstacle that the signora at first tried to pass on the right still finding him before her since he had moved to bar her way and then on the left again finding the unwanted young man in her path since he was more agile than she and so she went from left to right without resolving the problem though she gradually gained ground toward the bed where poor Maria was doing nothing but sob with little interest in the progressive maternal approach which was not to be taken lightly because despite Antonio's constant urging to be calm and perhaps to sate her dire wrath on him the sole guilty party the mother seemed quite determined to reach her own offspring to strangle her as she never tired of proclaiming in a loud voice, I'll strangle you if I get my hands on you I'll strangle you she shouted in fact as if she had taken leave of her senses and certainly Antonio even at the cost

of using physical force would never have allowed her to carry out
her wicked plan, but Maria at a certain moment seemed to revive
and seeing her mother coming closer and being unable to read in
Antonio's spirit his firm intention of opposing the signora at all
costs Maria perhaps overcome by fear jumped from the bed thus
causing her defender to lose his position and making him unable
to prevent the signora from grabbing her daughter though he still
managed to hinder the action to such an extent that Signora Borghetto succeeded in grabbing only Maria's slip and that garment
was then almost ripped in two and so Maria stopped abruptly with
one of her tender breasts exposed and there she remained in the
attitude of one who even after having submitted to the worst outrages is heedless of receiving still others and indeed offers herself to the extreme blows of destiny or of her mother, and instead
perhaps it was this very unconditional surrender that caused a collapse in Signora Borghetto whose aggressiveness fell away abruptly
so far as could be seen and in fact after having told her daughter
in a low and almost subdued voice to dress herself she sank into
the room's only chair and burst into tears manifesting her maternal torment asserting that after all the sacrifices that had been
made here was her recompense and declaring that she would have
preferred a thousand times to die rather than suffer what she was
suffering as she saw her daughter ruined in this way, and so the
scene had become somehow stabilized with the three characters
statically arranged at a suitable distance from one another or rather
the four characters because the landlady had remained on the threshold in the role of simple but quite alert spectator and Antonio
realizing this only now in this first pause in the action and finding
the lady's presence unsuitable moved toward the door to close it
and the landlady perhaps because she had already seen and heard
more than she had ever hoped or because she was of a kindly
nature took no offense and on the contrary quite gracefully managed to whisper to Antonio that she had done everything she could
to stop the violent lady without succeeding of course anyhow she
could assure him that she would never tell a living soul anything

of what had happened before her eyes and finally just before Antonio slammed the door in her face the good woman even managed to signal to him to button his fly, and this was useful to Antonio because it gave him the opportunity not only to repair the indecent oversight but also to draw breath a moment in his confusion and shame at his own carelessness, however once the pants had been buttoned he had again to concern himself with greater troubles and turning he saw Maria moving with heartbreaking resignation here and there to pick up her scattered clothes while Signora Borghetto was still slumped in the chair weeping with an occasional subdued return of aggressiveness which caused her to express her intention of shutting Maria in a cloistered convent or to send her God knows why to an obscure place in Africa but more often she allowed herself to be overwhelmed with self-pity and commiserated with herself aloud because they had ruined her daughter that is a fortune-hunting no-good scoundrel had ruined her and surely also made her pregnant in order to marry her and fix himself up for life, oh what a misfortune poor her who would now have the courage to tell her husband that fine man who had worked like a dog all his life to give his family but most of all his daughter a position, in short she lamented with such abundance and variety of themes that Antonio though he was the chief object of her recriminations and insults once again felt himself gripped by a kind of compassion so that at a certain point he thought of giving the signora a piece of good news and he told her that what seemed to grieve her most hadn't happened that is he could give her his word of honor and even swear on the memory of his dead mother that basically he hadn't even touched Maria so to speak and therefore the girl despite the signora's fears was still a virgin as the signora herself had procreated her, and at the beginning it seemed that this good news brought the procreatress some relief but immediately thereafter she returned to her former intention of not seeing Antonio nor even hearing him and so she went back to lamenting with unchanged desperation almost as if she were really of the opinion that the membrane in itself counted for little or nothing, and then suddenly Maria was ready and motionless in the center of the room with her eyes downcast her fur coat on and her purse in her hand, and it was only when he saw her like this that Antonio became fully aware of the situation, that is the incident until then had been so horrid and grotesque that it seemed without any real capacity to cause suffering provoking mostly amazement and similar emotions, and in addition the events in their succession were so beyond the ordinary that they contained a kind of probability of producing others still more outrageous and absurd which at the end would prove somehow unreal but now with Maria so submissively on the point of leaving the idea of farce vanished and the disaster became irreparably concrete and full and without any imaginable remedy what's more, now that Signora Borghetto unbelievably hard and rigid went toward the door ordering her daughter to follow her at once, now that Maria obeyed her and went off not even raising her eyes for a last look and only stopping when she was on the threshold to say without turning around that she was ashamed and sorry about what had happened but in any case she loved him and would love him forever, and before she disappeared entirely Antonio too managed to tell her he loved her and would love her forever, and immediately afterwards with the sudden awareness of having been left alone he felt himself engulfed in universal sorrow.

In which Antonio suffers unspeakably and
finally goes back to the family home

It was a good thing for our young hero that the catastrophe which descended on him without his having prepared for it to any extent and indeed just at a moment when he was exceptionally inclined toward optimism and about to give his love a fairly stable if not definitive order was so outside all normal canons that it offered to one who could interpret it properly a certain consoling exaltation and in fact Antonio felt himself almost exalted by it and he derived no little support by putting himself ideally on a plane with the young Werther and Jacopo Ortis his celebrated predecessors in great misfortunes and he felt a sense almost of superiority toward them since a misfortune as unusual as his had certainly never happened to them, however a man couldn't expect to keep himself indefinitely on such a demanding plane and in fact as the minutes gradually passed and the event lost its hot general magnificence and revealed more than one dismaying and petty aspect his spirit also lost its extraordinary capacity for tolerance so that in the end he would no doubt have been overcome if luckily at the same time the universal sorrow that had accompanied the immense misfortune instead of continuing to appear as a single homogeneous and lofty grief hadn't begun to show itself composed of many griefs smaller of course which Antonio perhaps involuntarily but still obeying his unconscious defense mechanisms could face separately one at a time even receiving some satisfaction from certain ones because for example it was quite true that Signora Borghetto had heaped on him crushing waves of contempt and insults however it was indubitable that in the last analysis she herself had received the biggest screwing since it wasn't any joke to discover your only daughter and heiress in bed with a poor boy in a furnished room though it wasn't a trifle either for the daughter to be caught by her mother in such a spot and so his way of taking things became highly disloyal toward Maria who had suffered God knows how much poor thing at the shame and the insult, except that precisely through the atrocious suffering of that disaster their love had received the greatest confirmation anyone could wish and in fact at the very moment when they were being so disastrously separated one from the other they had in turn renewed their vows of undying love though how this undying love was going to be concrete in the future they were in no position to foresee and to tell the truth not even heaven could say when he and Maria would again be able not to lie in the same bed of course but at least to meet and talk, absolutely never if they considered the existence of Signora Borghetto and perhaps of her husband Cavalier Ilario if by some mischance he were to learn of the mess, still in three years or even less Maria would become adult legally and then she could dispose of herself even against her parents' will if necessary and to be sure Antonio could hardly wait to take such tasty revenge which was certain as Maria's love was certain, and so what with minimizing on the one hand and rethinking on the other and underlining in such details the most favorable aspects all that great mountain of grief which at first seemed God knows what risked being reduced to nothing or almost nothing but Antonio just when he was on the verge of the reasonable conclusion that after all the world hadn't come to an end sprang back from it frightened like Dorian Gray when he went to take a peep at his decaying portrait and truthfully it was too hard for him to wriggle out of whatever circumstance cheaply because his every misdeed stirred up again a profound sense of guilt that required the most enormous torments in compensation and so after having made an effort to deflate the catastrophe now he was busy inflating it again and the thing was less difficult than might be thought because it was easy to say three years but three years were a monstrous length of time especially if you contrasted them with the mere quarter of an hour that had gone by since Maria had left or rather since she had been torn from him, and Antonio at this juncture was certainly not ready to admit that the days as they passed would gradually make his sufferings more tolerable on the contrary he was firm in his resolve that during every minute of those thousand and some days he would suffer with the same boundless intensity of the present moment, and so this well-composed combination of time and grief both infinite or at least beyond measure restored to his misfortune the fullness and grandeur that became it and then from whatever side he examined it there was only one way out namely the act which had been conclusive both for Ortis and for Werther and which lacking other more suitable devices he could have performed by going and jumping into the canal below the Rio delle Ostreghe however he didn't really want to give Signora Borghetto a satisfaction of that kind and moreover even from a polemical point of view death by heart failure would have been entirely preferable and also so appropriate to the situation that just thinking about it Antonio was seized by a kind of giddiness that made him feel this outcome was entirely probable and near, and so it was on that very evening that after having straightened up his room which was rather in disorder as a consequence of the signora's visit he adopted the habit of wearing clean pajamas so he wouldn't make a bad impression if by any chance they were to find him a corpse the following morning.

To tell the truth in addition to putting on the least old of his pajamas he would also have liked to attend to his will not just to make a display of leaving Maria the few cents left him and to give instructions for his funeral which he wanted very simple and made with the inferior and economical public transport but also to have an opportunity to draft a few awesome pages properly explaining the real reasons for his premature demise and in other words a merciless accusation not of one woman alone but of the countless Signora Borghettos in the whole world who are accustomed to trampling on the rights of young lovers, however it wasn't so simple to write pages of this sort in his present state of prostration and in fact he didn't write them however by imagining he was writing them he could still release ideally the aggressiveness which in his lack of a direct clash with the signora had remained bottled up inside him, and moreover not actually drawing up this testament it came out more abundant and significant than it would have been if he had really had to write it and in fact he could see that his story with Maria contained at the same time both normal qualities common that is to many other cases of boys and girls who one way or another made love solving their problems somehow and also exceptional and very evident symbolic qualities especially in the final phase with Signora Borghetto's irruption into the room and with that ignoble cry of sow which better than any other phoneme or syntactical locution could indicate the low level of animality that a mother could attribute to her daughter's love only because she had unhappily fallen in love with a poor boy instead of the son of the Agha Khan or the rubber-tire king, and in short it was clear that his story with Maria more and better than the story of Romeo and Juliet could demonstrate what and how many misfortunes were always lying in wait for two young people guilty only of loving each other.

Still it was not through daydreaming of beautiful messages for posterity or improbable triumphs over Signora Borghetto that Antonio could hope to go beyond this nasty pass in his story because the reality of the situation and the inherent demand for a moral judgment simply came in through the window as he was making every effort to push them out the door and for example no cavil or argumentation was capable of making him forget that the true painful fulcrum of the affair was Maria whose condition could easily be imagined as worse than his if for no other reason because she remained legally in her mother's hands, however on this same point he had to ask himself if the laws really had that superior ethical value one supposed since Signora Borghetto's right to keep Maria in custody until her twenty-first year though sanctioned by the law as he knew was not ethically valid in his opinion but once he had established this fact he didn't know what to do with it or rather he fell right into one of the problems which gnawed at him most since as he now saw again with his mind's eye the things that had happened from the moment of the signora's disastrous arrival had been announced to the moment when she had gone off dragging Maria after her he was led to wonder if he had behaved in that admittedly critical juncture with sufficient virility since despite every law or custom it might have been best to slap that mother who kept shouting sow at her daughter, still the question was less one of law and more one of final wisdom since it wasn't clear whether slapping the signora would have bettered or worsened the situation, perhaps worsened despite the personal satisfaction he would have derived and therefore from a pragmatic point of view not slapping her had shown true firmness, even if it had to be admitted that someone observing the events from outside that is without an intimate knowledge of them might find in Antonio's conduct a certain lack of decisive action which could also be taken for cowardice whereas in effect it was simply wise prudence, however he lingered a bit too long on this subject of his basically passive attitude toward the signora and in fact he decided he would dispel any insinuation of cowardice by being found dead of heart failure, but apart from the fact that the two things were not so closely linked that the one had perforce to dispel the other he also had to take into account the serious embarrassment in which Maria would find herself in that event since she would mistakenly consider his decease from a competitive point of view and who knows might even commit suicide and instead he didn't want Maria to die in fact he pictured her living long after him healthy and free of her mother and of course in love with him to the distant day of her death, but

even having her live like that a prisoner of a memory which however lofty would certainly not be cheery couldn't be called a beautiful and generous thing so not even death by heart failure turned
out to be the great solution it had seemed in other respects and
therefore the best thing was to suffer and to wait for a countless
number of days, and now that grief which with some cleverness he
had seemed to keep in check for a while suddenly regained the
desired immensity where with a suffering after all not very far
from enjoyment he drowned his thoughts or rather confounded his
feelings in that nightmarish night which among other things was
very long since it had practically speaking begun around four in
the afternoon and in the confusion of his torments he couldn't remember and didn't know to what occasion or moment of the day to
link the sound of the bells which at longer or shorter intervals from
this or that spire of the neighborhood came oppressive and grim
to die in the air over the Fondamenta della Parona, and on sober
reflection those sounds of bells were his only remaining tie with
the outside world but through lack of faith he ran the risk of losing
himself also in the pious waves of sound which were so many cir-
cles of infinity where if he had wished he could glide dazed and
drained but then when he was perhaps already much closer to losing awareness of time and even of place his eye happened to fall on
his watch which had a luminous dial and seeing that it was barely
twenty-five past seven or a quarter to nine it occurred to him that
after all if he felt like it he could even take in a movie an idea
which naturally immediately altered the dimensions of his suffering
and in fact he hastened to reject it as sacrilegious even imagining
that there should be no film showings in a city plagued by such
grave injustices and then he went back to raving of vengeance and
highly complex solutions all grazing death more or less closely and
so he inflated his tangle of tribulations until he had brought it back
up to a decent level and then everything underwent a new sudden
reversal as the kindly landlady after discreetly knocking asked him
from outside if by chance he wanted a cup of coffee or even some
beef broth and he wanted nothing of course except to suffer his

enormous misfortunes with increasing anguish however proceeding at this pace weariness joining with suffering and maybe even a bit of fever or at least some terrible shudders produced almost forms of hallucination where the darkness and the silence were abstractly combined with the other immensities by which he already felt himself tortured and still he couldn't continue much longer in those annihilating expanses and then to pull himself together in order to give himself also some contentment of a narcissistic type after so many blows he thought of scaling the outside of the campanile of San Marco or better still of saving several dozen children on the verge of drowning in the Grand Canal, but then somebody passing over the Ponte della Parona made so concrete a noise that he was led to guess whether the person was going toward the Calle della Mandola or toward the Campo San Fantin and then at a certain point the footsteps were no longer the steps of just anybody passing by but those of Maria coming back to him and he hadn't the strength to get up and go into the hall to press the buzzer opening the door and that meant he had fallen asleep and was dreaming but in a curious fashion which didn't entirely preclude perception of reality and of the many sufferings connected with it so it was best to make an effort to draw himself out of this dangerous torpor and look at his watch which said three twelve, and after spending a little while meditating on the strange dimensions of that night he looked at the watch again and saw again three twelve and so he had lost the sense of the passing of time and perhaps for all eternity he would remain motionless in a non-time or practically speaking the three years which separated him from his reunion with Maria would never go by and at that thought his whole body stiffened and he counted with punctilious slowness up to three thousand and then looked again at his watch which still said three twelve so it was clear he had forgotten to wind it and this deprived his sufferings of a lovely metaphysical quality but in compensation it gave him back the hope that Maria would reach her twenty-first year within the pre-established period and he could dream of the triumph of that day with an infinity of progressively dramatic scenes in which

Maria announced to both her parents that having now attained her majority she was going off to join her one true love taking only the dress on her back, you who have trampled on the rights of my spirit are unworthy of my affection the courageous girl said, keep your wretched wealth I would rather suffer hunger with the man I love than stay another hour under your ungrateful roof she then said and in addition she made sufficient references to their egoism and their pettiness since it was beyond doubt that they would have wanted her to be the bride of some milksop some stupid offshoot of a rich Venetian family who would surely make her unhappy whereas she with the wisdom of her heart chose a poor young man from the country endowed however with excellent qualities with whom she would live happily ever after despite her parents, and immediately afterwards Antonio recognized the sound of many people passing over the Ponte della Parona and saw from the broad cracks in the blinds that a light was entering which wasn't anything much but was nevertheless daylight so he had slept God knows how many hours and even in the most blissful way that circumstances allowed namely dreaming of Maria's twenty-first birthday and the consequent pleasures however instead of feeling reassured and of passing perhaps with probability of good results to a more conscious consideration of his present state he promptly felt guilty at this oneiric evasion as if by suffering less he had diminished himself or at least evaded his duties of torment and now to make up he tried to reconstruct as quickly as he could the previous night's climate of lofty suffering and in all truth it wasn't hard to reconstruct since nothing had changed and in fact the new day when it came to dreariness and uncertainty could well serve as a model for the countless days that would follow so it surely was no gain to have eluded death by heart failure which however could come even in any daylight hour if his sufferings were to increase a bit as they were in fact doing, still at the moment far more probable than death by heart failure was death through weakness or malnutrition since calculating that the day before in view of Maria's arrival that is in the joyous expectancy of that meeting subsequently so disas-

trously concluded he had taken very little nourishment and naturally after the sudden change in his destiny he hadn't touched
food so now he was quite a few hours behind in his eating but he
didn't worry in the least about that on the contrary it seemed to
inspire a good idea namely his making himself worthy of his own
great grief by persevering in his fast and thus giving it that voluntary character halfway between expiatory and propitiatory which is
usual in any religion, in short he was about to reach the point it
was right for him to reach nor did he lack the two necessary things
which were hunger on the one hand and food to sate it on the other
and in fact besides the big cake and the pastries brought by Maria
he also had cheese and bread and fruit hidden in a drawer of the
dresser so it was absolutely meritorious to refuse nourishment and
even to begin to shudder with superior pleasure imagining how he
would go on refusing it until he starved to death and as far as he
knew he might also hope this wouldn't even be very painful because as he proceeded in his total abstinence from food the contractions of his guts of which he now was irritatingly aware would
in all likelihood be attenuated, anyhow it seemed to him that since
he had already come a long way he had best insist and in fact he
didn't answer the light knocking at the door that he heard twice at
some interval but then when a concomitant sound of bells from all
the surrounding spires informed him that it was noon allowing him
among other things to set his watch and when a third and less discreet knocking was heard at the door he couldn't refuse to listen to
the landlady who quite concerned at what was happening or rather
not happening in the room wanted to know if he was still alive,
however the kindly lady didn't phrase the question so brutally but
rather asked if he was feeling well and if he needed anything and
he answered that he felt well and didn't need anything and after
having overcome this test modest as it was that is after refusing
further succor he felt he had now passed the hardest part of the
course he had to follow in order to die of starvation and he was
already led to reflect quite sweetly on the uselessness of his own
life and in fact of life in general hasn't life a useless fruit wretched-

ness and this was what was left him today of all his hopes, thank God for the consolation of poetry even if written by another that is to say a relative comfort since among the strongest causes of his dejection there was the thought that he hadn't had time to become a poet especially since the funeral of a young poet who has died for love would have been more effective than that of a young man who died for love without being a poet, anyhow death would erase also this accessory suffering death which was the end of all grief according to the universal opinion, and thinking in this way he happened to fall asleep again or rather to fall into delirium because by now his weakness was great and he was already unable to achieve full consciousness in the rarer and rarer intervals between one lapse and the next, and then it was night again to judge from the darkness visible beyond the cracks in the shutters however perhaps not night but late afternoon since a number of people were still crossing the Ponte della Parona, but what did it matter whether it was night or day or with people or nobody best to allow himself to be overcome again by his torpor also to escape the disturbing temptation to eat the whole fruitcake weighing a good three pounds something that the young Werther surely wouldn't have done nor the young Ortis either, and so at last with swirling mists and shadows the succoring nothingness advanced again, and then again a very resolute knocking at the door and the annoyance of asking what they wanted and the landlady's fervid voice announcing the arrival of a special-delivery letter which in the present situation could only be an urgent message from Maria.

Trembling he took from the landlady's hands the envelope bearing the words special delivery written in large red letters heavily underlined and he had to go back to his bed immediately since because of his weakness but certainly also because of his emotion his head was spinning so that standing on his feet he wasn't able to read even the beginning of those four pages crammed with writing in neat well-ordered lines as might be expected of Maria even in tempestuous circumstances, my love she began by saying but then went on to ask if she still had the right to call him that after what

had happened solely through her fault of course since only a stupid
girl like her was able to think the evil-eye woman was a bad omen
when instead she had been following Maria on behalf of an agency
her mother had engaged to find out if she was meeting Antonio
outside the house despite all the promises and so this terrible disaster had come about which almost made her die of shame and not
as Antonio might be tempted to think at shame in her mother's
eyes but of shame in his Antonio's because of the way her mother
had behaved toward him but also because of her shouting what she
had shouted without a minimum of understanding, in any case since
he had assured her at the end that he loved her and would always
love her she had recovered a little and now despite her great suffering she was looking toward the future with a ray of hope provided
he went on loving her of course, the only thing that really counted
was their reciprocal love because as far as the rest was concerned
they would find a solution, for example she considered it a great
stroke of luck that her mother hadn't understood what he had revealed perhaps a bit naïvely on the subject of her virginity or perhaps she had understood it but hadn't believed it and anyhow as
her mother thank heaven thought her ruined forever she might
resign herself despite her enormous fury to considering marriage
inevitable and though she had decreed that the two of them were
never to meet again or to speak not even on the telephone she had
conceded that they could write each other letters and in conclusion
things could even have gone worse than they had and she only regretted she was still a virgin and not already pregnant, and as far
as virginity was concerned she recalled certain ancient Roman cus-
toms involving the god Priapus and if necessary might do something herself but on the subject of fecundation it seemed inevitable
for them to wait until her majority because her mother had further decreed she would for no reason allow her daughter to go out
of the house without accompanying her herself, she couldn't even
go to the University and this after the separation from Antonio of
course was the thing that grieved her most because she wanted to
take her degree while she was young and if possible cum laude, in

any case she would study for her exams at home and that would perhaps speed the passing of the three years minus seventeen days between now and her twenty-first birthday that is one thousand seventy-nine days considering leap year and this was a long time however the two of them were not to be excessively frightened because she was sure the days would go by faster than they could suppose at present they had only to go on loving each other and so now she was waiting with indescribable anxiety for a letter from him reassuring her of this fact and finally she sent him an enormous quantity of kisses and hugs and further still that is in a rather concise postscript she affirmed that she was naturally also prepared for a Sicilian-style solution so to speak that is she was ready to run away from home somehow or other if he felt she should.

Though there was nothing particularly upsetting in Maria's letter Antonio had felt a growing agitation and almost an inner upheaval as he proceeded in the reading of the four pages and as far as he could tell it derived from a natural inevitable comparison between Maria's positive and so to speak practical sufferings and his own torments which God knows why always tended toward the absolute and in a sense toward evasion, and in effect by forcing as many universal motives as he could to combine with their personal affairs he did produce an appreciable opposition to brutality to bestiality to compromise to conformism to normal procedure to liturgy however he ended meanwhile by losing sight of the very nucleus of his own sufferings or at least he made them so vast and out of proportion to himself that he was exonerated from the obligation of facing them on the level of reality and so he wandered lyrically amid perfect and hypothetical griefs with which Maria in the final analysis no longer had anything to do except as a symbol or allegory that is to the extent that the sufferings of Alighieri or Petrarch involved the real-life Beatrice or Laura, and if that was all right for Dante and for Francesco who had based on them exercises that were narcissistic if you like but still poetically valid it couldn't certainly be all right for him since he was lagging way behind in the poetry department, and in short after having read Maria's modest letter Antonio could reasonably isolate in his own way of suffering in fantasy or of fantasticating as he suffered a new motive of unworthiness in fact he came to feel himself so inferior to her as to think it would have been wrong not to lose her, oh yes she would rightly abandon him and he would remain forever suffering in his lost solitude since this was no less than he deserved, and at this point our young man had tears welling up in his breast and in his throat however he didn't know whether it was decorous to cry because at the head of his bed the helpful landlady had remained eager to participate insofar as she could in his vicissitudes, and naturally he felt annoyed by her presence but at the same time he understood its inexorability since his suffering also involved witnesses that is it wasn't clear whether the fact that the landlady was standing there looking at him was a restraint or a stimulus to his tears however it was sure that if he were to start crying with that woman underfoot he would do so more clamorously and in fact at a certain moment unable to control himself any longer he turned his face to the pillow and burst out sobbing really without restraint as for that matter knights cried in the lovely poems of chivalry the rare times when they did cry also for love as it happened in most cases, in short there was perhaps a bit of theatricality in his weeping but surely no pretense since it was the very magnitude of his sufferings that demanded manifestations of this fashion which would arouse the participation of others in such a way as to assist him in bearing somehow the otherwise unbearable grief and so it didn't even seem strange to him when he felt the landlady's hand rest charitably on his head and her voice say with suitable agitation that she couldn't bear to see him suffering so much and that he should try to console himself otherwise she too would burst into tears in a little while and since Antonio showed not the slightest sign of consoling himself after a moment she also began to cry poor woman putting her head on the pillow next to his and telling him in fits and starts how she was no less unfortunate than he was since she loved a married man who treated her like a slave and had even taken away her telephone because he was jealous or more likely stingy or maybe he had to save every penny to give to his wife because all his promises to press for an annulment were false and on that very evening which was Christmas Eve she was all alone and unhappy because he was spending the holiday with his family, in short it seemed that Antonio should recover from his own troubles by thinking of hers a thing he hadn't the least desire to do obviously since his suffering at Maria's rightful abandonment was so full that he could be destroyed by it without any need of external assistance, still this destruction could go smoothly as long as the loving land-lady's support was kept within decent limits but when he became aware that O God she was pressing her whole body to his and now rather than sobbing she was sighing and as if that weren't enough she was moving one hand to caress his shoulders and his chest and even farther down and he stiffened at once hoping it wasn't true however there was precious little to hope as the charitable hand with slow change of direction was gliding straight there it seemed, my God if he allowed her hand to move a few inches farther he would be lost in depths of unfathomable wickedness, why just look what was happening to him and at the least suitable moment, any-how if he didn't want to lose virtue and honor he had to put a stop to that wretched woman's impudence and do it fairly fast that is before it was too late from every point of view, so gathering all his strength both physical and spiritual he sat up in bed abruptly and pushing the unfortunate landlady from him with an anchorite's resolve he ordered her to be ashamed of herself and to have at least a shred of respect for his searing grief and the poor woman who wasn't expecting this much looked at him first amazed and incredu-lous and then seeing there was absolutely no hope of being mistaken she burst into real tears and ran out covering her face with her hands.

This fairly energetic action in defense of the integrity of his suf-ferings as well as of his loyalty to his one love inspired in our hero a dispassionate examination of his situation in the most literal sense namely his residence in that room which in addition to not being a sufficiently virtuous place had also the drawback of costing money,

and in fact since even in the happiest moments of his love he had
been unable to forget how in Venice his money was flowing away
like water you can be sure he could hardly forget it now in these
nasty moments, in short perhaps the right time had come for him
to ask himself what he was doing in a city where he was no longer
allowed to see Maria and where there was certainly no point in
talking about advantages for his studies since he had never made
less progress in learning than during his stay in Venice, and finally
if he didn't go away quickly he would also have to pay another
month's rent in advance in fact not having announced his departure in time he would have to pay the month in advance even if he
left, however his contractual relations had also been modified by
the new factor of the landlady's enterprise which for example he
would never have dreamed of exploiting in order to stay there without paying whereas it seemed fair for him to exploit it by going
away without paying advances therefore it was best to take advantage of the indignation that still inflamed him and resolve to leave
this now unbearably sad place only to go however to a still sadder
place, in short the best thing was to get moving without giving the
matter too much thought and so he jumped immediately out of
bed and started collecting his belongings and throwing them at random into the leatherette suitcase meanwhile eating the bread and
the cheese and the pastries but not touching the fruitcake which
since it had remained intact could serve as a Christmas present for
his father and sister, and really it was a shame not to take away the
Christmas tree too but he just didn't know where to put it with all
his belongings which seemed to have increased incredibly since he
had come there, but with some effort he managed to shut his suitcase and then after looking at that room where for better or worse
his loved had reached very high peaks with subsequently suitable
abysses he devoted some emotional thought to it and then tiptoed
across the vestibule and went down the steps leaving the house in
the Fondamenta della Parona and going toward the Campo Sant'-
Angelo and the San Samuele dock to take the direct motoscafo for
the Piazzale Roma but then halfway there he changed his mind

because he was so dejected among all those people with packages and packets going home to celebrate Christmas and his only support in the world was Maria after all so before leaving Venice for Marocco he preferred to go to the main post office on the Rialto and there write her saying he had changed his address and without her he felt like dying.

In which Antonio resolves to compose
his future collected letters

Contrary to what generally happens with the misfortunes of this world which at the first blow seem irreparable and unbearable whereas perhaps all too swiftly they assume new proportions and at times even reach a satisfying solution the more Antonio thought about the misfortune which took place in the room in Fondamenta della Parona the more it took on the consistency of a fairly stable and definitive disaster and this was not so much because Antonio imagined he would never see Maria again because if he was able to maintain his sanity in that period it was precisely because he was sure their love was of a practically indestructible quality but rather because Signora Borghetto's inopportune intervention had begun a series of negative phenomena of which the separation from Maria was only the high point since other minor calamities existed which on the one hand completed and so to speak embellished the greatest and on the other hand they also had a pungent validity of their own and moreover stimulated him to draw up a balance sheet which could only show the bankruptcy of his brief and intense Venetian adventure which after having begun very well had ended in a way that could hardly have been worse. In fact despite his comprehensible tendency to be charitable toward himself at least in the moments when that was necessary our hero couldn't forget the spirit of what we might well call civic exaltation in which his removal from Marocco to Venice had taken place less than a month before as if going to rent a furnished room in the so-called historical center of the city meant in some way conquering it and so now the reverse process inevitably appeared an overall defeat as if not only the Borghettos but the whole city in its sum of houses and streets and inhabitants were rudely driving away one who basically had no right to stay there and he was brusquely being put back into his humble condition of country youth at the very moment when the Marocco countryside rigid with frost and opaque with fog plumbed the depths of its depressive power and in short also the atmospheric factor helped provide Antonio with a singular acumen in understanding the vastness and the profundity of his misfortunes even the apparently minor ones naturally, such as his savings so disastrously reduced during his sojourn in the city or the scarce progress he had meanwhile made in his studies.

So not even the passing of time made it easy for the unhappy Antonio to find relief or some avenue of escape especially because those disasters that had befallen him all contained something petty or at least unstimulating also from the intellectual point of view and truly even a traditionally dramatic scene like the violent separation of two lovers had been enacted with complete lack of grandeur dominated so to speak by that ignoble cry of sow re-echoing too often for Antonio to be able to overcome the constant distress of his own inadequate conduct and in fact he began to be more distressed than ever but with twinges more of regret than of grief that is what he found hardest to swallow at the time was that despite the situation which was quite favorable in some of its aspects he hadn't been able to achieve that big clash with Signora Borghetto which without worsening things very much would have given them quite a different flavor and naturally he compensated by returning again and again to the scene and perfecting more and more virile and contemptuous answers to fling in the vulgar matron's face, with

every right of one who loves and is loved he could sustain that
Maria by now belonged more to him than to anyone else especially
if this anyone else was as mean in spirit as the base insult unequivocally showed, and then he could speak of the chasms between gen-
erations and the absurd demands of those who having sadly wasted
their own lives now wanted to lay down the law to the young and
deprive young love of its most beautiful season, he could say a collection of lofty and just things in short however imagining them
now while it brought relief in one way depressed him in another
because by contrast he was reminded of what he had in reality
said asserting faint-heartedly that he hadn't really touched Maria
and her virginity was actually safe, a real piece of stupidity as
Maria had rightly pointed out and he was now the first to bite his
fist however he didn't much like that business of the god Priapus
either and he had written this to Maria arguing that defloration
should be more than anything else a moral act, in any case the truth
was that he hadn't performed this act and when he started thinking
how much better it would have been if he had performed it since
if Maria were now at least properly violated if not downright pregnant then his personal position though at first sight it might seem
much more ambiguous and generically not very distinguished
would at least have been solid not only with regard to Maria and
the Borghetto family but also to the whole city of Venice where
Cavalier Ilario's motorboats zoomed around rather ostentatiously.

Having thus been only a step from good fortune without having
had the spirit or the sense to take proper advantage of it was for
Antonio now that he thought of it after the right moment had
passed a source of great bitterness too great in fact to be borne without making an effort to reverse it at least partially and there was
really no denying that at least insofar as Maria herself was concerned his foolish behavior might also reveal some noble and generous aspects and it wasn't at all improbable that if Maria judged
the facts objectively as they should be judged she would understand
the true meaning of his renunciation and would therefore come to
love him more and more and better and better, in fact it was precisely

this sort of nobly motivated sentiment that was best suited to her at present in other words driven also by the mishap that the poor girl for better or worse had remained intact Antonio was becoming involved in a spiritual reconstruction opportune from whatever point of view it was examined since it was no longer possible to see and hear Maria and still less to touch her now it was best to incline toward abstraction returning to that musical angel impression which had been among the first if not the very first she had aroused in him on the occasion of their fatal meeting, or else to go a little farther with the adaptation to models of the Laura and Beatrice type whose depictions were almost as lacking in sexuality as those of the angels and also offered the hope of marginal utilization of his griefs in the field of poetic or generally artistic production which however difficult at present thanks to certain vulgar aspects of his misfortunes and who knows also because of the excessive pressure of his suffering was still the most probable scope of an existence as ill-starred as his was.

To tell the truth this theory of marginal utilization of misfortunes connected for that matter with the more general and generally recognized worthwhile principle that every cloud has a silver lining was something Antonio had flattered himself he was able to put into practice perhaps too quickly and in reality a certain amount of fervor or creative stimulus had made itself felt in him the very evening in which he had turned up again at his home that is just at what according to every rightful prediction should have been the conclusive and surely also the most squalid phase of his wretched Venetian adventure when arriving with the three-pound fruitcake he had found his old father and his sad sister watching the television Christmas show and his father though he still evidently had a large supply of dire prophecies to utter had preferred at least for the moment to turn back to the tiny screen's images rather than make predictions concerning this prodigal son's unannounced return while his sister having learned he hadn't yet eaten his supper had gone to fix him something to eat and then while he was eating and at the same time thinking how bitter it is why death is hardly

worse referring clearly to the dark wood in which he had become
lost like Dante his sister had started rummaging in the leatherette
suitcase and in the various packages he had brought home search-
ing mostly for dirty clothes to be washed and so without really
meaning to she had discovered two splendid pairs of slippers and
two equally splendid dressing gowns and the fact that these objects
had apparently never been used led her to the mistaken conclusion
that they were Christmas presents for herself and her father from
a brother and son who had seen the error of his ways and our Antonio though surely not unaware of the value allegorical and otherwise of those objects in which still a shred of hope might linger
allowed them to go to new owners without any repugnance indeed almost enjoying it like a man who feels calamities falling on
him thicker and faster and more unforeseen and finally is overcome
chiefly by wonder and by curiosity to see where it will all end and
yet reaching also by this path a deeper level of sadness so that later
in his icy room he came to the conclusion that death must be a little
less rather than a little more bitter than his present condition and
truly if it hadn't been for the consoling thought of Maria and her
letter which he reread extracting every drop of comfort from it he
would perhaps on the very night of his Christmas homecoming
have arrived at a conclusive act of desperation but luckily there
was Maria and there were also some unsettled scores with the Borghetto family and the whole city of Venice which he would show
who he was the youth they had driven out almost ignominiously,
and besides that inhospitable and common room with the help of a
bit of willpower and perhaps also a little kerosene or liquid-gas stove
could become a place sufficiently adequate for distinguished actions,
firmly shut in there he would divide the many hours of his empty
days between the study necessary for him to achieve a position and
the creation of works designed to bring him fame in fact as far as
the latter were concerned he vowed already that he could catch two
birds with one stone dedicating himself as a start to a series of letters to Maria designed not only as pure and simple correspondence
but also and especially as an opportunity to give his misfortunes

and griefs that universal divulgation they unquestionably deserved, and this seemed doubly profitable to him since on the one hand he would attain literary glory which in the absence of wealth or aristocratic splendor would still make him worthy of Maria and on the other hand it would somehow insert into the literary history of the current century the immense debt he owed her for the sole fact that she existed or rather that she lived in his same world even if in the hands of a despicable mother.

In reality also on the subject of these collected letters which according to every reasonable prediction would belong to the consolatory genre in the sense that they would be largely disconsolate Antonio imagined things would be easier than practically speaking they were and in fact to be able legitimately to express on a recognized artistic plane the thought that life is useless and wretched you need not only a suitable number of misfortunes but also application and discipline which we might regard as contradictory since if life is really useless and wretched there is certainly not much point in working very hard to say so, anyhow our Antonio skipped questions of this sort and was youthfully confident that the magnitude of the disasters would correspond directly to the grandeur of his artistic offspring since the idea of putting together a good collection of letters seemed really clever especially since he could count on the landscape in the sense that there existed an indubitable and obviously fertile concordance between the unfortunate young man's state of mind and the winter desolation of the Marocco countryside and in fact Antonio's first and most important letters to Maria consisted above all of descriptions of gray furrows whitewashed by morning frost and of bare rows of poplars along the winding river Desse and of trunks in which it was hard to believe the sap would once more rise in the spring and similar things but he couldn't go much farther along that road nor could he go much deeper and though Maria in her answers always remembered to say his letters were very beautiful and moving Antonio himself realized they could be so only within what you might call family boundaries that is to say moving for her who was already quite moved but for the hypothetical general reader the letters would hardly be an occasion for congratulations and praise.

Naturally at such a delicate moment and in such a brusque fashion to come up against the well-known esthetic theorem according to which intuition is expression was bound to cause considerable concern especially since things didn't grow better if it was taken in the opposite sense that is conceding that expression could be intuition and truth to tell if in the first case the meager epistolary results were explained by insufficiency of suffering which was scarcely credible in the second case he was forced to admit a lack of sensitivity or at least of inspirational power and in conclusion from whatever angle he examined the matter it was basically disagreeable so Antonio at the risk of boldly disagreeing with Benedetto Croce finally elaborated a principle of his own by which sorrows that were too great and searing couldn't be cheaply transformed into art and it could be seen for example that Maria whose sufferings could unquestionably be considered inferior to his since she surely didn't have financial worries and lived in a house that was downright overheated still managed to write letters not only full of common sense but also of poetic grace however involuntarily whereas he whose sufferings were greater produced forced and monotonous letters more similar to the little compositions he had put together in high school on days of listlessness than to the elevated missives of the young Ortis and this continued to be the case even after the purchase of a liquid-gas stove permitted him to make the air of his room much more temperate and in fact it was precisely the thermic well-being he achieved that made him realize it wasn't a question of Centigrade or Fahrenheit but of some other thing, a harsh realization since before when it had been cold he had been able to blame his scarce productivity on the low temperature but now that there was the stove he didn't know where to find further excuses for the progressive stiffness of his letters which also were becoming shorter and shorter so he had to fear that also as far as bulk went his collected letters would not amount to much, but for that matter no new events took place and once he had described the winter countryside in its length and breadth if he was to avoid painful repetition he had to concentrate on his sentiments but here too there wasn't much room for variety since the basic ideas were always the same namely that he loved her more and more and was suffering unspeakably at their separation but the certainty that they would be reunited one day supported him in his suffering and after having repeated this again with words perhaps a bit fresher there were days when he remained idle before a sheet of paper three quarters blank until he was seized by a great anger at his own impotence and went to play cards at the tavern on the Terraglio, in short within all too brief a period his life at least from the standpoint of organization had found a fairly comfortable rhythm because he got up at noon in time to eat hastily in order to deprive his father of the opportunity of making excessive prophecies and then he went to the tavern until suppertime and then after supper he went back there until midnight when they closed though if you took a good look at his way of life it was fairly wretched since he really didn't enjoy himself much at the tavern because in addition to the familiar sufferings he acquired new ones derived from stern bitterness at his waste that is he went on playing distressed by the thought that in addition to his time he was also squandering the expensive warmth of the stove he had left burning in his room with the idea of going back there after only a couple of games, and so it took only a trifle such as one of the many paternal prophecies or reproaches or even a tiny loss at cards to plunge him into bottomless dejection and to make him feel condemned by an incredible number of unfavorable circumstances to a dreary mediocrity at the end of which obviously there would also be the loss of Maria and he might even yearn for this loss as the expiation of faults to a large extent not his own faults beginning with the crime of having happened to be born and how many times as he went home with the icy stars of winter over his head or as he waited for sleep which delayed its coming in the still silence he continued to tell himself he would lose her thinking of her as a kind of cumulative goodness of life and then he reacted thinking he would finally write a letter that would be marvelous but more and more often he didn't react at all and allowed himself to be drawn on by an ambiguous desire for the worst finding himself at last in a dangerous balance between immortality and nothingness with obscure inclinations toward nothingness which resolved all suffering and ambition, and this was a very exhausting state which must also be taken into consideration if you want to try to understand what happened to him when he received the incredible letter.

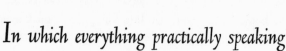

In which everything practically speaking

comes to an end

The incredible letter hit Antonio
like what is generally called a bolt from the blue because it took
him completely by surprise after about thirty or more credible letters which not being presumably intended for later publication were
very reasonable and in fact they enabled Maria above all to make
daily and sometimes twice-daily report on what was happening to
her and it was extraordinary how she always found something to
narrate even though nothing special ever happened since neither
her father nor her mother spoke to her any more as if she were in
some way nonexistent that is with only her skin outside and inside
no blood or soul and only once had her mother said come with me
and had taken her to buy a new pair of shoes a very mysterious
event as she had no need of shoes and now less than ever did they
let her walk anywhere and so it remained to be seen whether Signora Borghetto's incongruous enterprise was to be catalogued
among her manifestations of mental cruelty or among her attempts
at conscience-easing however since it was unthinkable that the
signora had a conscience it was more likely an act of mental cruelty,
anyway Maria's letters with their sobriety and admittedly their
uniformity and with their regular sequence had finally led Antonio

to the conviction that apart from the literary question things were really not any worse than what was to be expected after the disaster that had happened and in any case it was consoling to think that time was working in favor of love and youth because in the Borghetto home Maria was standing her ground on the one hand and her parents were equally standing theirs on the other stabilizing the situation into a kind of cold war that is into a tacit and reciprocal renunciation of big offensives aiming at the capitulation of the enemy but it turned out that the relations between opposing forces were stable only in appearance because instead day after day that situation was changing though not sensationally in Maria's favor since with each passing day she came closer to her majority that is to the longed-for moment when she would finally shed both maternal and paternal prohibitions, and since the final outcome of this sort of escalation or climb to the twenty-first year had to be clear to anyone who thought about it not excluding the Borghetto parents then their present obtuse and narrow-minded stubbornness was substantially nothing but a form of livid resignation to seeing in a period unfortunately still not very near the triumph of the two lovers who had right on their side thanks if nothing else to the irresistible progress of time, and our Antonio was fonder of this solution which engaged him only at a remote distance than of any other possibility so that having immediately rejected the Sicilian-style flight he had settled down with a thousand sorrows of course in this idea and at the close of his letters he never forgot to urge prudence and patience on Maria confident that thanks to these cardinal virtues the plum as they say would fall into his mouth the moment it was ripe and instead all of a sudden the incredible letter arrived to ruin everything that had painfully been salvaged from the preceding disasters.

The letter began with the following words my darling love I would rather be dead than locked here in my bathroom writing this desperate letter which perhaps will never reach you and this letter was defined incredible by Antonio not because he thought the things however unusual that Maria narrated in it were lies or even only exaggerations but because in their brutal cruelty and singularity they went beyond the limit of acceptability and passed into the roster of events of which it is said that they are simply not of this world precisely because of their outrageousness which in the final analysis is the quality which makes them somehow bearable since they are also dumfounding that is to say thanks also to the amazement they normally arouse and the surprise with which they usually present themselves and in fact there really are things that the human spirit wouldn't be able to bear twice whereas once if caught so to speak off guard it faces them and overcomes them perhaps at first taking them in only partially and acquiring full awareness of having been screwed only at the end, and this presumably was the condition of unawareness and let us also say incredulity to which Maria had come after the outrages and profanations of her body no less than of her spirit concerted by her unspeakable mother, however on thinking them over afterwards they aroused that stimulus of revolt and radical evasion which Maria quite unequivocally expressed at the opening of the letter with the words I would rather be dead and such words written by a creature alien as she was to bombast and superficial histrionics assumed a painfully tragic significance which the rest of the missive did not contradict but rather accentuated and increased because Maria after this clear and orderly beginning became as she went on rather confused which was more than forgivable in view of the agitated state and who knows perhaps also the terror in which the poor thing must have written however the result was that you couldn't exactly understand which things had really happened and which were merely feared, and in this second category it wasn't clear which were feared because of precise threats from Signora Borghetto and which sprang instead from the confusion of a mind already subjected to far too much inhuman violence and for example when Maria referred to rather extreme pressures to which she would very soon be subjected defining them roughly as brainwashing one might believe this would simply be a sleep cure to be taken perhaps in Switzerland or at most a course of electroshock which were both absurd treatments however one could expect anything from the grim signora even brainwashing or exile in Upper Volta which Maria also included among the probable events because the Borghettos had some distant relations there and in fact what had already happened was enough to inspire well-founded fears of even more outrageous deviltries since at this point it was legitimate to suspect that Signora Borghetto's psychological structure had more than one nasty kink or at least a large sadistic component obviously derived from God knows what sexual frustrations and there was really no other way to explain the cruelty and the diligence with which the unworthy mother had carried out her plan to ascertain scientifically the degree of her daughter's chastity leaving in the city of Venice no trace of the exploit performed one hoped without the knowledge of her husband Cavalier Ilario, so on leaving the house with Maria she had said she had to go to Chioggia on behalf of the San Simeone Grande Ladies Aid and she was taking Maria along because she didn't dare leave her unguarded at home but at San Marco instead of the vaporetto for Chioggia they had taken the Alitalia motorboat for Tessera and from there the seven-thirty jet which an hour later landed at Rome's Fiumicino airport where Signora Borghetto heedless of the expense hired a taxi to take her daughter to the Pro Bono Pacis Gynecological Clinic where everything had been prearranged for a rapid examination without any formalities and so Maria was asked to lie down naturally without her pants on a little hospital bed with specially designed stirrups to keep the legs apart and an illustrious gynecologist after looking with great care and with a special instrument into her vagina had issued to Signora Borghetto's relief a report of objective virginity or to be exact he had announced that the membrane known as the hymen though it did reveal some light dents had not been actually broken, after which since there wasn't a plane back to Venice immediately the mother had taken the still confused daughter to visit the Basilica of Saint Peter's and then to eat in some nearby restaurant where however not even the signora had been able to eat much and finally not knowing what else to do they had gone to Fiumicino to wait on a sofa in the entrance until time for the plane to Venice where they arrived at seven p.m. so that well before eight they were in the Campo San Polo not having exchanged a single word all day despite the unusual events and it had been a rather beneficent silence from which however no good could be expected and in fact when on entering the house Maria told her mother of her intention to retire to her room without taking part in the evening meal because she was tired and had no appetite her mother immediately granted permission adding however that if her daughter was in such a hurry to retire in order to write her fancy man her usual daily report then she could spare herself the trouble because from now on she would not be allowed to write letters to anyone or to receive them from anyone, and since Maria bursting into tears then told her she was an inhuman monster who didn't deserve to live her mother first stated that it was all for her own good and then came out with threats of brainwashing and exile in Upper Volta and of legal interdiction and in a word she had displayed with excessive clarity her determination now that Maria had so unexpectedly been proved a virgin to employ every means to make her get the idea of marrying Antonio right out of her head.

So Maria had more than ample reason to express at the opening of her letter that acute desire to be already dead which for that matter was the only clear and firm thing in her mind at the moment since death seemed to her not so much a surely fast way of getting out of the sad situation as a tenebrous means of expiation since even in her limpid and well-balanced mind they had managed with their insults to arouse a sense of guilt and so now she longed cathartically to die to pay for a sin not hers though in a certain way it affected her closely since it was the mishap of being the daughter of such a mother however she also sought out other blemishes in which despite her previous nonchalant talk of ancient Roman usages connected with Priapus she now regarded with great shame and for instance the fact of being subjected in a state which she herself didn't know whether to consider petrified resignation or cold insensitivity to that gynecological examination which had lacerated in her a virginal veil far more significant than the hymen whereby to the indignity of being Amalia Borghetto's daughter she could now add this other indignity of having lent herself without sufficient resistance to that kind of technological rape which she described in the letter with extraordinary detail and crudity as if she had wanted to suffer in recalling it the pain that for obscure reasons she hadn't managed to suffer when they were doing it to her, and in any case her grief over offenses already undergone was nothing compared to the alarm that assailed her at the thought of the future which she envisioned as darker than ever since for God knows how long she would lack the solace of his letters which had been until then a kind of proof of a certain final validity of her misfortunes whereas now at the idea of not being able to receive any mail she already felt plunged in an uncertainty that weakened her frightfully but even in this uncertainty she was fairly sure that any pressure her parents applied to uproot her love for Antonio would have no effect at all unless they had decided for this purpose to drive her mad and her chief terror was precisely that they would make her lose both her mind and the love which was now more than ever the sole support of her life, and so with repeated and somewhat ambiguous exhortations to remember her whatever might happen to her she ended the letter properly speaking which as usual had a postscript in which Maria returned to her simple and well-ordered style to explain how she would try to send this message which in all probability if it did reach him would be her last at least for an incalculable period namely by throwing the missive into the Campo San Polo with a thousand-lire note attached and a fervid plea to the unknown finder to put a special-delivery stamp or at least the usual forty-lire one to the envelope keeping the change as a reward.

Now the detail that the letter had reached its destination in a rather roundabout and basically aleatory way also helped strengthen Antonio's first impression fairly deducible from the contents, an impression of a generic incredulity which meditation attenuated

into one of exaggeration or partial credibility but this was basically
a defensive move that is an attempt however unconscious to annul
by denial this new pile of troubles which had poured over him
now when as we have seen his strength was already sapped by his
previous travail and above all by his inability to extract proper
literary benefit from it however apart from the fact that the new
troubles were certainly not the kind to be dismissed with a simple
definition of incredibility it must also be recognized that once
the moment for reflection came which with him generally occurred
sooner than necessary Antonio was not a man who even unconsciously evaded his own responsibilities and was rather inclined to
assume them in a quantity often superior to what would have been
reasonable and this time too he rather quickly reached the conclusion that the sudden worsening of the situation was entirely his
fault since it was all too clear that even overlooking his discouraging of the Priapesque enterprise which perhaps not even Maria
had meant seriously the new wave of ills derived from the imprudent though well-meant declaration which had escaped him the
day of mother Borghetto's horrible invasion because that very
remark apparently received then with inattention had prompted
the unspeakable signora to arrange the treacherous and well-calcu-
lated mechanism which led to the verification of objective virginity
and in consequence to the unleashing of a plan of atrocities which
would become steadily worse if one were by chance to lend credence
to Maria's expressed fears of brainwashing or exile to Upper Volta
or both, and as he kept thinking about it Antonio believed it more
and more also because he found something surprising in the undeniable fact that all those stratagems and ferocities which among
other things must have cost the earth had only one aim namely to
make Maria give him up so even in Signora Borghetto's eyes after
all he was the one who counted and thus from the tangled mass
of new griefs and fears he arrived without too much effort at a
new sense of importance and immediately thereafter of power
which on the one hand compensated for the suspicions of ineptitude
that all his behavior and finally Maria's proved virginity might

have aroused in anyone but on the other hand thrust him into that fervid spiritual state in which a man feels above all the inspiration to act.

Unfortunately it usually happens that when the inspiration to act is born from somehow contradictory forces and as in this case slightly imaginary ones like the sense of guilt and even more the sense of power it easily leads to senseless or at least not very sensible actions and this is because the inspiration to do something is formed and takes on substance before one knows what is the best thing to do so it ends by dictating only the level or at most the quality of the action but not its form, in short our Antonio felt driven to do anything perhaps even something mistaken provided it was on the same heroic level as the events of which he and Maria were the victims and the fact that these events were generally absurd naturally didn't help him find a reasonable way of acting if a reasonable way existed also because to be sincere Maria's attitude perhaps unintentionally limited the field of action severely that is while he now had the impression he was really ready for any enterprise however strange or reckless her letter in its many and confused themes didn't contain one that even remotely might suggest the Sicilian-style solution or flight which she had longed for on other occasions so one could also infer that her present passive acceptance of thoroughly unjust conditions namely her weak submission to her mother's maleficent will without any other resistance beyond a generic desire for her own demise denoted an already existent and highly dangerous mental derangement and so he not only had to act but to act urgently especially since he could see with what nonchalance Signora Borghetto approached jet airplanes and electroshock and modern technological devilishness which in themselves also because of their expense annoyed Antonio considerably so perhaps in reaction against the technological aspects he tended to linger on the picturesque aspects of Maria's condition in fact he imagined the poor girl as a maiden bound to a cliff and her mother as a dragon advancing from the sea to devour her and then himself as a bold knight who would confront and disembowel

the horrible monster, in short even looking at the situation pic-
turesquely there was no time to lose although practically speaking
it wasn't conceivable that the little palazzo in the Campo San Polo
could be attacked with weapons and spears even if he went there
only to beat up Signora Borghetto also because as he had clearly
remarked there was nothing in Maria's letter to encourage such
behavior and on the contrary if the letter suggested anything at all
it suggested prudence though it was hard to see what good prudence
would do and in conclusion after having meditated very laboriously
from noon when on waking up he had found the incredible missive
until five in the afternoon when his inspiration to act had become
irrepressible he took the bus to Venice because he had become convinced that the only opening or access to the complicated matter
was through Cavalier Ilario Borghetto of Maritime Supplies.

All things considered the line of reasoning that led Antonio to
this fine idea was not wholly without foundation though it sprang
from a somewhat factious premise namely that the adult male by
nature possesses more common sense than the female in other words
he felt that a sound businessman like Cavalier Ilario though concerned or perhaps dismayed by the idea that his only daughter and
heir was going to end up in the hands of a poor devil without a
cent would never arrive at those paroxysms of hatred not to say
hysteria which his wife seemed to achieve without any difficulty,
and then reflecting on the meticulous skill that hatred had shown
in organization one could reasonably deduce that Signora Borghetto
had constructed her masterpiece the trip to Rome and the gynecological examination of her daughter and had executed the plan
without saying anything to her husband because these were women's
affairs anyhow and so Antonio was under the impression that he
had only to go to Cavalier Ilario and spill out all the filthy things
that were going on in his house behind his back and he would thus
secure the cavaliere's decisive intervention, though decisive in what
direction Antonio frankly avoided imagining as he traveled quite
swiftly on the bus toward the Piazzale Roma in whose immediate
vicinity Borghetto Maritime Supplies had its headquarters espe-

cially since Cavalier Borghetto might very well not be in the office or being there he might refuse to receive Antonio which Antonio also foresaw and even desired ardently not so much to evade a conversation which could present surprises and considerable difficulties as to face it because that was in his view also one of those risks faced only if supremely improbable and there was the further consideration that a new and important humiliation would on one hand bring him closer to Maria who at the moment was having the worse time of the two of them and on the other hand would give him that impulse of overall revolt which would finally spark the heroic action so powerfully yet confusedly demanded by his inspiration to act.

It's all too evident that at this point poor Antonio was proceeding blindly or that his behavior had at least a piecemeal quality in the sense that he was concerned only with the most immediate step making no attempt to anticipate the following and consequent ones and though he vaguely placed his hope in a certain talent for improvisation which he had nevertheless only rarely displayed before and which in the particular circumstance drew indirect support from a serene sunset light which once they had passed the factories at Marghera he could see over the lagoon and from the comforting observation that the days had already grown a bit longer and therefore the better season was approaching, in reality he was preparing himself for the most enormous folly that is he was at the mercy of those unconscious forces of a predominantly masochistic nature which led him to enrich and perfect the series of disasters begun at the very moment when he had been brought into the world or rather conceived and which had then continued thick and fast up to the present moment with no sign of letting up if you excepted the brief parenthesis of happiness with Maria which he now had to pay for and to pay for heavily, and so by the time he reached the Piazzale Roma the corroborating effect of the days' lengthening had vanished for good and Antonio now felt very uncertain as to the rightness of his idea of going to talk with Maria's father and indeed he wouldn't have gone at all if he hadn't

195 / Giuseppe Berto

had reason to hope Cavalier Ilario would refuse to see him but
instead the moment the cavaliere was informed of Antonio's
presence in the waiting room he had him shown in at once and
Antonio found himself facing a lean little man with an obvious
desire to get things done in a hurry but at the same time indicating
that for this exceptional visit he was willing to spend all the necessary time and in fact first of all he asked his young visitor what he
would have as an aperitif a Campari or a Carpano which the
young man refused with well-planned dignity above all since he
found this man likable and felt no animosity of any kind toward
him especially after he had told his secretary solemnly he didn't
want to be disturbed not even by the telephone, and it was obvious
that he had a great gift for dealing with people this cavaliere who
managed even to put Antonio at his ease announcing he wasn't at
all surprised by this visit in fact he had been expecting it or rather
hoping for it because it was easier for men to understand each
other, and Antonio was so in agreement with him that in fact to
complete that agreement as quickly as possible he immediately
asked the key question namely whether the cavaliere knew or
didn't know what was going on in his house and the persecutions
of which Maria was the victim especially since the day before
yesterday that is when her mother had taken her on a carefully
planned trip to the nation's capital and the cavaliere with the
greatest naturalness answered that he knew everything but was
amazed that Antonio knew however two young people in love
could always find a way to communicate with each other no matter
how many precautions are taken, and then Antonio who had been
expecting quite a different answer asked with some firmness if the
cavaliere had also heard talk of brainwashing or exile to Upper
Volta and the cavaliere answered politely that there was no cause
to exaggerate with talk of persecutions and brainwashing and in
any case these were matters he left to his wife who enjoyed his
complete trust though at times she weakened and allowed certain
nonsense to go much farther than it should and at this point Antonio became fully aware that this conversation was a huge act of

stupidity and in his mind he began to search desperately for an even more stupid course which might well be that famous heroic action which was needed however it wasn't easy to find since at the moment he lacked the indispensable scorn or contempt and the whole business seemed perhaps only temporarily to have become theoretical that is his consciousness examined it not as an exactly extraneous case since he and Maria were still involved in it body and soul but as something virtually foreordained and in any case inexorably binding so their sufferings for God knows what reason had the same inevitability natural events generally have on the basis of some superior logic and arranged in advance so there was nothing to be done against them and the poor boy assuming at least in this pass the very marginal role of executant of his own destiny explicitly asked the cavaliere if one shouldn't consider his own and his wife's behavior toward their daughter monstrous and inhuman and the cavaliere without taking the slightest offense answered in a roundabout way by first explaining that he had worked like a dog all his life accumulating a fortune of seven hundred million lire and since he hoped to work another ten years before kicking off it was likely that the fortune would reach three billions which after all is three thousand millions and here he paused to ask Antonio parenthetically if he had the remotest idea of what three thousand millions were but then didn't wait for an answer since it was evident Antonio could have no such idea and then he returned to his main theme saying he could see no reason why three thousand millions should come to such an end and that is without any counterweight on Antonio's part so it was quite natural that as his ill-advised wife had neglected to break the thing off at the right moment he now had to go back to strong measures with Maria for her own good obviously, and Antonio felt so to speak on the very brink of the heroic action just about to burst from him though of course he didn't yet know what it would consist of however it was certain that though he felt a disarming lack of hatred for this man he would have been ready to shoot him for example if he had had the good sense to provide himself with a pistol in time but in any case he might strangle him or at least slap him and then spit in his face but this wasn't the point and here he realized almost with a start that he was forgetting the core of the question which was certainly Maria or rather the maiden bound to the rock who was now being faced not by one but by two fierce dragons ready to tear her limb from limb and so finally the necessary heroic action came and he was himself amazed he hadn't thought of it before since it was an action of complete magnanimity which not only saved Maria from exile and brain-washings but also included the satisfaction of his own deepest re-quirements of self-punishment and life-long frustration and in another sense it didn't overlook his exhibitionism since he would show that ignoble merchant who could think only in terms of self-interest what a true man was capable of when necessity de-manded it and in short what had come into Antonio's mind was to renounce Maria provided she would be safe that is he wouldn't write to her any more and wouldn't try to see her or speak to her provided her parents would stop persecuting and tormenting her, and when Antonio suggested this course Cavalier Ilario thought it over for a moment since obviously the bargain seemed too good to be true but then he realized he could trust this respect-able and honest young man and he held out his hand to seal the agreement and Antonio after very brief hesitation finally shook that hand feeling even proud and not only of himself but also of the whole affair and therefore also of the detail that he was being treated so to speak as an equal by Cavalier Ilario whom he then asked notwithstanding the agreement if in conclusion he could write a final message to Maria then and there to explain the most recent events to her and the reasons for his painful renunciation and the cavaliere finding the idea unquestionably good or even excellent immediately turned him over to the secretary who would find him pen and paper and some place to write, and Antonio in a corner of the office the secretary shared with two typists despite all his determination could only scrawl a few lines in which he told Maria that they had the whole world against them and therefore it was pointless to struggle and then he went out and the cold air and the cold lights of the Piazzale Roma gave a dreadfully hard blow to his insistent belief that he had performed a heroic action and still he insisted on believing it and even decided he wouldn't take the bus and would cross the long bridge on foot to think better and in any case now that he had really lost Maria he felt he loved her as never before and that he was one with her, because he also wished he were already dead and buried.

CHAPTER
XVI

In which Antonio in his despair visits the
café on the Zattere and encounters a blonde

Immediately after his confused
and senseless renunciation of Maria who was the only good thing he
possessed on this earth our Antonio fell ill with an illness really not
very serious but not entirely negligible since the doctor was unable
to diagnose it precisely in all its aspects because on the one hand it
seemed common influenza with bronchial complications and fever
which toward evening rose to a maximum of a hundred and one
whereas on the other hand it had characteristics not necessarily
included under the heading of major illness and though they chiefly
consisted in discomfort and stomach-aches in the absence of more
precise clues they had perforce to be associated with mental distress
which gave Antonio some solace since it would really have been
disappointing if his immense grief hadn't manifested a more pertinent disease than influenza though on closer consideration even the
influenza in itself could be connected with his spiritual sufferings in
a much less aleatory way than you might imagine because on coming out of Cavalier Ilario Borghetto's Marine Supplies office he had
gone on foot not only the whole length of the bridge linking Venice
to the mainland which was about a full mile but also the successive
mile to the Mestre overpass and he had done this at a brisk pace

though already after the first half-mile his feet hurt but with just the sort of pain he needed to punish himself for the folly he had committed and also to distract his thoughts from it at least for a few moments and so completing the journey in half an hour or even less he had reached the top of the overpass with duly aching feet and bathed in sweat of course but instead of going to wait for the Number Eight in the little waiting room which was for that matter quite squalid he stood outside purposely unbuttoning his overcoat and then also his jacket exposing himself to the bora that is to say the wind from the east which often blows dry and chill over the Veneto plain in the winter months and which there on the overpass that evening was blowing so hard it slashed your face in a temperature of about twenty below zero and in his exaltation Antonio managed even to personify this wind to which he addressed invocations begging it to kill him if possible with dispatch and not too painfully and it would have been a huge humiliation if after such an offer some holocaust hadn't cropped up besides an influenza with a temperature of barely a hundred so thank heaven there were also those pains and stomach disturbances which though ignoble and depressing by nature were still the palpable evidence of his loftier mental tribulations.

To tell the truth these tribulations were not so much lofty as muddled because naturally when a man suffers he doesn't just limit himself to suffering period but tries to realize the why and the wherefore of its happening to him and often the necessary and sufficient causes of human griefs and all the nonsense that accompanies them seem lacking or are so concealed in the deepest recesses of one's being that you can't make head or tail of them and thus the search for motives becomes in itself an occasion of torment also because the causes of your errors when you happen to find them turn out to be errors in their turn and so on therefore Antonio can't be blamed too severely if as soon as he stuck his nose into that muddle he instinctively drew it back or rather if he devoted his will power first of all to convincing himself that in renouncing Maria he hadn't committed the greatest stupidity he could have

committed in the situation in which he had come to find himself
also because if he had considered it stupidity he would have been
forced to admit having succumbed to the fascination or at least the
cleverness of Cavalier Ilario to a fairly remarkable degree and
precisely where the man was most despicable and certainly it wasn't
that our hero hadn't behaved like an idiot and a fool with Cavalier
Ilario however anyone attributing his miserable surrender to foolish-
ness would have been judging superficially since in going to the
Maritime Supplies for the incongruous encounter our Antonio
bore within himself his renunciation of Maria all nicely ready and
he was out looking for precisely the best opportunity to produce
it and surely a better occasion than that couldn't be found however
it was still an occasion and not a cause and God only knew where
the cause was or rather the many highly complicated causes however it was certain that in his heart Antonio had never firmly
believed in the possibility of happily marrying a nice girl laden with
millions or rather billions apparently and moreover his love which
seemed almost perfect to him betrayed on the contrary frightful
weaknesses derived from ignorance and from doubts that existed
or counted even if they rose to the surface of his consciousness only
rarely and never completely, so it wasn't surprising that this love so
resplendent on the outside coming up against enormous difficulties
and sufferings should give way almost at one blow but apart from
the fact that Antonio was convinced his love hadn't in the least
given way and had on the contrary established itself definitively
even though in a nobler sphere as we shall see what he obstinately
denied for the moment was that his renunciation was stupid because
reflecting on the singular conditions in which poor Maria had then
to live it seemed clear that renouncing her was the only means to
save her from further insult and persecution, and in the face of
such a result which also seemed inviting because it could be achieved
on the spot with the cavaliere's word of honor as guarantee the
renunciation he bore all ready and waiting inside him then exploded
in his mind endowed in addition with such characteristics of abnegation and heroism that he felt he had to accept it quickly and with

the same speed propose it to the incredulous cavaliere, and in short as he was committing the stupid act he was filled with a fervent spirit of altruistic sacrifice so much so that in his yearning for self-laceration and a bit also because of his haste to conclude things he had completely forgotten the value that rightly or wrongly he himself had in Maria's eyes that is he forgot the grief the poor girl would suffer at being abandoned by him just at the most unfortunate moment of her life however to tell the truth in the unhappy creature's last and contradictory letter there were a number of passages completely lacking in any hope that their all too thwarted love could somehow survive and in fact one couldn't deny that the lachrymose missive all in all gave Antonio up as lost, true she put this conjecture forward with the hinted expectation that heaven and earth equally pitiless would be moved to prevent such torment however Antonio predisposed in the wrong way had taken her special and surely transitory remissiveness too much to heart and in fact a keen observer would have no trouble in discovering in his renunciatory impulses some traces of counterfrustration or to put it more bluntly a bit of wounded pride.

In short from whatever direction you tried to penetrate it to make even a rough analysis the situation was a fine mess where the forces of good and those of evil were so tangled up that there was no action or thought which didn't seem both good and bad and since the only fixed point in the business seemed to be the very painful fact that Maria was now lost forever Antonio during those first days insisted not surprisingly in his idea that having been denied the good fortune of not coming into the world he had best leave it as soon as he could, but since a temperature of a hundred and one and a touch of diarrhea were certainly not afflictions which could foster any reasonable hope of decease it was inevitable to attempt some other method of elaboration of his grief in view of his unavoidable survival and in the hope of a somehow less miserable life, and so his defense mechanism first of all attended to the suppression of Maria's physical appearance which became progressively hazier in his memory and therefore progressively more convertible

into allegory and the same mechanism increased the rapid spiritu-
alization of his love and led Antonio to the conviction that he now
loved Maria much more firmly and fully than before moreover in
an unchangeable and indestructible way thanks to its metaphysical
perfection a process which as is well known had taken place previously both in Petrarch and in Dante Alighieri concerning their
ladies, and the fact that this had happened to them after their ladies
had died didn't make much difference since anyone could see that
Antonio's love for the living Maria was now equally if not more
cruel and desperate than what he would have felt for Maria dead,
and in short the themes of love and death so akin in their spirituality and durability after they reach a certain level continued to min-
gle in him chiefly as a means of literary evasion and in this sense
also the fever and the diarrhea were finally useful because they
managed to provide that state of physical weakness and heart-
broken spiritual tenderness which tempering the grief at the imagined deceases gave the prospect a resigned and almost sweet
quality which if Antonio were to survive could quite well be translated into poetry or in a subordinate fashion of course also into
prose.

But as always happens when things long dreamed of come within
our reach they tend to vanish or at least to change their aspect and
so also this hypothesis of poetic death or mortal poetics once Antonio had overcome his visceral and influenzal disturbances and was
therefore in a position to compose showed an inclination to vanish
into laziness which in a way and on another level involved the all
too conclusive settling of his great grief in a universal concept of
existential frustration or even only within the frame of general
bitterness which bound his life even before the latest and greatest
upsets, and this settlement can be criticized or deplored only up to
a point since it is well known that disasters however huge if they
are definitive have a much greater power of assuefaction than
smaller disasters which one thinks are transient, anyhow Antonio
didn't surrender without resistence to the irresistible pacifying
tendency of what's done is done and let the dead bury the dead and

in fact all things considered he was very sorry that the sensation of undergoing one of the most important sorrows that can befall a living being should become attenuated and with it the hope of reasonably deriving from it suitable poetical compositions and so as soon as he was back on his feet that is to say two weeks after the great renunciation since there was no point in thinking of poetry for the moment he preferred to think about reinforcing both his sorrow and his inspiration by returning to its scenes that is by going every afternoon to Venice but not to the vicinity of the palazzo in the Campo San Polo where Maria still was or to the neighborhood of the Fondamenta della Parona where memories were too recent and harsh but to the airy Zattere and among and through churches and back streets around the warehouses and the gas plant where in a chiefly deambulatory way his exceptional love had first blossomed.

Antonio's choice of these backgrounds and itineraries was not entirely casual however it wasn't appreciably determined by a sudden return of interest in art history though to tell the truth our hapless lover was careful to drag his sufferings before the Paolo Veronese paintings in San Sebastiano and to the disputed Guardi choir stalls at the church of the Angelo Raffaele and he didn't avoid carrying them to the gate of the Ca' Foscari courtyard but only late in the evening when the University was already long since closed and he ran no risk of encountering Maria, and Antonio was actually quite aware of his desire not to say his necessity to reconstruct his past love in its most elevated aspect from both a sentimental and a cultural standpoint and he didn't worry too much about the fact that the operation required some sacrifice of the truth that is the elimination more or less of that part of Maria connected with the weaknesses of the flesh which was no small part after all, so in going back to the places where his love had been freshest he preferred the spots that recalled the birth of noble and edifying thoughts while he skipped the back streets and dark passages where she had leaned against walls and had acquired the habit of abandoning herself all too willingly to his intimate caresses and similarly he made every effort to erase the memory of her mouth when it was open and gasping with desire or her expression when at the approach of her orgasm it became fixed with her eyes staring and almost frighteningly vacant losing for that matter a good share of her beauty, instead he put some emphasis on the improvement of tiny details in his opinion far removed from sensuality like her freckles or the crooked tooth or certain looks and smiles which in their opportune purity seemed to omit the weight of the flesh and naturally this course of selection also helped confuse Maria's image in his memory or rather it was a tiny aspect of that vaster task of suppression which he was carrying out to force the flesh-and-blood Maria into the realm of the unconscious and this not so much for the comprehensible reason that in erasing Maria he tended also to erase the memory of the stupidities he had committed for her or against her as because by eliminating her sensuality in favor of her spirituality he was constructing for himself a completely stabilized though somewhat improbable creature that is to say he was performing one of those toilsome processes of angelification which not only lead to good literary results but are also beautiful in the absolute sense.

Now this idea that angelifications are beautiful in the absolute sense was not something Antonio had found in his head ready-made or had constructed opportunistically for this present circumstance instead it constituted the junction of other equally mistaken ideas almost all linked to countless prejudices which in their turn had originated in defective sexual education or to put it more clearly in the general tendency of educators of every kind to make young people hate sex so this scission of Maria which our young man was making to eliminate what we might call the faulty part could indeed tend to poetic results or to the shifting of that unfortunate love on to practically indestructible bases but substantially it manifested a retarded and antisexual zeal which when you thought about it wasn't generous even toward Maria because though Antonio did everything to believe he was the sole possessor of those carnal stimuli which had led them both to their ruin the fact re-

mained they had got into the mess together with at least equal
enthusiasm and for that matter also on the subject of the ruin they
had come to through the fault of their dissoluteness Antonio was
being very naïve if he thought the Borghettos would have been
capable of letting their only child end up in the hands of a young
man who was virtuous and chaste but without a cent, and at this
point one could also infer that in his present repugnance for the
pleasures of the flesh our hero was animated unconsciously of
course by the resistance he set up to the thought of what an ass he
had been not to give it to Maria when he had his hands on her
and when she wanted nothing else and in short there was plenty
of reason to abhor sexual sins from original sin on and to feel the
stimulus to angelicize not only Maria but also himself, though here
the operation proved much more difficult as the days passed and
his abstinence was prolonged and in fact Antonio eventually came
to prefer among all the places connected with Maria's memory the
terrace of that café on the Zattere.

Now it's quite true that on this terrace he had seen Maria for the
first time and hence in her most absolute integrity and purity both
in the sweetness of her face and the charm of her Venetian blond
hair which had made him compare her at once to a musician-angel
in the nearby Accademia Gallery, and it's also true that an open and
luminous place with more than one spire in view helped in the formation of completely desexualized thoughts, however it's equally
true that since Antonio's and Maria's misfortunes had wrought no
visible changes in the habits of the Venetians the terrace continued
to be crowded especially on fine days with a number of girls who
enjoyed taking that midwinter sun and Antonio precisely because
he knew there were girls there finally preferred that place to any
other and indeed he was especially happy when he came upon a
pretty one because he could exercise his own capacity for renunciation on her more than on the others thus making himself all the
more certain his love for Maria really was undying so he sat there
looking at the pretty girls purposely even staring at their breasts or
their waists or their hips and in short at whatever was most admi-

rable about them and sometimes when for example they had also pretty legs he scrupulously imagined moving his hands slowly up those legs to the soft groin and the labia to caress them, but just when he was beginning to feel some pleasure in these fantasies he cut them short abruptly concluding he didn't give a damn about that girl and meaning to offer up this conclusion to the memory of Maria his one love, however anybody could realize this game was fairly dangerous in the long run and in fact one day which was probably Thursday of Carnival week or perhaps even the last day of Carnival because people were rather gay and were amusing themselves by throwing streamers at each other and confetti and little balls of colored paper Antonio's way of staring which a person unaware of his private situation might even consider provocative and insolent finally attracted the attention and the confetti of a pretty blonde.

Now it must truthfully be said that Antonio didn't in the least want this to happen and he wasn't even remotely thinking about it and in reality though he had been practicing his powers of renunciation on this blonde for some time if anybody had asked him how she wore her hair or whether her legs were plump or slim he wouldn't have known what to answer that is he had the vague impression she was a pretty girl with a rather full bosom but this impression merely proved the validity of his renunciation however he hadn't had the curiosity to investigate in what other way she might be beautiful and only after the girl had succeeded in stirring him from his renunciatory meditations by throwing confetti at him was he able to see she was a beautiful blonde who oh my God seemed rather full of freckles but happily all her teeth were straight, still he didn't allow himself to be overcome by any smugness in observing he had been fairly lucky in his spiritual exercises in fact he was rather disturbed and even saddened when the girl with gestures more than with words asked him what made him look at her so much, and then she immediately burst out laughing evidently because Antonio caught off guard must have assumed a comical expression perhaps a bit confused and in fact boldly raising her voice she asked him if by any chance this was the first time he had happened to see a woman, and this behavior on the blonde's part was not really so improper in view of the carnival atmosphere however it still seemed to irritate a brunette who was in her company at the same table since they began to argue in a lively and at times harsh manner in a language evidently not Italian, and then the blonde whose face had become flushed during the argument went back to throwing confetti at Antonio mostly to spite her girl friend who seeing that her words were in vain tried to stop the blonde's arm at a certain point and then the blonde turned on her roughly saying something which in all probability was a string of insults and then as if that weren't enough she stood up and while the other girl seemed really angry the blonde came over to Antonio to announce that she was bored sitting there on the terrace and since Antonio had been looking at her for a good half hour in a really indecent way now he had to buy her a drink somewhere else preferably in the neighborhood of the station where there was a place with records and they could dance the shake, and though he was upset by more than one dark presentiment and also by the discovery that the girl was almost taller than he was our Antonio finally went off with her toward a new and extraordinary adventure.

CHAPTER
XVII

In which, it appears, Antonio is

quickly consoled

Taking his place all too obediently at the side of that tall blonde girl who had started off at a brisk pace toward the Gesuati probably with the intention of turning into the Rio Terrà Foscarini to go to the Accademia and catch the vaporetto or better still the direct motoscafo for the station Antonio was as usual in the grip of many confused and contradictory sentiments among which as was only natural a bit of remorse stood out in any case somewhat mitigated by his satisfaction at being in the company of a blonde whom the more he looked at her the more he found attractive and this increased the obscure sensation he was heading for something which if not evil would nevertheless have to be painfully expiated, anyhow distracting him at least partially from these metaphysical fears he was now tormented by the necessity of confessing to the girl who obviously overestimated him and considered him smarter and more up-to-date than he was that he simply didn't know how to do the shake and indeed he could just manage slow dances and it was strange he should be so timid about saying such a thing that is something simple and of no importance to a girl who for that matter seemed born to put people at their ease since she was open and straightforward, however as this fear and embarrassment rightly or wrongly did exist they must have been inspired by an emotion for which there was really no reason unless naturally it was connected with the freckles with which the girl's face seemed sufficiently supplied and in short that emotion which surely existed and complicated relations with the present girl had in the final analysis also to be traced back to Maria who was the first and only source of all emotion and once this was established it was hardly worth suffering so much about revealing his inability to do the shake because at worst this girl would drop him and go find a boy more suited to her or else after going with him to the dance hall she would there join a sufficiently expert partner however the first solution seemed to Antonio the more opportune from every point of view and in fact he was about to advise her to find a more suitable companion when the blonde who had stopped at the Accademia dock and seemed hesitant whether to take the motoscafo or the vaporetto suddenly announced that she would now go back to the café on the Zattere because she had invented this whole business chiefly to spite her cousin Vera who was so bossy, and when Antonio caught off guard like this and unable to show his relief at the sudden change in program stood there without saying anything so that he could appear cross or even insulted that she should drop him abruptly after she had invited him dancing she smiled at him sweetly or who knows perhaps only coyly and asked him to forgive her rudeness but she simply had to go back to her cousin, and finally since Antonio mostly out of slowness but also because he was a bit affected by the coyness which made her much prettier delayed in telling her not to worry and besides he couldn't dance the shake she added before she ran off not giving him time to answer that the day after tomorrow at five o'clock sharp whatever the weather was she would be at the Zattere café without her cousin Vera and she would be happy to see him again since he seemed really terribly nice.

And so once again our Antonio without any great merit could look good in his own eyes confirming for himself the idea that his one undying love was Maria and that this blonde though she was hardly to be thrown away meant less than nothing to him especially since even judging her in the most benevolent fashion you had to call her bold and wild thus absolutely not comparable to Maria, and still despite this firm conclusion Antonio on finding himself suddenly alone at the foot of the Accademia bridge felt a certain uneasiness which he promptly and not altogether mistakenly attributed to the sudden time vacuum that is to the fact that he didn't know what to do now since it would have been silly and in a sense imprudent to go back to the Zattere in view of that blonde whom he vaguely felt he should keep clear of, and as he went off he took the direction away from the Zattere though not exactly on purpose that is he crossed the Accademia bridge going on to the Campo Santo Stefano and then still finding nothing to do he went on absently to the adjoining Campo Sant'Angelo and here perhaps because he found himself only a few steps from the famous Fondamenta della Parona it suddenly occurred to him that it wouldn't be a bad idea to drop in at that house perhaps to make love with the amiable landlady, but he recoiled from this idea with appropriate haste trying more than to condemn it not to pay any attention to it though it would have been reasonable and wiser to pay it some attention because such a notion was not only a hint that he had suffered the humiliation of being dropped by the blonde more than he wanted to admit but also a symptom indicating that all his intellectual labor to attain the desexualization of himself and the pacification of his senses in the memory of Maria was basically wasted effort and also that his future would be much more complicated than he might foresee at the moment.

Anyhow for the time being our hero had so many problems and griefs to which he could devote himself that the blonde simply didn't exist and in fact he didn't dedicate any special thought to her during those next two days indeed he wouldn't have thought about her at all if it hadn't been a question of re-establishing how serious and responsible Maria was by comparison and the outcome was so evident that he was finally even irritated at those superfluous comparisons he had been making which if he thought about it were quite unseemly because of the very juxtaposition they implied, and then once irritated he released his irritation on the blonde who however wasn't really to blame for being so much worse than Maria also because if other girls hadn't been so much worse than she was Maria wouldn't have been able to be so much better than they, in short in this highly roundabout way the new girl risked assuming an importance which objectively wasn't her due, and so Antonio precisely to counteract this false overestimation went to the Zattere café two days later at five o'clock also in order to behave normally since now he went there almost every afternoon and thus not going there on that specific afternoon would have been tantamount to admitting that one way or another he allowed the blonde to condition him whereas he wanted to prove to himself of course that he certainly wasn't going to change his own habits because a completely crazy and therefore quite unreliable blonde had made a kind of backhand date which obviously she wouldn't keep, but instead there she was sitting all alone at a little table apparently waiting just for him all pink and white with her freckles and an air of gaiety just slightly malicious as if halfway between joy at seeing him arrive and the determination to amuse herself again at his expense by teasing him and Antonio who needless to say had a special sensitivity in perceiving dangers of this kind was at first very reserved until the girl at a certain point asked him if by any chance he was still offended because the other day she had dropped him at the Accademia and naturally Antonio could only answer that he wasn't in the least offended however his tone of voice or something must have given the answer a low degree of conviction because the blonde immediately said she was born crazy and people shouldn't be upset by her craziness which according to Antonio might also be correct however when the association with her was the result not of an initiative on her part as had happened to him but on the part of the person who had to undergo the craziness, still in answering the girl he certainly didn't express himself that frankly in fact he finally said not without a hint of gallantry that craziness in a beautiful girl can be borne gladly and probably this was one reason why there were more girls in the world who were beautiful and crazy than girls who were ugly and crazy, and at this point perhaps encouraged and in any case already sated with the admiration Antonio was abundantly lavishing on her face the blonde asked him with a touch of provocation if Antonio didn't find that besides her face she also had nice legs and so Antonio who for that matter had already observed her legs discreetly on his own was forced to shift his attention to the girl's lower limbs and as she was wearing a skirt that was almost a miniskirt they were visible to quite an extent above the knee however instead of taking pleasure in what he had to look at he suddenly felt a sharp irritation which he didn't yet know whether to attribute to the girl's rather shameless exhibitionism or to the unfortunate notion that occurred to him that the legs before his eyes were slimmer and perhaps also better shaped than Maria's, the fact remained that he answered somewhat harshly and unpleasantly saying he was accustomed to appreciating girls not so much for their pretty legs as for their intelligence and sensitivity and the girl's only answer was to say stupid giving him in addition a prompt sidelong glance after which she shut up turning her face to the sun as if the only thing she cared about at least at the moment was to become sunburned and Antonio for his part was quite happy she had been irritated and vowed he would do nothing to restore a cordial atmosphere and so much the better if this casual and basically also inopportune acquaintance were not to continue because it was obvious he had nothing in common with that girl or with any other girl in the world outside of Maria thank God, and to prove to himself how true this was he wanted to take his mind off her and forget her devoting himself meanwhile to looking for a little canary chirping festively somewhere lucky bird but then he saw it hanging out of a window in a cage and although the association was merely marginal he shut his eyes and went over in his memory Leopardi's Solitary Sparrow and he felt his fervor increase with the perception of universal vanity which so it seemed was a condition of poetry, oh he would be quite capable of giving complete expression to the evil of living perhaps using only the sounds of that hour which he was very alert in detaching from one another and from the improbable silence, cries of gulls and various thudding of engines and slap of water under the bellies of the boats that went by and the waiting for sounds that weren't there at present but which might come any minute like the sound of bells or in the other direction the grim sirens of ocean liners or tugboats and with them a sharp longing to go he couldn't say where though to the Orient if possible, and he really had forgotten the girl though the satisfaction of having forgotten her also implied an awareness of her existence, in any case she counted less than nothing he could be sure of that since it was totally indifferent to him whether he remained seated there or went off perhaps even without saying good-bye, but then at a certain point that is after an endless pause which detached the new words from what they had already said or thought before she asked him rather aggressively what could he know of her unhappiness, a remark against which our Antonio instinctively defended himself thinking My God what a lot of unhappy girls there are in this world only slightly protecting himself with that thought because immediately afterwards he considered that if he were to judge by his own state then unhappiness really might be the most common and credible human condition and thus moved by nothing more than a feeling of solidarity he asked the girl why she felt unhappy considering this still a foolish question at least from his point of view since he had sound reasons for believing in existential unhappiness and therefore if necessary in unhappiness free of any contingent cause since the original one of having come into the world was enough, anyway the girl who was probably not yet up to the concept of existential unhappiness suddenly started talking about her own misfortunes which even objectively considered were numerous and big since in a few words she managed to tell him that they had killed her father in Budapest during the revolution of fifty-six that is when she was a little girl not nine years old and her mother had escaped at once bringing her to the West but she had died shortly thereafter of a terrible disease leaving her in the care of an uncle and aunt who ran a little hotel called the Magyar Hotel near San Gregorio where she worked for her living because besides being an orphan she was also poor and as if that weren't enough stateless that is really nobody's child, in short when it came to reasons for being unhappy even independently of existential frustrations it seemed she had more than enough and Antonio certainly didn't want to deny her them and he felt a kind of heart-rending compassion for her but a cautious one at the same time because he couldn't forget how the girl only a short time before had asked him so boldly if he liked her legs which even now when she was concerned with serious thoughts she didn't take the least trouble to cover even to the extent her miniskirt would allow, and so torn and not finding anything pertinent to say to comfort the unfortunate girl he finally asked her simply but in a tone of great tenderness what her name was and he was thunderstruck to hear that her name was Marika that is practically speaking Maria.

This coincidence of names which after all he shouldn't have found so amazing considering the popularity of the name Maria in every country on earth instead produced in Antonio an extraordinary effect and a quite irrational one when you think that he took it as a kind of warning of destiny or for one of those providential obstacles that heaven customarily puts in the way of the trespasser, however a moment's thought was enough to make him realize how thoroughly mistaken this was because he viewed this new girl like all others a mere abstraction useful to confirm the stability and the superiority of his feelings for Maria and still the fact that this one was also more or less named Maria led to some confusion between the two which for many reasons was best avoided and conversely to a forced differentiation through which this Marika acquired perhaps an undue autonomy that is she became an independent entity with a spiritual nucleus obviously centered around a concept of unhappiness and a body which though a bit too large and heavy for a boy like Antonio who was engaged in a process of angelification still presented a notable shapeliness in the lower limbs, in short it wasn't easy to see clearly into this coincidence or rather in the confusion it had aroused and the girl seeing him so gripped by thoughts anyone could safely have imagined were sad asked his forgiveness for having bored him with the list of her woes and added that by now it was all water under the bridge except for the special misfortune of being poor and stateless obviously and in any case as she luckily had a jolly disposition she managed to console herself whenever something good happened to her such as for example attracting Antonio because she had realized he liked her the other day from the way he stared at her slipping his eyes so to speak under her clothes and Antonio who couldn't of course explain to her the remote and basically antisexual reasons for his way of staring and who anyhow was still pondering her name asked her why she happened to be called Marika or rather if in her country all the Marias were called Marika and the girl explained that she herself didn't exactly know whether it was a corruption of the original Hungarian name which was Marinka or else the fusion of two names like Maria Enrica or Maria Federica the fact remained she had always been called that and in the kind of passport she had been issued she figured as Marika Ronay, and having said this she rightly wanted to know what his name was and where he lived and having learned he came from Marocco and not from Venice she was pleased because she had a friend from high school who had gone to live at Mogliano just a bit past Marocco and she had always promised to go visit her and had never gone but now that she had met Antonio she would go not tomorrow however because she had to work in the afternoon but the day after tomorrow provided Antonio would wait for her after her visit to her girl friend about six in the afternoon in the pastry shop right in the square at Mogliano under the arcade so he could bring her back to Venice in his car and Antonio answered that he would be glad to wait for her in the pastry shop however he felt obliged to warn her he didn't have a car since he was a student from a poor family and therefore almost always short of money and she looked at him for a moment as if she wanted to reproach him but then she shrugged and half-laughing said she was always unlucky in her acquaintances because she never found a boy loaded with money and then having taken a look at her watch she was suddenly in a hurry and went off leaving him to pay for a total of three cups of hot chocolate with whipped cream, an action which our Antonio judged rather severely.

Apart from the three chocolates he had to pay for however Antonio was rather broad-minded in forming a general opinion of the girl since it seemed to him for that matter quite incongruously that once he accepted the fact that her name was more or less Maria then everything else should go well also because she didn't matter much to him and so it would have been ridiculous to demand perfection of a girl to whom he devoted such slight interest, besides he had to remember that the poor thing was a foreigner after all and so some of her free or even fast attitudes should be blamed more on different background than on a facile character or corrupt soul, and finally Antonio knew all too well that it would have been excessive to assume as a criterion of moral judgment his ideas which were surely outdated and out of tune with the free and easy behavior of modern girls which in the final analysis was almost always innocent and so to put it bluntly without any pointless circumlocution he had no right to insist that every girl he met possess the special virtues of Maria with whom this Marika surely couldn't compete though actually this girl also had some fine qualities including her long legs and the jolly disposition which despite her numerous misfortunes she managed to display also benefiting her fellow man of course, anyhow comparing her to Maria would have been ungenerous toward her as well as improper toward Maria who was to be left in her higher spiritual sphere so keeping the levels distinct as was no doubt wise Antonio felt there could be nothing wrong if he went to wait for this Marika in the Mogliano pastry shop since he had now promised her and also since nothing prevented their becoming good friends eventually and he might even consider her sufficiently worthy of hearing of his love troubles which he still suffered abundantly, and so he went to wait for her at the pastry shop with a completely clear conscience and well in advance of the agreed hour however by six she hadn't come and not even by six-thirty an hour when Antonio began to perceive a bit of moral discomfort intimately connected with his gradually mounting annoyance at that waiting in other words he was so adept at remorse that he could easily reverse the normal course from sense of guilt to expiation which in this case was constituted by his tiresome wait in the pastry shop to go back and discover or even create a guilt which in the present instance could only lie in an excessive interest in the girl who was late coming so it wasn't true that there was nothing wrong in their engagement and that he didn't give a damn about her, guilt was present though at the moment it hadn't taken a specific shape and it would be better not to let it take on any shape at all since now nobody could reasonably reproach him if he stopped waiting for a girl who was already half an hour late and in all likelihood since he didn't even have a rattletrap Fiat five hundred she would never turn up at all, however it was precisely in the uselessness of waiting for her that he found a reason for waiting namely to punish himself thus for the excessive importance he had given her finally and in short when she arrived at five to seven our Antonio frankly didn't know whether to be pleased or not just as he didn't know whether he was more irritated with himself for having waited for her beyond every dignified limit or with her because she didn't bother about arriving on time for appointments however he was fully determined not to buy her even one chocolate with whipped cream so he went straight up to her forestalling any desire she might have for refreshment and said it was better for them to go and talk outside.

The evening really wasn't ideal for outdoor conversation because though the cold wasn't very severe there was a fog so heavy it seemed almost like rain and in fact the plane trees of the broad road they started walking along were dripping as if it were raining and Antonio was already fairly dissatisfied with his idea of taking a walk while Marika who was wearing a nice lined raincoat seemed not to worry about the dampness also because she was very angry with her cousin Vera who for some unknown reason hadn't wanted her to come to Mogliano, and this cousin Vera must have had a downright nasty nature if Marika had had to argue such a long time before she could leave which was why she had been so late in short practically speaking she had come with the Number Eight and naturally hadn't gone to see her old school friend and she wouldn't go now being happy to stay with Antonio and to walk with him in the rain even if it wasn't precisely rain however she liked it because apparently this awful weather reminded her of her childhood in some village in Hungary but without especially saddening her on the contrary she declared explicitly that she didn't want to be sad especially because she was terribly hungry but she still didn't want to go and coop herself up someplace to eat and since a mile or so farther on there was a restaurant she suggested they walk there because she was really happy to be in the country and she even liked the headlights of the endless cars which went by one after the other making a loud noise on the wet asphalt, in short she talked all the time with an animation which finally became suspect as if she weren't really in the mood she was displaying but in another secret humor Antonio finally recognized as desperation, and from this still unsure discovery he proceeded along a whole chain of sentiments each more desolate than the next which in their haste seemed to be founded not so much on an inner reality as on external things, that is he felt destroyed not by his own misfortunes or by his own nature but rather by the drops that were falling and by the noise of the passing cars and the rows of lights which soon died in the fog and actually by things that here and now he had in common with this Marika and thus he suddenly came to perceive an irremediable affinity with her precisely in what might be her most temporary and dangerous aspect and at the same time he knew as painfully as it could be known the void Maria had left in him and the necessity to fill it without any pretense of complete replacement but to satisfy in some way an anxiety for extreme and perhaps mortal ruin of which this new girl so pitifully ambiguous might be the instrument therefore all of a sudden he said he couldn't live without her and she didn't answer but leaned back against a plane tree and made him kiss her at once as if during all that time she had been waiting for nothing else.

CHAPTER XVIII

In which Antonio, giving way to meditation, finally enjoys himself less than he should

This Marika's surprising rapidity in deciding to have him kiss her was beneficial to Antonio since on the one hand it allowed him to shore up his self-confidence which after the latest developments of the story with Maria had become rather rickety and at the same time through the constant comparison which never stopped churning in his mind he was enabled to establish some new points in Maria's favor though if he thought about it he realized Maria hadn't had to be coaxed to let him kiss her either, still rather than stress the time involved in the process it was better to remark the essential and profound peculiarities of the matter that is Marika's kisses betrayed a kind of disposition toward more or less anybody who came along whereas with Maria it had been a unique and somehow definitive encounter which in fact he had immediately incorporated into the theory of the two souls seeking each other forever in the infinity of the worlds though in view of how things had ended it would have been better if they had gone on seeking each other for a while longer, anyhow the excellence of Maria's kisses lay especially in the undeniable singularity of the whole story because Marika's kisses were also very sweet and wonderful for that matter and Antonio only regretted that instead of enjoying them as they deserved he was ruminating over them as if they had been not kisses but algebra problems and for example it seemed to him that Maria's kisses were more autonomous and complete in the sense that in the beginning at least one knew that there would be nothing beyond them whereas these kisses of Marika's seemed a fluent preface to swift ulterior actions for which however there would be obstacles at least of a practical nature that is Antonio perhaps exaggerating a bit to Maria's advantage considered that the biggest hindrance to going to bed with this Marika was the lack of a bed, if the weather had been fine without thinking it over too much they would have made love as best they could on the grassy bank of some canal nearby but under the present meteorological conditions it would certainly be pointless to count on conveniences of the sort but on the other hand since Marika was visibly below the age of twenty-one in Antonio's opinion it was impossible to go with her to some hotel so it was best for the moment not to think about it and to take things as they came, and the things which came for the present were kisses that grew more and more enjoyable that is to say the two of them moved from one plane tree against which they had been kissing till they were breathless to another plane tree a bit farther on and Marika with her back leaning against it pressed forward the rest of her body to adhere to him as closely as possible especially with her abdomen and so he thought the moment had come to venture a caress or two but curiously enough when he tried to touch her breast the girl pushed his hand away and when he tried to arrive at her abdomen she even stopped kissing him and said that all those kisses had made her weak and if they didn't move on quickly they would never reach the restaurant.

This unforeseen behavior disturbed Antonio somewhat not because he really felt much like giving her orgasms against the plane trees but because Marika's surprising restraint upset a scale of minor values already firmly established according to common sense and reason or in other words it seemed contrary to the logical order of things that Marika should resist where Maria on the contrary had surrendered with extraordinary ease so the girl's inexplicable hesitation could derive only from her capricious nature and for this reason Antonio could feel toward her a slight bitterness which in any case helped him to reconsider the excessive impulsiveness which a short time before had led him to tell her he couldn't live without her, a remark to be given a merely contingent value limited to a mood which might also be transitory and which anyway had changed through another cause, and Antonio was already thinking how to explain all this to her and perhaps confess to her with absolute honesty how desperately and eternally he was in love with another when luckily in the fog he glimpsed the red glow of the sign of the Park Hotel dei Dogi for which they were heading and Marika said thank goodness here we are with such great joy that Antonio hadn't the courage to preach her a moralistic sermon then and there so he postponed it till later, however even later that is when they were sitting opposite each other at a secluded little table and Marika seeing him glum asked him what was wrong Antonio couldn't summon the courage to explain himself and in fact he said oh nothing but with such audible self-pity she couldn't help laughing and she began to tease him rubbing her legs against his under the table and then taking one of his legs between hers and squeezing it hard but while she did this she kept on eating bread and butter and drinking white wine waiting for the seafood risotto they had ordered and Antonio hardly knowing what to think about her finally considered her a bit too free and easy even for a foreigner and therefore quite unworthy of receiving confidences on the subject of Maria, and so having got Maria out of the way Antonio also began to drink white wine and to devote some attention to the leg game Marika was playing under the cover of the tablecloth in a really very enjoyable and not at all vulgar fashion since while she was doing it her face retained a gaiety which if you didn't know what she was up to with her legs might even have been taken for spiritual and in fact it seemed that this boundary between what was spiritual and what was not after a certain point became somewhat uncertain and anyhow Marika's face so flushed with sensuality or if you like also with spirituality was at this point very beautiful and a man could devote himself with great satisfaction to examining it in all its details such as the line of her hair at her temples or her mouth which was broad and full or her nose which on the contrary was small or her freckles, and at the thought of the freckles he was seized by such tenderness that he almost told her he was afraid of falling in love with her that is he almost said something quite inappropriate from whatever point of view you might choose to examine it.

Our Antonio in that first and generally quite favorable stage of the new adventure suffered therefore from abrupt shifts of mood and judgment connected of course with a certain instability and incongruity in the girl's behavior but even more with the circumstance that in keeping with his own nature he hadn't the slightest idea what to do or to desire and even when the food and especially the wine had given them both greater felicity of movement and ease of expression he remained ready to accept any brusque change that might come from her but at the same time he succeeded God knows how in abandoning himself to erotic even boldly erotic fantasies so his wish to make love was easily legible in his expression and this seemed to make Marika laugh with increasing gaiety and perhaps also with a bit of malice but Antonio by now was completely disarmed and certainly didn't dream of being offended and in fact when perhaps with the intention of arousing him for nothing she asked him if he wanted to make love he answered candidly that he was dying to but he didn't know how to manage it she burst out laughing evidently because she hadn't understood what he meant by not knowing how to manage it and she may have imagined an excessive inexperience on his part or even physical inability but when he had explained it was simply a matter of logistic obstacles or rather the inadvisability of going to make love on the bank of a canal in this weather she said she didn't see why they shouldn't do it right where they were since it was a clean and comfortable hotel presumably with many free rooms in the off season, and with immediate resentment because he was already

imagining she had told him a lie about her age at the time of the
Budapest revolution Antonio asked her what made her think they
would give the two of them a room when she was still a minor
since by calculating the years she should be little over eighteen and
she first of all took from her purse the sort of passport she had and
put it under his nose to show him she had been born at Szolnok
in Hungary precisely on the twenty-seventh of March nineteen
hundred and forty-eight and then she said for him to produce his
identity card and to go to the desk and engage not a double room
which they wouldn't give him but two communicating single
rooms with bath in between if possible or rather now that she
thought about it she wanted a double for herself and a single for
him communicating of course and hers at least she wanted facing
the countryside because she didn't like the noise of the trucks going
by on the highway, and she said all this firmly and even harshly so
Antonio though going to ask for rooms embarrassed him enor-
mously went and reserved them, on the other hand it would have
been indelicate to expect her to do it though of the two of them
he surely was the one with less experience of hotel routine but this
of course might derive not so much from a special familiarity with
the hotel where they were as from her work at the Magyar Hotel
of Venice though trucks surely didn't pass in front of the Magyar
Hotel, in short Antonio couldn't stifle at the bottom of his spirit
which still seemed bottomless the suspicion that the girl with whom
he was running the risk of being infatuated was a professional or
perhaps only semiprofessional a suspicion which from a certain
point of view was not even so offensive since she had never asserted
she wasn't and as far as sentiments went she hadn't committed herself beyond the affirmation that she liked him which meant in consequence she was ready to go to bed with anybody she found likable,
anyhow apart of course from the fee that would have to be paid
there would be cause only for rejoicing if she were a semiprofessional because that fact would strip the adventure of any extraneous
glamour and would give it the proper dimensions of a commercial

transaction which couldn't do any harm to his sublime love for Maria.

And so Antonio forced himself to find grounds for contentment in everything that might support his hypothesis or supposition that this Marika was a kind of small-time tramp though pretty as she was God knows what she would cost if she were one of those who do it for money and as usual he didn't know what to wish for since there was a positive side and a negative side to everything so it was best to trust to fate and stick to the objective facts which he had to admit led mostly to the reasonable conjecture that the girl wasn't exactly a saint or a beginner and true enough her nonchalance was remarkable and quite unlike Antonio's behavior when she headed for the upper floor passing the clerk and even the manager who for the occasion had come to the door of his office, and also amazing from Antonio's viewpoint was the lively not to say arrogant ease with which she ordered the chambermaid to provide extra towels and to bring her some good soap since arriving without baggage she didn't even have the necessities for her toilette, and there was also something abundantly experienced about the way she examined the two rooms and the bath and the bed however in this case too her behavior might be connected with her customary work if she really did work at the Magyar Hotel and therefore purchasing for once what she normally sold she wanted to be sure she was spending her money well even if the money after all was Antonio's, still it was possible there was something excessive in her behavior as if in a rather cockeyed way she wanted to show ill-humor or spite toward that all too pensive young man who had befallen her or conversely to mask disappointments and preoccupations she chose to bear alone of which Antonio had a vague hint when she went to the phone and asked for a Venice number beginning to speak in Hungarian a language which seemed to rush out at prodigious speed with words spilling one after the other and she spoke first with a sweetness which in view of her visible mood was unquestionably feigned and then with increasing harshness at the end that is to say before slamming down the receiver to break off the conversation with downright fury after which she remained sitting on the edge of the bed by the night table all flushed and breathless with her teeth clenched and for a while she avoided looking at Antonio not however out of fear of him but probably because she was absorbed in thoughts which had nothing to do with him but after a while she looked at him pityingly or rather with great pity for herself and asked him to excuse her but she had been forced to tell them at home she was spending the night with her friend at Mogliano but by ill luck her cousin Vera had answered and as usual had started preaching at her and so they had quarreled, anyhow she concluded with a shrug she didn't give a damn and she certainly didn't want to spoil her evening on that idiot's account and then she went into the bath singing softly but crossly a song in which the expressions night of love and night of passion recurred frequently and though she had left the door open as if to invite him to keep her company Antonio preferred to fling himself on the double bed and guess from the sounds what she was doing and since at a certain moment she turned on the faucet of the tub surely to take a bath it occurred to him that he should do the same to show her patriotically that the Italians are also fond of cleanliness, however it was dubious whether you could consider a girl a foreigner when she spoke Italian with great spontaneity and with the accent everybody has in Venice, still with great spontaneity she also spoke Hungarian and meanwhile the rather strange thoughts and the sounds of sloshing and faucets induced a kind of weary bitterness whereby this adventure which with one thing and another was going to cost at least twenty thousand lire lost its charm and even seemed a bit squalid indeed on closer inspection it might not appear worth experiencing even if Marika was quite beautiful though it surely wasn't beauty that counted most in matters of the sort as he knew all too well by now, in short Antonio went over and over this event which he was about to enjoy so as to prepare some remorse which at that moment could only be generic since the crime properly speaking hadn't yet been committed but it was more than enough to make Maria's memory crop up again if nothing else as a symbol of sincere and disinterested love, and though this wasn't the best moment to do it Antonio abandoned himself even excessively to that memory which among other things confirmed the fact that the void left by Maria became more impossible to fill the more he went on but having reached this point he luckily realized he was heading straight for such a state of uneasiness and desolation that if he didn't draw back as fast as he could he would end by wasting the money he had invested in the operation so it was advisable to put Maria aside once again and to concentrate on what would happen when in a short while shiny and clean Marika from the bath would enter the room a bit like Venus being born from the waves, ready and waiting in other words to perform the functions for which she had been born.

Antonio was sufficiently expert in erotic fantasies to which he often devoted himself so as to compensate somehow for the scarcity of memorable experiences and to react at least with his imagination against the melancholy of the life he had been dealt by destiny and besides this Marika's body which he could rightly imagine as solid and quite free of any fetters of chastity seemed made especially to help a man imagine himself loving it in the most fervent and extravagant fashions kissing and caressing it in every direction to extract perhaps guilty pleasures but unquestionably luscious ones, however the fact that it was now within easy reach seemed to put a largely inexplicable restraint on his imaginative faculties and indeed thinking that after her bath she was now drying that beautiful body and hearing her sing no longer crossly but with a kind of abandoned distraction night of love and night of passion Antonio instead of becoming aroused as might have been expected was gripped by a kind of fear which was basically only a sense of responsibility for what he would have to do in a few moments not moral responsibility in this case of course but so to speak technical responsibility, in short from this point of view also love was a fairly odd thing if a man let himself daydream about it for days and days and then when the moment came he felt paralyzed or at least felt such torments of the spirit as to wish for some reason or other that everything could be called off, anyhow Antonio hoped that the singing girl was sufficiently professional to help things along however even on the question of professionalism he no longer felt so reassured that is his spirit alternated wildly between the fear she might still be a virgin and the fear she had syphilis or some other disease of that sort, and the matter wasn't clarified much even after she came out of the bath wearing a large towel which however she didn't seem to want to cover herself with in any special way but simply to dry herself as was no doubt right, nor did she dedi-cate any special attention to him thank goodness that is she didn't notice his torments but seeing him still fully dressed she asked jokingly if he was waiting for her to put him to bed poor baby, thank goodness she was in a good humor and also occupied with drying herself and in fact without her paying any attention to him Antonio managed to undress rapidly and slip completely naked under the covers and from there feeling protected as if he had reached safety he could finally start examining her with some zeal or at least with the desire to have some, and certainly she had a vigorous full body with a pair of firm well-shaped thighs not heavy in their lines and her breasts too were rather robust that is fairly large and because of their very weight obviously they hung down a bit so they were also quite far from the divine perfection of Fouquet however no idea of virtue was involved here so they were all right and in conclusion from what he could tell hers was all in all a young and beautiful body which nevertheless seemed to lack something not easily defined but which might be a capacity to move him to tenderness for example and this precisely because of her solidity and vigor, anyhow it wasn't very clear and all things considered Antonio preferred to limit his attention to the girl's face which was more familiar and intelligible to him though at present not even her face was much help in understanding what sort of a girl she was or rather in the final analysis what importance she gave to the fact that in a little while she would be making love with somebody she knew barely more than by sight, it seemed she

accepted it as the most natural event in the world since she worried
only about drying herself and when she had finished she slipped
under the covers trembling and grumbling that the central heating
didn't work properly and though she seemed to overlook Antonio's
presence when he saw her there beside him in the big bed he felt
his heart pound and began to wonder whether despite all appearances her trembling with cold wasn't somehow to be interpreted as
an invitation to him to start moving with kisses and caresses to
warm her if for no other reason and still she might also seem removed in her private chill and it wasn't easy to tell whether if he
started kissing and caressing her he would be doing something
really welcome or not so even though by now he was finally full
of desire for her and was eager to do something he didn't move
waiting for a sign of encouragement which in fact came after a
while when without looking at him and even closing her eyes she
asked him what he was waiting for and Antonio thought but naturally he wasn't sure he sensed a singular emotion and who knows
perhaps even tenderness in her voice which might only be intended
to mitigate the basically brusque substance of the question, but one
way or another her asking what he was waiting for unquestionably
denoted impatience and had to be interpreted as an incitement to
act but how for God's sake when she didn't offer any indication
and lay there on her back motionless with her eyes closed her
breathing almost calm or in any case not panting with passion and in
the present uncertainty it occurred to Antonio that he might still
go take that bath he had planned for reasons of national pride above
all however when he announced this intention of going and taking
a bath with her eyes still shut she answered afterwards and evidently that was her really all too moderate way of letting him
know that she was raging with desire and that in any case she
didn't welcome further delays and being finally fit for the act Antonio fell to work but as ordinarily happens with those who haven't
great experience in amatory matters he fell to work over-hastily that
is he dropped straight to the breast and started kissing it with perhaps exaggerated and in any case artificial transport which accord-

ing to him should have left no doubts about how much he desired
her and loved her, but surprisingly she showed no signs of warm-
ing to his ardent maneuvers and erroneously assuming that her
coldness derived from the fact that the maneuvers weren't sufficiently ardent he redoubled the ardor or at least the vehemence of
the kisses until almost annoyed she pushed him away from her
breast and not mincing matters said she didn't like this business of
slobbering over her at all and she wanted to be taken as nature
meant and the way she liked best namely with her underneath and
him on top.

This surely wasn't a great mishap and yet Antonio was a bit
upset even if he couldn't clearly understand the reason for his vexa-
tion surely it wasn't pleasant for him that this girl should show so
little appreciation of the kisses other girls on the contrary had
liked very much however what mattered was to establish the
motives for her peevish revulsion which Antonio was naturally led
to blame on himself more than on her since for example he could
hardly dismiss the supposition that in love matters she was no
novice and perhaps disdained his preliminary effusions because they
weren't sufficiently refined and expert and similarly there was the
suspicion that she wanted to make love with herself underneath and
him on top which was indeed the most natural way but also the
most banal one because she judged him a poor lover or worse still
a crude one, and so just to let her know that he wasn't inexperienced
to the degree she perhaps thought he asked her with the tone of
somebody who has been around whether he should take some precautions so she wouldn't be made pregnant but she answered very
calmly that he needn't worry since she had already taken the precautions on her own account and Antonio was reassured by the
news but also curious to know what kind of precautions she had
taken or rather if she was relying only on her private calendar and
the Ogino-Knaus system or whether she used the oral pills he had
heard so much about, anyhow this fact that she provided personally
and so serenely for her fecundative immunity also confirmed the
hypothesis that she belonged to the professional ranks though if

he thought about it she didn't seem a shining example that is to say from a girl who made love a mercenary trade one could also expect more enthusiastic collaboration than what was offered by this girl who lay there with her eyes shut and apparently more concerned with thoughts of her own waiting for him to mount her, anyway by now he couldn't help but mount her and his desire to do so hadn't passed either however he did it ill-humoredly and with scorn and anger so he would really have liked to hurt her penetrating her with violence and in fact he put into the act as much force as he could but he felt himself received by such softness and warmth that his first thought was you want to bet I catch a disease since it was possible to connect the softness with abundant secretions of a blennorrhagic nature for example but still the second and immediate thought was that he didn't give a damn that is the thing was so voluptuous and extreme that nothing lay beyond it that could matter or better still nothing lay beyond it at all and in short he felt his moral sense rapidly dissolve in the most unsuitable fashion namely swept away by that force of pleasure which united him to her despite the fact that a great part of her remained outside it since her eyes were still closed and her lips clenched and her breathing only a bit more rapid than before and the whole expression of her face suggested more than anything else a form of suffering whereas instead her womb seemed to experience its pleasure on its own and almost furiously it stretched forward meeting his movements in order to be penetrated more deeply and so to enfold and draw him into mysterious and almost frightening regions and Antonio clearly understanding her sex was calling him to pour himself forth inside her labored without hesitation or delay toward his orgasm and yet he still had a stubborn desire to stir also the upper part of her to draw her into the passion with him to the breaking point and to whatever final eruptions that might involve and to achieve this he felt his only course was to redouble the frenzy and the violence of his own assaults and he did so with such furious increasing determination that at a certain point she emitted some moans perhaps of pain and that was enough to make him finally flow into her with rage and potency and triumph, and immediately thereafter with a sense of bitter perdition in the last contractions, and of precariousness and incompletion since exhausted as he was he now only wanted to let himself go in a loss or renunciation of himself which would then unite him to her in a sphere perhaps of common wretchedness and damnation however he felt blocked by the suspicion that she hadn't had her pleasure together with him and that she had remained behind isolated in a spiritual state higher perhaps and in any case colder from which she could also look down in disgust at his unseemly ejaculation, and all of a sudden it seemed so important to make sure she had her pleasure that he asked her and from a torpid and even hostile distance she answered what do you care and this was a very harsh answer under the circumstances but on thinking it over or rather on accepting the idea that she was nothing more than a little tramp whose services consisted in bringing him to orgasm without necessarily sharing it he shouldn't have cared very much but still he did care because of the bitterness of feeling alone and somehow diminished while he was still on top of her and within her having poured himself out also because of his sensation of debasing impotence since he hadn't succeeded in sweeping her off with himself like himself, in short he was in exactly the right state to perceive the squalor of his sin and he already heard from on high a voice asking Adam Adam where art thou and he surely wouldn't like to be found so dirty and exhausted in a position so related to his guilt, if nothing else he should withdraw and in fact summoning his strength he started to draw back but he had barely hinted at the movement when she surprisingly clasped her arms around his waist and said stay there in a hoarse but sweet voice which was contradicted by her behavior till then or at least what Antonio had managed to understand of it and naturally he did stay there but awkwardly and as if suspended waiting for some clarification which in fact came a little later when she reopened her eyes and almost laughing reminded him that she had already told him once before she was crazy but at the moment she felt more stupid than crazy because love was such a happy thing

and instead she managed to make it a torment anyhow to pay for
her misdeed she wanted to make love again right away happily this
time and though grateful for the request and in some ways flattered
Antonio was mostly seized by the suspicion of not being up to performing twice in a row which was an undertaking he had indeed
heard mentioned but in which he had never had the opportunity
nor felt the need to try himself, anyhow doubt was unquestionably
the most harmful emotion at this juncture in other words the more
he thought about it the less probable it was that he could do it
whereas she seemed determined to grant no intervals and had
started caressing him all over however there was also the suspicion
that she was caressing not so much with passion as with tenderness
and sweetness and therefore in a way Antonio considered generally
dangerous in the sense that by abandoning himself to rather subtle
sentiments he ran the risk of never emerging from his present state
of weakness so it was best for him to give the matter a more resolute beginning or at least to force himself to concentrate his
thoughts on sex and on the infinite pleasures to be derived from it
and he also sought help in ratiocination arguing that he had desired
this too often in vain to be able to allow himself to throw it away
now even if it was offered in such precipitous abundance, in short
he had to convince himself he could make it and he would make it
and in fact he was soon about to resume moving inside her though
without mature conviction that is little more than mechanically also
because his distrust continued that is he was always on the lookout
for some craziness or change of mood in her, and still she seemed
now totally devoted and her caresses lost a little of their previous tenderness to become more profound and expert and aimed at the most
sensitive regions of the body and also her movements while remaining harmonious had gained new energy and decision and moreover with her voice still hoarse and more voluptuous than ever she
now did nothing but repeat how beautiful and oh you're wonderful and you're driving me wild and obviously Antonio was greatly
encouraged however he also had the impression that in doing and
saying those fervid things she was trying chiefly to keep up her own

morale that is she was working hard to convince herself she was experiencing an extraordinary pleasure that in reality she didn't feel or felt only to a minimal degree, and in fact before much time had passed she stopped proclaiming her delights in a loud voice and as before she became closed in herself with lips and eyes closed in an expression which might also be one of suffering and then Antonio who after all had forced his desire to be aroused and had no intention of arriving at another solitary orgasm stopped being concerned about the reasons for the girl's eccentric behavior which made him think of physical defects or at least sexual disturbances but naturally it wasn't easy to get to the bottom of such conjectures and for that matter she didn't give him time because perhaps realizing only now that he had stopped she began to wriggle her abdomen angrily and wildly as if she intended to oppose his defection by performing alone the movements necessary to carrying the matter forward and Antonio for a while punctiliously resisted her but then he also started slamming against her angrily with all his strength determined to master or to crush her until he realized in any case she would be the stronger and so decided that by now he didn't care about anyone but himself he let himself go in a hasty and almost insipid orgasm which luckily already contained its own expiation, and then as if fearing the possibility of her holding him there for a third of those poor performances he withdrew rapidly and went into the bath with a desire for sincere purification and when he came back into the room she had already fallen asleep on her side lying across the big bed and she looked so like a little girl with her face relaxed and her mouth half open that the thought of her being filled and soiled with his seed profoundly disturbed Antonio who stood awhile to look at her imagining an absurd and ambiguous relationship between himself animated by true renunciation and her really a little girl with her freckles intact in her purity, still in this way he couldn't go back and avoid the sin which anyhow as far as he could tell was original sin itself and so he might as well think of the next morning when with fresh strength he would force her to genuine and complete pleasure but meanwhile he wanted most of all to sleep and to sleep alone so he turned out her light and went and threw himself down on the narrow bed in the other room and before falling asleep he allowed the desolation within him to spread out beyond the boundaries of the occasion until it covered the whole continuity of his life and the bitter relations between himself and others and he allowed himself to be penetrated by this vast and profound sadness until with difficult and ambivalent solace the memory of Maria emerged from it now that she was really lost forever.

CHAPTER
XIX

In which Antonio, as usual, tries

to comprehend

The fine resolution our Antonio
had made for consolatory purposes to enjoy himself in the morning
a bit better than he had managed to do the previous evening
couldn't be put into effect since when he woke up that is to say
very late as was now his habit he no longer found Marika as it
happened but a note from her which curtly explained that since
she had seen him sleeping peacefully like a little angel and hadn't
had the heart to wake him she was leaving and she begged him not
to come looking for her on the Zattere or worse still at the Magyor
Hotel but to wait and she would get in touch with him as soon as
possible, and obviously Antonio wasn't too happy at finding a note
which wasn't even very affectionate in the place of a blonde and
also beautiful girl to make love with but once he had mastered his
first disappointment or annoyance he didn't become too angry
about it in the sense that it wasn't altogether wrong that an adventure of this sort coming when his grief at losing Maria was still
fresh should finish so miserably and indeed the more his disenchant-
ment bit into him the more he squared his conscience however this
didn't prevent him from feeling a great melancholy weigh on him
not to say a great bitterness which on top of everything else he

hadn't the strength and perhaps not even the wish to fight so he took to brooding over it in the best possible manner that is by looking out of the window at the landscape which needless to say was locked in by fog not too thick however but luminous though not sufficiently to suggest that the sun would manage to break through since it was past noon already, in short what could be seen were fields without a living soul and the plowed and heavy earth and lines of hazy trees motionless probably with the white incrustations of frost which excluded them forever from any hope of spring or at least that was what Antonio thought as he concluded that the landscape in both its ideal and its realistic aspects was not basically very dissimilar from the one he could enjoy at the window of his room in Marocco with the difference that the Marocco landscape was completely free of charge whereas this one cost money and naturally making such calculations was even more dispiriting and enough to send him back to bed when a sudden association of ideas reminded him that Marika had gone off without asking to be paid unless of course she had paid herself taking from his wallet whatever was due her or she needed leaving him perhaps without the amount necessary to pay the hotel bill and though this supposition was in some respects paralyzing he rushed to examine his wallet which he had left in the rear pocket of his pants and he found she hadn't touched a cent and was of course relieved but at the same time depressed at having suspected her of such a thoughtless action, and immediately afterwards confused because if she really didn't do it for money then he had no clear idea of what his relationship to her was.

Now the opinion that this Marika was a professional or at least one of those girls who want money for making love even though they themselves enjoy it was something Antonio himself couldn't say when or how he had conceived that is he remembered clearly having thought it particularly on seeing her walk without the slightest embarrassment past hotel clerks and maids but since this specific casualness found its more than ample justification elsewhere then he must have brought the idea of Marika's professional-

ism along already in his mind in short it was a prejudice inspired
not by Marika's typical behavior but by his disbelief that he was a
youth capable of arousing spontaneous impulses in fairly attractive
girls and even more from his secret necessity to avoid confusing
Marika and Maria and so now that the false and hasty differentiation had collapsed he was rather consoled on the one hand by the
undeniably valid circumstance that he had gone to bed with Marika
and hadn't given her a cent while on the other hand he was all at
sea in the question of the girls' differences that is he felt the danger
of too great a proximity of two girls who on sober reflection seemed
to have their age and their freckles in common but not many other
qualities and in fact the sentiments he felt toward them were substantially quite dissimilar, so it was urgent and right to produce
some new diversity since the one which had previously worked so
well no longer subsisted, and for example the difference might be
that while for Maria he was or rather had been the only boy in the
world with whom she felt the desire to make love so that it was
licit to raise her to a state of restored and remote purity it would
have been absurd to attempt the same process with Marika who
was to be placed if you really wanted to be generous in the category
of the many modern girls who make love with anybody who comes
along just to keep up with the times perhaps deriving more disappointment than pleasure as far as he could see, and in short if he
reasoned calmly he couldn't possibly confuse the spheres to which
the two girls belonged so this Marika though she wasn't strictly
speaking a professional was still immersed in her condition of sin-
fulness though the condition was not sufficiently clear and was
indeed quite debatable and something he should reflect on soberly,
and to reflect better Antonio slipped under the covers in the big
bed namely the one where Marika had slept and where he redis-
covered her perfume and beyond it an undefined odor that might
also be hers that is to say of her hair and her skin and her sex and
naturally he didn't manage to reflect long because with disturbing
immediacy and violence he was reminded of how he had penetrated her the evening before or rather that effortless and unre-

strained introduction of himself into a softness that had no end or at least so it seemed to him now and of how he had lost himself there even if he had been lost there alone.

Naturally all this recollection though intense and warm remained confined to the field of sexuality and in effect he forced himself to think of Marika merely as a big body what's more without freckles and he even managed to overlook her hair which was blond and fine as a little girl's and he also erased the unfortunate fact that she was an orphan and stateless precisely in order to picture her as a firm big body to be penetrated even more deeply than he had the evening before and he imagined having her beneath him and possessing her now fully since he was much stronger than she and dominating her until he had drawn from her the deep animality of orgasm, and then lying over her exhausted and satisfied body while he still remained separated from her in perdition and in the condemnation to crawl on the ground on his belly because she wasn't Maria that is she wasn't one who could be loved with complete love, and then he couldn't restrain himself from imagining he was penetrating Maria as he had Marika no longer to create for himself a position in which he could deal with Ilario and Amalia Borghetto as an equal but to experience even for only one time a sweetness surely greater than what he had felt with Marika and infinitely fuller since Maria knew how to love to the point of orgasm that is to the moral abandonment of herself the very thing Marika couldn't or wouldn't do, and so without precisely wanting to he was destroying the defense of ideal purity which he had built up around Maria that is at the worst moment he started creating the very confusion he had previously tried obstinately to avoid mixing both girls in a sexual excitement where Maria was not at her best and in a fuller and deeper sentiment which was not Marika's due, and to obviate sacrilege he forced himself to concentrate on a painful and inhibiting thought which moreover was very handy since he couldn't forget that Maria was lost and now lost forever, however this must have been also the worst moment for such a thought because after he had imposed it on himself with some effort he was almost overcome by it and he had such a frightening sensation of diminution and of emptiness that if he didn't fill the void at once he risked being distraught in the most awful way and to fill it at present there was nothing better than imagining he was making love bringing to the act an immensity of love, and of course since it was only a matter of imagining he could quite well have imagined making love with Maria plunging however into the desperation of having lost her so he let his fantasy run riot with Marika risking the danger still of falling in love in an unsuitable manner and to an unseemly degree assigning sentiments to her that belonged to another girl, and he felt frightened since it was like going toward something wicked and punishable such as a longing to masturbate not for the precarious pleasure he could draw from it but for the squalid desolation into which he fell afterwards when he remained spent in his sin with no desire to rise again with his body or with his soul.

So it was precisely this sense of frustration that impelled him in the pursuit of a special unworthiness whose aim he didn't yet want to recognize but whose increasing torment he perceived with obscure satisfaction and masochistic desire to expand therefore he broadened the theme of his own waste until he included the vanity and error of his existence itself and then the languid torture that it wasn't true at all perhaps nothing was true in the entire world that is no more space or time in which to become concrete and exist, it was now an abyss of more total negation which attracted him but since despite everything he felt it was excessive to involve in his own refusal others who perhaps enjoyed living he contented himself as usual with a pathetic and personal desire to die a surrogate of the profounder aspiration never to have existed, all the advantages of his own nonexistence were now clear to him such as absence above all of uncertainty and of grief however they were obviously unattainable inasmuch as he now existed and thus while he waited for this desired conclusion he had best adapt himself somehow to the misfortune of being obliged to live in a condition which was also humble and disagreeable and one which would have been absurd even if it had been possible to think of uniting himself to a noble and also nobly situated creature like Maria, and discovering then even if indirectly an equality and almost an affinity with Marika which he had been unable to have with Maria of course he somehow gained the right to summon Marika to unite with him in their common calamities no longer merely as a body but now also with freckles and fine hair and the pathetic look of a stateless orphan, but also as a body of course wherein to seek profundity of pleasure and who knows perhaps also profundity of protection but where first of all he had to discover what was confused and perhaps sick, probably however sick more in soul than in body and far from dismaying him this was what attracted him with the greatest strength because it required also spiritual penetration to cure her or at worst to involve himself in her hidden illness to a limitless extent since he had nothing to lose because he himself was nothing, so it wasn't clear whether he was being stimulated toward perdition or redemption by thus considering Marika in neither temporary nor superficial terms the fact however remained that he also felt ardently prepared to renounce possessing her body provided he was allowed to love her a bit like Jesus used to love the women who followed him around Galilee, but taking into account the poverty and instability of his own strength and the attitude Marika had manifested thus far such a spiritual development was not highly probable so progress finally consisted in his deciding to make love with her more completely than it had been possible to do and also without remorse or even the goading thought that he was wronging Maria.

Now it isn't that our Antonio in all these twisting tormented thoughts and second thoughts felt completely in the right or free from the suspicion that by yanking his thoughts this way and that he might rid himself a bit too quickly of Maria and the numerous burdens of conscience connected with her, however he was almost automatically achieving a kind of providential split of his personality thus having to one side a Maria who could always be maintained in a higher sphere where nothing would touch her and on the other hand a second historically accurate Maria whose conduct at present might also seem to him less irreproachable than it had seemed formerly in the sense that it wasn't really hard to discover in this Maria weaknesses and errors which had been fundamental to the unhappy progress of the affair for instance just to name one a certain lack of resolution since though it was true that she had several times declared herself ready to flee with him anywhere he liked it was equally true that she hadn't made this declaration on the proper occasion so it might be supposed that when she said she wanted to run away it was one of those slightly too extreme resolutions which when the cards were down proved worthless and in fact he would have liked to see what would have happened if he had taken her at her word at some point and had proposed fleeing to Marocco not because he liked Marocco of course but because after all he had no other place to flee to, in short it would have been better if instead of these heroic plans she had produced more down-to-earth ideas for example to keep the affair secret as long as possible instead of spilling it in haste to her parents whom he had clearly never shown any desire to know not even by sight and whom with a minimum of common sense she would never have involved given their nature, anyhow in thinking that if Maria had been an orphan like Marika and perhaps also stateless things would have turned out very differently he didn't mean to reproach in any way the unhappy girl who surely had suffered more than he from the disaster and perhaps was still suffering though it was also legitimate to suppose that since she was unquestionably a bit submissive family pressures had probably oriented her by now toward some urgent and profitable engagement which would make her forget the past so it wasn't then entirely wrong to decide that on the practical level he could now tend to his own business without worrying too much about anything else provided of course that the story's ideal values were saved which in Antonio's view were not only saved but also more active than ever in the sense that they had increased the store of his humiliations from which sooner or later his only possible form of revenge would spring forth namely art.

So our hero allowing himself to be seduced more than anything else by Marika's perfume lingering in the bed came to a conclusion we can't call very consoling or even loyal deciding that it wasn't right to remain bound by eternal regret to a girl who after all hadn't done enough to remain bound to him so now he could think about getting on with life putting a bit more desire for living with his great desire for dying a concept which meant bluntly he felt ready to launch himself on a new adventure with that minimum of sentimental involvement which seemed indispensable for making love with some satisfaction, however the two stories the one barely ended and the other not yet begun would perforce be of a different order since he certainly was not now setting out with illusions of souls seeking each other forever in the infinity of the worlds to be joined finally in a dream of eternity but rather he moved from the ac-knowledgment of human precariousness and decay, and perhaps it wasn't beautiful to begin a story in that way but obviously there was no better way to begin one on this earth where evil was so great and omnipresent that two people couldn't love in hope but only in defense, therefore he and Marika were simply two people who decided to travel together for a certain span of existence surely not interminable being united more in wretchedness than in hap-piness and yet granting each other such reciprocal comfort in their wretchedness as mortals are able to grant, namely by making love with the greatest possible frequency and the greatest possible enjoy-ment.

CHAPTER
XX

In which Antonio still doesn't understand

very much

Antonio's decision to start loving Marika in a sensible and insofar as possible enjoyable manner came up against a big obstacle in that she had practically disappeared forbidding him to look for her where he would have been most likely to find her a fact which led him to consider that though an orphan she might nevertheless have relatives or at least other people eager to stick their noses protectively into her affairs and Antonio still fairly distraught by his encounters with the persons concerned with Maria's fate didn't want to run even a remote risk of meeting those who might worry about Marika's fate so prudent counsel prompted him to bide his time patiently until she got in touch with him spontaneously as she had promised however waiting was also irksome since he couldn't forget that Marika by her own definition was rather crazy and so there was the possibility she might take say a week or even more before getting in touch and a week from Antonio's point of view was a very long period of time and not only for the good reason that when a young man has decided to make love with a sufficiently desirable girl the hours that delay the event seem never to pass but also because he was confident though with slight basis for confidence that the beginning of a harmonious relationship with Marika would rouse him from that state of inertia into which he had fallen with the beginning of the misfortunes connected with Maria or even before if he thought about it, and naturally he was the first to lament such a protracted loss of time however he was also aware that it would have been senseless to think of studying or still less of writing with his mind constantly occupied either by plans of what he would do when Marika had finally got in touch or by the memories of the story with Maria for though in a moment of special coherence he had realized the story was best put behind him nevertheless his memories seized the slightest opportunity almost slyly to reappear.

Obviously this couldn't have happened even slyly if there hadn't been a minimum of indulgence on the part of our Antonio that is if he hadn't opposed a quite inadequate resistance to the memories which tended to reappear and on the other hand it was also possible to find good excuses for this indulgence since it surely wasn't easy to sit dreaming twenty-four hours a day of a beloved who never turned up and not feel toward her a slight resentment which then sought its natural counterweight in the memories of another love which though admittedly only in the early phase had furnished great satisfactions, moreover Antonio didn't consider his meeting with Marika the decisive event of his life and still less did he feel that beyond the foreseen and fore-enjoyed amorous pleasures he needn't expect also a due amount of nuisances and troubles which it was best not to think about too thoroughly or foresightedly and certainly there was no more suitable way to avoid contemplating future troubles than by contemplating past ones which at least were past and therefore likely to grow faint in the caldron of diffuse sadness that is to say in that atmosphere of bitterness in which Antonio felt more protected from the blows that destiny somewhat inexplicably but persistently rained down on him, and obviously also his habitual and generic attitude of pessimism toward anything that might happen favored his taking refuge in the past however painful and besides once he had accepted the definitive loss of Maria as he had in fact accepted it afterwards thinking of her involved no particular responsibility or impulse to reconstruction and so he was more free from woes than one might imagine and this encouraged a certain resignation and certain sensations of confusion which Antonio had always been even too fond of because they led him to a downright beneficial spiritual relaxation when you think what he might have been otherwise, and in fact at present his inattention was such that he not infrequently attributed to Maria some feeling or expression that had instead been Marika's and vice versa and this not so much because he was mixing up the virtues and faults of each as because in his general view of life at the present delicate impasse the future often appeared to him only as a series of events through which he would pay for past errors accumulating also some new ones so from a certain point of view one girl was worth as much as the other since each was merely an illusory means of escaping an ungrateful lot which fate had meted out to him by making him come into the world at the wrong time and in the wrong place and above all in the wrong family.

Now it's not as if everything were perfectly logical in the line of reasoning followed by poor Antonio whose condition certainly didn't foster orderly marshaling of thoughts however among the many foolish thoughts he harbored in those hard days his malevolence toward his family was perhaps the least ill-founded not only because he could fairly reasonably blame his lack of patrimony for his misfortunes with the Borghettos but also because his father and his sad sister did nothing but demonstrate luckily more with silence than with words their disapproval of his conduct taking not the least trouble to grasp its determining causes which they would have been incapable of grasping anyhow, and he surely didn't need others to point out or underline the fact that he was throwing away his days unprofitably and it grated on his nerves to hear his father proclaim that somebody would soon regret spending his days at the tavern and his nights God knew where also because Antonio had spent only one night out of the house after his return to his family at Christmas, and he was even more irritated when the disapproval touched a really sore spot for example if his father started grumbling that somebody would soon be in direst poverty since he was behaving like the grasshopper and not like the ant and after having had the fine idea of giving up his steady job at the local school he was squandering his inheritance with cards and orgies, in short Antonio's home didn't offer him that comfort a home should offer anyone no matter how prodigal and sinful and so immediately after the visit of the postman who he felt might bring him any day the letter through which Marika would finally get in touch with him he hastened to leave the paternal roof and went off walking around the countryside looking for the rare signs of spring and when the weather didn't encourage excursions in the fields he went straight to play cards at the tavern next to the bus stop and when he noticed the arrival of a bus he examined the people arriving to see if by chance Marika instead of getting in touch by letter had decided to turn up in person.

However he himself understood that it was feckless to hope she would turn up point-blank on the Number Eight instead of announcing her arrival first by mail and so it was the post that he awaited with greatest anxiety even going to meet the postman partly to gain time and partly to shield from family curiosity the possible missive which nevertheless was delayed beyond what was right and predictable, anyhow a full week hadn't passed after the questionable night of love at the Park Hotel dei Dogi when the postman handed him a letter which however wasn't from Marika but from someone who signed himself a devoted friend and being devoted to Antonio the friend wanted to inform him that it was idiotic to trust Marika or worse to fall in love with her since the poor Hungarian refugee was nothing more nor less than a whore and a liar and among other things what she constantly asserted to give herself airs wasn't sure by any means namely that her father had been a hero of the revolution in Budapest and had given his life since her mother had also been a woman of easy virtue and nobody could tell exactly who Marika's father had been and as far as the girl's other defects went Antonio's unknown informer listed with their full names about ten certified lovers who divided into professional categories were three students of business administration three students of architecture a student of the Academy of Fine Arts two insurance agents a waiter at Quadri's married with children and a basso who sang at the Fenice, and when Antonio had reached the end of the letter he was more upset by having received an anonymous letter than by anything else though it was fairly depressing after all to read that detailed list of men who had gained notoriety by having had carnal traffic with the poor orphan, but as to the simple fact that she was no good he learned this as if it were the most obvious thing in the world and he was even delighted or at least aroused in a not entirely unpleasant and somewhat liberating fashion, that is to say thank heaven she was a whore as for that matter he had believed all along because from now on he would treat her as such and for a start he would promptly end the ridiculous and interminable waiting to which she had condemned him and would go straight to look for her exactly where she had ordered him not to go and so much the better if he were to catch her at it namely with one of the ten listed lovers or with an eleventh or twelfth since at this point he couldn't see why there should be only ten, in any case if these characters numbered a dozen or more or less he would be happy to meet any one of them face to face though it wasn't clear what he would have done if the incident had actually occurred, anyhow deciding to think it over along the way he ran to catch the first bus to Venice and naturally during the journey brief as it was the happiness or excitement of his spirit or whatever it was became slightly deflated in fact even before the bus had passed Mestre and the industrial zone of Marghera it was deflated completely dissolving into a generic self-pity which though centered on the circumstance that he basically had no rights over Marika and on the contrary should be grateful to her for the couple of amatory exercises she had let him perform without any disbursal extended to include all his habitual reasons for feeling ill-starred and so he crossed the whole Venice causeway with his face stuck to the window pretending to be interested in a wan lagoon inhabited by a few desperate gulls but in reality trying to conceal the grimaces he was making in his effort not to cry in a bus though he had more than enough reasons for crying there or elsewhere since it would have been hard to discover on the face of the earth a more unhappy creature than he, however the detail that Marika was a whore touched this unhappiness only marginally as an accessory motive more than anything else and he had almost lost his desire to go look for her and in fact on reaching the Piazzale Roma he was sorely tempted to go straight back to Marocco without even getting off the bus however what would he have done at Marocco he asked himself what would he do there as Marocco could hardly be called a place of special solace for the unhappy so he might as well take a little stroll in Venice until he had got rid of the lump which as long as it stayed in his throat threatened to make him burst into tears any minute.

Naturally as he now lacked a specific destination Antonio chose a direction at random joining one of those streams of people who in Venice move among the tangled streets and taking advantage of the opportunity the city offers to walk with your head completely plunged in sorrows or in joys even exceptional ones without the risk of being run over by an automobile he paid no attention to where he was walking but only to brooding on his sorrows and it was strange he didn't give a thought to Maria at that juncture since the memory of Maria always popped into his mind at his unhappiest moments and you certainly couldn't say that the present moment wasn't sufficiently unhappy however the thought of Maria even if absent from his conscious mind must have been quite active in his unconscious because instead of for example joining the stream going from the Piazzale Roma toward San Simeone Piccolo and the station or the other stream which was heading roughly for the Campo Santa Margherita and the Carmini he joined the one that went along San Pantaleone toward the Rialto and so after he had passed the Salizada San Pantaleone and the long street called Crosera he came out at the end of the Calle Larga Foscari right at the point where the Calle di Donna Onesta begins and there without his expecting her Maria burst upon him clearly and violently just as she had looked that first day they met with her innocence and her uneasiness and uncontaminated charm not yet daughter of Cavalier Borghetto of Maritime Supplies, oh it was at this very spot that they had called each other tu and she had immediately run off and he hadn't yet known who she was or what her name was and he was now tempted to imagine what would have happened if he hadn't followed her and they had never seen each other again but he felt this wouldn't have been right and perhaps not even possible in other words even after things had gone so badly he could find in the sorrows that had befallen him with Maria a quality of necessity perhaps even in the finalistic sense whereas in his sorrows with Marika there was only dismaying uselessness and lack of propriety, and once he had established this fundamental difference his spirit was eager to suffer in the loftiest and worthiest way for example by seeking in the courtyard of the Ca' Foscari which for that matter was only a step away the wall where they had leaned and exchanged their first kiss that terribly rainy evening the day after their meeting and the wall was there naturally the same as then or rather not the same without her because that evening she had been there and it was the first time she let herself be kissed by anyone deciding at that very moment to give him all that was hers to give and who knows if she would have repeated the same experience if possible heedless of errors and suffering he would surely have repeated it if it had been possible even at the cost of suffering infinitely more, and so as if made more meritorious by this fine aspiration he headed for the large hall where groups of students visible through the plate glass were standing and chatting perhaps between lessons and naturally he hadn't the slightest idea of finding Maria there instead he was certain she couldn't be there almost as if she were denied the faculty of existing in a place where he could find her, so he wasn't going to look for her but simply for some information about her and he moved from one group to another asking if anybody was in the second-year English course until they pointed out a girl in a group and he went to ask her if by any chance during these past few days she had seen a girl in the second year named Maria Borghetto and this girl answered that Borghetto hadn't shown up at classes since before Christmas and she had heard that she was sick and Antonio didn't know whether he should grieve or rejoice at this news which could obviously make him both sad and happy anyhow before he came to a decision in the matter another girl spoke up and said Borghetto wasn't sick at all but was happily skiing at Cortina where she had been seen by a number of mutual friends.

Although this was also news which might make one happy or sad to varying degrees Antonio felt suddenly saddened by it in fact he took it as a personal insult since at the very moment when he had scaled the greatest heights in loving her with purity and generosity and self-sacrifice there was Maria apparently spending the peak of the winter season at Cortina d'Ampezzo namely a place where it wasn't very probable one could suffer at length or deeply the pains of love, and naturally it wasn't that Maria couldn't go off wherever she pleased but even conceding that she really needed to ski or to breathe fresh mountain air or to restore her spirits a bit after the disasters she had undergone she could just as easily have gone to Asiago for example or Cansiglio or Nevegal that is to alpine or even subalpine localities less frivolous than Cortina where according to reports corruption was the fashion, and obviously Maria being his no longer could if she liked become as corrupt as she pleased however he also was entitled to be saddened by it and in a sense to be offended and even to take refuge out of pique in the thought of other women, and obviously there was one all ready whose name besides was not very different from Maria who was, true enough, connected with other sorrows however these new ones were at least of a sort that with a bit of effort could be faced and fought and in fact Antonio resolved to do exactly that and he abandoned both Maria's memory and the noisy hall which he suddenly found unbearably irritating and he set out to look for Marika on the Zattere or possibly even at the Magyar Hotel at San Gregorio only a few steps from the Zattere, but no matter how much he wandered back and forth between the Zattere and San Gregorio for all the rest of the afternoon he couldn't catch a glimpse of

Marika in one place or the other in fact there wasn't a living soul now on the terraces of the various cafés of the Zattere because it was damp and cold and as for the desk of the Magyar Hotel when he passed along the street in front of it he could see an angular no longer young girl there whom it was possible to identify as the disagreeable cousin Vera and in all likelihood it was she who when Antonio decided to telephone from the nearest café and ask for Marika answered with considerable rudeness that Marika wasn't in and wouldn't be coming back for supper.

And so nothing remained for our Antonio to do but go back to Marocco where on top of everything else he would now arrive too late for the evening meal but he wanted to make it even later so that on his arrival he would find his family firmly settled before the television set and could avoid the inquiring glances and the more or less mute reproaches and the apologues on the vices of grasshoppers and the virtues of ants, so it was best for him to go on foot to the Piazzale Roma taking a long way round by Santo Stefano and the Rialto and Santi Apostoli but this longer way was not only to kill time but more to avoid the normal itinerary which would have led him past too many places connected with his story with Maria since in the vast quadrilateral between the Zattere and the Harbor Station and between San Polo and the Tre Ponti there was no street or square or passage or bridge where they hadn't at least kissed exchanging abundant vows of undying love so it was better to stay away from all that because as he had gone up and down the Zattere the lump produced by the anonymous letter and that other even greater lump caused by the news that Maria was happily skiing at Cortina had been gradually reabsorbed in the general and habitual sadness with which it was wisest for him to content himself so to speak keeping as clear as possible not only of regrets or remorse concerning the past but also above all of hopes and plans concerning the future since he felt that as the past had also been liquidated in such a sad way he had to be on guard also against the future resigning himself precisely to a policy of static ordinary suffering although this involved the anticipated acceptance of several large afflictions as for example the uselessness of existence which was not after all so difficult to accept since now it would have been very arduous to find any sort of reason to justify his appearance in the world, or to give another example his irreducible solitude which in a sense was a consequence of the uselessness of existence unless of course it was its cause, in any case the lesser evil seemed to be to resign himself even though this solution was very mean and to remain quietly in fruitless solitude or in solitary fruitlessness since his attempts to get out of it had released that excess of sufferings which had fallen on him in recent times, and therefore if deceiving oneself with the hope of avoiding ills caused only disappointment that is ruinous plunges into worse ills then it was better to keep far away from any opportunity of deceiving himself and indeed turn his back on such opportunities before they took shape since he certainly wasn't the type to elude tribulations and disasters the minute it was possible not to elude them, in short he was coming to terms and adapting himself to the unhappy condition that was his own without trying to evade it in any way and with this practical and sensible idea well established in his mind he reached home at almost ten o'clock but before crossing the threshold he saw that the extraordinary adventures of his intense day were not yet ended indeed it seemed they had barely begun since on casting his usual prudent glance through the window at the family atmosphere instead of seeing the corner of the cleared table with his plate of soup left there kept warm with another plate turned upside down over it he saw his gruff father and his sad sister still seated at their places however the former didn't seem gruff and the latter didn't seem sad because opposite them blonde and beautiful and at least apparently filled with gaiety was sitting the orphan Marika.

Now this outlandish sight wasn't surely an event Antonio could logically have expected though the expression get in touch which she had used in her farewell note could also quite legitimately cover the ineffable little picture he had before his eyes however it took surely a good measure of impudence on the part of this Marika to present herself directly at his house especially if there was any truth in the information of the anonymous friend according to whom she was of the easiest virtue still at the present moment he didn't feel particularly inclined to give full credence to an anonymous letter an unquestionably base and ambiguous means of information also because when observed through the window of his home the blonde foreigner seemed really an ordinary young and beautiful girl in moral as well as physical health and indubitably exploiting such a favorable appearance she had succeeded in winning the affection both of his sister who was listening to her all intent and obliging and above all his father who had brought out a bottle of grappa with herbs reserved for the happiest occasions and now each had a little glass of this cherished grappa before him and they were drinking it in little sips conversing meanwhile with a liveliness and a good humor so unusual in his home that Antonio was even a little piqued as it was clear this happened not only in his absence but precisely because of his absence, that is if he had been in they surely wouldn't have created that atmosphere of festive brotherhood and he almost felt like going in to see whether his presence wouldn't immediately ruin the atmosphere but experience had already sufficiently taught him how wise it was to leave families out of all matters of love so he had best wait outside for her to make up her mind to say good-bye unless of course she chose instead to spend the whole night there which would have been quite easy since from what he could see through the window both his father and his sister had been won over by the fascination and we may also say the cleverness of the young adventuress and would no doubt have given her one of their own beds if she had wanted it, certainly as she was involved there had to be some scheme behind this some murky purpose which might also be to trap him into a kind of official engagement or at least a relationship recognized by his family which though it wasn't much of a family was still the only one available under the circumstances since she had been without one perhaps since birth, that was then the intention and target of her incredible visit to become an honest woman again at the expense of people humble if you like but respectable after all and simple even too simple seeing how they let themselves be ensnared by chatter and smiles and theatrical looks, he in any case would not go along with this dirty little game which anyone with a head on his shoulders would give a wide berth and in fact he started walking fairly far from the house along the road to the bus stop also irritated because he had actually done nothing but go back and forth all day long and he certainly had no need of more walking especially since he had also skipped his midday meal in his agitation after reading the anonymous letter and now he felt a terrible hunger and perhaps more than jealousy at the welcome given Marika it was the knowledge of his right to the unattainable bowl of soup that made him very painfully aware of his true solitude which dated back at least to the time when his mother had died and he now thought he could feel with disturbing immediacy and as a kind of ideal abstraction like something in an elementary reader the beauty of being surrounded by affection and family warmth and naturally this wasn't the moment to let himself be moved by facile sentimental fictions however he couldn't help being aware that this different and more joyous manner both in his father and in his sister which had never been shown him was instead lavished on a stranger who turned up for the first time, and though he didn't in the least regard her as a rival for his family affections since he clearly cared less than nothing now for these affections it was nevertheless annoying that she should enjoy the same easy success with his family she had achieved with him and what's more with not entirely untainted aims considering her past, therefore he was eager for her to come out so he could confront her in the way she most deserved but she seemed to be in no hurry to leave that hospitable home and meanwhile he was forced to remain out there in the cold and the damp where thank God a bit of wind had shifted the fog and now the moon was even shining in the sky not very limpid however sufficiently luminous and the wind wasn't exactly the icy one from the north or the east but another that probably came from the south and brought a hint of distant lands and presentiments however unstable of spring that is of events at least

meteorologically happier, anyhow he wouldn't let himself be influenced by that to the point of feeling more compassion than rancor
toward a person who was deceitfully trying to insinuate herself into
his home and trap him in a situation from which he would then
have a hard time extricating himself if he did manage to extricate
himself, in short the astute refugee certainly wasn't worthy of any
indulgence and to begin with he would throw those ten lovers in
her face whose names and professions he now knew by heart, now
he had every right to demand an explanation of them seeing that
she was plotting a family arrangement entirely to his damage and
deception and so when she finally did come out followed from the
house by ample displays of affection and warm invitations to come
back soon he hid behind the trunk of a plane tree on the road fully
determined to do something but not having yet decided what was
to be done or in other words placing himself precisely in the best
position to behave in the worst possible way, and in fact as soon as
the poor thing had come within convenient range he suddenly appeared from his hiding place and not recognizing him at that moment she was uncertain and almost ready to scream as in a murder
story when he gave her a violent slap on the right cheek simultaneously calling her tramp, and having reached this point our hero
was already aware of the ridiculous situation into which he had
driven himself that is he had chiefly the impression he was on a
stage playing *Camille* or even singing *La Traviata* however understanding you are caught in a laughable mess doesn't mean seeing
also the way to get out of it indeed it seemed the only way out was
to press forward and so he placed the anonymous letter in her hand
and peremptorily commanded her to read it but naturally even if
she had wanted to read it she couldn't have since the nearest light
was too far away so still maintaining the operatic atmosphere and
his tone of outraged dignity he proclaimed that there it was written
that she had ten lovers at the very least and he asked her if this was
true assuming of course that she would in any case answer no and
instead she answered with a sentence she had also pronounced
once before namely what do you care but putting into it if possible

even more dejection and shame than the first time and still denying nothing or rather denying him the right to intrude into her private affairs and at this point Antonio understood only one thing namely that he had to behave like a man giving her presumably another couple of slaps and then striding off the stage forever, but apart from the fact that keeping up this theatrical tone was a bit in contrast with his tastes and convictions he didn't feel he had the strength to do what he had in mind because in the uncertain light of the distant lamp she seemed rigid and offended and extraordinarily beautiful my God it was easy to imagine striding off the stage forever but he didn't want to lose her and then finally his not wanting to lose her was a fixed point in the mass of his foolish actions and so he told her he didn't care if she had not ten but a hundred lovers maybe all at once however he wanted to find out from her and not from a coward who made accusations hiding in anonymity, and there was such eagerness for compromise and forgiveness in his words and in his way of saying them that she took the letter and looked at it holding it toward the distant light and though little or nothing could be seen she immediately affirmed with anger and bitterness that her cousin Vera had written it, and though Antonio had made a thousand suppositions he had never thought of that and even now it didn't seem very logical to him so he asked her what made her think that but she didn't answer and stood there angrily not saying anything until from a jerking movement of her shoulders and then from interminable sobs he realized she was crying and then after she had let herself go and wept for a while she began saying Vera was envious and wicked because when something nice happened to her Vera always tried to spoil it and she couldn't bear being a slave in that hotel any more in fact she couldn't bear to go on living because all the misfortunes in the world happened to her and Antonio who knew this sort of feeling only too well was now slipping dangerously toward compassion however it seemed right for him to ask at least one more thing namely why Vera behaved so cruelly and Marika still sobbing said that Vera wasn't so wicked as she was crazy or not normal anyway

because she played Vivaldi records and the music aroused her so
that she masturbated, and at this point Antonio again didn't know
what to think that is he would have liked to know how Marika
had found out about her cousin's disturbing musical tastes and then
how this cousin had learned his name and address and above all if
it was conceivable that she could invent a complete list of ten lovers
with full name and profession, however as he was developing all
this curiosity he was also thinking how strangely other people lived
masturbating while they listened to Vivaldi and oddly enough he
didn't feel any great repugnance toward that masturbation but only
distress because the girl who indulged in such practices instead of
being beautiful was disagreeable and angular anyhow on examining the muddle more profoundly his dominant feeling was not this
but a boundless pity for Marika who was not speaking now but
hanging her head and sobbing quietly the way children do when
they've forgotten what they're crying about and so he recalled viv-
idly the sight of her asleep like a child in fact at the Park Hotel dei
Dogi all relaxed with her mouth half open and her fine hair scattered over the pillow so from the great rage of sentiments of a
moment before nothing waas left but tenderness and a completely
Christian desire to ask no further explanations of her but to keep
her as she was since in her heart there could only be innocence or
whatever else there was it would be something that could be overcome with charity and love, so this was just the right moment to
make her forgive him for his foolish excessive violence touching her
face gently to free the fine hair stuck to it by her tears and telling
her at the same time not to cry please to stop crying because he
couldn't bear to see her so downcast in this way especially since it
was his fault and if she went on crying it meant she would never
forgive him, and then though she did go on crying for a little while
she obediently raised her face where even in the faint light it was
possible to see her mouth wet and open and lascivious, in all her
face only that mouth seemed to assume a form which wanted to be
kissed God how strongly it asked him to kiss it as complelely and
profoundly as was possible, and obviously he couldn't help kissing

her even though he had the impression it was premature that is he would have preferred to dwell a bit on that charity and tenderness which alone could give a reason to all the rest from his point of view and instead her final tears were already mixed with a kind of frenzy to act fast and she was no longer content with being kissed and kissing but having opened his overcoat and jacket she clasped him or rather clutched him furiously all over with her hands soon heading straight for his sex heedless of modesty or obstacles wanting to reach it without waste of time and Antonio caught off guard by the great rapidity with which apparently contradictory things were following one another didn't know exactly how to behave though in his doubt he still felt obliged to do something too and he began to caress her trying to move under her skirt toward her sex but she promptly and even a bit roughly told him please to keep still however she wasn't still and at this point it was all too clear that she wanted to give him an orgasm there in the road and she also proved fairly expert in doing it that is she was caressing him with sufficient gentleness and speed of movement and though deeply upset by her refusal he was no longer in condition to refuse himself and for God's sake why should he refuse a pleasure he now felt rising from every part of his body as her mouth glued to his ear kept whispering with mounting agitation tell me you like it tell me you're enjoying it, and he obviously was enjoying it but in a kind of furious confusion where pleasure was mingled with rancor and dismay at his own submission and malleability and weakness, and a sense of impotence at his own animality and bitterness in the presentiment that she would leave him alone in the headlong dismissal from paradise, and the cruel conviction now that perhaps the ten lovers listed in the letter were too few because there was no telling how many men she must have serviced in the way she was doing and even the thought of her cousin Vera who masturbated to records cropped up as the only possible hope that is the sharing a common indignity from which she still wanted to remain somehow excluded though wanting to flay herself in other ways as far as he could understand, and in addition a chaos of other thoughts that rapidly assumed value but no meaning and tore him with sudden flashes of intelligence and power or remained absolutely incomprehensible or unbearable so now what was the importance of struggling to understand much better to abandon his last foothold and let himself go and she perceived also this final temptation or resistance of his and tried to favor it and conquer it accelerating her movements and whispering raving words into his ear come oh please come quickly and with weakness and invocation and terror and confusion he struggled still against the pleasure as long as he could and then in the end he decided there was no sense in struggling and he let himself go with disintegration and furor to the orgasm staring into a new abyss of life while she with her mouth in his ear gasped and moaned as if she were enjoying his pleasure with the same angry intensity and this was more than he could bear now that he was driven from paradise mortified and exhausted so he said that if she didn't want to miss the last bus for Venice they had better start walking and head without delay for the stop.

So they set off toward the distant lights of the highway he at her side on the very brink of total dejection that is fairly close to the perception and acceptance of a single mystery which was the common wretchedness of toiling after forms of vanity beyond which degradation and ignominy lay on the borderline with death or probably with something worse like an eternal chain of sin and repentance, and if he had reached such a general understanding of the problem it would certainly have been a good thing because his quite unjust feeling now was great rancor toward Marika as if she had been the essence of evil that is solely responsible for his wasted pleasure and the abjection that had derived from it and she really might have been solely responsible but then it would have been more reasonable to descend into her obscurity to seek the roots of a disease or at least a way of being that once known perhaps wouldn't have been so hostile and frightful and which in any case could have been accepted with a little love but it was precisely love that he felt lacking in him now as if he had spent it all in the wretchedness of his orgasm of a moment before and then nothing had remained to him but intolerance and the wish for her to go away as soon as possible leaving him to face a bitterness that he wanted to be his alone, however he also wanted to release that rancor aggressively against her and not to heal but to wound her and so at a certain moment he asked her what pleasure she took in procuring in this or in other ways orgasms in which she didn't share and she answered harshly that as far as she could tell he must have enjoyed it all the same so he was to leave her in peace or if he preferred he could go on home since she could get to Venice by herself, but later while they were at the stop waiting for the bus which seemed never to come she spontaneously resumed the subject saying with humility that what happened to her wasn't her fault and naturally she was the first to suffer from it but perhaps there was something wrong with her or else the misfortunes of life had already ruined her anyhow the fact was that when she made love she felt a kind of great warmth inside which couldn't come out because she never managed to have an orgasm and therefore she was seized by this kind of rage to make others enjoy it still she didn't think she was hurting people that way on the contrary, in any case if he had been hurt she was sorry she could only apologize to him and as for the rest it meant that they would never see each other again and Antonio hearing her speak like this was already regretting his unjust bitterness toward her and shifting his mood he felt he loved her now as perhaps no one had ever loved her that is with such transport as to be able to sweep her into complete love where in the end she too would find ultimate pleasure and perdition, now he wanted her not to go to Venice any more but to spend the whole night with him so he could love her in a way she surely had never experienced before and she was clearly tempted and wasn't lying when she said she would have gladly stayed with him to make love all night the way he promised but it was impossible she absolutely had to go home, and it was strange she should feel this obligation so strongly since she surely didn't like it however she did feel it so Antonio couldn't budge her from her decision and when the bus was already in sight and they had only a few moments left she told him three times in a row that she loved him so much and she also said rather incongruously that she was in despair at loving him so much and in any case if he wanted to tomorrow night they could be together all he had to do was come to the Magyar Hotel at ten in the evening but not before ten.

CHAPTER
XXI

In which Antonio, after giving
the situation much thought, comes to
an important decision

After the bus with Marika making hasty gestures of good-bye at the back window had disappeared beyond the curve with a long sound of tires Antonio instead of feeling dispirited or even only puzzled as would have been right or at least suitable for once remained quite strangely filled with a vague sensation of triumph and satisfaction which he hadn't the desire or probably the strength to oppose though he knew very well it hadn't genuine grounds since it was based on factors of a more sentimental than rational nature and this was diametrically opposed to the sage resolution he had made that very afternoon to be content with what was and not to indulge in unfounded hopes or in the illusion that something new and at the same time beneficent could happen to him of all people and in effect his pleasant excitement wasn't occasioned by the fairly valid circumstance that Marika had promised him a complete night of real love but rather by the much vaster but entirely hazy and not at all solid impression that he was so to speak only a step away from happiness and that it was enough somehow to want it and he could even enter into that state permanently.

Now Antonio was quite aware of how dangerous this could be in the sense that he risked coming a cropper immediately and for a second time in an amorous misadventure which moreover was being born under far more worrisome auspices than the first, but he so rarely felt in the vicinity of any kind of happiness that it was forgivable for him to grant himself some leeway and also when it came to contentment he was accustomed to speak of it to himself as if it were a sorrow that would soon pass or dissolve even before turning into concrete facts and precise events so it really wasn't worth the effort to spoil it even more prematurely by attempting a slightly deeper and naturally destructive analysis also because he didn't want at this moment to admit the concomitance of external and occasional factors in the formation of his precious even if precarious sensation about Marika that is he was annoyed at recognizing that in this matter too as always Maria was involved though in a very complicated and even contradictory fashion because no one and himself least of all could have detached in his spirit the desire to wreak just revenge on her for having gone skiing at Cortina from the exactly opposite desire to seek new and perhaps more tormenting catastrophes with which to punish himself for the guilt of having lost her.

Still from whatever direction it was born or nourished this surrender to optimism once begun became progressive and in fact as he now walked toward home and dwelt also on absolutely extraneous circumstances like the fact that the moon was almost full or that the sirocco hinted at a probable spring Antonio took refuge in exaltation to elude reality that is he couldn't stop remembering how before climbing into the bus Marika has said fully three times and with unquestionable agitation that she loved him so very much and obviously such a spontaneous and confirmed sentiment of love seemed designed purposely to create the impression that he was only a step away from happiness especially if he gave up for the moment the idea of defining happiness or better defining the step still to be taken in order to enter that state and settle there, and these hesitations were unfortunately inevitable as Antonio still harbored a number of resentments even if subterranean ones since for example despite his fervor his mind hadn't lost certain doubts which moreover could only benevolently be called doubts since Marika had not provided an answer to his question whether the ten lovers listed by the self-styled friend male or female of the anonymous letter were real or invented, or rather she had given an answer and it had been mind your own business or an analogous expression which without denying the existence of the ten lovers aimed at denying him any inherent concern with them, in any case that had happened before the triple declaration of love which obviously had changed everything at least in the sense that even a girl who had had ten lovers might still be capable of offering true or genuine love as had been demonstrated for that matter by numerous literary masterpieces, and for the rest what would really have been serious and unpardonable in this case would have been falsehood and she hadn't in the least lied thank heaven since she had made an admission even if an indirect one telling how her mysterious difficulty in achieving orgasm gave her a kind of furious longing to make others enjoy sex and how many of these others there were or rather had been couldn't be established with the information Antonio had at his disposal however it wasn't farfetched to hazard even more than ten and for that matter once her state of non-virginity had been accepted a lover more or a lover less made no difference and everyone knew that virginity cannot always be taken as a guarantee of virtue since there were for example the curious habits of her cousin Vera who derived from Vivaldi quite unpredictable and surely not virtuous pleasures though males were excluded from them, however they might also include Marika somehow and to begin with it was odd that she should know about them and should talk about them so calmly as if it were an ordinary matter only worth mentioning because casually connected with an anonymous letter, in short if one thought it over calmly it might turn out that this Marika was on an even lower moral level than one had attributed to her at first that is she might possess defects even greater than her habit of arousing orgasms along the road or of popping into bed and messing around with anybody who caught her fancy, however comically enough it happened that not even the most outrageous suppositions succeeded in damaging effectively the predisposition to happiness that quite exceptionally Antonio felt in himself that evening on the contrary they seemed in a way to enrich and enliven it.

Now all this was happening thanks to a singular but not entirely rare psychological procedure which allowed our Antonio to derive from the contemplation of his own misbehavior with Marika not so much satisfactions of the masochistic type having to do with degradation or whatever as a kind of hope naïve if you like but very elevated at least from the literary point of view since it was firmly attached to certain great Russian novels he had read when he was still young that is without understanding much of them but remaining touched by them as if by grace and thanks to them he now tended to place his present and still uncertain relationship with Marika in a pattern of redemption which obviously was the more effective the more she was corrupted so if it had been a question of setting out with her toward Siberia to be redeemed together from the sins which were hers more than his he wouldn't have thought twice about it however practically speaking Siberia remained in an unattainable fictional sphere whereas he was proceeding on the level of banal realism between the city of Venice and its most immediate hinterland and he had to find less heroic and more plausible justifications for his unusual mood and he had to agree for example that at least for the moment he intended to use Marika not so much for redemptive experiments as for making love first of all and secondarily to console himself after a previous and recent story which had ended badly so seeing the use he wanted to make of her it wasn't clear why he kept caviling over her vices and her virtues as if to spend a night of pleasure with a girl it was absolutely indispensable for her to be helpless and in love and if possible also chaste unless of course the use he wanted to make of her wasn't quite so elementary as he still insisted it was and involved an indefinable extra something which by chance precisely because it was indefinable might also coincide with the famous step still to be taken which would lead him definitively into the condition of happiness.

In short our hero moved over a terrain bristling with dangers and we might even say traps where his inclination toward logical reasoning was helpful only up to a point because of both the instability and the ambiguousness of the elements to be examined and because of the constant and excessive intrusion of casual incidents which became interpolated into his ratiocination driving it in one direction rather than another and for example now that he entered his home and finally removed himself from the romantic influence of the moon and the sirocco he was conditioned by the circumstance of being in fact at home though his being there wasn't in itself exactly a novelty in the sense that the condition wasn't visibly different from that of so many other evenings when he came in after his family had gone to bed and he ate the cold gluey pasta left there for him at the end of the table, nor could it be said that Marika's passing through the house had left any traces since his hard-working sister before allowing herself her nightly rest had neatly removed everything and had washed dishes and glasses so that if he hadn't happened to see the girl through the window he would certainly never have guessed Marika had been in his house, still he had seen her and that memory went through his mind as he ate the pasta with a good appetite remarking at the same time with dutiful equity that in the course of his reasoning along the way home he had neglected the innocent part of Marika that is especially her little-girl look with her fine hair and her blue eyes and her many freckles all things that had to correspond to good inner qualities, anyhow it was mainly in the field of symbolic meanings that Marika's passing through his home proved positive gradually acquiring richer and higher values since though the family for

some years now had been more than anything else a nuisance for
him there still must have been a time perhaps before his mother
had died when it had meant warmth and protection and this idea
of the family must have remained active in him without his knowledge so now it had no trouble emerging perhaps slyly as he brooded
over the ineffable scene glimpsed a short while before from the
window until without even realizing it he reached that fervent state
of prediscovery which Galilei must also have reached when he
noticed the swaying of the lamp in the Pisa Cathedral and of course
he felt a moment's hesitation in the face of wonder expected or
rather predestined and now within reach, and as immediately afterwards Galilei had his inspiration of the pendulum so now our
Antonio suddenly felt his mind opening to the idea that he had
to marry Marika.

That marrying Marika was precisely the step to take to reach
permanent happiness or at least a condition in which living wasn't
too oppressive was something Antonio had no reason to doubt nor
on the other hand was it to be thought that marriage wasn't in itself
a joyous event yet neither the necessity nor the joy of the act could
prevent the matter from appearing a tiny bit complicated perhaps
even dangerous and in any case hasty since it was all too clear that
the idea of marrying Marika like the discovering of the pendulum
had had largely visual origins connected with what he had seen
through the window however unlike the pendulum which fell
within the schemes and limitations of physical laws the matrimonial
idea remained free and disputable in the field of moral events, in
any case even within the nondefinitiveness of morality one could
attempt rational interpretations of the visible and in fact if by
looking through the window he had had proof of Marika's great
speed in winning people's affection this didn't authorize him to
suspect her of malice or accuse her of trickery since apart from the
fact that she didn't know he was looking at her from outside and
therefore certainly wasn't acting at least directly for him he had to
take into account her normal inclination to be gay and friendly

with anyone whenever possible, and in addition it was easy to understand how being an orphan or at least being without her parents from childhood she might be fascinated by a family especially not having yet had time to discover the sort of family it was namely a glum and depressing pair ready to grumble at anything even if for the occasion they had presented themselves in quite a different light so if anybody was being deceitful in the idyllic scene visible from the window it wasn't surely the poor stateless orphan whose need for family love in a secure nest must have deep and very sad roots, but now he with a single blow could provide her with a family and a house and as it happened also a nationality since there was no overlooking the detail that by marrying her he would furnish her a permanent citizenship and the good part was that despite all this he didn't have the impression of being a benefactor but rather of receiving benefaction since the nuptial operation if you looked at it carefully brought advantages especially to him as it gave him that reason for living or at least that justification for his coming into the world he often lacked and which he had also recently lost after having deceived himself with the illusion he had found it at the time of his love with Maria, but there was no doubt of its being an illusion after the news that she was skiing at Cortina and in fact it was downright senseless to think Maria might need him whereas Marika precisely because of her poverty and degeneration asked for nothing better than his helping her and saving her.

Having thus arranged the matter in its proper ideal frame he still had to examine it in its practical aspect which truthfully speaking wasn't simple especially economically and so before facing it Antonio decided to go to bed and make himself nice and warm under the blankets with the principal aim of being in a sufficiently protected and inviting atmosphere associated with certain sensations of well-being from his early childhood and with the desire to reconstruct them as far as possible in a matrimonial context, but despite all these precautions the problem remained serious because the ineffable little picture observed at the window though implying seriousness and duration in his father's and sister's benevolence toward the orphan could at most nourish the hope that Marika would be received without any great hostility into the house as daughter-in-law and sister-in-law and could also suggest the old saying that when there is food for three mouths in a home they can easily without increase in expenditure also feed four however apart from the fact that his father surely wouldn't have agreed with this old saying Antonio himself had to admit that eating was nothing compared for example to clothing and shoeing even though Marika didn't dress in an elegant or expensive fashion and was indeed inclined to the slightly sloppy style of the young still it was a well-known fact that the simplest dresses also cost money and moreover Marika could be suspected of an inclination to go out dining and dancing and amusing herself and this of course was not censurable since she was young and gay but in the final analysis amusements also cost money, in short the financial problem existed and there could be no thought of solving it by letting Marika continue to work at the Magyar Hotel since in all probability that would have contradicted the impulse of redemption which was the prime mover of the whole business, and so even not dismissing the thought that she might even readily find a less shady job than her present one in the hotel the fact remained that for the moment she would be jobless and quite presumably also penniless since she was hardly the saving type and in conclusion the task of providing for her maintenance and well-being would fall entirely on his shoulders but luckily it wasn't so desperate as it might at first seem since Marika wasn't in the snobbish position of Amalia and Ilario and we may as well also say Maria Borghetto that is she had no class motives for despising the social position and even less the salary of an elementary school teacher so if he chose the solution was handy, namely a good Act of Contrition recited at the Marocco elementary school where luckily there were always positions vacant.

Now it mustn't be thought that Antonio didn't see all the oppres-

sive squalor in this return to a post he had abandoned a little over
three months before with high hopes and bold confidence, in fact
he could see it all too well and as the act of leaving had held out
some promise however illusory that his progress toward distinguished things would be considerably accelerated so his return
aroused the sincere worry that progress would be slowed down since
this was no mean leap backward he was preparing to take to put
himself in a position to marry Marika immediately, but at this
point in his reasoning he had to be honest and admit that his matrimonial project merely made him anticipate that nasty backward
step and not by very much either really since with one thing and
another the eight hundred ninety thousand lire his beneficent and
deceased grandfather had left him had for the most part been dis-
sipated and at the moment he had no more than a hundred and
seven thousand lire in part deposited in the Mestre Savings Bank
and in part kept in cash in his wallet and since there was no hope
that his father with his meager pension or his sad sister with her
share of the inheritance would be willing to keep him for a little
while longer in idleness and orgies his squalid return to the elementary school desk seemed inevitable with the sole difference that he
would now have to go back at once instead of in a month or two
however considering that the immediate return was connected
with a marriage ideally more than opportune then the return wasn't
so repellent in fact the vision of an immediate existence divided between school and home where his bride Marika would be waiting
for him with all her freckles and her fine hair seemed so beautiful
that he felt impelled to achieve it as soon as possible and though it
wasn't strictly necessary he also worked out a plan somehow to
force the course of events that is by burning his bridges behind him
so to speak freeing himself at once of that hundred and seven thousand lire which now that he thought about it was only an obstacle
to the future and there was no more elegant and marvelous way to
be free of it than to buy a worthy engagement present for Marika
which he would take to her the following evening or rather that

same evening since it was now after two a.m. and the nearness of the event was such that though the big problems had roughly been solved and though his weariness after his day of travail still weighed on him considerably Antonio couldn't sleep and he didn't even want to because it was sweet to lie in the bed's warmth and review in his mind the beautiful things the future had in store for him.

CHAPTER
XXII

In which Antonio suffers great losses

After such fervid if not exactly sensible preparation our Antonio naturally arrived in Venice well ahead of the hour Marika had so carefully indicated for his presentation at the Magyar Hotel and so after he had drunk a couple of coffees in different places he spent the final half hour walking back and forth on the Zattere at Santo Spirito between the Incurabili Bridge and the tip of the Salute in the immediate vicinity of the Abbey of San Gregorio near which stood the little hotel where he was to turn up not before ten, and he walked in the midst of a thick fog which had risen from the lagoon in the early afternoon and had then gradually increased in density until it had become a kind of whipped cream in which the insistent sound of the sirens of the few vessels that dared go about in this weather and the melancholy and almost funereal sound of the little signal bell attached to the buoy off the island of San Giorgio to indicate to navigators the entrance of the Giudecca Canal were expanded, in short if our hero that evening had been sensitive to meteorological conditions as he had been the previous evening when he had allowed himself to be reassured by the moon and the sirocco perhaps the step he was preparing to take wouldn't have seemed so joyous or so sure but of course like every other living creature in his struggle against the unhappiness of life he considered favorably and perhaps factitiously everything that happened to him and therefore also the heavens and their mutations and so the fog which was unusual that evening even for a city like Venice made him rejoice after all as if it had risen on purpose to shield his delicate feelings from the gaze or interference of others but more than feelings they were as usual fantasies that is he was trying to imagine how the important meeting between himself and Marika would take place in the little lobby of the hotel and he felt it would be very beautiful if they were to look each other straight in the eye in an ardent but chaste way and if then without pronouncing superfluous words he were to hand her the tiny case containing the ring with the cultivated pearl bought in Mestre that afternoon at the sacrifice of fully eighty thousand lire and when amazed by the gesture and the gift she then looked at him with emotion and incomprehension he would say in the softest possible voice that as she had said she loved him and as he felt he loved her he meant to marry her at once or in other words as soon as the necessary papers could be got ready.

In daydreaming like this Antonio was obviously making numerous mistakes of which the worst was to suppose he would find the orphan Marika in the mood he had left her in the previous evening or to be precise fervent with love and ready to tell him three or even more times in a row that she loved him so much but instead when he made his entrance not without some pounding of the heart into the Magyar Hotel just after ten he saw her behind the desk looking like a secretary remote from any sentimental concerns and even too reserved since it was only with her eyes that she risked giving him a very rapid sign of understanding but for the rest she treated him just as an ordinary customer or even worse making him give her immediately his identity card with a bored air and telling him she could only give him a room on the fifth and last floor which however was very quiet finally inquiring if he had other luggage besides the rather ancient attaché case he was carrying in his hand, and after this she called a bent little man in a porter's apron who was yawning nearby and ordered him to show the guest to number forty-two and the man without making the slightest effort to disguise the annoyance this caused him preceded the new

guest up the four flights of stairs since obviously the hotel lacked
an elevator but finally thank God Antonio found himself alone in
a room with rather commonplace furniture including a bed that
was neither large nor small but of an intermediary measure Antonio
had always considered hybrid or to be more explicit ambiguous,
however it wasn't on the substantially rather unpleasant appearance
of the room that he could blame his ill-humor if it could be called
that since it would have been more correct to define it as a slight
disappointment or melancholy and in any case a mood that was
habitual with him and therefore not even to be connected with
Marika's rather cold welcome because for that matter lacking clair-
voyant gifts the poor girl certainly couldn't imagine he was going
to turn up with all those serious intentions and therefore she
thought erroneously of course but plausibly that he had come there
to spend an intense but so to speak self-contained night of love
with her, and for that matter he should have been the first to rejoice over her reserved welcome since if that was the treatment
generally given young male customers it meant that the hotel where
Marika had to work and live was a respectable hotel where even
assuming she had wanted to be affectionate toward him she couldn't
surely have been with that half-bent porter near her and a couple of
fat foreign ladies sitting on the little sofa in the entrance waiting
for God knows what perhaps only for bedtime so he should be
grateful she had given him that rapid sign of understanding whose
unequivocal meaning was that the two of them despite fat ladies
and bent porters and the whole world could consider themselves
united, in any case this was only an awkward transition phase they
were in now because they would soon be married and therefore
free to display reciprocal tenderness and love in front of anybody
without explanations and in the meanwhile it was foolish to become
sad because of little contretemps or petty obstacles especially since
now the most disagreeable part of the hotel operation had been
completed and he had only to wait for Marika to join him and then
that room would indeed become a world for them however my God
it was a less cozy world than expected also because there was no

adjoining bath but only a sink with hot and cold running water and under it a quite primitive bidet one of those painted iron ones on a metal tripod which have to be used in a complicated way filled and emptied by hand, and this instrument gradually became the focus for much of the ill-humor Antonio had worked up from other motives.

To tell the truth he felt toward that useful object all too evidently associated with sexual activities an unquestionably excessive repugnance which he himself didn't really understand in the sense that he didn't grasp its fundamental sexophobic origin and exalted instead its esthetic origin which was underlined especially by the circumstance that there wasn't even a protective screen in front of it so it was horrifying to think of Marika seated there for hygienic reasons observed by him not to mention the opposite namely himself observed by her while astride the implement performing lowly ablutions, in any case while not overlooking the uneasiness he had also to consider positively the fact that his repugnance for the device in a way gave the measure of how much ideal progress he had caused Marika to make in this short time since he was now able to liberate her from physiological necessities and this of course was only a secondary or even very humble aspect of the vaster process of redemption in which he felt involved up to his neck though it all ended by complicating his life considerably because for example undressing in front of a gay little tramp as he had supposed Marika was before evaluating her better was something that embarrassed him only up to a point whereas now to perform the same operation before her after he had greatly spiritualized her was far more awkward therefore practically it was best for him to undress and wash at once so that she would find him already in bed in his good pajamas which he had brought along in his case and which until a few days before he had worn chiefly with funereal thoughts but now he put them on with exactly the opposite idea however in the meanwhile it had occurred to him that finding him in bed in his pajamas Marika might imagine he was raging with desire to make love whereas on the contrary in the amorous stage he had reached now sensual satisfaction interested him only up to a point and in any case much less than many other things, still he was already in bed and to dress again would have been stupid too because she could arrive any moment and who knows what she would have imagined if she had found him dressing again though on second thought if she caught him so to speak with a sock in his hand she would have had a hard time telling whether he was taking it off or putting it back on, in short these were rather idle and elusive arguments which he indulged in to ease the tension of waiting for Marika who showed no sign of arriving and he hadn't had the good sense to bring along a book or at least a newspaper which still it would have been rather unusual to bring along on a full night of love but now he didn't know what to do to give his thoughts some occupation more worthy and less annoying than the primitive bidet or sex bath which instead dominated the room exerting a number of psychological pressures all of the antiromantic type so in the end it was best to eliminate the object by closing his eyes and concentrating on the sounds which were various and not all irksome because in addition to the hisses and gurgles of the plumbing and an almost evanescent muttering of the television set which rose up the stairwell from below he could hear footsteps and voices of people outside passing along the street five stories down and from time to time though at long intervals he heard the gloomy sound of a boat's siren and in the moments when all other sound was lacking he heard or had the impression he could hear the clang of the buoy off San Giorgio and therefore in the comparison between what could be seen and what could be heard the winner was unquestionably and rightly what could be heard until unfortunately there came a series of loud bizarre sounds which our Antonio even before managing to define them properly judged horrible and sufficient to make him look back with regret even at the repugnant influence of the sex bath and in fact though he stubbornly forced himself to imagine somebody was drowning in a room not far away it was soon clear that the sound was gargling also because between one wave and the next of the horrible sounds there were interspersed vocalizings based on the famous aria of Gioacchino Rossini *La calunnia è un venticello* and in conclusion it was indeed a basso who was performing those vocal exercises and prophylaxis before granting himself his nightly repose and certainly nobody even with all the good will in the world could have failed to associate this fact with the circumstance that a basso who sang at the Fenice had been included among the ten lovers listed in the famous anonymous letter.

Now it isn't as if Antonio at this really quite advanced stage in his plans wanted to turn back and summon up difficulties for himself which when he thought about it had already been overcome however even without taking into consideration the sudden and we could well say provocative arrogance with which the basso asserted his existence the fact was that the question of Marika having relations with ten lovers perhaps even simultaneously hadn't been so much overcome as suppressed by Antonio that is to say he had stored it away in a subterranean part of himself where it survived doing no harm provided it wasn't disturbed or aroused but with all those offensive noises the gargling basso emitted Antonio surely couldn't maintain a state of agnosticism or better still of agnosia but was willy-nilly driven to cognitive activity with such force that he could even imagine himself bursting into the basso's room to play perhaps another operatic scene not entirely inappropriate to the present circumstances wherein he would ask the wretch if he was one of Marika's lovers, however even admitting that the character agreed to answer instead of unceremoniously kicking out the intruder he would have answered a yes or a no and anyone could see that the only valid answer was yes since no could have been too easily suspect as a chivalrous lie, but why the hapless man should have answered yes even in the event that he had enjoyed or God forbid was still enjoying Marika's charms no one could understand and in short the pointlessness of the irruption seemed evident even to an unfortunate in the state of mental confusion that our Antonio was in at the moment especially since it wasn't only a matter of ineffectiveness of the cognitive process but also and above all of the uselessness of the knowledge even if it could be known, that is even admitting that the basso confessed his intrigue or affair with Marika Antonio wouldn't have known what to do about the confession as it seemed already taken for granted since with reference to the past it was precisely from what we might call a certain vicious condition of Marika's that he had moved on to the idea of redemptive marriage, in short all that concerned the past of his promised bride even the basso of the Fenice or the married waiter from Quadri's or the other eight lovers put together was something he had to accept with patience if not with downright joy as the indispensable premise to the redemption-filled future, and as far as the future was concerned to have sufficient guarantees he had only to marry Marika as soon as possible taking her immediately afterwards to Marocco of course.

So everything led Antonio to a confirmation of his good matrimonial ideas which despite the constant obstacles and contretemps were becoming more and more dear to him and when thank God the basso finally stopped his gargling and vocalizing and the hotel returned to its tolerable sounds he devoted himself entirely to his plans and setting the engagement ring in full view on the night table where Marika would see it the minute she arrived he began to enjoy in advance her various expressions of wonder and delight and her many words of gratitude and since Marika delayed her arrival he had time to savor a great abundance of words and actions still not guessing correctly what she actually did when she arrived at last which was simply on opening the door to signal to him not to utter a word after which she immediately turned off the light without having a chance to notice the ring on the night table of course, then leaving the door open surprisingly she approached the bed and still completely dressed slipped into it clinging passionately to Antonio who caught off guard by her abrupt behavior didn't know what to do and in fact the more her transports and clutchings increased the less he felt capable of doing anything in other words he was so obviously at sea that at a certain moment thinking to facilitate matters she whispered into his ear that she had taken off her underthings before coming up and even a deaf man would have

understood this was an invitation she was addressing to him to take
without delay that part of her which presumably pleased him the
most and though Antonio understood the invitation it seemed somewhat too brisk a way of proceeding and rather indelicate though
she couldn't be held altogether responsible for it poor thing she was
surely ignorant of the enormous progress he had made since the
previous evening along the road of higher sentiment, anyhow even
more than by her lack of tact Antonio was disturbed by the door
being left wide open and rightly attributing to this a good part of
his own temporary incapacity he asked her if she had forgotten to
close it or if it had to stay open and she answered that unfortunately
it was impossible to shut it because she was on duty and had to listen
out for sounds even from the ground floor to hear if by chance number twenty-two or number twenty-four should come in since they
hadn't come in yet and moreover her cousin Vera might arrive
who naturally had the keys and could come in without ringing
however she had gone to the movies and surely wouldn't be back
before twelve-thirty and since it wasn't yet midnight they had presumably a good half hour to be together and in half an hour they
could make love comfortably if they wanted to without his having
to worry about the open door because she would be very careful and
nobody would surprise them and it wasn't by accident that she had
given him room forty-two on the top floor at the end of a corridor
where nobody had any reason to come, in conclusion according to
her there were no obstacles of any kind therefore she couldn't understand why he didn't get a bit busier and at one point she even asked
him with some apprehension if he was still fond of her and of
course he was in fact thanks to the redemptive mechanism he had
the impression he loved her more than ever perhaps to an inhibi-
tive degree in the sense that if he had loved her a bit less he might
not have been so disturbed by the bidet or by the open door or even
by her nonchalant behavior, in any case this was a temporary condition since he would have had only to tell her for example about the
engagement or even just hint at it and she would suddenly be elevated to more virtuous conduct but how the hell could he talk to

her about that now apart from the fact that in this darkness and
with the door open the thing would have been unquestionably
diminished and spoiled, better then to postpone the ceremony to a
more suitable moment and meanwhile adapt himself as best he
could to the actual situation bearing in mind that if she were short
on spirituality it was abundantly compensated by her being long
on availability and her ample desire to please him therefore to reject what she offered with great liberality and convenience was to
risk humiliating or even insulting her so at the point they had
reached there was nothing to be done but take her especially since
this would undoubtedly be the last time the thing would happen
so squalidly because afterwards their engagement would give quite
a different tone to their sexual relations, and in short summoning
his courage he climbed on her following her tastes also in this since
this was in fact the way she preferred to be possessed however despite his best intentions it was no easy undertaking because knowing
she was intent on the sounds he too though involuntarily lay there
with his ear alert to hear if by chance number fourteen was coming
home five stories below, and although he kept telling himself he
was enjoying a young and beautiful and even beloved girl what he
was doing was indubitably one of the most difficult and least pleas-
urable exertions of the kind that had ever befallen him in his life
however it had one good feature namely as the effort lasted so long
perhaps she too might be extraordinarily aroused and also reach an
orgasm and in fact at a certain point she seemed to display a bit of
participation even forgetting to listen carefully and he took advantage of this to bring the matter as best he could to its conclusion
with relief for both it seemed since as soon as she noticed he had
finished without wasting a moment she got out of the bed and after
hastily whispering that she would be back later she ran off shutting
thank God the damn door behind her.

Although he had nothing to reproach himself with and after all
nothing to reproach her with either since he could hardly expect
her to change overnight especially when she remained in ignorance
of the good reasons for which she should change Antonio was

rather downcast by the miserable outcome of that first part of the evening which in fact had brought less satisfaction than could have been expected so he couldn't help wondering if he usually so prudent in hope hadn't this time driven himself to yearnings well not exactly rash but at least a bit hasty and ill-timed also thinking that as he hadn't yet had time to speak of these yearnings to her he could if necessary establish between his decision to marry her and its consequent announcement to her a phase of transition or waiting facilitated also by the circumstance that on buying the ring he had reached an agreement with the jeweler who would exchange it if the fiancée didn't like it and interpreting this agreement in its broadest sense Antonio might also be allowed to give it back and have his money returned perhaps losing a few thousand lire in the transaction, in short the possibilities were ample also from the economic standpoint however at this stage in his reasoning Antonio drew back in disgust at his own cowardice and wickedness since what was happening was that he who had always done nothing but complain about the misfortunes visited upon him by heaven was now about to turn his back on the one piece of good fortune that destiny had finally decided to set before him since anyone would have realized that Marika was not so much corrupt as she was wild as she herself for that matter had honestly admitted from the very beginning and if by chance beyond that wildness she could also be accused of dubious conduct it derived from the fact that she had been born so to speak under an evil star exactly like himself when he thought about it therefore saving her was a trifle since he had merely to hold out a comradely hand and love her naturally in that protective way which is generally possible among the disinherited, in short it really didn't seem to require much effort and our Antonio on thinking it over managed to restore that bit of faith in life and in the future that the situation had allowed him to muster up and sufficiently encouraged by this he prepared to wait for Marika's return paying attention to the sounds noticing the progressively rarer steps of passers-by in the street below and then toward one o'clock a shuffling downstairs which in all probability signified the return of the famous cousin and then more footsteps outside and an occasional shout and in between longer and longer stretches of silence when he could hear from time to time the little bell on the buoy off San Giorgio unless it was an impression caused by the effort of remaining intent and in fact at times the barely perceptible noise tended to swell like a remote but full sound of church bells which expanded in his head until it filled it completely beyond reality of course since after a day spent chiefly in nerve-racking waits he now felt considerably out of sorts as well as of course debilitated by the joyless amorous exercise performed a short while before which on second thoughts had been all a misunderstanding but one that luckily could be cleared up quite easily as soon as Marika arrived providing she did arrive finally since it was by now past two a.m. and our hero with the swollen sound of imaginary bells happened to fall asleep from time to time for periods that seemed to him frighteningly long whereas in reality they lasted only a few minutes as was evident when he glanced at his watch and thank goodness they were brief because in his heart he felt guilty at these lapses into sleep which if you judged them severely might also be symptoms of insufficient fervor in his waiting, anyhow it seemed that even indulging his weariness he couldn't manage to sleep more than five minutes at a time so he indulged it more and more often until opening his eyes with a start after a sleep that had perhaps been more profound he saw her bent over him with a malicious and amused look tickling him by drawing her fine hair over his face and she asked him if by chance he had come here to sleep seeing that he slept so well, and to Antonio she appeared so beautiful and sweet that with his mind still a bit hazy he was tempted to relate her to some paradisiacal vision except that her dress was a bit in contradiction to the idea that one generally has about the costume of the inhabitants of paradise that is to say in her case a robe which she hadn't put on but was thrown around her shoulders and under it a kind of little shirt that at most came to her navel leaving the rest free but if it didn't have much to do with paradise it might have some connection with conjugal life so this could also be the right moment to direct her eyes to the ring on the night table so plainly in evidence that it was surprising she hadn't noticed it by herself anyhow if she hadn't noticed it that meant her eyes were only for him and in fact she continued looking at him intensely no longer amused but passionate and yet without excessive sentimentalism as at a certain point she announced she was terribly cold and couldn't wait to warm up against him that is if he would make up his mind to leave a little room for her and only then did he realize that absorbed in his own abstruse ideas he wasn't paying sufficient attention to her well-being in other words he couldn't forget himself for her and so one might think his love still had considerable progress to make in the field of generosity anyhow to begin with he moved eagerly to one side and she immediately stretched out beside him pressing herself against him trembling with cold no doubt but at the same time burning with passion and certainly not hiding the fact because she did nothing but say to him darling darling and take me take me and so once again he had first to postpone the business of the ring but at the moment he was about to get busy he remembered the door wondering if she had left it open as before and now with the light on so he raised himself up to look and found it shut thank heaven but his concern made her wonder if she had locked it carefully on the inside and so she wanted to go and check making a rapid leap then running back to press herself to him in the bed and observing her movement he had the opportunity of admiring her body agile and strong at the same time which the transparent little nightgown concealed slightly from the navel up and not at all from the navel down and now he held her tight with great pleasure and desire to possess her perhaps at once but meanwhile to explain perhaps why she had rushed to make sure the door was locked she started saying she was a bit afraid of her cousin Vera with whom unluckily she shared a room who might wake up and come looking for her not finding her in her bed in any case it wouldn't be very easy for Vera to guess what room she was in since she had been too smart to write Antonio's name in the register, and Antonio agreed with her that is he was also of the opinion that under these circumstances it wouldn't be easy for Vera to come and catch him however he was of the further opinion that this Magyar Hotel was one of the worst possible places for love-making and in addition the mention of the irruption of an outsider however improbable had recalled to mind another episode that might be considered analogous which had happened to him fairly recently and though on second thoughts it was completely improbable at least from a statistical point of view that he should be caught twice running in quite delicate situations it could also be that he was born with this peculiar destiny and in short even on this score he didn't feel completely comfortable in facing the sexual duties which were assigned him in the situation and though Marika had by now forgotten her cousin Vera and at least judging by the way she clung to him and rubbed against him she was thinking exclusively of him he hadn't really any great desire to make love at once especially because he suspected that if he didn't broach the subject of the engagement first the situation would as usual be resolved in his virtually solitary orgasm whereas if on the other hand in the most suitable and kindly way he suggested to her the eventuality that she might already consider herself his promised bride then in all probability she would entrust herself to him body and soul and their love-making would be sublime in reaching a simultaneous and reciprocal pleasure, so putting kisses and caresses aside for the moment he started talking about what had happened to him the previous evening telling how gradually as he was going toward home after she had left on the bus and therefore while he was under the marvelous influence of her triple declaration of love it had almost abruptly come into his mind that he could resolve his life in a different way from what he had until then believed possible and advisable that is no longer wasting time in playing cards at the tavern or idling around Venice seeing the days go by fruitlessly and he could instead devote himself to a secure and respectable though modest profession such as teaching in the Marocco elementary school but this of course without closing himself off forever in a narrow and mediocre position namely not abandoning his higher aspirations which were first of all to take his degree and then who knows to achieve presumably in the literary field a notoriety or even fame for which he didn't feel entirely ill-suited and of which he sincerely didn't consider himself undeserving, however he clearly realized that even if he was sufficiently gifted struggling alone he would never manage to get out of the dismal rut into which he had fallen partly through his own fault as he was ready to admit but also because of certain disastrous events, still he now had the impression that the series of adverse happenings was about to end and what's more he was convinced that if he had beside him a person from whom he could receive encouragement and comfort and for whom above all it was worth sacrificing himself he would surely find the strength to climb back up the downward path of misfortune, and this indispensable person in his view was precisely herself Marika for that matter he might even say the idea had come to him through his pondering a simple and decent scene which he had had so to speak the opportunity of glimpsing as he looked through the window unseen while she was happily chatting with his father and sister arousing thoughts directly associated with a proper married state and in conclusion if on an entirely temporary basis she could adapt herself to living with his family in the house at Marocco he thought it would be a fine and beneficial thing for them both to be married as soon as possible, and at this point though he had already said the most important thing he could have easily gone on listing other advantages which their marriage would surely bring but instead he stopped because Marika's appearance wasn't quite as radiant as might have been reasonably expected in fact at the very beginning when he had started talking generically about destiny and misfortunes she had moved away from him as if concentrating on his talk with the probable aim of making an effort without great success however to foresee what he was getting at with this argumentation which admittedly was a bit too rambling and prolix however when he had finally blurted out the marriage proposal loud and clear the reason for all her continued perplexity and meditation was obscure and the least he could have thought was that she had some secret hesitation probably connected with her not exactly virtuous past and therefore also with the welcome she might have had as his bride in the rather bigoted household in Marocco still on this score he was quite happy to reassure her that she would be received with open arms since though naturally he had made no mention of his matrimonial plans to his father and sister from the pleased and even conspiratorial manner with which his sister had brought him his morning coffee and from the moderation of the nasty prophecies of his father in the morning he could infer that they would be quite happy if he were to settle down with that girl so pretty and sweet and happy who had come to visit them, but when even this news failed to inspire the proper contentment in the presumed fiancée he decided to hint discreetly of course at the fact that by marrying him she would also escape the annoying condition of being stateless since she would ipso facto acquire the citizenship of her husband and she did appreciate this advantage to its full extent because she nodded her head to signify she understood it quite well however she still showed no sign of being overjoyed as she should have been so then falling back on the surest and most convincing gesture he took the ring from the table and held it before her eyes saying it was his engagement present and she took it with a slow and apparently pensive movement and slipped it on the ring finger of her left hand actually with some difficulty because it was tight and then she looked at her finger with the ring on it not uttering a word and he couldn't make out her behavior also because he couldn't see her face which she obstinately kept down, however just as he was beginning to feel a bit annoyed and we might even say embittered by her inexplicable and obstinate lack of reaction he saw a tear fall on her hand and then another and another still and frankly he would have expected anything before he would have thought of seeing her cry and though this was certainly better than nothing he had no idea how to interpret it or consequently how to be guided by it toward more coherent conduct and so he stayed there watching her with even less idea than before what was opportune and suitable to do or say and it was only after a while when in fact she had stopped crying that he pulled himself together and asked her what there was to cry about and without raising her head she replied with a negative gesture and afterwards also pronounced the word nothing meaning in all likelihood that since it was too complicated to explain in words what she felt in her spirit she preferred at least for the moment to remain silent and this was more than comprehensible since her emotions and feelings couldn't have been very simple perhaps not even definite and by their very nature they set up a resistance to being expressed in words which inevitably diminished them, and having understood this Antonio wanted to help her somehow but more to make her realize that words after all counted only up to a point so he gently took her left hand which was the one bathed in tears and at present also adorned with the symbol of engagement and she meekly let him take it however without changing expression or attitude and in short it was still a difficult relationship which however already was or at least already could be on the way to solution in the sense that any moment she might predictably come out with an explanation which if not absolutely happy would at least be somewhat intelligible and in fact he could already glimpse signs in her that led him to hope for an imminent outpouring but at that very moment they heard a loud noise on the floor below as if an object had fallen or a person had bumped into a chair or a table and Marika abruptly sat up staring toward the door listening tensely and Antonio of course also listened carefully but no matter how he pricked up his ears he couldn't hear anything whereas Marika to judge by her concerned and irritated expression must have continued to hear something because at a certain point to discover more clearly what was going on outside she hastily and silently got out of bed and picking up her robe went to listen at the door remaining motionless and concentrated in her listening and then not content she turned out the light and opened the door a crack to listen again and she peered out for rather a long while and finally after having made a sign which in the semidarkness wasn't very clear but perhaps meant she would be back soon she went off like a ghost that is to say without making the slightest sound.

And so the fine gesture of engagement which our Antonio was making as best he could amid huge and unexpected complications was actually interrupted at its most delicate point and he was temporarily shut off from events left alone in a dark room and in a state of mind still wavering between wonder and dismay though it was rapidly veering toward dismay and he could only return in his mind to what had so far happened and analyze it to attempt afterwards some prudent predictions for the immediate future, and obviously on drawing up even a partial and temporary balance of that night which anyone would have foreseen as simple and joyous he had nothing to congratulate himself about because as yet there had been precious little joy and as for simplicity it was best to forget it because in addition to Marika's complicated and enigmatic reactions to the marriage proposal there was also that complex movement of characters both visible and invisible like the catarrh-ridden basso and the spectral cousin Vera thanks to whom he seemed to have fallen not into an intimate engagement ceremony but into the heart of a suspense drama and Antonio was rightly the first to regret having chosen as the setting of his matrimonial declaration this Magyar Hotel which from every point of view seemed unsuited to a normal fulfilment of the matter and certainly if he had been able to retrace his steps at least taking back the ring he would have begun the whole thing over from the beginning in another hotel or any place but this one which without exaggeration also taking into account the visible bidet could be judged repellent, however at this point he also had to be the first to admit that blaming his surroundings for this intense revulsion was only a subterfuge to remove as much importance as possible from the disagreeable things that had happened in these surroundings especially Marika's attitude when he had confided he loved her in such a way and to such a degree that he had resolved to marry her, and though he had to reproach himself for a momentary tendency to see everything through rose-colored glasses a tendency pardonable for that matter in a man who only occasionally won the privilege of feeling generous and beneficent still it was undeniable that what

Marika had done and said would have been disheartening even for a man who had waited for her with a less rosy outlook since to a proposal which on several counts elevated her she had reacted chiefly with indifference and thank God immediately afterwards there had been those few tears which could also bring everything back onto the carpet as their motive was still obscure because Marika hadn't been given time to explain them, however when she did come back to furnish proper explanations the situation might suddenly be reversed for example it would suffice for her to confess that an acute and immediate awareness of her own moral unworthiness had led her to display first a hesitation he had erroneously taken for indifference and then an emotion clearly revealed in her tears at which point he would immediately take her in his arms with more love than he would have given her without all those obstacles, and so thanks to elaborations of this thought and also perhaps thanks to a few subterfuges Antonio succeeded in mastering his dismay and in directing his spirit toward cautious hope keeping it in that state for the time Marika remained absent which after all wasn't very long because before ten minutes had gone by she reappeared that is she opened the door and turned on the light coming forward two or three steps looking straight ahead with an air that couldn't conceivably have been more downcast and stopping she told Antonio in a low and sad voice her cousin Vera wanted to speak to him.

Among the many things Antonio could expect and perhaps even hope for in a night as strange as this one you could certainly not include a conversation with this cousin whom he vaguely remembered having seen at the café on the Zattere about ten days before and then glimpsed behind the hotel desk forming both times a bad impression of her so he would not have liked to see her or listen to her but apparently in the situation into which he had thoughtlessly got himself on entering the Magyar Hotel his every desire and legitimate viewpoint were trampled in the dust almost deliberately and in fact before he could express an opinion the cousin had already come in approaching him with a determined bearing

that could without exaggeration be called masculine so Antonio
realized that to tell her to leave would be useless and he prepared
himself to sustain this conversation whose nature he still couldn't
predict and in fact it even occurred to him that they meant to trap
him more rapidly and more definitively than he wished to trap
himself however he quickly realized he was quite wide of the mark
with his suppositions because cousin Vera in a harsh but low voice
out of obvious regard for the other guests in the hotel presumably
asleep at that hour told him Marika had informed her of his proposal and in her position as close relative and therefore responsible
in view of the orphan's minority she was of the opinion that such
a marriage was not advisable for Marika who with her fresh beauty
and youth could aspire to something better than a poor country
schoolteacher, in any case to console Antonio she wanted to tell him
that the marriage wouldn't have been advisable or sensible from
his point of view either since Marika was not only very demanding
and capricious but was actually eccentric for example after having
arranged this mess of having him come to the hotel with God
knows what promises Marika had then come to her to say she
didn't love him enough to risk marrying him and this cruel information gave the coup de grâce to Antonio's last shreds of hope but
in compensation it also gave him the so-called courage of despair
that is the indispensable power despite his being in bed and in a
horizontal position to achieve a sufficiently dignified tone and attitude to tell that disgusting cousin he appreciated her concern but
the opinions of people accustomed to writing anonymous letters
didn't interest him in the least so he directly addressed Marika to
find out from her and not from others if she really didn't love him
enough to accept his proposal of marriage and Marika at this fron-
tal attack couldn't remain to one side as a secondary and passive
and subdued figure which she would perhaps have preferred and
sadly summoning her strength she looked up at him with hard and
desolate desperation and he understood that this concealed or rather
miserably betrayed a painful inner murkiness from which she still
wouldn't or couldn't free herself then unable to bear looking at him

any more she hung her head as if guilty or penitent and coming to
the bed she said in the low voice that it was true she didn't love
him enough and as if to underline the squalid finality of the declaration she wanted to take the ring off her finger where she herself
had pensively put it a short while before but as the ring was tight
it wouldn't come off easily and then with a sudden resolution
which he already knew he would later regret a thousand times but
whose magnificence then and there seemed irresistible Antonio told
her she could keep it as a reminder of their unfortunate love or if
she preferred as a compensation for the favors she had granted him
since even though he was only a poor country schoolteacher he insisted on paying generously for services especially sexual ones, and
hearing him express himself with such sarcastic crudity Marika de-
sisted from every effort to remove the ring and turning brusquely
ran out of the room and after her thank God cousin Vera also went
without a word and Antonio left alone and feeling for some reason
short of breath got up and went to the window flinging it open and
outside the fog was still thick however not dark but a little clear so
he could think it was near dawn and that meant the days had already grown longer compared to those other times when he had
also lain awake in anguish and sorrow and so spring was coming,
and not a sound could be heard in the circumscribed immensity of
the fog except for the distant throb of a motorboat which could
easily have been one of those bearing the glorious name of Cavalier
Ilario and Antonio listened at length to that sound not because it
really interested him much despite the blows it gave his soul but
because somehow he thought that all the cold penetrating him
would produce a definitive disaster and yet before the sound of the
boat died in the interminable distance he heard it drowned out by
the sound of bells perhaps from San Marco which up there on the
fifth floor arrived broad and airy and not heavy and somehow
stifled as on the Fondamenta della Parona, and Antonio who at the
moment couldn't bear hurting himself too much by remembering
the Fondamenta della Parona as he had happened to remember it
forced himself to associate the sound of the bells with something

else like the recollection of when he was a boy and served Mass and the Mass began with *Introibo ad altare Dei ad Deum qui laetificat juventutem meam,* to God who makes joyful my youth oh my youth Antonio thought and then since this too was hardly a good direction for his thoughts he tried to go on with the Mass but he couldn't remember any more and into his mind came only the phrase fiant aures tuae intendentes which God knows may not have had anything to do with the Mass, *fiant aures tuae intendentes* our hero repeated in any case again and again not paying much attention to the meaning of what he was saying, and then realizing that the illness even if he caught it as he hoped wouldn't be sufficiently rapid to resolve his present misfortune on the spot he took off his pajamas and began to dress.

CHAPTER
XXIII

In which Antonio, as usual, thinks things over, deriving, unusually, some consolation

Having left the Magyar Hotel with his attaché case in his hand and in his wallet the last twelve thousand of all the eight hundred and ninety thousand lire inherited a few months before from his poor maternal grandfather Antonio was now walking at random rather stiffly along some streets which in all likelihood would have brought him to the Zattere where it seemed right he should arrive though the motives for this at the moment weren't very clear to him or rather they were quite nebulous and in fact the only thing that at present had for him any importance and a very limited one at that was somehow to maintain his self-control whence his stiffness which more or less corresponded to an instinctive chiefly animal impulse toward coherence and the phrase *fiant aures tuae intendentes* which he kept repeating in his mind with tenacious passiveness but not entirely by chance if you think about it since in some way it too corresponded to his incessant need to account for things which had temporarily been a bit quelled because of the big setback he had just received but which lay in wait inside him summoned so to speak by the superior capacity for suffering which belongs to youth especially unfortunate youth and in effect he hardly hoped to go on for very long turning

over in his mind *fiant aures tuae intendentes* or exploiting the tenu-
ously consolatory impression that as the days were growing shorter
they were progressing as one might logically suppose toward spring
however it was a fact that the big setback just received was so big
that it offended altogether his human condition his decorum and
affections and hopes so it wasn't wise and perhaps not even possible to face it all at once therefore at a certain point just as he was
coming out of the Rio Terrà dei Catecumeni onto the Zattere ai
Saloni turning immediately to the right of course because if he had
turned to the left he would have ended up at the Salute and who
knows perhaps again at the Magyar Hotel, coming out then on the
Zattere which naturally was a sea of fog like a Stygian swamp
where a man overwhelmed by abandonment and desolation could
find very little to cling to and realizing on the other hand that he
could no longer forestall his sufferings with enigmatic Latin phrases
or astronomic predictions connected with the succession of the sea-
sons which anyway seemed less probable in that foggy morning
our hero resolved to face harsh reality taking it however a bit at a
time and beginning with the easiest aspect that is since he had to
start suffering perforce it occurred to him concretely to suffer first
and with an unquestionably disproportionate intensity for an entirely secondary misfortune namely that he had been a big block-
head or rather an outright fool to waste eighty-eight thousand lire
which practically speaking was the last of his money on that noble
gesture of flinging the cultivated pearl ring in her face an action
which at the time had seemed rather grand and at least designed to
restore his pride which had then been in rather bad shape but when
he thought about it now with detachment it appeared in its true
essence as an enormous idiocy so it was easy to imagine those two
women laughing behind the back of the poor bum who with ridiculous braggadocio had wanted to act like a great gentleman and
for that matter he couldn't exclude the possibility that Marika had
made only the slightest effort to slip off the ring which couldn't
have been quite as tight as she pretended because it was also possible that the wretched orphan was dishonest in more ways than one,

and stimulated by this supposition he was also tempted to let himself go perhaps only to relieve his anger in a series of massive execrations but he felt a kind of painful pang in his spirit and not because beyond his scorn he remembered how much he had loved her until a few minutes before but because it was evident that his great bitterness toward her as well as the excessive grief for the squandered eighty-eight thousand lire served to disguise the really sore spot of the business since there had been a moment when Marika directly called on by him to answer had been close to letting him see what was murky or perhaps sick in her and he now knew how close she had been to the truth and who knows perhaps also to redemption but it was then bitter and hard to realize that even then he had known it at that moment when if he had called her with the necessary charity she would have opened herself and perhaps would also have been saved from that turbid submission to her cousin who in all likelihood wasn't even her cousin, however who had ever said all this was up to him who had burdened him with such a mass of duties that they only crushed him under mountains of guilt because he couldn't perform them and for that matter if on his part help hadn't been offered with sufficient charity it couldn't be said that on her part it had in any way been requested so if he had been inspired to step forward with intentions of saving or rather redeeming her there was also the possibility that he would have met other and worse humiliations, and in conclusion since it still wasn't established that he had been born with Messianic tasks his mistake had been to put himself on the same level with a corrupt and vicious girl like Marika and above all to fall in love with her then looking like a dope and losing no small sum of money, in short by thinking about it he was again straightening the thing out however precariously when the course of his thoughts came to a new and brusque arrest followed by a deviation caused by another inner pang this time through the circumstance that having crossed the Ponte del Bacalà and that of the Incurabili and that of the Calcina obviously he had now reached the Zattere dei Gesuati in the immediate vicin-

ity of that café terrace which though invisible at the moment thanks
to the great fog that engulfed everything was surely there just ahead
so now it was all too clear why on coming out of the Magyar Hotel
he had walked in one direction rather than another namely he had
to come to this terrace not however because he had met Marika
there but because there he had met Maria who now that is after all
the new knowledge he had lately acquired about life and love was
returning to his mind quite cleansed of the sin of going skiing in
Cortina as of all other sins to tell the truth, and in fact the place
also inspired him to remember her as she had been at the beginning
with her adolescent appearance and smile and crooked tooth and
even freckles if you like restored in other words to her original
integrity and perfection and not so much to underline ungenerous
differences and consequently to liquidate perhaps at once and with
suspect haste the story with Marika but rather to affirm honestly
and not entirely to his own advantage that the second story had
after all been only an erroneous appendix to the first since surely it
had been the intolerable sense of emptiness after Maria's loss that
had driven him so precipitously into the adventure with Marika
and indeed to go still deeper it had been the sense of his own guilt
in losing Maria that had instilled in him that great eagerness expiatory no doubt to compromise himself permanently with Marika
through a marriage that would have been foolish to say the least and
that only the benign protection of heaven had allowed him escape
in extremis, and in short though from one point of view it wasn't
nice to do it so briskly he could now see Marika in her true role
as instrument of self-punishment thus depriving her of any autonomy and also of the capacity to make him suffer if he didn't feel
like suffering, he could even forget her then and there if he chose
and take Maria as the sole and true source of his nourishing sorrows and in fact as he stepped onto the damp and slippery planks
of the terrace naturally deserted at this hour and in this weather he
completely ignored the spot where Marika had first appeared to
him concentrating entirely on the spot where for the first time
Maria had appeared to him, now finally with his spirit freed of

successive superimpositions and resentments and completely resigned to the irreversibility of events that is with Maria lost lost lost
he attained the capacity to judge her absolute perfection when he
had glimpsed her on the terrace with her back to the October sun
and when he had dared stop just there at the foot of the Ponte
Lungo and when nearby under the portico of the Cassa di Risparmio she had arrived the next day in her brown raincoat with her
hair all sticky because it was raining cats and dogs that day and so
instead of strolling they had gone into the café to drink a punch
and had come out convinced of the ineluctability of their love and
of the more than probable sufferings connected with it and then
in the rain they had headed for the Ca' Foscari walking along that
same Fondamenta Nani where he was now walking without her in
the fog facing for the second and thousandth time the problem of
solitude, then he thought until it hurt of something he had worried
about that same rainy day his concern to fix in his memory every
detail of their being together so confusedly and shyly happy in order
to nourish with memories his solitude when he would be left alone
and the thought of solitude then had been a kind of fiction invented
naturally to savor with greater trepidation the happiness of their
being together but now he was alone and of the details he had resolved to memorize that day he couldn't recall a single one except
his distress over his new shoes since he had just bought the shoes
to look smart for her and he thought the rain would completely
ruin them, and perhaps in that concern lay the guilty origin of his
misfortunes and misadventures in his always putting himself or
even his shoes before others including loved ones and nothing was
more likely yes it was precisely because of his constant egoism that
he had lost her, meanwhile he had reached the Ponte delle Maravegie almost at the end of the Fondamenta that is only a few steps
from the Accademia bridge where he could catch a motoscafo or a
vaporetto to reach the Piazzale Roma sitting down at least but instead he decided to cross the bridge and continue on foot and surely
this time not to save the motoscafo fare but because it was painful
to walk with all the weariness of the horrible night on his back so

it could serve as a beginning of the expiation of at least a part of this final guilt he had discovered namely his placing after himself even the most beloved persons, and also as far as the other numerous and much vaster guilts were concerned his walking with weariness and suffering could be of some utility since it was always better to settle scores with oneself in a state of exhaustion if possible, and in any case his only course was to continue on foot because he had walked those same streets with her the first and the second days of their love and many other days afterwards of course as their story developed and at the same time became inevitably corrupted a little, and now the fact that he was egocentric or even an egoist couldn't entirely explain his loss of her or his cowardice at not having deflowered her when it would have been right to do so or the other still greater and inexcusable cowardice of having quickly given way to disheartenment without struggling enough before allowing her to be lost, all these basically were only incidents in which one could find more weakness than wickedness and in any case it hadn't been for this reason that he had lost her but for another more remote one which became all the more evident as in his anguished clutching at the past he kept thinking of Maria's perfection since certainly he bore within himself some atavistic contradiction between the divine and the demoniacal whereby on the one hand he worshipped purity and on the other he couldn't wait to contaminate it, and the fact that this was a contradiction common to nearly all mortals didn't console him much since he suffered much more than the others at being unable to adapt himself to it so he would in any case have lost Maria since he certainly couldn't keep her uncontaminated in spite of time which came from God and the profanations which might also come from Him seeing that travail and decay were apparently the only sure destiny granted man and if you couldn't admit that you were bound to suffer, it was necessary in other words to accept in a kind of monstrous compromise the odor of sex and the imperfect breast and the animality of the orgasm and the crouching and the blood and the pollution and the resurgent desire for an interminable search for expiation after the sin, but then why did they teach that we are made in God's image instead of preparing us for what seemed to be life as he only now began to understand and still so imperfectly that he wanted to recognize it only in Marika for example but not in Maria, and this was the lofty and painful measure of his love for her and this boundless impossible love also accepted her loss and preferred to have lost her and wanted to lose her again since it was as if he had her still with him walking through the foggy and almost deserted streets of the early morning still knowing he wouldn't hold her for himself not even in that fiction of purity, and there they had already reached the Campiello degli Squelini with its eight naked dripping plane trees and beyond it was the Calle Foscari with the university building on one side and opposite the little café called so vainly the Café della Speranza where one day they had drunk coffee together a day that hadn't been easy in their story insofar as he could recall but one they had in any case overcome as best they could, and the café was open now however he didn't feel like going in though a coffee would surely have done him good in his present condition but it was as if he didn't have time he felt he had to hurry to cross the bridge and go along the Calle Larga Foscari which for that matter was fairly short to arrive at the very spot where the first day she had told him it was best for them to separate, and in fact they had separated because he had let her go toward her home without following her this time however first he wanted to tell her that apart from the cowardice and the egoism the suffering that had happened wasn't all his fault because he had come to her and she was the most beautiful and the greatest thing in his life presumably also in what was left to him still to live but he had come to her without understanding anything because no one had ever taught him anything or rather they had taught him not to understand and to be confused and lost, they had told him only of the horror of the flesh and the shame of carnal sin and of contamination and diseases and duties and humiliation and decay, above all they had insisted on expiation and disappointment and the gall that lies at the bottom of every pleasure, in fact he said all this to her in a humble attempt at exculpation before letting her definitively go along the Calle di Dona Onesta toward San Polo and maintaining his resolution he didn't follow her but turned to the left and went off along the Crosera toward San Pantaleone and the Piazzale Roma through streets where the rare passers-by were heard before they were seen which wasn't much help in overcoming a sense of solitude and in fact his walk had again stiffened slightly since he felt again the need of making some effort to preserve his self-control however when he thought about it he now seemed a bit better than before that is though in one sense it was all too evident that there was little to understand about life in itself he had the funny impression that he nevertheless had understood something which at least was useful from a practical point of view connected chiefly with survival, that is life was a fairly cockeyed business with which it was best in any case to come to terms without taking humiliations and sufferings too much into account, or to put it in other and worthier words being a man meant acquiring a disposition of humble tolerance toward that not very clear or very clean mixture which was existence paying no matter how or how much and it also seemed that only a sizable capacity for supporting evil and sorrow enabled a man to go on and perhaps even to produce something, and having luckily understood at least this on coming out of the enormous misadventures that he was now still struggling out of he was in some way directed toward a future that perhaps wouldn't just be a succession of days each grayer and more vain than the last but perhaps the achievement of he didn't yet know exactly what, in any case the fact that he had reached this sort of sensible arrangement regarding his life in a condition so exceptionally burdened with recognized errors and conscious suffering could also help him toward something positive in the sense that both errors and suffering were not to be underestimated and still less despised or rejected because they alone if only through the theory of marginal utilization of misfortunes could support his hope of one day becoming somebody a hope he had to cling to with all his strength and good intentions at least here and now to keep from falling into God knows what abyss and for example just when he had once again lost Maria and once again the splendid if foggy city was driving him out disagreeably addressing him without choice or remedy toward a place like Marocco and a profession as elementary school teacher perhaps temporary but who could say he managed to think with a still tenuous but also undeniable form of comfort that the days were growing longer that is he had a kind of constructive vision of study and work in the spring in his room whose window overlooked rows of poplars and plowed fields which would soon turn green, and of course he had felt the same or similar forms of comfort at the approach of the preceding spring and with different reasons at the approach of autumn when he still hadn't met Maria however it was beyond doubt that this time he came to it fortified and in the final analysis at an advantage if it could be thought that sorrow might have a kind of final destination, in any case it was best to believe or hope in something if he didn't want to end in a confused uselessness which still despite all his careful arguments seemed among the things within reach at present to be the thing most within reach along with fear and anguish so abandoning all broader speculation he felt he should go back to the eighty-eight thousand lire thrown away with his magnanimous and ridiculous gesture of the ring, it was prudent to linger a little longer and suffer a limited petty grief waiting until the rest moved off a bit and became more accessible to miraculous compromises and adaptations, and in any case it might well be said that the same mean and sad situation into which he had plunged and remained almost swamped substantially stimulated his powers of reflection and perception making him at least hypothetically and hopefully capable of deriving what little good it was possible to extract from the world and from nature and from the unfathomable depths of the spirit, and so for example as the days were already much longer and spring was coming . . .

POSTSCRIPT

I believe a novel like this one, constructed more or less in the traditional manner even with a line of preface at the beginning, requires also a line at the end. However since I have by now said what I had to say and the possible meanings that can be derived from it are best left to the readers, who can derive them on their own if by any chance they want to, I can only take my leave, quoting prudently and for my own amusement, what his Holiness Pius XI said to a group of parish priests complaining about I forget what: "For our part, we knew from the beginning we wouldn't make everyone happy, something which as a rule not even the good Lord succeeds in doing."

A Note About the Author

Giuseppe Berto was born at Mogliano Veneto, near Treviso, in 1914. He won a degree in classical studies at the University of Padua, and for some time was a teacher. He served as an officer in the Italian army both in the Abyssinian War and in the North African fighting of 1941–3; captured at the surrender in Tunisia, he spent two and a half years as a prisoner of war in a camp near Hereford, Texas. Since then he has devoted himself to writing. His first novel, *Il Cielo è rosso,* was published in 1947, when it won the Firenze Prize, and appeared in the United States as *The Sky Is Red* in 1948. His second book, *Le Opere di Dio* (*The Works of God*), was issued in 1948. After it came *Il Brigante* (1951), known here as *The Brigand.* Then, after a long silence, he published (1963) a book of short stories, *Un Po' di successo* ("A Little Bit of Success"), which has not appeared in English. The year 1964 saw the publication of his successful novel *Il Male oscuro,* issued as *Incubus* by Alfred A. Knopf in 1966; it won both the Viareggio Prize and the Campiello Prize. The Italian title of the present novel, *La Cosa buffa,* is taken from a passage in Joseph Conrad's *Heart of Darkness*: "Droll thing life is—that mysterious arrangement of merciless logic for a futile purpose. The most you can hope from it is some knowledge of yourself—that comes too late."

A Note on the Type

This book was set on the Linotype in Granjon, a type named in compliment to Robert Granjon, type-cutter and printer—1523 to 1590, Antwerp, Lyons, Rome, Paris. Granjon, the boldest and most original designer of his time, was one of the first to practice the trade of type-founder apart from that of printer.

Linotype Granjon was designed by George W. Jones, who based his drawings upon a face used by Claude Garamond (1510–61) in his beautiful French books. Granjon more closely resembles Garamond's own type than do any of the various modern faces that bear his name.

This book was composed, printed and bound by
The Colonial Press Inc., Clinton, Massachusetts.
Typography and binding design by
Bonnie Spiegel